A TEXT BOOK OF

APPLIED
THERMODYNAMICS

For

Semester - II

SECOND YEAR DEGREE COURSE IN MECHANICAL ENGINEERING AND AUTOMOBILE ENGINEERING

As Per New Revised Syllabus of North Maharashtra University, Jalgaon, June 2013-2014

Er. N. K. PATIL

M.Tech. (Energy Mgt.), M.E. (M/c Design), M.B.A.
Associate Professor
Dept. of Mechanical Engg.,
SSBT's College of Engg. & Technology
Bambhori, JALGAON.

Prof. S. S. GHORPADE

B.E. (Mech.), M.E. (Mech.)
Assistant Professor,
Sinhgad Academy of Engineering
Kondhwa (Bk.), PUNE.

Dr. S. N. SAPALI

B.E. (Mech), M.E. (Mech) Ph.D. (IIT) Kharagpur
Professor & Head of Mechanical Engg. Dept.,
College of Engineering (COEP), PUNE.
(An Autonomous Institute of Govt. of Maharashtra)

Dr. S. S. KORE

B.E. (Mech.), M.E. (Mech.), Ph.D.
Associate Professor,
Sinhgad Academy of Engineering,
Kondhwa (Bk.), PUNE.

NIRALI PRAKASHAN

Advancement of knowledge

N3088

APPLIED THERMODYNAMICS (NMU - SE Mech. / Auto)   **ISBN 978-93-83971-34-3**

First Edition : January 2014

© : **Authors**

Published By :
NIRALI PRAKASHAN
Abhyudaya Pragati, 1312, Shivaji Nagar,
Off J.M. Road, PUNE – 411005
Tel - (020) 25512336/37/39, Fax - (020) 25511379
Email : niralipune@pragationline.com

DISTRIBUTION CENTRES
PUNE

Nirali Prakashan
119, Budhwar Peth, Jogeshwari Mandir Lane
Pune 411002, Maharashtra
Tel : (020) 2445 2044, 66022708, Fax : (020) 2445 1538
Email : niralilocal@pragationline.com

Nirali Prakashan
S. No. 28/25, Dhyari,
Near Pari Company, Pune 411041
Tel : (020) 24690204Fax : (020) 24690316
Email : bookorder@pragationline.com

MUMBAI
Nirali Prakashan
385, S.V.P. Road, Rasdhara Co-op. Hsg. Society Ltd.,
Girgaum, Mumbai 400004, Maharashtra
Tel : (022) 2385 6339 / 2386 9976, Fax : (022) 2386 9976
Email : niralimumbai@pragationline.com

DISTRIBUTION BRANCHES

NAGPUR
Pratibha Book Distributors
Above Maratha Mandir, Shop No. 3, First Floor,
Rani Jhanshi Square, Sitabuldi, Nagpur 440012,
Maharashtra, Tel : (0712) 254 7129

JALGAON
Nirali Prakashan
34, V. V. Golani Market, Navi Peth, Jalgaon 425001,
Maharashtra, Tel : (0257) 222 0395
Mob : 94234 91860

BENGALURU
Pragati Book House
House No. 1, Sanjeevappa Lane, Avenue Road Cross,
Opp. Rice Church, Bengaluru – 560002.
Tel : (080) 64513344, 64513355,
Mob : 9880582331, 9845021552
Email:bharatsavla@yahoo.com

KOLHAPUR
Nirali Prakashan
New Mahadvar Road,
Kedar Plaza, 1st Floor Opp. IDBI Bank
Kolhapur 416 012, Maharashtra. Mob : 9850046155

CHENNAI
Pragati Books
9/1, Montieth Road, Behind Taas Mahal, Egmore,
Chennai 600008 Tamil Nadu, Tel : (044) 6518 3535,
Mob : 94440 01782 / 98450 21552 / 98805 82331, Email : bharatsavla@yahoo.com

RETAIL OUTLETS
PUNE

Pragati Book Centre
157, Budhwar Peth, Opp. Ratan Talkies,
Pune 411002, Maharashtra
Tel : (020) 2445 8887 / 6602 2707, Fax : (020) 2445 8887

Pragati Book Centre
Amber Chamber, 28/A, Budhwar Peth,
Appa Balwant Chowk, Pune : 411002, Maharashtra,
Tel : (020) 20240335 / 66281669
Email : pbcpune@pragationline.com

Pragati Book Centre
676/B, Budhwar Peth, Opp. Jogeshwari Mandir,
Pune 411002, Maharashtra
Tel : (020) 6601 7784 / 6602 0855

PBC Book Sellers & Stationers
152, Budhwar Peth, Pune 411002, Maharashtra
Tel : (020) 2445 2254 / 6609 2463

MUMBAI
Pragati Book Corner
Indira Niwas, 111 - A, Bhavani Shankar Road, Dadar (W), Mumbai 400028, Maharashtra
Tel : (022) 2422 3526 / 6662 5254, Email : pbcmumbai@pragationline.com

www.pragationline.com   info@pragationline.com

Preface ...

It gives us an immense pleasure to present this Text Book of **"Applied Thermodynamics"** for Second Year Degree Course in Mechanical/Automobile Engineering students of North Maharashtra University, Jalgaon. **Thermodynamics** has been a part of the curricula of many disciplines like Mechanical, Automobile, Engineering students. The object of this book is to present the subject matter in the most precise, compact and in a lucid manner.

Authors have tried to introduce the subject to the average students, with a simple and lucid language. The subject matter has been developed in a logical and coherent manner with neat diagrams along with a fairly large number of solved examples and exercises. Answers to many unsolved numerical problems are also given.

The main objectives of this text are :

- **To cover the basic principles of thermodynamics.**

- **To develop a very good understanding of the subject matter.**

- **To give practice to solve the numerical examples in thermodynamics.**

We are very much thankful to Shri. Dineshbhai Furia and Shri. Jignesh Furia of M/s Nirali Prakashan, Pune for giving a platform to provide good inputs the students community. We are grateful to Mr. Mallikarjun Munde, a Senior Manager for his endless efforts to make this book as best as it can be. We are also thankful to Mr. Malik Shaikh, Mrs. Anagha Kaware and Mrs. Anjali Muley for their co-operation throughout the work.

We also thankful to **Mr. Pruthviraj M. More**, Branch Manager, Jalgaon Office, for his valuable help and efforts for promotion of our books.

Although every care has been taken to check mistakes, and errors, yet it is difficult to claim perfection. Any errors, mistakes and suggestions for the improvement of this book, brought to our notice will be thankfully acknowledged and incorporated in the next edition.

January 2014
Pune.

Authors

Syllabus ...

1. Boiler and Boiler Performance   **(Number of Lectures - 8, Marks: 16)**

(a) Steam Power Plant layout, Classification and selection of boilers, Stocker fired boiler.

(b) Modern boilers with various fossil fuels, IBR act, Energy conservation opportunities, waste heat recovery boiler.

(c) Boiler performance - Equivalent evapouration, boiler efficiency (direct and indirect Method).

(d) Numerical on boiler performance.

(e) Heat balance for a boiler.

(f) Numerical on boiler Heat balance.

(g) Boiler Draught, Natural and Artificial draught, losses, Condition for maximum discharge through chimney.

(h) Numerical on draught.

2. Vapor Power Cycle and Steam Condenser

(Number of Lectures - 8, Marks: 16)

(a) Fundamentals of Vapour Processes, Steam power cycles- Carnot Cycle, Rankine cycle.

(b) Analysis of Rankine cycle for work ratio, efficiency, Power output, specific steam consumption, heat rate. Comparison of Rankine and Carnot cycle.

(c) Numerical on Rankine cycle

(d) Methods to improve Rankine cycle efficiency - Regeneration, Reheating, Co-generation. (Elementary treatment).

(e) Numerical on reheat Rankine cycle, regenerative Rankine cycle.

(f) Condenser, Classification of condenser, Necessity of condenser, Vacuum measurement, Condenser efficiency, Vacuum efficiency, Calculation of cooling water required.

(g) Air leakage and its effect on condenser performance, Air extraction pump, cooling towers.

(h) Numerical on condenser performance.

3. Compressible Flow and Steam Nozzle   **(Number of Lectures - 8, Marks: 16)**

(a) Compressible fluid flow, Static and Stagnation properties, numerical.

(b) Sonic velocity, Mach number, type of nozzles and diffusers.

(c) One dimensional steady isentropic flow through nozzles and diffusers, Critical pressure ratio, maximum discharge, choked flow.

(d) Numerical on flow through nozzles and diffusers.

(e) Effect of variation in back pressure on nozzle characteristics, Effect of friction and nozzle Efficiency.

(f) Numerical on Effect of friction and nozzle Efficiency.

(g) Super saturated flow, Fanno line, Rayleigh lines (No numerical).

(h) Normal and oblique shock losses. (No numerical)

4. **Reciprocating Air Compressor**   **(Number of Lectures - 8, Marks: 16)**

(a) Introduction, use of compressed air, terminology used in compressor, Classification of compressors.

(b) Construction and working of single stage compressor, Thermodynamic analysis of reciprocating air compressor without clearance volume, Isothermal Efficiency, Double acting Compressor.

(c) Numerical of reciprocating air compressor without clearance.

(d) Effect of clearance, analysis of reciprocating air compressor with clearance volume, volumetric efficiency, FAD, Actual Indicator diagram.

(e) Numerical of reciprocating air compressor with clearance.

(f) Improvements in volumetric efficiency, multistage compression, Condition for minimum work of compression, Intercooler, after cooler, heat rejected.

(g) Numerical on reciprocating air compressor.

(h) Numerical on reciprocating air compressor.

5. **Rotary Air Compressor**   **(Number of Lectures - 7, Marks: 16)**

(a) Introduction, classification of rotary compressors; construction, working, analysis and application of roots blower.

(b) Construction, working, analysis and application of vane type compressor

(c) Construction, working, analysis and application of screw type compressor

(d) Introduction, classification of fans and blowers, Fan characteristics.

(e) Construction and working of centrifugal fan and axial flow fan.

(f) Numerical only on fan.

***

Contents ...

***

Unit I

BOILER AND BOILER PERFORMANCE

1.1 INTRODUCTION

The economic development of any country is measured by the per capita energy consumption/generation.

It is to be noted that developing countries like India are required to generate more power, as there is large gap between demand and supply.

Generally energy is available in various forms:

(i)   Mechanical energy.

(ii)   Thermal energy.

(iii) Electrical energy etc.

Out of these electrical energy is most preferred, because of following advantages:

(i)   Less transmission and distribution losses.

(ii)   Electrical energy can be easily converted into other forms etc.

1.2 STEAM POWER PLANT WORKING

Fig. 1.1 shows simple steam power plant. It mainly consists of:

(i) Boiler,

(ii) Turbine,

(iii) Condenser,

(iv) Feed pump etc.

In this fossile fuels such as gas, oil, coal are used. Combustion of air and fuel takes place to generate hot gases. Heat of hot gases is used to heat the water and convert the water into steam.

This steam after it is being superheated, is expanded in the turbines for generating power. The steam afterward is exhausted either into the atmosphere or in the condenser. If it is exhausted in the condenser, it gets condensed and if the condensate is pure, it is pumped back to the boiler by means of feed pump.

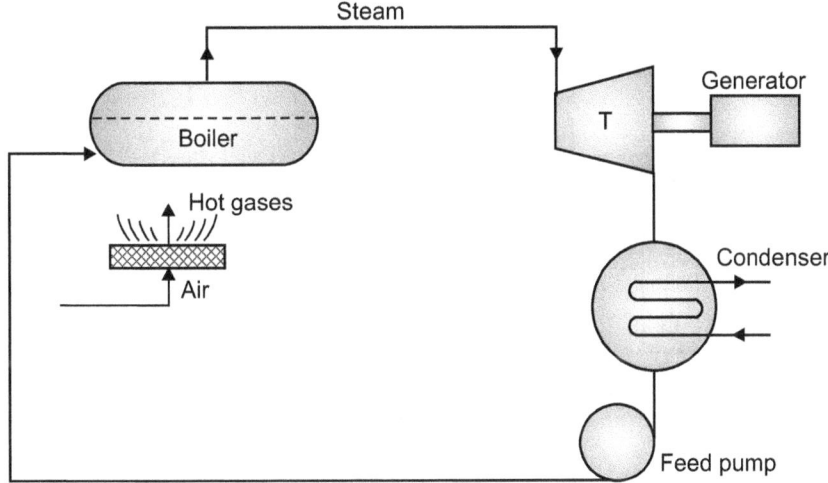

Fig. 1.1: Steam Power Plant

1.3 STEAM POWER PLANT WORKING

Fig. 1.2 shows schematic diagram of a modern steam power plant. It consists of four circuits:

(a) Air and flue gas circuit.

(b) Coal and ash circuit.

(c) Feed water and steam circuit.

(d) Cooling water circuit.

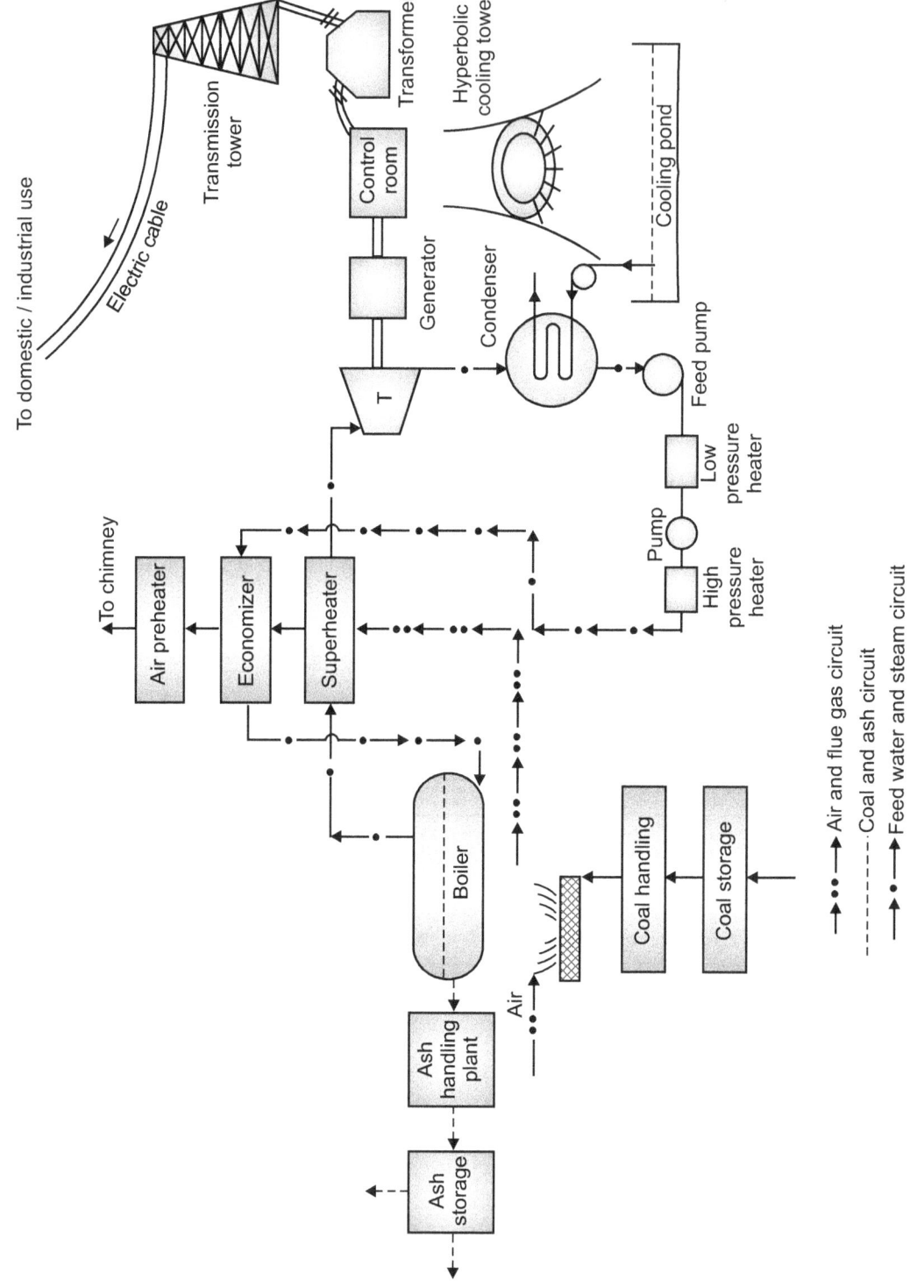

Fig. 1.2: Modern steam power plant and its circuits

(a) Air and flue gas circuit:

(In Fig. 1.2, represented by – ·· →) Air for combustion will be supplied from the atmosphere, because of forced draught, induced draught or balanced draught system. Fuel is supplied to the combustion chamber from the fuel feed system. In the combustion chamber, combustion of air and fuel (coal) takes place and hot flue gases are generated. These hot gases are made to flow through superheater, economizer, air preheater. After recovering heat from the flue gases are exhausted high in the atmosphere, through chimney to reduce the air pollution.

(b) Coal and ash circuit:

(In Fig. 1.2, represented by – – – –) Coal will be received from the coal mines and is stored in the coal yards. Coal is pulverized (grinding or sizing of coal to proper size or even fine powder) as per requirement of the plant. The coal is supplied to the combustion chamber through coal conveyors. After combustion ash produced is collected in ash storage yards through ash handling equipments.

Note that normally a 100 MW plant requires 1200-1500 tonnes of coal/day and a reserve of 15 days is generally maintained.

(c) Feed water and Steam circuit:

(In Fig. 1.2, represented by – · →) Steam when expanded into the turbines it produces power and then it is condensed in the condensers. Condensate collected will be pumped by means of feed pump through low pressure heater and high pressure heater for primary preheating of water and then it is made to pass through the economizer, where heat of hot gases will be used for preheating of water and preheated water is supplied to the boiler drum.

In the boiler, water is heated and steam is generated. After it is being superheated, it is expanded in the turbine.

In passing through all these equipments, there is some loss of water and this is compensated by adding make-up water. The make-up water is treated so as to avoid scale formation on the inner surface of tubes and boiler drum.

(d) Cooling water circuit:

(In Fig. 1.2, represented by →) When the steam is exhausted in the condenser, heat of the steam will be taken up by condenser cooling water and cooling water becomes hot and steam gets condensed.

This hot water is cooled in the cooling tower and is recirculated.

If the cooling water is available freely from lake or river then this water is used for cooling purpose.

1.4 BOILER

A steam generator or boiler is a closed vessel to transfer the heat produced by the combustion of fuel (solid, liquid or gaseous) to water and ultimately to generate steam. The steam produced may be supplied :

- To steam engines and turbines.

- At low pressures for industrial work in cotton mills, sugar factories, breweries, printing, textile industry etc.

1.4.1 Selection of a Steam Boiler

While selecting a boiler, following factors should be considered.

1. The power and the working pressure required,
2. The rate at which steam is to be generated,
3. The fuel type and water available,
4. Comparative initial cost,
5. The probable load factor,
6. The geographical position of the power house,
7. Operating and maintenance cost,
8. Erection facilities.

1.4.2 Essentials of a Good Steam Boiler

A good boiler should possess following features:

1. It should produce quantity of steam efficiently as per requirements,
2. It should be capable of quick starting,
3. It should be light in weight,
4. It should occupy a small space,
5. The tubes should not accumulate soot or water deposits and should have a reasonable margin of strength to allow for wear or corrosion,

6.   It should rapidly meet the fluctuation of the demand,

7.   It should be easy for inspection and repair,

8.   It should comply with safety regulations as laid down in the Boilers Act,

9.   It should be easy to install,

10.   Boiler components should be transferable without difficulty,

11.   It should need less attention during operation.

1.4.3 Important Terms for Steam Boilers

Following are important terms used in steam boilers.

1.   **Boiler shell:** It is made from metal plates bent into cylindrical form. The ends of the shell are closed by means of end plates. A boiler shell is designed to have sufficient capacity to contain water and steam as per requirement.

2.   **Combustion chamber:** It is the space, meant for burning fuel in order to produce hot gases or flues which transfer heat to water.

3.   **Grate:** It is a platform, in the combustion chamber, on which fuel (coal or wood) is burnt. The grate consists of cast iron bars which are spaced apart so that air required for combustion can pass through them.

4.   **Furnace:** It is the space, above the grate in which the fuel is actually burnt. The furnace is also called *fire box.*

5.   **Mountings:** These are the essential fittings which are mounted on the boiler for its proper functioning. For example, Water level indicator, pressure gauge, safety valve etc. A boiler cannot function safely without mountings.

6.   **Accessories:** These are the devices which improve efficiency of boiler. They are not essential for the operation of boiler but play an important role to run boiler efficiently. For example, Superheater, economiser, feed pump etc.

1.4.4 Classification of Boilers

The boilers may be classified as follows:

1. **According to the Position of Water and Hot Gases:**

(a)   **Fire Tube Boiler:** In fire tube steam boilers, the flues and hot gases pass through the tubes which are surrounded by water. The heat is conducted through the walls of the tubes from the hot gases to the surrounding water.

Examples: Simple vertical boiler, Cochran boiler, Lancashire boiler, Cornish boiler, Scotch marine boiler, Locomotive boiler etc.

(b) **Water Tube Boilers:** In water tube steam boilers, the water is contained inside the tubes (called water tubes) which are surrounded by flues and hot gases from outside.

Examples: Babcock and Wilcox boiler, Stirling boiler, La-Mont boiler, Benson boiler etc.

2. **According to the Position of the Furnace:**

   (a) **Internally Fired Boilers:** In these boilers, the furnace is located inside the boiler shell. Most of the fire tube steam boilers are internally fired.

   (b) **Externally Fired Boilers:** In these boilers, the furnace is located outside the boiler shell. Water tube steam boilers are externally fired.

3. **According to Circulation Method of Water and Steam:**

   (a) **Natural Circulation Steam Boilers:** Here, the circulation of water is by natural convection currents, set up during the heating of water. Most of the steam boilers use a natural circulation of water.

   Examples: Babcock and Wilcox boilers.

   (b) **Forced Circulation Boilers:** In forced circulation steam boilers, circulation of water is by using a pump. Forced circulation is used in high pressure boilers.

   Examples: La-Mont boiler, Benson boiler, Loeffler boiler etc.

4. **According to the Number of Tubes:**

   (a) **Single Tube Boilers:** In single tube steam boilers, there is only one fire tube or water tube.

   Examples: Simple vertical boiler and Cornish boiler.

   (b) **Multitubular Boilers:** In multitubular steam boilers, there are two or more fire tubes or water tubes.

   Examples: Lancashire boiler, Locomotive boiler, Babcock and Wilcox boiler etc.

5. **According to the Mobility:**

   (a) **Stationary Boilers:** The stationary steam boilers are used in power plants and in industrial process work. They do not move from one place to another.

   Examples: Babcock and Wilcox boiler.

   (b) **Mobile Boilers:** The mobile steam boilers are those which move from one place to another.

   Examples: Locomotive and Marine boilers.

6. **According to the Axis of the Shell:**

   (a) **Horizontal Boilers:** In horizontal steam boilers, the axis of the shell is horizontal.

   Examples: Lancashire boiler, Locomotive boiler, Babcock and Wilcox boiler etc.

   (b) **Vertical Boilers:** In these boilers, the axis of the shell is vertical.

   Examples: Simple vertical boiler, Cochran boiler etc.

1.5 FUEL FEED AND BURNING

1.5.1 Introduction

Fuels burn in a confined space called furnace. The principal requisites for proper combustion of fuel in a furnace are:

   (1) Supply of requisite quantity of air to the furnace.

   (2) Efficient mixing of air and fuel.

   (3) High flame temperature to maintain ignition.

   (4) Enough time to complete the burning process within the furnace enclosure.

The process of steam generation can be divided into two parts:

   (a) furnace, where heat of the fuel is liberated,

   (b) heat transfer surface for the absorption of heat so released.

The way in which fuel is supplied and burned in a furnace has got the maximum influence on the quantity of heat liberated from the fuel. Different methods of firing fuel depend primarily on the physical state of the fuel, for example, solid, liquid or gas. In this chapter, the methods used for the solid fuels will be discussed.

Based on the type of combustion equipment used, boilers may be classified as:

   (1) Solid fuels fired

   (a) Hand fired,

   (b) Stoker fired,

      (i) Overfeed stokers (chain grate),

      (ii) Underfeed stokers (Single or multiple retort type).

   (c) Pulverised fuel fired,

      (i) Unit system,

      (ii) Central system,

      (iii) Combination of (i) and (ii).

(2) Liquid fuel fired

    (a) Injection system,

    (b) Evapouration system,

    (c) Combination of (a) and (b).

(3) Gaseous fuel fired

    (a) Atmospheric pressure system,

    (b) High pressure system.

Following considerations should be taken into account while selecting a combustion equipment for solid fuels:

(1) Initial cost.

(2) Adequate combustion space and its ability to withstand high flame temperature.

(3) Grate area over which fuel burns.

(4) In case it is decided to supply air in parts (for example, primary, secondary, tertiary air etc.), than the ratio of these portions.

(5) Arrangements for thorough mixing of air with fuel for efficient combustion.

(6) Flexibility of operation.

(7) Operating cost of the equipment.

(8) Minimum nuisance due to smoke.

1.5.2 Mechanical Methods

Mechanical methods of fuel firing include an arrangement for "carrying" fuel into the furnace enclosure where it is burned and the ash so formed is collected at the bottom. Advantages of mechanical method of fuel firing are:

(1) There is always uniform layer of fuel on the fuel bed.

(2) Combustion conditions inside the furnace can be easily controlled, hence fluctuating load demands can be easily met with.

(3) The problem of draft control is not so severe as in case of hand firing.

(4) Poorer grades of fuel can be burned with some modifications.

(5) The quantity of fuel burned per hour is considerably higher than that of hand firing.

(6) There is no dependence on the manual skill and also there is saving in labour cost.

Principal mechanical methods of fuel firing are stoker and pulverised fuel firing. In stoker firing coal is carried into the furnace for combustion and the ash formed after the combustion is discharged at the appropriate point. In pulverised fuel firing, fuel is ground to powder form; which 'flows' to the furnace through burners with the help of primary air. Ash collected at the bottom of the furnace is discharged into the ash pit.

Economical working of a power station depends upon the efficient use of fuel. Whether this can be obtained more efficiently by stoker or pulverised fuel firing depends largely on the following factors:

    (a) Characteristics of the coal to be used.

    (b) Capacity of the boiler units.

    (c) Load fluctuations.

    (d) Station load factor.

    (e) Capital cost and maintenance cost of the equipment selected.

Merits and demerits of the two methods for example, stoker and pulverised fuel firing are given below.

1.5.3 Stoker Firing

Advantages of stoker firing are:

    (1) The coal is burned as obtained from the mines, so that there is no necessity of coal preparation plant. Sometimes it may be only necessary to 'size' the coal in order to suit the furnace conditions.

    (2) This method can be economically used for medium as well as large capacity boilers.

    (3) This method of firing is practically free from the dangers of explosions.

    (4) Usually, less building space is required.

    (5) Capital investment as compared to pulverised fuel system is less.

    (6) It involves less maintenance and operating cost.

    (7) Substantial reduction in auxiliary plant.

    (8) The method is more reliable.

    (9) Some reserve is gained by the large amount of coal stored on the grate in the event of coal handling plant failure.

Disadvantages of stoker firing are as follows:

    (1) Furnaces generally need fire arches or other modifications which increase the cost and are liable to give trouble.

    (2) Structural arrangements are not so simple and surrounding floors have to be designed for heavy loadings.

    (3) There is always some loss of coal through riddlings etc.

(4) There is excessive wear of moving parts due to abrasive action of coal.

(5) There is multiplicity of moving parts always under mechanical stresses and high temperature.

(6) Sudden variations in load cannot be met to the same degree of efficiency as in case of pulverised fuel firing.

(7) Troubles due to slagging and clinkering of combustion chamber walls are experienced.

(8) Banking and stand-by losses are always present.

(a) Features of Stoker Firing

Modern stoker-fired boilers exhibit the following features:

(a) The liberty of design enabling the specified continuous maximum duty to be met without excessively high rates of combustion on the grate surface or of heat transmission through the boiler heating surface.

(b) A furnace volume of very ample proportions with a correspondingly large area of radiant heat absorbing surface, whereby the temperature of the gases entering the convection zone of the boiler is kept well below the ash fusion temperature of the fuel or mixture of fuels which may be encountered.

(c) Admission of secondary air in such quantity, pressure and direction as to ensure thorough mixing of the gaseous products of combustion. The furnace design generally will aim at ensuring that all the products pass through a zone of luminous flame, the value of which features in inhibiting harmful deposits has been established by the researchers.

(d) The boiler surface proper will be disposed in well-defined banks and in lateral spacing to establish a regular temperature gradient between gases and metal surface of the tubes, and to afford accessibility both for on-load and off-load cleaning.

(e) Accumulation in contact with heating surfaces of dust or grit carried forward by the gases will be avoided by the provision of suitable pockets at appropriate points in the gas passes, whence on load dust extraction can be readily affected.

(f) On-load cleaning, in fact, will have received consideration as part of the fundamental design, an aspect facilitated by the general adoption of remote controlled sequence operated soot blowers, the location which can be determined without regard to the limits formerly imposed by manual operation of individual blowers.

(b) Principle of Overfeed Stoker

In overfeed stokers, coal is supplied on the top of the grate. As the coal burns, ash and clinkers are formed which collect at the bottom, then the next charges of coal are supplied and the process continues. Primary air is supplied under pressure from the bottom of the grate. As the air flows through the grate openings and the layer of ash, it becomes heated up and as it passes through the layer of incandescent coal, combustion is accelerated in that region. By the time it reaches the region of green coal, entire oxygen of the air is consumed. Combustion of green coal is promoted by supplying secondary air from the side. Gases leaving incandescent region consist of carbon dioxide, carbon monoxide, nitrogen, hydrogen and steam with oxygen usually missing. Fresh fuel undergoing distillation of its volatile matter forms the topmost layer of the fuel bed. Heat for distillation and eventual ignition comes from the following sources:

(1) by conduction, from the incandescent coal region.

(2) from the gases at high temperature diffusing through the upper layer.

(3) radiation from flames,

(4) hot gases present in the furnace,

(5) from the hot furnace walls,

(6) secondary air, if preheated.

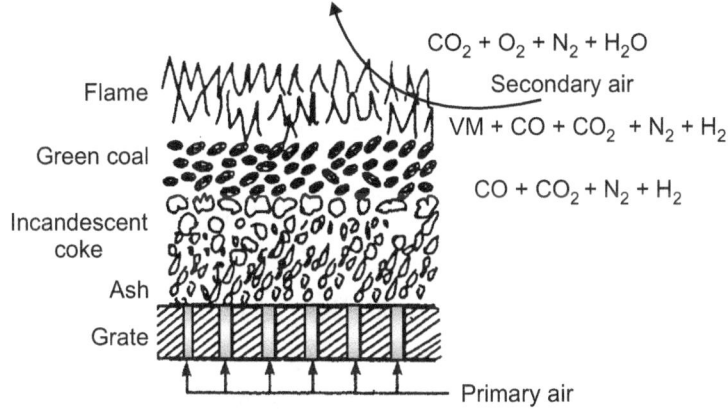

(a) Principle of overfeed stoker

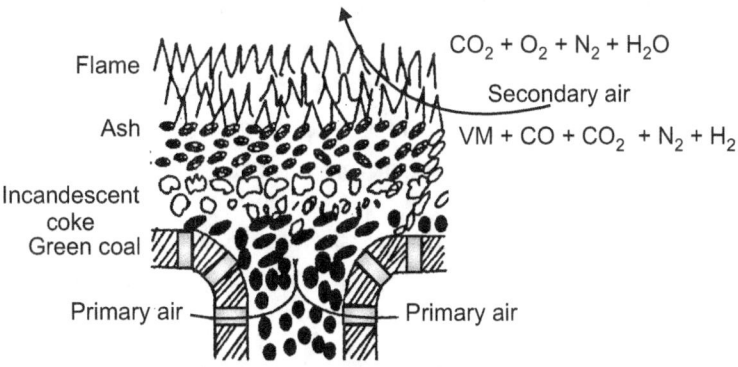

(b) Principle of underfeed stoker
Fig. 1.3

For complete combustion in the furnace:

    (i)   Secondary air is introduced at high velocity so as to create turbulence.

    (ii) A fire arch is usually provided for thorough mixing.

(c) Principle of Underfeed Stoker

Underfeed stokers utilize the gas producer principle. Green coal is fed to the lower layer of the fuel bed and is gradually pushed up and coked, giving up its volatile constituents and becoming incandescent by the time it reaches the top layer. Clinkers or ash which is formed on the upper layer is forced to the side or back of the fuel bed, where it is removed by suitable means. Air under pressure is supplied through small openings in the grate. First of all air diffuses through the pores of the raw fuel, thereby taking volatile matter along with it. Then it passes through the ignition zone and enters the region of incandescent coke. Usually the reaction is not complete in this region, so secondary air is required for the same. Underfeed stokers are best suited for semi-bituminous and bituminous coals high in volatile matter content and with caking tendency. The tendency of caking coals to swell augments, the action of the stoker in producing a fuel bed of unusual thickness and the pushing action of the feeding mechanism keeps the bed broken up and porous. All underfeed stokers are essentially forced draft stokers, since they operate with restricted air openings only. There are two general classes of underfeed stokers. For example,

    (i)   Single retort type, (ii) Multiple retort type.

(d) Underfeed Stokers

The essential principle of the underfeed stoker is a reciprocating ram or rams which feed coal from hoppers at the front of the furnace into the bottom of horizontal or slightly inclined retorts. The raw coal is underneath burning coal at the top of the fuel bed, which distills the volatile matter from the fresh coal. The liberated gases pass upwards through the burning coal, and are burned with air entering through tuyers at the upper edges of the retorts. The coke which remains after distillation of the gases gradually is pushed upwards by entering fresh fuel and burns on the furnace of the fuel bed. The entire fuel bed is worked towards the rear of the stoker or on to dead plates at the sides of the retort, ash and refuse being discharged into an ash hopper or removed by hand.

Forced draft is always necessary. Rams and pushers, and sometimes also the ash disposal equipment, are driven by a motor or engine. Fuel and air supply can be regulated automatically by variations in steam pressure. Arches are unnecessary, and considerable heat is transmitted to the boiler by radiation. This results in a relatively low temperature of gases passing through the boiler, even at high combustion rates.

Single Retort Stokers (Fig. 1.4) use a steam-driven ram or a screw feed, together with supplementary adjustable stroke pushers to distribute coal properly in the retort. From the surface of the fuel bed, refuse is deposited on dead plates where it is removed by hand through doors on the front. In some designs the dead plates may be dropped to dump to the ashpit. Access doors on the sides of the furnace are unnecessary.

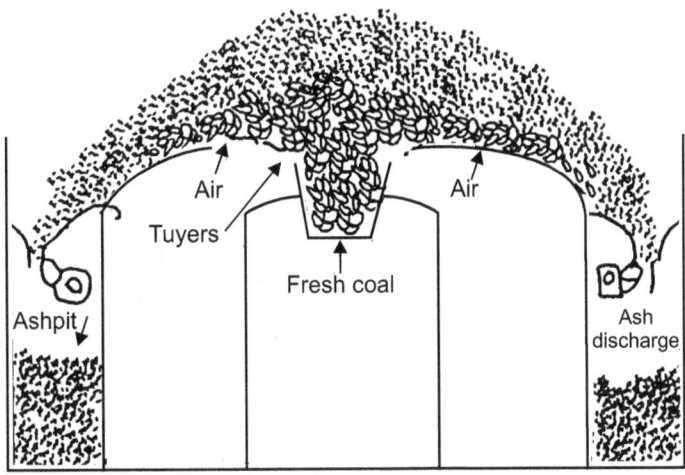

Fig. 1.4: Single retort type stoker

Fig. 1.5 illustrates underfeed link grate mechanism of the stoker. Link grate motion reduces resistance to air flow by keeping the fuel bed porous. Air flowing through the grates is not smothered, but is allowed to support combustion by thoroughly permeating all parts of the fuel bed.

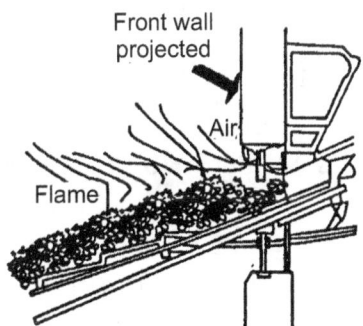

Fig. 1.5: Details of retort type stoker, showing coal feeding system

At moderate combustion rates, even with high volatile coal, combustion is complete within a short distance of the surface of the fuel bed. The capacity of stoker ranges from 100 to 2000 kg of coal burned per hour.

Multiple retort underfeed stokers occupy the fuel width of the furnace. The fuel bed consists of alternate retorts and tuyers for the supply of air. The furnace bed may be inclined at about 20°. Below the retorts, the grate surface is continuous so as to burn fuel completely before it is pushed off the ash supporting plates. The distinctive feature of this stoker is that the sides of the retorts reciprocate relative to the bottoms. This provides a means of moving the fuel uniformly along out of the retort. It also provides a moving grate surface on to which the fuel is passed as it leaves the retort. The same movement serves to push the refuse cross the rocker ash dumping plates where it continuously discharges through the adjustable opening next to the bridge wall.

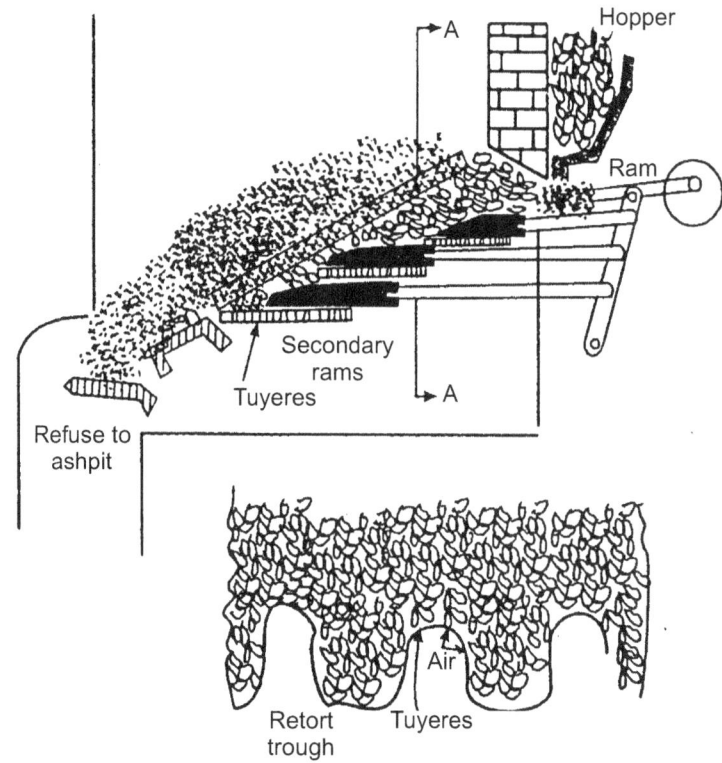

Fig. 1.6: Multiple retort type stoker

The number of retort units may vary from 2 to 20 with coal burning capacity ranging from 300 kg to 2000 kg of coal per hour per retort. Fluctuations in boiler load can be effectively met in this case. Part load efficiency of multiple retort type stokers is usually high.

Advantages of Retort Stokers
 (1) Higher thermal efficiency is possible as compared with chain grate stoker.
 (2) Part load efficiency is high particularly with multiple retort type.
 (3) Much higher steaming rates are possible with this type of stoker.
 (4) Higher temperatures of preheated air are possible.

(5) Substantial amount of coal always remains on the grate so that the boiler may remain in service in the event of temporary breakdown of the coal supply system.

(6) Overload capacity of the boiler is high as large amount of coal is carried on the grate.

(7) Ignition arches, if required, are simple in construction.

(8) With the use of clinker grinder, more heat can be liberated out of the fuel.

(9) The grate is self-cleaning.

(10) Tuyers, grate bars etc., ate always in contact with fresh coal and are not subject to high temperature.

Disadvantages:

(1) Initial cost is high.

(2) Large building space is required.

(3) Low grade fuels with high ash content cannot be burnt economically.

(4) Clinker trouble is usually present.

1.6 MODERN BOILERS

1.6.1 Fire Tube Boilers

The boilers that are used in now-a-days in process industry and power plants come with various mountings and accessories. These are fire tube or water tube boilers.

The various fire tube boilers are described below.

(a) Simple Vertical Boiler

- This boiler is suitable to produce small quantity of steam at low pressure where limited space is available.

- It consists of a cylindrical shell in which fire box and grate are placed near to the bottom as shown in Fig. 1.7. Fire box is surrounded by water in the boiler shell.

- Two or more cross tubes are fitted in fire box. These tubes are made inclined to improve water circulation and to increase heating area.

- A vertical tube is used to connect fire box with chimney at the top of fire box.

- Through the manhole, the boiler attendant can enter inside the boiler shell for cleaning, inspection and or maintenance.

- For draining out the mud and sediments settled at the bottom, a mud hole is provided.

- Its construction is simple, but efficiency of this boiler is less.

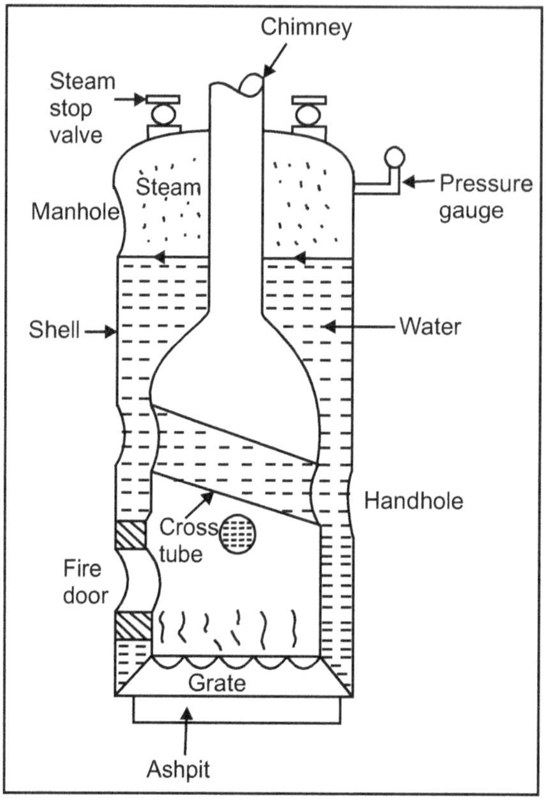

Fig. 1.7: Simple vertical boiler

(b) Cochran Boiler

- It is also a simple form of vertical fire tube boiler. It consists of the fire brick layer which prevents the overheating of the boiler shell. The hot gases pass through a large number of fire tubes surrounded by water as shown in Fig. 1.8 and convert it into steam. Then steam goes up to steam space.

- The crown of the boiler shell and grate are both hemispherical in shape.

- The waste gases entering the smoke box are released through the chimney. The amount of waste gases leaving the chimney is controlled by means of a damper manually.

- When the damper is partly closed, amount of the waste gases leaving the chimney will be reduced. Due to this action of the damper, the amount of air entering the grate will also be reduced and obviously, only limited fuel can be burnt and the amount of steam generated also will be reduced. Thus, the damper controls the rate of steam generated.

- Through the manhole, the boiler attendant can enter inside the boiler shell for cleaning.

- By opening the door in the smoke box, the fire tubes and the smoke box can be cleaned by a wire brush.

- The diameter of the boilers varies from 1 to 3 m and the height of the boiler varies from 2 to 6 m depending on steam requirement. The evapourative capacity of the boiler ranges from 20 to 3000 kg/h.

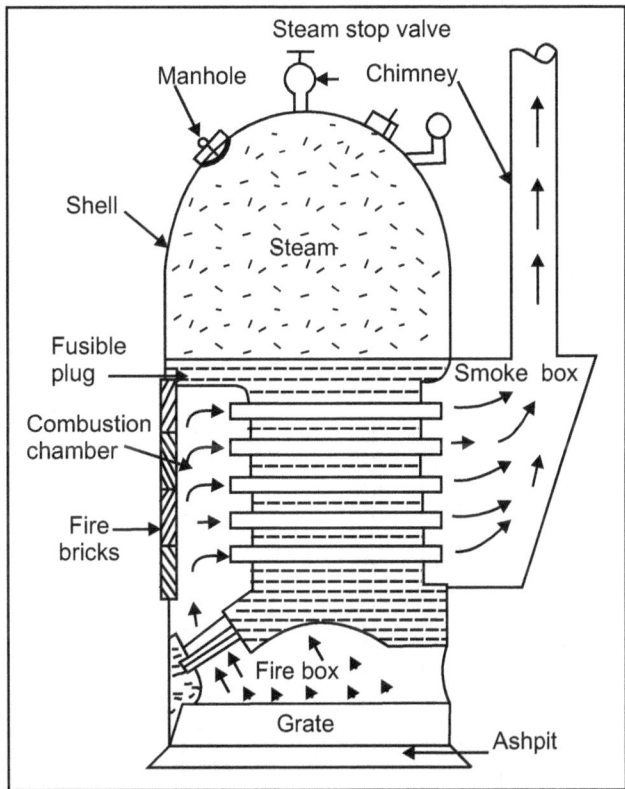

Fig. 1.8: Cochran boiler

(c) Lancashire Boiler

The Lancashire boiler is a fire tube, stationary, horizontal, internally fired, two tubular, natural circulation boiler. Fig. 1.9 shows constructional details of a Lancashire boiler.

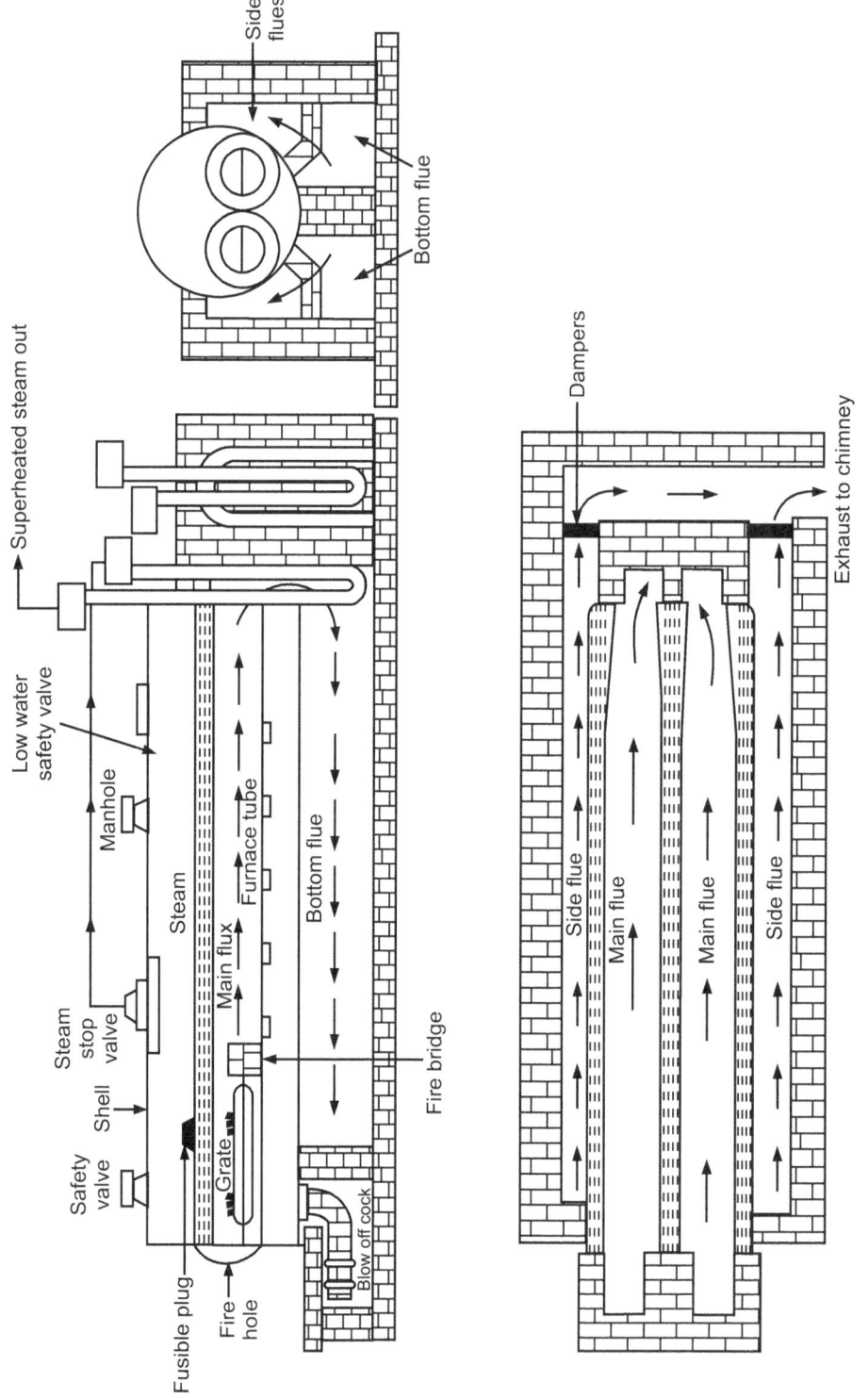

Fig. 1.9: Lancashire boiler

- This boiler consists of a cylindrical shell usually of 2 m in diameter and 8-10 m in length. It has two large internal flue tubes having diameters between 0.8-1 m in which grate is situated at the front end of the main flue. The coal is fed to the grate through the fire doors.
- The internal flue tubes are reduced in diameter at the back end to provide access to the lower part of the boiler. One bottom flue and two side flues are formed by brick setting.
- A low fire brick bridge is provided at the end of the grate to prevent the flow of coal and ash particles into the interior of the furnace tubes. The dampers operated by chain in the form of sliding doors are placed at the end of side flues to control the flow of gases. The damper regulates the combustion rate as well as steam generation rate.
- Then all mountings required for safe working of boiler are fitted and are shown in Fig. 1.9.

Working :
- These hot gases from the grate pass up to the back end of the tubes (main flue) and then is the downward direction.
- Then they move through bottom passage from back end to the front of the boiler (bottom flue).
- At front end they are divided and passes through two side passages (side flues).
- Then they move along two side flues and come to the chimney.
- This particular arrangement increases the heating surface to large extent.

(d) Cornish Boiler
- In construction it is similar to Lancashire boiler in all respect, except it has one main flue passage instead of two, as shown in Fig. 1.10.

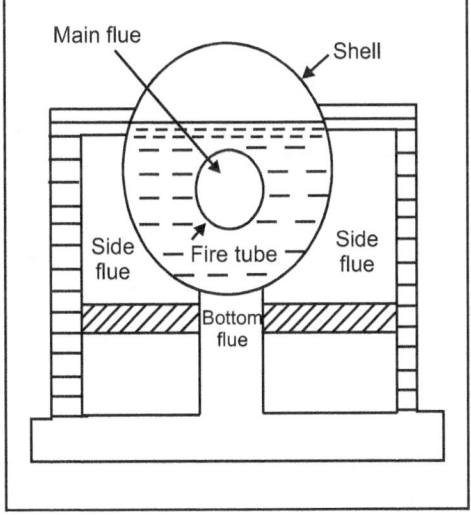

Fig. 1.10: Cornish boiler

- Its cylindrical shell is usually of 1 to 2 m in diameter and 5-7.5 m in length. The diameter of flue tube may be about 0.6 times that of the shell.
- The steam generating capacity and pressure of a Cornish boiler is low as compared to Lancashire boiler.

(e) Locomotive Boiler

- It is a horizontal fire tube type mobile boiler. It consists of a shell having 1.5 m in diameter and 4 m in length. Fuel is fed into the fire box through the fuel door and air enters through the damper and the slots in the grate plate.
- The rate of combustion and the amount of steam generated is controlled by the dampers. The fire brick arch deflects the hot gases and improves the combustion efficiency.
- The hot gases pass through large number of fire tubes and enter the smoke box. The circulation of air and hot gases is improved by means of induced draft produced in the smoke box.
- Waste steam from the engine enters the smoke box through the blast pipe and expands.
- Due to the expansion, it produces a partial vacuum which improves the movement of hot gases and air.
- Waste gases go out through a short chimney. A door is provided in the smoke box for inspection and cleaning.
- To remove the moisture from the wet steam and to increase the temperature of steam, it is superheated as shown in Fig. 1.11.

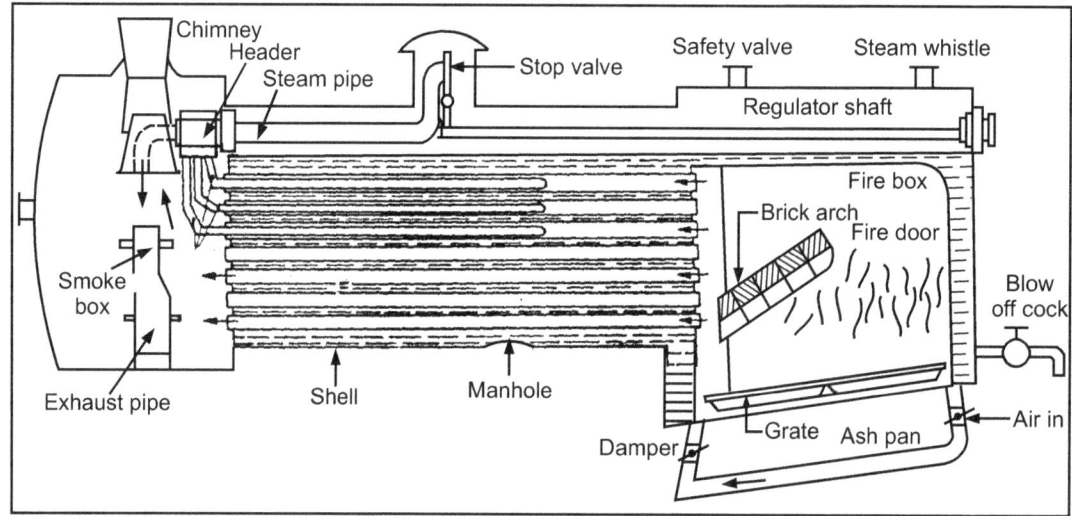

Fig. 1.11: Locomotive boiler

- The wet steam through the regulator enters the wet steam header, passes through large number of superheated tubes and finally comes to the superheater header. Then the superheated steam goes to the engine. To accommodate the superheater tubes, some of the fire tubes are larger in diameter.

- There are about 160 fire tubes of 47.5 mm diameter and 24 fire tubes of 130 mm diameter. By superheating, the heat energy per unit mass of steam is increased and the thermal efficiency of the steam plant is considerably increased.

1.6.2 Water Tube Boilers

(a) Babcock and Wilcox Boiler

- This boiler consists of a steam water drum mounted on fire brick work. Hot gases from the furnace (placed below water tubes) follow zig-zag path through the fire brick baffles before going to the chimney through the damper.
- The damper controls the rate of burning and thereby the steam generation. The damper is operated by a chain passing through a set of pulleys.
- Water from the steam water drum comes down to the down take header and then goes to the uptake header through a large number of water tubes, inclined at about 15° for better circulation as shown in Fig. 1.12.

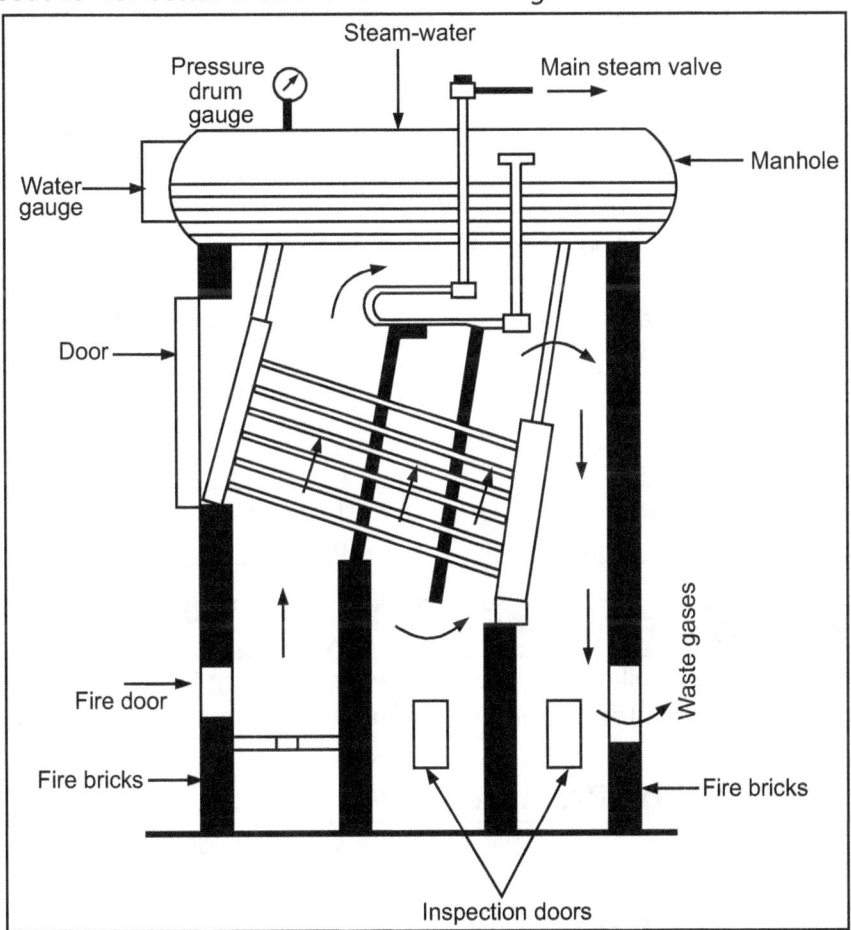

Fig. 1.12: Babcock and Wilcox boiler

- The wet steam comes to the wet steam header through an anti-priming pipe. The anti-priming pipe removes some moisture from the steam.
- Then, it passes through a large number of superheater tubes and reaches the superheater header. From the superheater header, it goes to the main steam valve and finally to the steam turbine.
- At the end of the down take header, a mud drum is connected from where impurities can be removed. Boiler is provided with two inspection doors and other mountings such as the water gauge, the pressure gauge and the safety valve.
- Compared to a fire tube boiler, evaporative capacity, the pressure of steam and the thermal efficiency of this boiler will be higher.

1.7 DIFFERENCE BETWEEN WATER TUBE AND FIRE TUBE BOILERS

	Water Tube Boiler		Fire Tube Boiler
1.	The water circulates inside the tubes surrounded by hot gases.	1.	The hot gases pass through the tubes which are surrounded by water.
2.	The rate of generation of steam is high.	2.	The rate of generation of steam is low.
3.	Overall efficiency is upto 90%.	3.	Its overall efficiency is only 75%.
4.	For a given power, the floor area required for the generation of steam is less.	4.	The floor area required is more.
5.	It can generate steam at a higher pressure.	5.	It can generate steam only upto 25 bar.
6.	The direction of water circulation is well defined.	6.	The water does not circulate in a definite direction.
7.	It is used for large power plants.	7.	It is not suitable for large plants.
8.	It can be transported and erected easily as its various parts can be separated.	8.	The transportation and erection is difficult.

1.8 HIGH PRESSURE BOILERS

The modern high pressure boilers are used for power generation having capacities 30 to 650 tonnes/hour with pressure upto 160 bar and maximum steam temperature of about 540°C.

1.8.1 Features of High Pressure Boilers

The unique features of high pressure boilers are as described below:
- **Method of Water Circulation:**

In all modern high pressure boiler plant, forced circulation is used for water circulation. Circulation of water is maintained by using pump which forces the water through boiler plant. The use of natural circulation is limited to subcritical boilers due to its limitations.

- **Type of Tubing:**

Most of high pressure boilers are water tube boilers. In these boilers, if the flow takes place through one continuous tube, the large pressure drop takes place due to friction. This loss is reduced by arranging the flow through parallel tube set system. This also results in better steam quality.

- **Method of Heating:**

    High pressure boiler uses following heating methods to increase heat transfer.

    (i)   Superheated steam is mixed with water during heating. This gives high heat transfer coefficient.

    (ii) Heat transfer coefficient is improved by increasing water velocity.

    (iii) By maintaining gas velocity above sonic speed, heat transfer coefficient is improved.

    (iv) Heat is saved by evaporating water above critical pressure of the steam.

1.8.2 Advantages of High Pressure Boilers

1. Heat of combustion is used more effectively by using tubing set of small diameter.
2. The efficiency of the plant is increased upto 40 to 44 percent by using high pressure and high temperature steam.
3. All parts are uniformly heated. It reduces overheating and simplifies thermal stress problem.
4. Compact in size and requires less floor space.
5. Quick response to load change without complicated control devices.
6. Use of pump ensures positive water circulation and increases evaporative capacity.
7. No scale formation because of high water velocity.
8. Use of high pressure and high temperature steam is economical.

1.9 INDIAN BOILER REGULATIONS (IBR) ACT

- IBR stands for The Indian Boiler Regulations Act. It is an Act of Indian National Law.
- It governs the manufacture, installation, operation and maintenance of steam boilers.
- The IBR is not a "type" approval, in which once a certain type of design is approved. It is a specific approval for each and every unit – every boiler, every valve, every trap, every pipe and so on.
- Every item used in an IBR steam system has to be manufactured, installed, tested, operated and maintained under inspection of local inspector.
- The Act defines anything connected to an IBR Boiler as an IBR system i.e. all boiler mountings, steam distribution pipes, valves, traps, strainers etc. are all under IBR.

1.10 IBR BOILER AND NON-IBR BOILERS

- A steam boiler is defined in the IBR Act as a vessel containing greater than 22.5 litres of water which is used to generate steam.
- Generally, any boiler above 1000 kg/hr capacity is an IBR boiler.
- Non-IBR boilers are coil type water tube boilers, available in a capacity of 200-850 kg/hr.
- The pressure of steam is dropped below 3.5 kg/cm², the system becomes Non-IBR. So most process plants use 3.5 kg/cm² as process steam.
- At the last valve before the process equipment (the process equipment is again Non-IBR).
- Condensate is not steam. It is water and is therefore, exempted from IBR.
- Steam traps on the main lines have to be IBR, but traps installed on the process equipment are Non-IBR.

1.11 ENERGY CONSERVATION OPPORTUNITIES IN BOILERS

(a) Reduce Stack Temperature

- Stack temperatures greater than 200°C indicates potential for recovery of waste heat.
- It also indicate the scaling of heat transfer/recovery equipment and hence the urgency of taking an early shut down for water/flue side cleaning.
- 22°C reduction in flue gas temperature increases boiler efficiency by 1%.

(b) Feed Water Preheating using Economiser

- For an older shell boiler, with a flue gas exit temperature of 260°C, an economizer could be used to reduce it to 200°C, Increase in overall thermal efficiency would be in the order of 3%.
- Condensing economizer (N. Gas) Flue gas reduction up to 65°C.

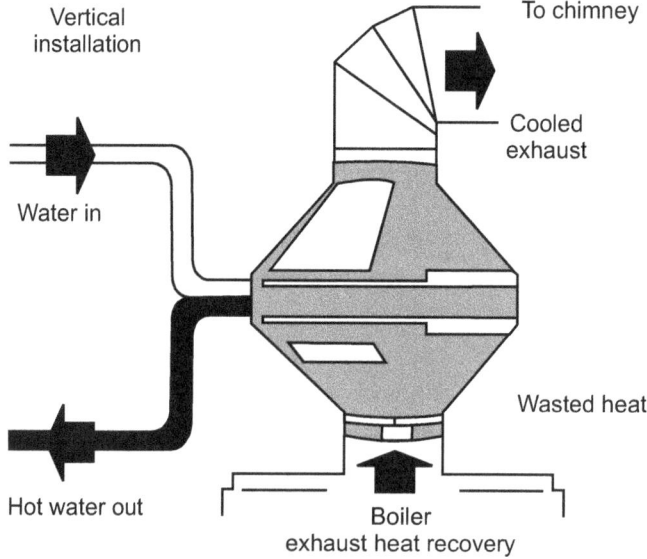

Fig. 1.13

6°C raise in feed water temperature, by economiser/condensate recovery, corresponds to a 1% saving in fuel consumption

(c) Combustion Air Preheating

- Combustion air preheating is an alternative to feedwater heating.
- In order to improve thermal efficiency by 1%, the combustion air temperature must be raised by 20°C.

(d) Complete Combustion

- Incomplete combustion can arise from a shortage of air or surplus of fuel or poor distribution of fuel.
- In the case of oil and gas fired systems, CO or smoke with normal or high excess air indicates burner system problems.

  Example: Poor mixing of fuel and air at the burner. Poor oil fires can result from improper viscosity, worn tips, carbonization on tips and deterioration of diffusers.

- **With coal firing:** Loss occurs as grit carry-over or carbon-in-ash (2% loss).

  Example: In chain grate stokers, large lumps will not burn out completely, while small pieces and fines may block the air passage, thus causing poor air distribution.

  Increase in the fines in pulverized coal also increases carbon loss.

(e) Control excess air

The optimum excess air level varies with furnace design, type of burner, fuel and process variables. Install oxygen trim system.

Table 1.1: Excess air levels for different fuels

Fuel	Type of Furnace or Burners	Excess Air (% by wt.)
Pulverised coal	Completely water-cooled furnace or slag-tap or dry-ash removal.	15-20
	Partially water-cooled furnace for dry-ash removal	15-40
Coal	Spreader stoker	30-60
	Water-cooler vibrating-grate stokers	30-60
	Chain-gate and travelling-grate stokers	15-50
	Underfeed stoker	20-50
Fuel oil	Oil burners, register type	15-20
	Multi-fuel burners and flat-flame	20-30
Natural gas	High pressure burner	5-7
Wood	Dutch over (10-23% through grates) and Hofft type	20-25
Bagasse	All furnaces	25-35
Black liquor	Recovery furnaces for draft and soda-pulping processes	30-40

(f) Blowdown Heat Recovery

- Efficiency Improvement - Up to 2 percentage points.

- Blowdown of boilers to reduce the sludge and solid content allows heat to go down the drain.

- The amount of blowdown should be minimized by following a good water treatment program, but installing a heat exchanger in the blowdown line allows this waste heat to be used in preheating makeup and feedwater.

- Heat recovery is most suitable for continuous blowdown operations which in turn provides the best water treatment program.

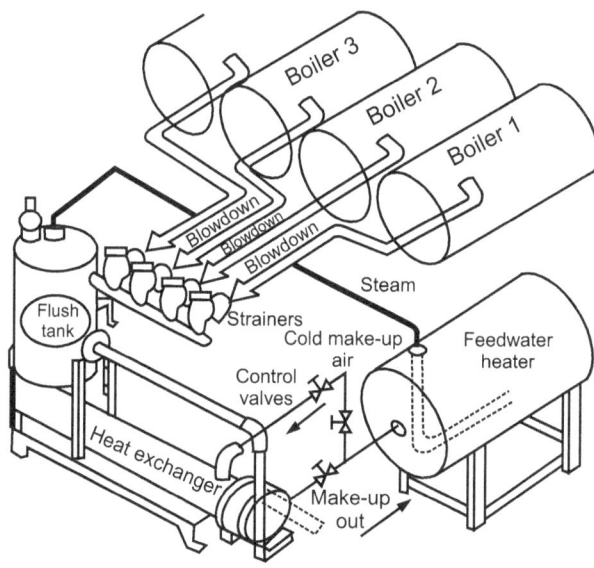

Fig. 1.14: Blowdown Heat Recovery System

(g) Reduction of Scaling and Soot Losses

- In oil and coal-fired boilers, soot buildup on tubes acts as an insulator against heat transfer. Any such deposits should be removed on a regular basis. Elevated stack temperatures may indicate excessive soot build-up. Also same result will occur due to scaling on the water side.

- High exit gas temperatures at normal excess air indicate poor heat transfer performance. This condition can result from a gradual build-up of gas-side or waterside deposits. Waterside deposits require a review of water treatment procedures and tube cleaning to remove deposits.

- Stack temperature should be checked and recorded regularly as an indicator of soot deposits. When the flue gas temperature rises about 20°C above the temperature for a newly cleaned boiler, it is time to remove the soot deposits

(h) Variable Speed Control for Fans, Blowers and Pumps

Generally, combustion air control is effected by throttling dampers fitted at forced and induced draft fans. Though dampers are simple means of control, they lack accuracy, giving poor control characteristics at the top and bottom of the operating range.

If the load characteristic of the boiler is variable, the possibility of replacing the dampers by a VSD should be evaluated.

(i) Optimum Loading of Boiler

- As the load falls, so does the value of the mass flow rate of the flue gases through the tubes. This reduction in flow rate for the same heat transfer area, reduced the exit fuel gas temperatures by a small extent, reducing the sensible heat loss.
- Below half load, most combustion appliances need more excess air to burn the fuel completely and increases the sensible heat loss.
- Operation of boiler below 25% should be avoided.
- Optimum efficiency occurs at 65-85% of full loads

(j) Boiler Replacement

- Boiler is replaced if the existing boiler is old and inefficient, not capable of firing cheaper substitution fuel, over or under-sized for present requirements, not designed for ideal loading conditions replacement option should be explored.
- Since boiler plants traditionally have a useful life of well over 25 years, replacement must be carefully studied.

1.12 COGENERATION

In all cycles discussed so far, the sole purpose was to convert a portion of the heat transferred to the working fluid to work, which is the most valuable form of energy. The remaining portion of heat is rejected to rivers, lakes, oceans, or to the atmosphere as waste heat because its quality (or grade) is too low to be of any practical use. Wasting a large amount of heat is a price we have to produce work, because electrical or mechanical work is the only form of energy on which many engineering devices can operate.

Many devices or systems however require energy input in the form of heat. The industries that heavily rely on process heat are chemical, pulp and paper, oil production and refining, steel making, food processing and textile industries. Such process heat is obtained with the use of cogeneration.

Cogeneration is the simultaneous generation of electricity and steam (or heat) in a single power plant. Cogeneration has been used since long by industries and municipalities that need process steam as well as electricity. Cogeneration is not usually used by large utilities which tend to produce electricity only. Cogeneration is advisable for industries that use large amount of process heat and also consume large amount of electric power. Therefore it makes economical as well as engineering sense to use waste heat.

From energy resources point of view, cogeneration is beneficial only if it saves primary energy when compared with separate generation of electricity and steam (or heat). The cogeneration plant efficiency is given by

$$\eta_{co} = \frac{E + \Delta H_s}{Q_A}$$

where, E = Electric energy generated

ΔH_s = Heat energy in process steam

Q_A = Heat added to the plant

1.12.1 Types of Cogeneration

There are two types of cogeneration (i) The topping cycle and (ii) The bottoming cycle.

(i) The Topping Cycle:

In which primary heat at the higher temperature end of the Rankine cycle is used to generate high pressure and temperature steam and electricity in the usual manner. Depending on process requirement, process steam at low pressure and temperature either (a) extracted from the turbine at an intermediate stage, much as for feed water heating or (b) taken at the turbine exhaust, in which it is called a back pressure turbine. Process steam pressure requirement vary widely between 0.5 and 40 bar.

(ii) The Bottoming Cycle:

In which primary heat is used at high temperature directly for process requirements. An example is the high temperature cement kiln. The processed low grade (low temperature) waste heat is then used to generate electricity obviously at low efficiency. The bottoming cycle has thus a combined efficiency and is below that to given in equation above and thus of little economic interest.

Only the topping cycle, therefore can provide true saving in primary energy. In addition, most process applications require low grade (low temperature) steam.

The topping cycle cogeneration plant is shown in Fig. 1.15.

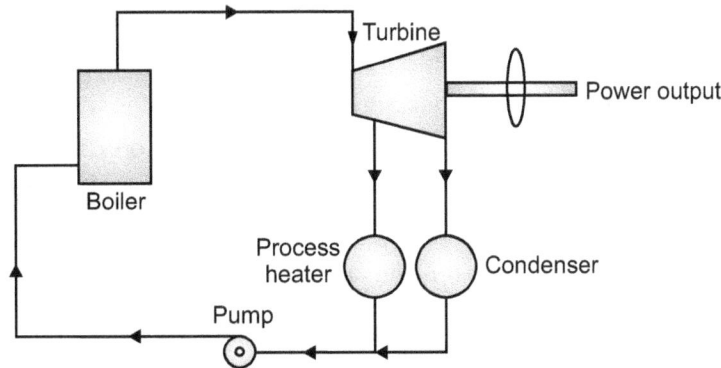

Fig. 1.15: An ideal topping cycle for cogeneration

There is no condenser in this system. Thus no heat is rejected from this plant as waste heat. In other words, all the energy transferred to the steam in the boiler is utilized as either process heat or electric power. Thus it is appropriate to define a utilization factor E_u for a cogeneration plant as

$$E_u = \frac{\text{Net work output + Process heat delivered}}{\text{Total heat input}}$$

$$= \frac{W_{net} + Q_p}{Q_{in}}$$

or $$E_u = 1 - \frac{Q_{out}}{Q_{in}}$$

where, Q_{out} = Heat rejected in the condenser

$\quad\quad Q_p$ = Process heat delivered

$\quad\quad Q_{in}$ = Total heat input

$\quad\quad W_{net}$ = Net work output

Thus theoretical cogeneration utilization factor is 100% but actual cogeneration plant have utilization factor as high as 70%. Future cogeneration plants are expected to have even higher utilization factor.

1.12.2 Combined Gas Power Cycle

The continued quest for higher thermal efficiencies has resulted in rather innovative modifications for conventional power plants. The binary vapour cycle discussed earlier is one such modification. A more popular modification involves a gas power cycle topping a vapour power cycle which is called the combined gas power cycle or just combined cycle. It consists of Brayton cycle topping a Rankine cycle, which has a higher thermal efficiency than either of the cycle operation individually.

Gas turbine cycle operates at considerably higher temperature than steam cycle. The maximum fluid temperature in steam cycle is 620°C in modern plants while gas turbine cycle operates at 1150°C. The use of higher temperature in gas turbine is made possible by recent development in cooling the turbine blades and coating the blades with higher temperature resistance material such as ceramics. Because of higher average temperature at which heat is added gas turbine cycles are efficient. However, the gas turbine cycle have one inherent disadvantage. The gas leaves the turbine at very high temperature (usually above 500°C) which wipes out the gain in thermal efficiency. The drawback can be overcome by using regeneration, but the improvement is limited. Therefore the thermal efficiency of gas turbine power plant is less than that of steam power plant. Therefore, if these two cycles are combined, then we can get the advantages of both cycles and overcome the drawbacks. For higher temperature range, gas turbine cycle is used while for low temperature range steam cycle is used. The result is a combined gas steam cycle.

Fig. 1.16 shows such a combined gas steam cycle.

In this cycle the energy of exhaust gases is used to generate steam in a heat exchanger which serves as a boiler for steam. More than one gas turbine is needed to supply sufficient heat to the steam. The steam cycle may be incorporated with regeneration and reheating. For reheating some more fuel can be burned in oxygen rich exhaust gases.

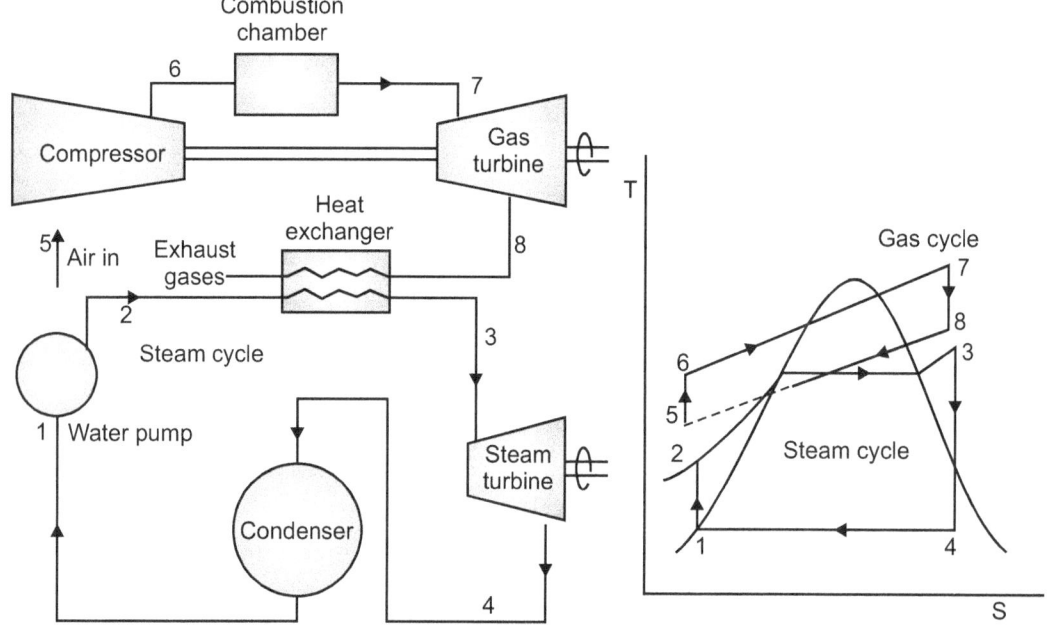

Fig. 1.16: Combined gas steam cycle

In the recent time, gas steam cycle proved to be more economical as it increases the efficiency without putting appreciable additional cost. Therefore such combined cycle have become more attractive. Thermal efficiencies well over 40 percent are reported as a result of combination.

1.13 Boiler Performance

The evapourative capacity of a boiler is the quantity of steam produced per hour at full load. It is also known as evapouration rate. The evapourative capacity of a boiler may be expressed in terms of:

    (i)   kg of steam/hr

    (ii)   kg of steam/hr/m^2 of heating surface.

    (iii) kg of steam/hr/m^3 volume of furnace.

    (iv) kg of steam/kg of fuel fired.

As per need boilers are producing steam of different qualities (wet, dry or super heated) at different pressure and temperature conditions. Their operating specifications such as temperature of feed water, fuel quality, firing methods, draught type are also different. In such conditions, it is not good to measure their performance in terms of quantity of steam produced per hour. Thus, a more logical method to express evapouration capacity, known as *equivalent evapouration* to compare steam generators has become popular.

1.14 EQUIVALENT EVAPOURATION

Equivalent evapouration is defined as the amount of water evaporated from water at 100°C to dry and saturated steam at 100°C.

As per standard conditions, 1 kg of water at 100°C requires 2256.9 kJ $\cong$ 2257 kJ to get converted into steam at 100°C.

Consider a boiler generating m_s kg of steam per hour at a pressure p and temperature T.

Let, h = Enthalpy of steam per kg under the generating conditions

Then,

For dry saturated steam at pressure p,

$$h = h_f + h_{fg}$$

For wet steam at pressure p with dryness fraction x,

$$h = h_f + x \cdot h_{fg}$$

For superheated steam at pressure p and temperature T_{sup},

$$h = h_g + c_p (T_{sup} - T_s)$$

If h_{f_1} = Specific enthalpy of water at given feed water temperature

Then, the heat gained by the steam from the boiler per unit time

$$= m_s (h - h_{f_1}) \text{ kJ}$$

The equivalent evapouration is given by,

$$m_e = \frac{m_s (h - h_{f_1})}{2257} = m_s \times F_e$$

where,

$$F_e = \frac{h - h_{f_1}}{2257} \text{ is known as \textbf{factor of evapouration}}$$

and its value is always greater than unity for all boilers.

It is defined as the ratio of heat received by 1 kg of water under working conditions to that received by water from and at 100°C.

1.15 BOILER EFFICIENCY

Boiler efficiency is the ratio of actual heat used in producing the steam to the heat liberated in the furnace. It is also termed as thermal efficiency of the boiler.

Boiler efficiency or thermal efficiency,

$$\eta = \frac{\text{Actual heat used in producing steam}}{\text{Heat liberated in the furnace}}$$

$$= \frac{m_s (h - h_{f_1})}{m_f \times C.V.}$$

where,

$$m_s = \text{Mass of steam generated in kg/hr}$$
$$m_f = \text{Mass of fuel burned in kg/hr}$$
$$C.V. = \text{Calorific value of fuel in kJ/kg}$$

If a boiler consisting of an economizer, and superheater is considered as a single unit, then its efficiency is known as **overall efficiency** of the boiler.

1.15.1 Factors Influencing Boiler Efficiency

Factors influencing boiler efficiency can be categorised into two groups :

(1) Fixed factors and (2) Variable factors.

1. **Fixed Factors:**

    (a) Boiler design which includes the shape and volume of the furnace, the flues arrangement, water and steam circulation arrangement, efficiency of heating surfaces,

    (b)   Properties of fuel burnt,

    (c)   Flue gas and ash heat losses.

2.   **Variable Factors :**

    (a)   The condition of heat absorbing surfaces,

    (b)   Humidity and temperature of combustion air,

    (c)   Effectiveness in combustion,

    (d)   Excess air fluctuations,

    (e)   Actual firing rate,

    (f)   Change in draught from rated, due to atmospheric conditions.

1.16 BOILER TRIAL

The main objectives of conducting a trial on an existing steam boiler are as follows :

    1.   To determine the efficiency and capacity of the boiler.

    2.   To check the performance with the rated performance.

    3.   To prepare account of the heat energy input and output including various losses for the purpose of corrective steps to improve efficiency.

1.16.1 Heat Losses in a Boiler Plant

The following heat losses occur in an boiler plant.

    1.   Heat loss through dry flue gases.

    2.   Heat carried away by steam in flue gases.

    3.   Heat loss due to unburnt fuel.

    4.   Heat loss due to incomplete combustion.

    5.   Heat loss due to radiation.

SOLVED PROBLEMS

Problem 1.1: 5500 kg of steam is produced per hour at a pressure of 7.6 bar in a boiler with dryness fraction 0.98. The feed water temperature is 51°C. The amount of coal burnt per hour is 650 kg of calorific value 30500 kJ/kg. Determine the boiler efficiency and equivalent evapouration.

Solution:

Given: m_s = 5,500 kg/hr, p = 7.6 bar, x = 0.98, T_1 = 51°C, m_f = 650 kg/hr, C.V. = 30500 kJ/kg.

Steam generated per kg of coal $= \dfrac{5,500}{650} = 8.461$ kg/kg of fuel

Enthalpy of feed water at 51°C from steam table,

$$h_{f_1} = 213.70 \text{ kJ/kg}$$

Enthalpy of steam at 7.6 bar from steam table

$$h_f = 711.68 \text{ kJ/kg}$$

$$h_{fg} = 2053.7 \text{ kJ/kg}$$

$$h = h_f + x\, h_{fg}$$

$$= 711.67 + 0.98 \times 2053.7$$

$$= 2724.296 \text{ kJ/kg}$$

Boiler efficiency,

$$\eta = \frac{m_s\,(h - h_{f_1})}{m_f \times C.V.} = \frac{5500 \times (2724.29 - 231.7)}{650 \times 30500}$$

$$= 0.6965 = \mathbf{69.65\%}$$

Equivalent evapouration,

$$m_e = \frac{m_s\,(h - h_{f_1})}{2257}$$

$$= \frac{8.461 \times (2724.29 - 213.7)}{2257}$$

$$m_e = \mathbf{9.42 \text{ kg/kg of coal}}$$

Problem 1.2: The following observations were recorded during a boiler trial of 1 hr duration. 700 kg of coal of calorific value 30,000 kJ/kg is used to produce 5,250 kg of steam at a pressure of 12 bar. Dryness fraction of steam is 94%. Temperature of steam leaving the superheater is 250°C and temperature of hot well is 45°C.
Calculate:

(i)   Equivalent evapouration.

(ii) Thermal efficiency of boiler.

(iii) Heat added in superheater.

Solution:

Given: m_s = 5,250 kg/hr, p = 12 bar, C.V. = 30,000 kJ/kg, x = 0.94, T_{sup} = 250°C, T_1 = 45°C, m_f = 700 kg/hr

(i)   Equivalent evapouration:

From steam table corresponding to feed water temperature 45°C, we can find,

$$h_{f_1} = 188.45 \text{ kJ/kg}$$

and corresponding to steam pressure of 12 bar,

$$h_f = 798.43 \text{ kJ/kg}$$

$$h_{fg} = 1984.3 \text{ kJ/kg}$$

For wet steam,

$$h = h_f + x \cdot h_{fg}$$

$$= 798.43 + 0.94 \times 1984.3$$

$$= 2663.37 \text{ kJ/kg}$$

Equivalent evapouration,

$$m_e = \frac{m_s\,(h - h_{f_1})}{2257} = \frac{5250 \times (2663.37 - 188.45)}{2257}$$

$$= 5757.61 \text{ kg/hr}$$

Mass of water evaporated per kg of coal,

$$m_e = \frac{5757.61}{700} = \textbf{823 kg/kg of coal}$$

(ii) Boiler efficiency:

$$\eta = \frac{m_s\,(h - h_{f_1})}{m_f \times C.V.}$$

$$= \frac{5250 \times (2663.37 - 188.45)}{700 \times 30000}$$

$$= 0.6187 = \textbf{61.87\%}$$

(iii) Heat added in superheater:

Heat added in superheater = Enthalpy of superheated steam – Enthalpy of wet steam

$$= (h_{sup} - h)$$

From steam table corresponding to a steam pressure of 12 bar, we find that,

$$h_g = 2782.7 \text{ kJ/kg}$$

and

$$T = 188°C$$

$$\therefore \qquad h_{sup} = h_g + c_p\,(T_{sup} - T)$$

$$= 2782.7 + 2.1\,(250 - 188) \quad \text{(Taking } c_p = 2.1 \text{ kJ/kg·K)}$$

$$= 2912.9 \text{ kJ/kg}$$

Heat added to superheater $= 2912.9 - 2663.37$

$$= \textbf{249.53 kJ/kg}$$

Problem 1.3: The following observations were made on a boiler plant during one hour test.

Steam generated = 37500 kg at 20 bar and 260°C

Temperature of water entering the economiser

= 15°C

Temperature of water leaving the economiser

= 90°C

Fuel used = 4400 kg

Energy of combustion of fuel = 31000 kJ/kg

Calculate :

(i)   The equivalent evapouration per kg of fuel.

(ii) The thermal efficiency of the plant.

(iii) The percentage heat energy of the fuel energy utilised by the economiser.

Solution:

Given: m_s = 37500 kg/hr, p = 20 bar, T_{sup} = 260°C, T_{ei} = 15°C, T_{eo} = 90°C, m_f = 4000 kg/hr, C.V. = 31000 kJ/kg.

(i)   Equivalent evapouration per kg of fuel:

Here boiler and economiser is considered as a single unit, so feed water temperature is 15°C and corresponding to this temperature from steam table,

$$h_{f1} = 62.9 \text{ kJ/kg}$$

Also at steam pressure of 20 bar,

$$h_g = 2797.2 \text{ kJ/kg}$$

and $\qquad\qquad\qquad$ T = 212.37 °C

For superheated steam,

$$h = h_g + c_p\,(T_{sup} - T)$$
$$= 2797.2 + 2.1 \times (260 - 212.37)$$
$$= 2897 \text{ kJ/kg}$$

∴   Equivalent evapouration in kg/hr

$$m_e = \frac{m_s\,(h - h_{f1})}{2257} = \frac{37500 \times (2897 - 62.9)}{2257}$$

$$= 47088.50 \text{ kg/hr}$$

Equivalent evapouration in kg/kg of fuel.

$$m_e = \frac{47088.50}{4400} = \textbf{10.70 kg/kg of fuel}$$

(ii) Thermal efficiency of the plant:

$$\eta = \frac{m_s\,(h - h_{f_1})}{m_f \times C.V.} = \frac{37500 \times (2897 - 62.9)}{4400 \times 31000}$$

$$= \textbf{0.7792} = \textbf{77.92\%}$$

(iii) Percentage heat energy of the fuel energy utilised by the economiser:

From steam table, at 90°C,

$$h_{f_2} = 376.80 \text{ kJ/kg}$$

Heat utilised by economiser,

$$Q_e = m_s\,(h_{f_2} - h_{f_1})$$

$$= 37500 \times (376.8 - 62.9)$$

$$= 11.77 \times 10^6 \text{ kJ/hr}$$

$$= \frac{11.77 \times 10^6}{4400} \text{ kJ/kg of fuel}$$

$$= 2675.38 \text{ kJ}$$

$$\text{\% heat utilised by economiser} = \frac{2675.38}{31000} \times 100 = \textbf{8.63\%}$$

Problem 1.4: The following data was recorded during a test performed on a steam plant consisting of a Lancashire boiler, economiser and a superheater.

Steam generated = 5,000 kg/hr at 14 bar pressure

Mass of coal burnt = 670 kg/hr

Calorific value of coal = 29500 kJ/kg

Temperature of feed water at entry and exit of economiser = 30°C and 130°C respectively.

Temperature of steam leaving superheater = 320°C.

Dryness fraction of steam leaving boiler = 0.97

c_p (superheated steam) = 2.3 kJ/kg·K

c_p (water) = 4.18 kJ/kg·K

Calculate:

(1)   Factor of evapouration.

(2)   Overall efficiency of the plant.

(3)   The percentage of available heat utilised in the boiler, economiser and super-heater respectively. Hence, determine percentage of heat lost.

Solution:

Given: m_s = 5000 kg/hr, p = 14 bar, m_f = 670 kg/hr, C.V. = 29500, T_{ei} = 30°C, T_{eo} = 130°C, T_{sup} = 320°C, x = 0.97.

1.   Factor of evapouration:

$$\text{Mass of steam per kg of coal, } \dot{m}_s = \frac{5000}{670} = 7.46 \text{ kg/kg of fuel}$$

From steam table, enthalpy of feed water at 30°C,

$$h_{f_1} = 125.68 \text{ kJ/kg}$$

and for steam at 14 bar pressure,

h_f = 830.07 kJ/kg, h_{fg} = 1957.7 kJ/kg, h_g = 2787.8 kJ/kg and T = 195°C.

Enthalpy of superheated steam,

$$h = h_g + c_p (T_{sup} - T)$$
$$= 2787.8 + 2.3 \times (320 - 195)$$
$$= 3075.3 \text{ kJ/kg}$$

Factor of evapouration, $F_e = \dfrac{h - h_{f_1}}{2257} = \dfrac{3075.3 - 125.68}{2257} = \textbf{1.307}$

2. Overall efficiency of the plant :

$$\eta = \frac{\dot{m}_s (h - h_{f_1})}{C.V.} = \frac{7.46 \times (3075.3 - 125.68)}{29500}$$
$$= 0.7459$$
$$= \textbf{74.59\%}$$

3. Percentage of available heat utilised:

(a) Heat utilised in boiler:

Water enters in boiler at 130°C and steam leaves boiler at 14 bar pressure (x = 0.97)

∴ Q_B = Enthalpy of steam at boiler outlet – Enthalpy of water at boiler inlet

$$= \dot{m}_s \, [(h_f + x \, h_{fg}) - h_{f_2}] \qquad (h_{f_2} \text{ at } 130°C = 546.3 \text{ kJ/kg})$$

$$= 7.46 \, [(830.6) + 0.97 \times (957.7) - 546.3]$$

$$= 16283.23 \text{ kJ}$$

% Heat utilisation in boiler $= \dfrac{Q_B}{Q_s} \times 100 = \dfrac{16283.33}{29500} \times 100 = \mathbf{55.197\%}$

(b) Heat utilised in economiser:

$$Q_e = \dot{m}_s \cdot c_{pw} \, (T_{eo} - T_{ei})$$

$$= 7.46 \times 4.18 \times (130 - 30)$$

$$= 3118.28 \text{ kJ}$$

% Heat utilisation in economiser $= \dfrac{Q_e}{Q_s} \times 100 = \dfrac{3118.28}{29500} \times 100$

$$= \mathbf{10.570\%}$$

(c) Heat utilisation in superheater:

$$Q_{sup} = \dot{m}_s \, \{[h_g + c_p \, (T_{sup} - T)] - [h_f + x \, h_{fg}]\}$$

$$= 7.46 \, \{[2787.8 + 2.3 \, (320 - 195)]$$

$$- [830.01 + 0.97 \times 1957.7]$$

$$= 2396.90 \text{ kJ}$$

% Heat utilised in superheater $= \dfrac{Q_{sup}}{Q_s} \times 100$

$$= \dfrac{2396.90}{29500} \times 100$$

$$= \mathbf{8.125\%}$$

(d) Percentage heat loss : 100 – % heat utilised in boiler, economiser and superheater

$$= 100 - (55.197 + 10.57 + 8.125)$$

$$= \mathbf{26.108\%}$$

Problem 1.5 : In an experiment on a small oil-fired boiler, the steam is produced at 6 bar pressure, with dryness fraction 0.96. The 75 litres of water is converted into steam in 9.5 minutes. Then 10 litres of fuel oil with specific gravity 0.85 and calorific value 43125 kJ/kg is consumed in 11 minutes 25 seconds. The feed water temperature is 35°C. Determine the boiler efficiency and equivalent evapouration.   **(P.U. May 2009)**

Solution:

Given: p = 6 bar, x = 0.6, water = 75 litres, 10 litres oil, C.V. = 43125 kJ/kg, T_1 = 35°C.

Mass of steam = 75 × 1 = 75 kg in 9.5 min.

$$\text{Mass of steam per hour} = 75 \times \frac{60}{9.5}$$

$$m_s = 473.684 \text{ kg/hr}$$

$$\text{Mass of oil} = 10 \times 0.85$$

$$= 8.5 \text{ kg in 11 min. 25 sec.}$$

$$= 8.5 \text{ kg in 685 sec}$$

$$\text{Mass of oil per hour} = 8.5 \times \frac{3600}{685}$$

$$m_f = 44.671 \text{ kg}$$

$$\text{Mass of steam per kg oil } (\dot{m}_s) = \frac{473.684}{44.67} = 10.60 \text{ kg/kg of oil}$$

Enthalpy of feed water at 35°C from steam table,

$$h_{f_1} = 146.56 \text{ kJ/kg}$$

and for steam at 6 bar from steam table,

$$h_f = 670.42 \text{ kJ/kg}$$

$$h_{fg} = 2085.0 \text{ kJ/kg}$$

$$h = h_f + x\, h_{fg}$$

$$= 670.42 + 0.96 \times 2085$$

$$= 2672.02 \text{ kJ/kg}$$

$$\text{Efficiency of boiler,} \qquad \eta = \frac{\dot{m}_s\,(h - h_{f_1})}{\text{C.V.}}$$

$$= \frac{10.60 \times (2672.02 - 146.56)}{43125}$$

$$= 0.6207$$

$$= \textbf{62.07\%}$$

$$\text{Equivalent evapouration,} \qquad m_e = \frac{\dot{m}_s\,(h - h_{f_1})}{2257}$$

$$= \frac{10.60 \times (2672.02 - 146.56)}{2257}$$

$$= \textbf{11.86 kg/kg of oil}$$

1.17 ENERGY BALANCE

- In a boiler, heat is produced by burning of fuel in the furnace. But all heat is not utilised for generation of steam. Some heat is lost by different ways.
- A systematic representation of heat release and heat distribution on minute, hour or per kg of fuel basis is known as energy balance sheet or heat balance sheet.
- The procedure to draw heat balance sheet on kJ/min basis is explained below:

(A) First of all compute heat release by the fuel.

Heat released by the fuel,

$$Q_s = m_f \times C.V.$$

where,

$$m_f = \text{Mass flow rate of fuel in kg/min}$$
$$C.V. = \text{Calorific value of fuel in kJ/kg}$$

(B) Calculate heat distribution in different ways.

1. Heat utilised to form steam

$$Q_1 = m_s (h - h_{f_1})$$

where,

$$m_s = \text{Mass of steam generated per minute}$$
$$h = \text{Enthalpy of steam generated, kJ/kg}$$
$$h_f = \text{Enthalpy of water, kJ/kg}$$

2. Heat lost through dry flue gases

$$Q_2 = m_g c_{pg} (T_g - T_a)$$

where,

$$m_g = \text{Mass of dry flue gas per minute}$$
$$c_{pg} = \text{Specific heat of flue gases, kJ/kg·K}$$
$$T_g = \text{Flue gas temperature, °C (K)}$$
$$T_a = \text{Temperature of air entering combustion chamber °C (K)}$$

3. Heat carried away by steam (moisture) in flue gases

$$Q_3 = m_m (h_g + c_{ps} (T_{sup} - T_s) - h_{f_2})$$

where,

$$m_m = \text{Mass of moisture per min.}$$
$$c_{ps} = \text{Mean specific heat of superheated steam in flue gases}$$
$$T_{sup} = \text{Temperature of steam leaving the superheater}$$

Sometimes steam formed by combustion of hydrogen is added to above mass.

Mass of steam formed $= 9H_2$

where, $H_2 =$ Mass of hydrogen present per kg of fuel

4. **Heat loss due to unburnt fuel**

$$Q_4 = m_{fu} \times C.V.$$
$$m_{fu} = \text{Mass of unburnt fuel per minute}$$

5. **Heat loss due to incomplete combustion of carbon to carbon monoxide**

$$Q_5 = m_2 \times CV_C$$

where,

$$m_2 = \text{Mass of carbon or CO in flue gases/min}$$
$$CV_C = \text{Calorific value of carbon or CO}$$

6. **Heat lost due to radiation**

$$Q_6 = Q_5 - (Q_1 + Q_2 + Q_3 + Q_4 + Q_5)$$

(C) Above calculated values are placed in a table as following :

Heat supplied	kJ/min	%	Heat utilised	kg/min	%
Heat released by the fuel	Q_s	100	1. Heat used to form steam.	Q_1	$\dfrac{Q_1}{Q_s} \times 100$
			2. Heat lost through dry flue gases.	Q_2	$\dfrac{Q_2}{Q_s} \times 100$
			3. Heat carried a way by steam in flue gases.	Q_3	$\dfrac{Q_3}{Q_s} \times 100$
			4. Heat loss due to unburnt fuel.	Q_4	$\dfrac{Q_4}{Q_s} \times 100$
			5. Heat loss due to incomplete combustion.	Q_5	$\dfrac{Q_5}{Q_s} \times 100$
			6. Heat loss due to radiation.	Q_6	$\dfrac{Q_6}{Q_s} \times 100$
	Q_s	100		Q_u	100

PROBLEMS ON ENERGY BALANCE

Problem 1.6: The following observations were recorded during a boiler trial.

Steam produced	= 540 kg/hr at 10 bar
Fuel used	= 65 kg/hr
Moisture in fuel	= 2% by mass
Mass of dry flue gases	= 9 kg/kg of fuel
Lower calorific value of fuel	= 32000 kJ/kg
Temperature of flue gases	= 325°C
Temperature of boiler house	= 28°C
Feed water temperature	= 50°C
Mean specific heat of flue gases	= 1 kJ/kg·K

Dryness fraction of steam $= 0.95$
Specific heat for superheated steam $= 2.3$ kJ/kg·K
Prepare the energy balance sheet for the boiler.

Solution:

Given: $m_s = 540$ kg/hr, $p = 10$ bar, $m_f = 65$ kg/hr, $m_m = 0.02$ kg/kg of fuel, $m_g = 9$ kg/kg of fuel, C.V. $= 32000$ kJ/kg, $T_g = 325°C$, $T_a = 28°C$, $T_1 = 50°C$, $c_{pg} = 1$ kg/kg·K, $x = 0.95$

(A) Heat released by the fuel per kg:

$$Q_s = \text{Mass of fuel} \times \text{C.V.}$$
$$= (1 - 0.02) \times 32000 \qquad (\because 2\% \text{ moisture in the fuel})$$
$$= \textbf{31360 kJ}$$

(B) Calculation for heat distribution:

1.   Heat utilised to form steam per kg of fuel.

Steam produced per kg of fuel, $\dot{m}_s = \dfrac{\dot{m}_s}{m_f} = \dfrac{540}{65} = \textbf{8.31 kg.}$

From steam table at 50°C,
$$h_{f_1} = 209.26 \text{ kJ/kg}$$

and at 10 bar pressure,
$$h_f = 762.61 \text{ kJ/kg}$$
$$h_{fg} = 2013.6 \text{ kJ/kg}$$

Now,
$$h = h_f + x\, h_{fg}$$
$$= 762.61 + 0.95 \times 2013.6$$
$$= \textbf{2675.53}$$

$$Q_1 = \dot{m}_s (h - h_{f_1}) = 8.31 \times (2675.53 - 209.26)$$
$$= \textbf{20494.70 kJ}$$

2.   Heat lost through dry flue gases,
$$Q_2 = m_g \cdot c_{pg} \cdot (T_g - T_a)$$
$$= 9 \times 1 \times (325 - 28)$$
$$= \textbf{2673 kJ}$$

3.   Heat carried away by moisture in flue gases.
From steam table at 1.03 bar,
$$h_g = 2776.0 \text{ kJ/kg}$$
and
$$T = 100°C$$

at 28°C h_{f_2} = 117.3 kJ/kg

$$Q_3 = m_m (h_g + c_{ps} (T_{sup} - T_s) - h_{f_2})$$

$$= 0.02 (2676.0 + 2.3 (325 - 100) - 117.3)$$

$$= \textbf{61.524 kJ}$$

4.   Heat lost due to radiation,

$$Q_4 = Q_s - (Q_1 + Q_2 + Q_3)$$

$$= 31360 - (20494.7 + 2673 + 61.524)$$

$$= \textbf{8130.78 kJ}$$

(C) Heat balance sheet on per kg fuel basis:

Heat supplied	kJ	%	Heat utilised	kJ	%
Heat supplied by 1 kg of fuel	31360	100	1. Heat used to form steam.	20494.7	65.36
			2. Heat lost through dry flue gases.	2673.0	8.52
			3. Heat carried away by moisture in flue gases.	61.524	0.19
			4. Heat lost by radiation.	8130.78	25.93
Q_s = 31360		100		Q_u = 31360	100.00

Problem 1.7: The following data was recorded during a test on a boiler:

Mass of feed water   = 650 kg/hr

Temperature of water at entry and exhaust of the economiser = 30°C and 50°C respectively.

Steam pressure   = 11 bar

Fuel used   = 60 kg/hr

Calorific value of fuel   = 45000 kJ/kg

Temperature of flue gases   = 300°C

Dryness fraction of steam   = 0.97

Boiler room temperature   = 32°C

c_p for gases   = 1.05 kJ/kg·K

c_p for superheated steam   = 2.2 kJ/kg·K

c_p for water   = 1.05 kJ/kg·K

The composition of fuel used by mass,

H_2 = 12%, C = 84% and remaining is ash.

The dry flue gas analysis by volume CO_2 = 13%, O_2 = 5%, N_2 = 82%.

Steam partial pressure in exhaust gases is 0.07 bar.

Draw heat balance sheet on the basis of one kg of fuel.

Solution:

Given: m_s = 650 kg/hr, m_f = 60 kg/hr, $\dot{m}_s$ = 650/60 = 10.83 kg/kg of fuel, p = 11 bar, C.V. = 45000 kJ/kg, T_g = 300°C, x = 0.97, T_a = 32°C, c_{pg} = 1.05 kJ/kg·K, c_{ps} = 2.2 kg/kg·K, c_{pw} = 4.18 kJ/kg·K, Steam partial pressure = 0.07 bar.

(A) Heat supplied by 1 kg of fuel:
$$Q_s = 45000 \text{ kJ/kg}$$

(B) Calculation of heat distribution:

1. Heat used to form steam per kg of fuel from steam table at 50°,
$$h_{f_1} = 209.26 \text{ kJ/kg}$$

and at 11 bar pressure, h_f = 781.12 kJ/kg

$$h_{fg} = 1998.5 \text{ kJ/kg}$$

Now, $h = h_f + x\, h_{fg}$

$$= 781.12 + 0.97 \times 1998.5$$
$$= \textbf{2719.665 kJ/kg}$$

and $Q_1 = \dot{m}_s\,(h - h_{f_1})$

$$= 10.833 \times (2719.665 - 209.26)$$
$$= \textbf{27195.21 kJ/kg of fuel}$$

2. Heat utilised in superheater,
$$Q_2 = \dot{m}_s \cdot c_{pw}\,(T_{eo} - T_{ei})$$
$$= 10.833 \times 4.18 \times (50 - 30)$$
$$= \textbf{905.64 kJ}$$

3. Heat lost through dry flue gases:

Air required to burn 1 kg of fuel

$$= \frac{N_2 \times C}{33 \times (CO + CO_2)} = \frac{82 \times 84}{33 \times (0 + 13)} = \textbf{16.056 kg}$$

Dry gases formed per kg of fuel,

$$m_g = 16.056 + 0.84 = \textbf{16.896 kg}$$

Then, heat lost through dry flue gases,

$$Q_3 = m_g \cdot c_{pg} \cdot (T_g - T_a)$$

$$= 16.896 \times 1.05 \times (300 - 32)$$

$$= \textbf{4754.52 kJ/kg of fuel}$$

4.   Heat carried away by moisture in flue gases :

The moisture formed per kg of fuel,

$$m_m = 9 \times H_2 = 9 \times 0.12 = 1.08 \text{ kg}$$

From steam table at 0.07 bar.

$$h_g = 2572.6 \text{ kJ/kg}, \; T_s = 39.025°C$$

and at 32°C

$$h_{f_2} = 134.02°C$$

Then,

$$Q_4 = m_m (h_g + c_{ps} (T_{sup} - T_s) - h_{f_2})$$

$$= 1.08 \times (2572.6 + 2.2 \times (300 - 39.025) - 134.02)$$

$$= \textbf{3253.743 kJ}$$

5.   Heat lost due to radiation.

$$Q_5 = Q_s - (Q_1 + Q_2 + Q_3 + Q_4)$$

$$= 45000 - (27195.21 + 905.64 + 4754.52 + 3253.743)$$

$$= \textbf{8890.88 kJ}$$

(C) Heat balance sheet on per kg of fuel basis :

Heat supplied	kJ	%	Heat utilised	kJ	%
Heat supplied by 1 kg of fuel	45,000	100	1. Heat used to form steam	27195.21	60.43
			2. Heat used by superheater	905.64	2.01
			3. Heat lost through dry flue gases	4754.52	10.57
			4. Heat carried away by moisture in flue gases	3253.743	7.23
			5. Heat lost by radiation	8890.88	19.76
Q_s = 45000		100		Q_u = 45000	100.00

Problem 1.8 : The following results were obtained from a boiler trial.

$$Feed\ water/hr\ =\ 700\ kg$$

$$Feed\ temperature\ =\ 27°C$$

$$Steam\ pressure\ =\ 8\ bar$$

$$Dryness\ =\ 0.97$$

$$Coal\ consumption\ =\ 100\ kg/hr\ (C.V.\ =\ 25000\ kJ/kg)$$

$$Unburnt\ coal\ collected\ =\ 7.25\ kg/hr\ (C.V.\ =\ 2000\ kJ/kg)$$

$$Flue\ formed/kg\ of\ fuel\ =\ 17.3\ kg$$

$$Flue\ temperature\ =\ 325°C$$

$$c_{pg}\ =\ 1.025\ kJ/kg{\cdot}K$$

$$Room\ air\ temperature\ =\ 16°C$$

Draw up heat balance sheet on kg/min basis. From the heat balance sheet, write the value of boiler efficiency.   **(P.U. December 2007)**

Solution:

Given: m_s = 700 kg/hr, T_1 = 27°C, p = 8 bar, x = 0.97, m_f = 100 kg/hr. (C.V. = 25000 kJ/kg·K), m_{fu} = 7.25 kg/hr, (C.V. = 2000 kJ/kg), m_g = 17.3 kg/kg of fuel, T_g = 325°C, c_{pg} = 1.025 kg/kg·K, T_a = 16°C.

Here heat balance sheet on minute basis is required. So first do following conversions.

$$m_s\ =\ 700\ kg/hr\ =\ \frac{700}{60}\ kg/min\ =\ \textbf{11.67 kg/min}$$

$$m_f\ =\ \frac{100}{60}\ =\ \textbf{1.67 kg/min}$$

$$m_{fu}\ =\ \frac{7.25}{60}\ =\ \textbf{0.121 kJ/min}$$

(A) Heat supplied/released by fuel per minute:

$$Q_s\ =\ m_f \times C.V.$$

$$=\ 1.67 \times 25000$$

$$=\ \textbf{41750 kJ/min}$$

(B) Calculation for heat utilization:

1. Heat used for steam formation

    From steam table at 27°C heat in water,

$$h_{f_1}\ =\ 113.13\ kJ/kg$$

and at 8 bar for steam,

$$h_f = 720.9 \text{ kJ/kg}$$

$$h_{fg} = 2046.5 \text{ kJ/kg}$$

Now,

$$h = h_f + x \, h_{fg}$$

$$= 720.9 + 0.97 \times 2046.5$$

$$= 2706.005 \text{ kJ/kg}$$

Then,

$$Q_1 = m_s (h - h_{f_1}) = 11.67 \times (2706.005 - 113.13)$$

$$= \textbf{30258.21 kJ/min}$$

2. Heat loss through dry flue gases,

$$Q_2 = m_g \cdot c_{pg} (T_g - T_a)$$

$$= 17.3 \times 1.67 \times 1.025 \times (325 - 16)$$

$$(\because 1.67 \text{ kg fuel burnt per minutes})$$

$$= \textbf{9150.50 kJ/min}$$

3. Heat loss due to unburnt fuel

$$Q_3 = m_{fu} \times \text{C.V.}$$

$$= 0.121 \times 2000$$

$$= \textbf{242 kJ/kg}$$

4. Heat loss due to radiation

$$Q_4 = Q_s - (Q_1 + Q_2 + Q_3)$$

$$= 41750 - (30258.21 + 9150.50 + 242)$$

$$= \textbf{2099.29 kJ/min}$$

(C) Heat balance sheet on minute basis:

Heat supplied	kJ/min	%	Heat utilised	kJ/min	%
Heat supplied per min	41750	100	1. Heat used for steam formation	30258.21	72.47
			2. Heat loss through dry flue gases	9150.5	21.92
			3. Heat loss because of unburnt fuel	242.0	0.58
			4. Heat loss due to radiation	2099.29	5.03
Q$_s$ = 41750		**100**		**Q$_u$ = 41750**	**100.00**

From heat balance sheet,

Efficiency of boiler, η = **72.47%**

Problem 1.9 : 20000 kg of feed weather at 25°C is supplied to a boiler during a trial of 8 hours. At the end of trial, 800 kg of water at 55°C is drained from boiler. Pressure of steam produced by the boiler was recorded as 12 bar with dryness fraction 0.95. The 2520 kg of coal is consumed during trial period with calorific value 30000 kJ/kg.

Calculate the actual evapouration rate, equivalent evapouration and prepare the energy balance sheet for the given data.

Solution:

Given: Water supplied = 20000 kg, T_1 = 25°C, p = 12 bar, x = 0.95, Coal burned = 2520 kg, C.V. = 30000 kJ/kg.

Total steam produced in 8 hours = Water supplied − Water drained

$$= 20000 - 800 = 19200 \text{ kg}$$

∴ Evapouration rate per hour $= \dfrac{19200}{8} = 2400 \text{ kg/hr}$

Fuel consumed $= \dfrac{2520}{8} = 315 \text{ kg/hr}$

Mass of steam per kg of coal, $\dot{m}_s = \dfrac{2400}{315} = 7.619 \text{ kg per kg of fuel}$

Heat in feed water at 25°C from steam table,

$$h_{f_1} = 108.77 \text{ kJ/kg}$$

Heat in steam at 12 bar pressure,

$$h_f = 798.43 \text{ kJ/kg}$$
$$h_{fg} = 1984.3 \text{ kJ/kg}$$
$$h = h_f + x\, h_{fg} = 798.43 + 0.95 \times 1984.3 = \textbf{2649.315}$$

Equivalent evapouration, $m_e = \dfrac{\dot{m}_s\, (h - h_{f_1})}{2257}$

$$= \dfrac{7.619 \times (2649.315 - 108.77)}{2257}$$

$$= \textbf{8.576 kg/kg of fuel}$$

Heat supplied during 8 hours,

$$Q_s = 2520 \times 30000 = 75.60 \times 10^6 \text{ kJ}$$

Heat used to form steam for 8 hours,

$$Q_1 = 19200 \times (h - h_{f_1})$$
$$= 19200 \times (2649.315 - 108.77)$$
$$= \textbf{48.778} \times \textbf{10}^{\textbf{6}} \textbf{ kJ}$$

Heat taken by 800 kg of water = (Heat content at 55°C − Heat content at 25°C) × 800

$$= 800 \times (230.17 - 108.77)$$
$$= \textbf{97.120} \times \textbf{10}^{\textbf{3}} \textbf{ kJ}$$

$$\text{Unaccounted heat} = 75.0 \times 10^6 - (48.778 \times 10^6 + 97.120 \times 10^3)$$
$$= 26.724 \times 10^6 \text{ kJ}$$
$$\text{Boiler efficiency, } \eta = \frac{48.778 \times 10^6}{75.0 \times 10^6} = 0.64 = \mathbf{64\%}$$

1.18 DRAUGHT

It is necessary to force the fresh air in combustion chamber and to exhaust the gases produced by combustion. This flow is possible by maintaining pressure difference. The pressure difference which causes flow of gas is called as draught.

Classification of Draught:

There are basically two methods of producing draught:
1. Natural or Chimney Draught.
2. Artificial Draught.
     (a) Steam Jet Draught
           (i)   Induced Draught
           (ii)   Forced Draught
     (b) Mechanical Draught
           (i)   Induced Fan Draught
           (ii)   Balanced Draught
           (iii) Forced Fan Draught

1.19 NATURAL DRAUGHT

Natural draught is also known as **chimney draught** because chimney is used to produce this draught. A chimney is a vertical tubular structure built either of concrete, steel or masonry. The draught produced by chimney is due to density difference between the column of hot gases inside the chimney and the outside cold air (cold compared to hot gases).

Fig. 1.17 shows schematic arrangement of a chimney of height H metres above the grate.

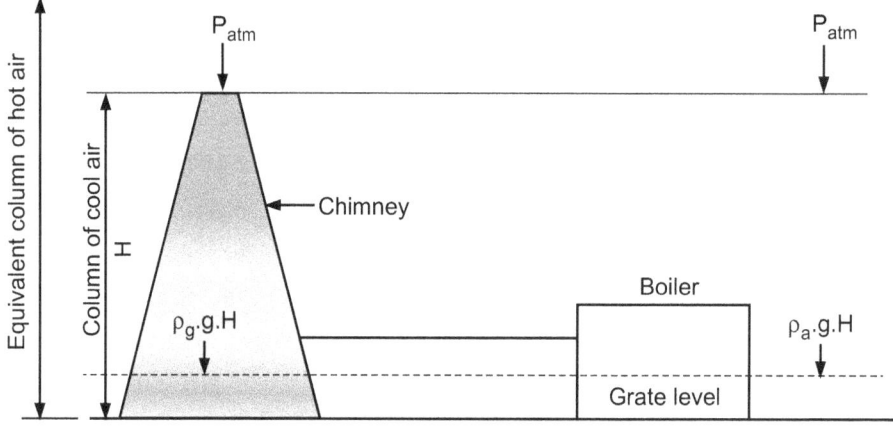

Fig. 1.17

Let,

H = Height of chimney above the grate in m

h = Draught required in terms of mm of water

p_a = Atmospheric pressure at chimney top

ρ_g = Average mass density of hot gas

ρ_a = Mass density of air outside the chimney

Now, pressure at the grate level (chimney side) (because of hot gases)

$$p_1 = p_a + \rho_g \cdot gH$$

and pressure acting on grate on opposite side (because of cold outside air),

$$p_2 = p_a + \rho_a \cdot gH$$

∴   Net pressure difference causing the flow through the combustion chamber,

$$\Delta p = p_2 - p_1 = (\rho_a - \rho_a) gH$$

This difference of pressure causing the flow of gases is known as **static draught**. Its value is measured by a water manometer and generally less than 12 mm of water.

1.20 HEIGHT OF CHIMNEY

The amount of draught depends upon the height of chimney, therefore, its height should be such that it can produce a sufficient draught.

Let,

H = Height of chimney above the grate in m

H_w = Draught required in terms of mm of water

T_a, T_g = Absolute temperature of outside air and flue gas respectively in K

V_a, V_g = Volume of outside air and flue gas in m^3/kg at temperatures T_a and T_g respectively

m_a = Mass of air supplied per kg of fuel

$m_a + 1$ = Mass of flue gases per kg of fuel

V_o, T_o, p_o = Volume, temperature and pressure at N.T.P. conditions

p_o = 1.013 bar = 1.013×10^5 N/m²

T_o = 0°C = 273 K

Volume of outside air per kg of fuel at N.T.P.

$$V_o = \frac{mRT_o}{p_o} \qquad (\because pV = mRT)$$

$$= \frac{m \times 287 \times 273}{1.013 \times 10^5} \qquad (\because R = 287 \text{ J/kg·K})$$

$$= \textbf{0.773 } \textbf{m}^3\textbf{/kg of fuel}$$

We know,

$$\frac{V_o}{T_o} = \frac{V_a}{T_a}$$

For outside air,

∴   Volume of outside air at temperature T_a,

$$V_a = \frac{V_o \times T_a}{T_o} = \frac{0.773\, m_a \times T_a}{273}$$

$$= \frac{m_a T_a}{353}\ m^3/kg \text{ of fuel}$$

Density of outside air at temperature T_a,

$$\rho_a = \frac{Mass}{Volume} = \frac{m_a}{\dfrac{m_a T_a}{353}} = \frac{353}{T_a}\ kg/m^3$$

Now, for hot flue gases,

$$V_g = \frac{m_a T_g}{353}\ m^3/kg \text{ of fuel} \qquad\qquad (\because \text{ similar to } V_a)$$

Density of flue gases at T_g,

$$\rho_g = \frac{Mass}{Volume} = \frac{m_a + 1}{\dfrac{m_a T_g}{353}} = \frac{353\,(m_a + 1)}{m_a T_g}\ kg/m^3$$

Draught is produced due to pressure difference. The draught pressure,

$$p = p_a - p_g$$

$$= \rho_a \cdot g \cdot H - \rho_g \cdot g \cdot H \qquad\qquad (\because p = \rho g H)$$

$$= \frac{353}{T_a} \cdot g \cdot H - \frac{353\,(m_a + 1)}{m_a T_g} \cdot g \cdot H$$

$$= 353 \cdot g \cdot H \left(\frac{1}{T_a} - \frac{m_a + 1}{m_a T_g}\right) N/m^2 \qquad\qquad \ldots (1.1)$$

Draught pressure in terms of mm of water as indicated by a manometer,

$$h_w = 353\, H \left[\frac{1}{T_a} - \frac{m_a + 1}{m_a T_g}\right] mm \text{ of water}$$

$$\left(\because 1 \text{ mm of water} = 9.81\, \frac{N}{m^2}\right)$$

Assume that draught pressure (p) produced is equivalent of H_1 metre height of burnt gases.

∴ $$p = \rho_g \cdot g \cdot H_1 = 353 \left[\frac{m_a + 1}{m_a}\right] \frac{1}{T_g} \cdot H_1 \qquad\qquad \ldots (1.2)$$

Equating equations (1.1) and (1.2),

$$H_1 = H \left(\frac{m_a}{m_a + 1} \cdot \frac{T_g}{T_a} - 1\right) \qquad\qquad \ldots (1.3)$$

1.21 CHIMNEY DIAMETER

Assuming no loss, the velocity of the gases passing through the chimney is given by,

$$C = \sqrt{2gH_1} \qquad \qquad \text{... (1.4)}$$

If the pressure loss in the chimney is equivalent to a hot gas column of h' metre, then,

$$C = \sqrt{2g\,(H_1 - h')} = 4.43\sqrt{1 - \frac{h'}{H_1}} \cdot \sqrt{H_1}$$

$$= K \cdot \sqrt{H_1}$$

where,

$$K = 4.43\sqrt{1 - \frac{h'}{H_1}}$$

and its value,

$$K = 0.825 \qquad \qquad \text{... For brick chimneys}$$

$$= 1.1 \qquad \qquad \text{... For steel chimneys}$$

The mass of gases flowing through chimney at any cross-section is given by,

$$m_g = \rho_g \cdot A \cdot C \text{ kg/sec} \qquad \qquad \text{... (1.5)}$$

Equation (1.5) is used to determine diameter of chimney.

1.22 CONDITION FOR MAXIMUM DISCHARGE THROUGH A CHIMNEY

The chimney draught is most effective when the maximum weight of hot gases is discharged in given time.

Velocity of gas through the chimney,

$$C = \sqrt{2gH_1}$$

$$= \sqrt{2gH\left[\left(\frac{m_a}{m_a + 1}\right)\frac{T_g}{T_a} - 1\right]}$$

... (H_1 from equation (1.3))

The density of hot gas is given by,

$$\rho_g = \frac{p}{R \cdot T_g} \qquad \qquad (\because \text{ From } pV_g = RT_g)$$

The mass of gas delivered per second,

$$m_g = \rho_g \cdot A \cdot C$$

$$= \frac{p}{RT_g} \cdot A \cdot \sqrt{2gH\left[\left(\frac{m_a}{m_a + 1}\right) \cdot \frac{T_g}{T_a} - 1\right]}$$

$$= \frac{p \cdot A \cdot \sqrt{2gH}}{RT_g} \sqrt{\left(\frac{m_a}{m_a + 1}\right) \cdot \frac{T_g}{T_a} - 1}$$

$$= \frac{K}{T_g} \cdot \sqrt{M \cdot T_g - 1}$$

where,
$$K = \frac{p \cdot A \cdot \sqrt{2gH}}{R} \quad \text{and} \quad M = \frac{m_a}{m_a + 1} \cdot \frac{1}{T_a}$$

$$\therefore \qquad m_g = K\sqrt{\frac{M \cdot T_g}{T_g^2} - \frac{1}{T_g^2}}$$

$$= K\left(\frac{M}{T_g} - \frac{1}{T_g^2}\right)^{\frac{1}{2}}$$

For maximum discharge differentiating m_g with respect to T_g and equating to zero,

$$\frac{dm_g}{dT_g} = \frac{d}{dT_g}\left[K\left(\frac{M}{T_g} - \frac{1}{T_g^2}\right)^{\frac{1}{2}}\right] = 0$$

$$\therefore \qquad \left(-\frac{M}{T_g^2} + \frac{2}{T_g^2}\right)K = 0$$

$$\therefore \qquad \frac{2}{T_g} - M = 0$$

$$\frac{2}{T_g} = M = \frac{m_a}{m_a + 1} \cdot \frac{1}{T_a}$$

$$\therefore \qquad \frac{T_g}{T_a} = 2\left(\frac{m_a + 1}{m_a}\right)$$

Substituting above value of $\frac{T_g}{T_a}$ to get $(H_1)_{max}$,

$$(H_1)_{max} = H\left[\left(\frac{m_a}{m_a + 1}\right) \cdot 2\left(\frac{m_a + 1}{m_a}\right) - 1\right]$$

$$(H_1)_{max} = H$$

The draught in mm of water column for maximum discharge,

$$(h_w)_{max} = 353 \, H\left(\frac{1}{T_a} - \frac{1}{2T_a}\right)$$

$$= \frac{353 \, H}{2T_a}$$

PROBLEMS ON BOILER DRAUGHT

Problem 1.10 : In a boiler plant, it is required to produce draught equivalent of 15 mm of water. The ambient and hot gases temperatures are 20°C and 250°C respectively. The amount of air required for combustion is 18 kg per kg of fuel. Determine the height of chimney.

Solution:

Given: h_w = 15 mm of water, T_a = 20 + 273 = 293 K, T_g = 250°C = 250 + 273 = 525 K

$$h_w = 353\, H\left[\frac{1}{T_a} - \frac{m_a + 1}{m_a \cdot T_g}\right]$$

$$15 = 353 \times H \times \left[\frac{1}{293} - \frac{19}{18 \times 523}\right]$$

$\therefore$ 　　　　　　　　　　　　$H = \textbf{30.5 m}$

Problem 1.11: A boiler having a chimney of 32 m height. The air-fuel ratio needed in combustion chamber is 20. Temperature of air at the grate entry is 28°C. Find minimum temperature of flue gases required to produce a draught of 18 mm.

Solution:

Given: H = 32 m, A : F = 20, T_a = 28°C, h_w = 18 mm

$$h_w = 353 \cdot H \cdot \left[\left(\frac{1}{T_a} - \frac{1}{T_g}\frac{m_a + 1}{m_a}\right)\right]$$

$$18 = 353 \times 32 \times \left[\frac{1}{301} - \frac{1}{T_g}\left(\frac{21}{20}\right)\right]$$

$$T_g = 607.37 \text{ K}$$
$$= 607.37 - 273$$
$$= \textbf{334.37°C}$$

Problem 1.12: A boiler uses 20 kg of air per kg of fuel. The fuel consumption is 33 kg/sec and actual draught required is 18 mm of water taking into account all losses.

Determine the chimney height and its diameter if the actual velocity of flue gases is 0.38 times the theoretical velocity due to friction. The surrounding is at 25°C and flue gases temperature is 230°C.　　　　　　　　　　　　　　　　**(P.U. December 2004)**

Solution:

Given: m_a = 20 kg/kg of fuel, m_f = 33 kg/sec, h_w = 18 mm of water, C = 0.38 $\sqrt{29\ H}$, T_a = 25°C = 25 + 273 = 298 K, T_g = 230°C = 230 + 273 = 503 K

Height of chimney,

$$h_w = 353 \cdot H \cdot \left(\frac{1}{T_a} - \frac{m_a + 1}{m_a \cdot T_g}\right)$$

$$18 = 353 \times H \times \left(\frac{1}{298} - \frac{20 + 1}{520 \times 503}\right)$$

$$H = \textbf{40.21 m}$$

Now,

$$H_1 = H \cdot \left(\frac{m_a}{m_a + 1} \cdot \frac{T_g}{T_a} - 1\right) = 40.21 \times \left(\frac{20}{20 + 1} \times \frac{503}{230} - 1\right)$$

$$= \textbf{43.54 m}$$

The actual velocity of gas,

$$C = 0.38 \times \sqrt{2g\ H_1}$$

$$= 0.38 \times \sqrt{2 \times 9.81 \times 43.54}$$

$$= \textbf{11.109 m/sec}$$

Density of flue gas,

$$\rho_g = \frac{353\ (m_a + 1)}{m_a \cdot T_g} = \frac{353 \times (20 + 1)}{20 \times 503}$$

$$= \textbf{0.7369 kg/m}^3$$

Mass of gas per sec,

$$m_g = (m_a + 1) \times m_f \text{ in kg/sec}$$

$$= (20 + 1) \times 33$$

$$= \textbf{693 kg/sec}$$

Also,

$$m_g = \rho_g \cdot A \cdot C$$

∴

$$693 = 0.7369 \times \frac{\pi}{4} \times D^2 \times 11.109$$

∴

$$D^2 = 107.78$$

∴

$$D = 10.38\ m \simeq 10.5\ m$$

$$\text{Diameter of chimney} = \textbf{10.4 m}$$

Problem 1.13: To provide natural draught, a chimney of height 16 m is used. Calculate,

(i)   The draught in mm of water when the temperature of chimney gases is such that the mass of the gases discharged is maximum.

(ii) If the temperature of flue gases does not exceed 350°C, find air supplied per kg of fuel for maximum discharge.

Take atmospheric temperature as 20°C.

Solution:

Given: H = 16 m, T_g = 350 + 273 = 623 K, T_a = 20 + 273 = 293 K.

(i) Draught:

$$(h_w)_{max} = \frac{353 \cdot H}{2T_a}$$

$$= \frac{353 \times 16}{2 \times 293}$$

$$= \textbf{9.64 mm of water}$$

(ii) Air supplied for maximum discharge :

The condition for maximum discharge is

$$\frac{T_g}{T_a} = 2\left(\frac{m_a + 1}{m_a}\right)$$

$$\frac{623}{293} = 2\left(\frac{m_a + 1}{m_a}\right)$$

∴ m_a = **15.87 kg/kg of fuel**

Problem 1.14 : At a location for installing a boiler plant, height of chimney is limited to 45 m. The temperature of flue gases and ambient air are 220°C and 25°C respectively. Pressure loss at grate is 8 mm of water. Also pressure loss in bends and chimney are 3 mm and 4 mm respectively. Determine diameter of the chimney, if a fuel burnt per second is 18 kg.

Solution:

Given: H = 45 m, T_g = 220°C = 220 + 273 = 493 K, T_a = 25°C = 25 + 273 = 298 K.

Pressure required to overcome losses = 8 + 3 + 4 = 15 mm of water

We know, $h_w = 353\,H\left(\frac{1}{T_a} - \frac{m_a + 1}{m_a \cdot T_g}\right)$

$$15 = 353 \times 45 \times \left(\frac{1}{298} - \frac{m_a + 1}{m_a \times 493}\right)$$

$$\frac{15}{353 \times 45} = \frac{1}{298} - \frac{m_a + 1}{m_a \times 493}$$

$$\frac{m_a + 1}{m_a \times 493} = \frac{1}{298} - \frac{15}{353 \times 45} = 2.41 \times 10^{-3}$$

$$m_a + 1 = 2.41 \times 10^{-3} \times 493 \times m_a$$

$$1 = 10188\, m_a - m_a = 0.188$$

∴ m_a = 5.32 kg

Now,
$$H_1 = H\left(\frac{m_a}{m_a + 1} \cdot \frac{T_g}{T_a} - 1\right)$$

$$= 45 \times \left(\frac{5.32}{5.32 + 1} \times \frac{493}{298} - 1\right)$$

$$= \textbf{17.61 m}$$

Density of flue gases,

$$\rho_g = \frac{353\,(m_a + 1)}{m_a \cdot T_g} = \frac{353 \times (5.32 + 1)}{5.32 \times 493}$$

$$= \textbf{0.85 kg/m}^3$$

Velocity of gas,

$$C = \sqrt{2gH_1} = \sqrt{2 \times 9.87 \times 17.61}$$

$$= \textbf{18.59 m/sec}$$

Mass of gas per second,

$$m_g = (m_a + 1) \times m_f$$

$$= (5.32 + 1) \times 0.18$$

$$= \textbf{113.76 kg/sec.}$$

Also,
$$m_g = \rho_g \cdot A \cdot C$$

$$113.76 = 0.85 \times \frac{\pi}{4}D^2 \times 18.59$$

∴
$$D = 3.02 \cong \textbf{3 m}$$

1.23 DRAUGHT LOSSES

The loss in draught may be due to the reasons mentioned below.
(a) Frictional losses offered by the flues and gas passages to the flow of gases.
(b) Loss near bends in the gas flow circuit.
(c) Loss due to friction head in equipments like grate, economiser, super heater etc.
(d) Loss due to imparting velocity to the flue gases.

The draught loss in a chimney is twenty percent of the total draught produced by it.

1.24 ARTIFICIAL DRAUGHT

For modern boilers static draught required is varying between 30 to 350 mm of water column. It may not be possible to build a chimney high enough to produce such large draught. To meet this requirement, artificial draught is used.

1.24.1 Forced Draught

- In this system, a blower is fitted near the base of the boiler (before grate) and the air is forced to pass through various elements as shown in Fig. 1.18.

- As air pressure throughout the system is maintained above atmospheric pressure, the system is known as positive draught system.

- Here function of chimney is to release gases as a height into atmosphere for better dispersion of ash particles and pollutants.

- Height of chimney is less than natural draught system.

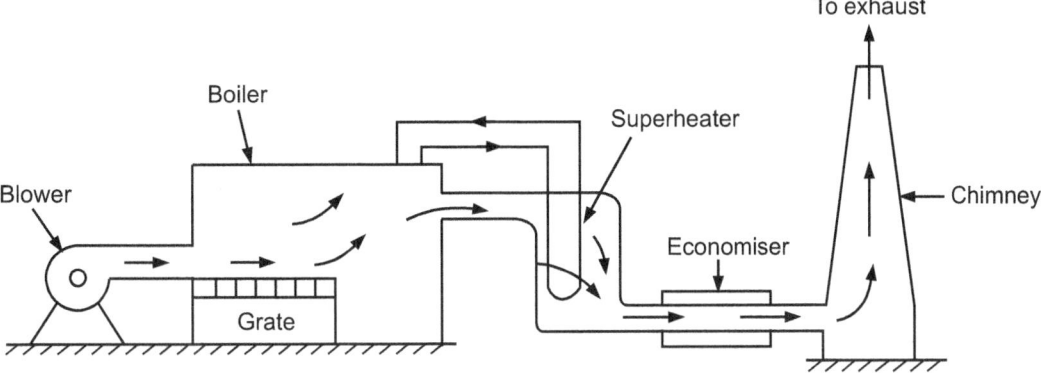

Fig. 1.18: Forced draught

1.24.2 Induced Draught

- In this system, blower is located near the base of the chimney.
- The air sucked into the system by reducing the pressure below the atmospheric pressure.
- By creating partial vacuum in the furnace and flues, the products of combustion are drawn from the main flue and they pass upto the chimney.
- This draught is used when economiser and preheaters are used in the system.
- The draught is similar in action to natural draught.

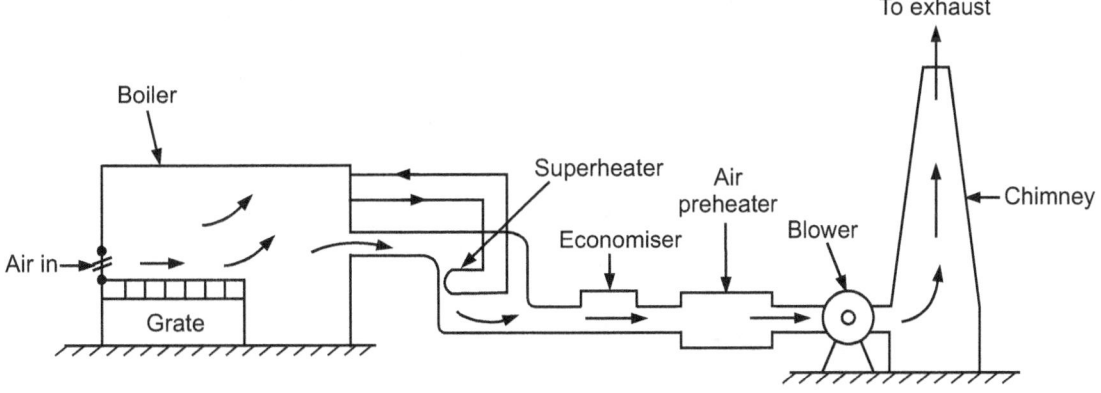

Fig. 1.19: Induced draught

1.24.3 Difference between Forced and Induced Draught

Forced Draught	Induced Draught
1. Blower is placed near the base of the boiler and is forced to pass through various elements of system.	1. Blower is placed near the base of chimney and air sucked to pass through various elements of system.
2. Comparatively less power is required for forced draught fan.	2. More power is required for induced draught fan.
3. No chance of air leakage in the furnace.	3. In this system, continuous air leakage takes place.
4. Flow of air is more uniform.	4. Air flow is not so uniform.
5. Does not require water cooled bearing.	5. Water cooled boring are required for induced draught.
6. Small fan size is required for same draught.	6. Big fan size is required for same draught.

1.24.4 Balanced Draught

- It is a combination of forced and induced draught system.
- In this system, forced draught fan overcomes the resistance in air preheater and chain grate stocker while the induced draught fan overcomes draught losses through boiler, economiser, air preheater and connecting flues.

1.24.5 Steam Jet Draught

- Steam jet draught is a simple and easy method of producing artificial draught.
- It may be forced type or induced type.
- Here steam jet directed into the smoke box near the stack induces flow of gases through the tubes, ash pit grates and flues.

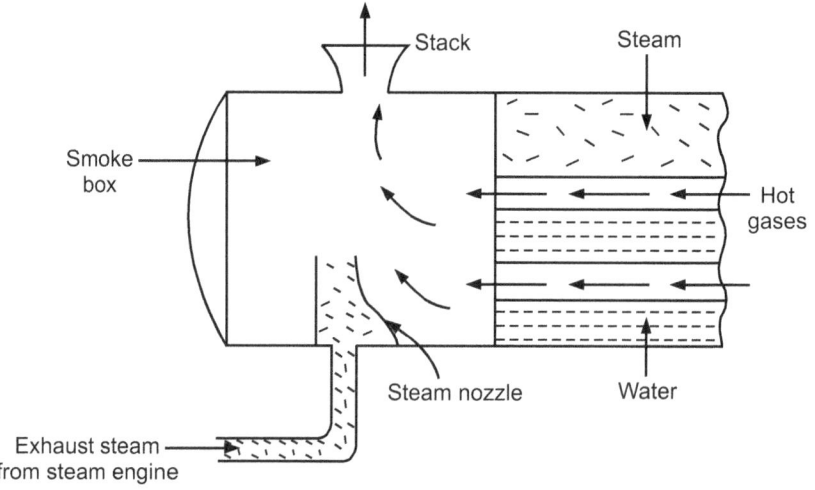

Fig. 1.20: Steam jet draught

The steam jet draught entails following advantages:

(i)   It is simple and economical.

(ii)   Occupies minimum space.

(iii) Maintenance cost is nil, very low attention is required.

Only disadvantage is, it needs high pressure steam for starting.

1.25 DIFFERENCE BETWEEN MECHANICAL DRAUGHT AND NATURAL DRAUGHT

Mechanical Draught	Natural Draught
Advantages	Disadvantages
1. The rate of combustion is more as the available draught is more.	1. The rate of combustion is low as the available draught is limited.
2. The height of chimney used is less and independent of draught needed.	2. The height of chimney used is more and designed by draught needed.
3. Fuel consumption per kW is 15% less than for natural draught.	3. Flue consumption per kW is more.
4. The efficiency of artificial draught is 6 to 8%.	4. The efficiency of chimney draught is about 1%.
5. Fuel burning capacity of grate is more.	5. Fuel burning capacity of grate is less.
6. Low capital cost.	6. High capital cost.
7. The running and maintenance cost is practically nil.	7. High running and maintenance cost of fan used.

EXERCISE

1.   Which factors you will consider while selecting a steam boiler?

2.   How boilers are classified?

3.   Differentiate water tube boilers with fire tube boilers.

4.   Explain a fire tube boiler with neat sketch.

5. Explain a water tube boiler with neat sketch.

6. Explain following mountings with neat sketch:

    (a) Water level indicator(b)Pressure gauge

    (c) Dead weight safety valve (d)Feed check valve

    (e) Fusible plug

7. Explain different accessories used in steam boilers with neat sketch.

8. What features of high pressure boilers are comparing with low pressure boilers?

9. Describe IBR and Non-IBR boilers in brief.

10. Explain the following terms with their significance:

    (a) Evapourative capacity

    (b) Equivalent evapouration

    (c) Boiler efficiency

11. What are the different sources of heat loss in a boiler plant?

12. Explain procedure to draw heat balance sheet for a boiler plant.

13. Compare natural draught with artificial draught.

14. Explain necessity of producing draught in boiler.

15. Differentiate between forced and induced draught.

16. Describe different types of stokers used for steam power plant.

17. Explain combined cycle power plant with neat sketch.

18. Write a note on energy conservation opportunities in boilers.

19. Write a note on cogeneration.

20. Explain factors affecting boiler efficiency.

PROBLEMS FOR PRACTICE

1. A boiler evaporates 3.6 kg of water per kg of coal into dry saturated steam at 10 bar. Find the equivalent evapouration if the feed water temperature is 32°C.

    (Ans. 4.2 kg/kg of coal)

2. Two kg of coal is required to produce 8 kg of steam (x = 0.98) at a pressure of 10.5 bar. Temperature of feed water is 45°C. Determine equivalent evapouration.

    (Ans. 4.2 kg/kg of coal)

3.   A boiler produces 9 kg of steam per kg of coal at 10 bar from water at 15°C. The dryness fraction of steam is 0.9. Determine efficiency of the boiler when calorific value of coal is 32 000 kJ/kg.   **(Ans.** 70.65%)

4.   The following observations were made in a test on a boiler :

Coal burnt per/hr	=	480 kg
Steam generated/hr	=	4375 kg at 3 MN/m^2
Feed water temperature	=	95°C
Temperature of steam leaving the boiler	=	260°C
Calorific value of coal	=	30 700 kJ/kg
Cp for superheated steam	=	2.093 kJ/kg K

Calculate:

(i)   The equivalent evapouration from and at 100°C in kg steam/hr.

(Ans. 4768 kg/hr)

(ii)   The efficiency of the boiler   **(Ans.** 73%)

5.   A chimney of 60 m height is used in a boiler plant. The temperature of atmospheric air is 27°C and 15 kg of air is required to burn 1 kg of air. For maximum discharge of hot gases, determine the draught pressure in mm of water. Also find temperature of hot gases.   **(Ans.** 35.3 mm of water, 327°C)

6.   A 30 m high chimney is used to produce a natural draught of 15 mm of water. The temperature of atmospheric air is 27°C and that of hot gases in the chimney is 287°C. Calculate mass of the air used per kg of fuel.

(Ans. 15.6 kg/kg of fuel)

Unit II

VAPOUR POWER CYCLES AND STEAM CONDENSER

STEAM AND VAPOUR PROCESSES

Introduction

Steam is a pure substance. A *pure substance* is defined as *'a homogeneous and chemically stable substance eventhough it undergoes a change of phase'*.

Steam is used in many engineering and chemical industries. It is used as a working substance for steam power plants and is used as a medium for heating in chemical, sugar and textile industries. Therefore, it is essential to study the properties of steam at different conditions.

Substances may exist in different phases. At atmospheric pressure and temperature conditions, copper is a solid, mercury is a liquid and nitrogen is a gas. Under different conditions, each may appear in different phase. So let us discuss the phase transformation of water at constant pressure.

2.1 PHASE TRANSFORMATION OF WATER AT CONSTANT PRESSURE

1. Assume 1 kg mass of ice at –20°C and 1 atm. pressure in a frictionless piston-cylinder arrangement. Weight W is kept on the piston to maintain a pressure of 1 atm. on the ice.

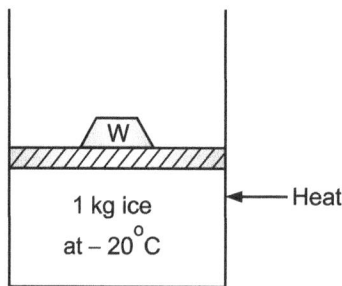

Fig. 2.1: At 1 atm. pressure and – 20°C, water exists in the solid phase

2. As we add heat, the temperature of ice will go on increasing till it reaches 0°C. At this stage, ice starts melting and there will be no rise in temperature till all the ice melts. (Process a – b in Fig. 2.7)

3. The addition of heat will be utilised to increase the temperature of water from 0°C to 100°C (Process c - d in Fig. 2.7).

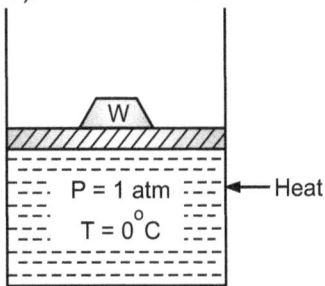

Fig. 2.2: At 1 atm. pressure and at 0°C, water exists in the liquid state (compressed liquid)

4. Now on further heating, water starts boiling and gets converted into vapour.

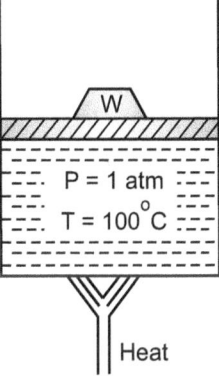

Fig. 2.3: At 1 atm. pressure and 100°C, water exists as a liquid which is ready to vaporise (saturated liquid)

5. Part of the water is evaporated. Therefore, there is a mixture of water and vapour.

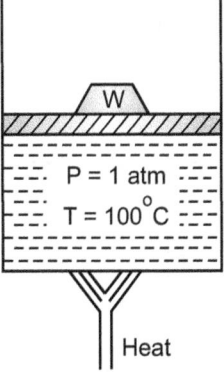

Fig. 2.4: As more heat is added, part of saturated liquid vaporizes (saturated liquid–vapour mixture)

6. See point 'd' in Fig. 2.7. The entire cylinder is filled with vapour. Any heat loss from this vapour will cause some of the vapour to condense.

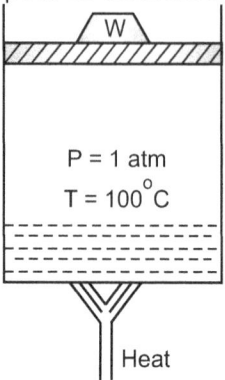

Fig. 2.5: At 1 atm. pressure, the temperature remains constant at 100°C until the last drop of liquid is vaporized (saturated vapour).

7. Further addition of heat will increase the temperature of steam. So, it is called as superheated steam.

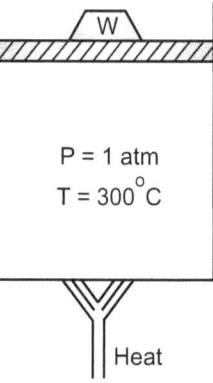

Fig. 2.6: As more heat is added, the temperature of the vapour starts rising (superheated vapour)

All the above steps are represented in Fig. 2.7.

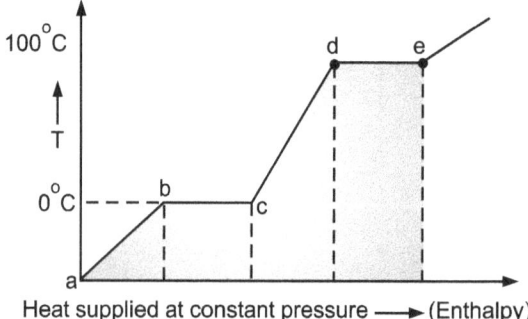

Fig. 2.7: Temperature - Heat supplied

In Fig. 2.7, a – b → Sensible heating of ice

            b – c → Melting of ice

            c – d → Sensible heating of liquid

            d – e → Saturated mixture of liquid and vapour

From point e – onwards, superheating of steam takes place.

2.2 EFFECT OF PRESSURE ON BOILING POINT

The boiling temperature of water increases with increasing pressure. The 'Boiling Temperature' of water at a particular pressure is known as "saturation temperature" and corresponding pressure is known as 'saturation pressure.'

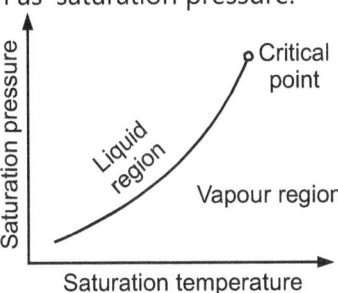

Fig. 2.8: Relation between saturation pressure and saturation temperature of water

The *critical temperature of steam* is defined as 'the temperature above which it is impossible to liquify the steam by pressure alone, irrespective of the intensity of temperature'. At critical point "the change of volume falls to zero".

For water, the properties are:

$$\text{Critical pressure } (P_C) \;=\; 221.2 \text{ bar}$$
$$\text{Critical temperature } (T_C) \;=\; 647.3 \text{ K}$$
$$\text{Critical volume, } (v_C) \;=\; 0.00317 \text{ m}^3/\text{kg}$$

2.3 PROPERTY DIAGRAMS

2.3.1 P-v Diagram of Water

The P-v diagram of a pure substance is shown in Fig. 2.9.

From Fig. 2.9, it is clear that as the saturation temperature is increased, the volume of saturated liquid increases.

Volume of the saturated liquid is very small compared with the volume of saturated vapour. As the pressure goes on increasing, the volume of vapour goes on decreasing upto critical point.

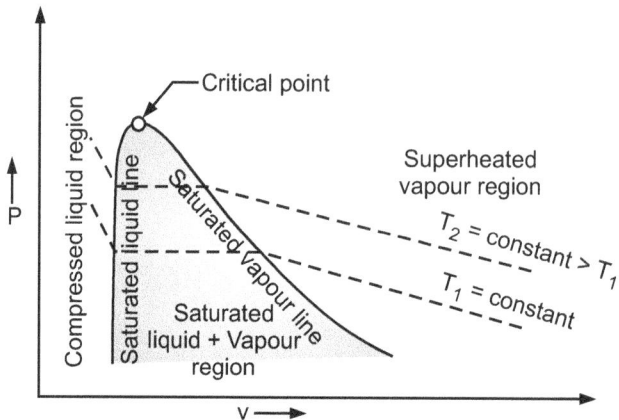

Fig. 2.9: P-v Diagram of a pure substance

2.3.2 Temperature Specific Volume Diagram of Water

The phase change diagram of water at 1 atm. pressure is described in Article 2.2. The process is repeated for different pressures to draw T-v diagram as shown in Fig. 2.10.

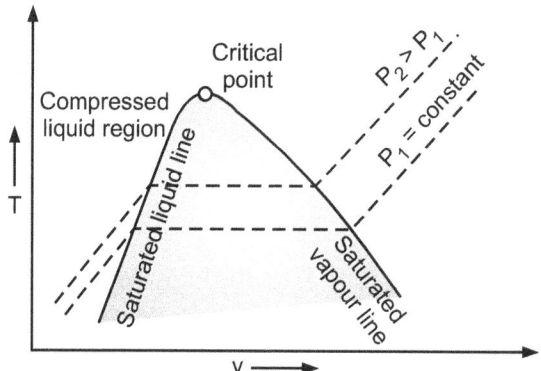

Fig. 2.10: T-v diagram for pure substance

From Fig. 2.10, we can draw the following conclusions:

1. Water starts boiling at a much higher temperature corresponding to higher pressures.

2. The specific volume of the saturated liquid is larger and the specific volume of saturated vapour is smaller than the corresponding values at 1 atm. pressure. It means, the horizontal line that connects the saturated liquid and saturated vapour states is much shorter.

2.3.3 Enthalpy – Entropy (h–s) Diagram of Water

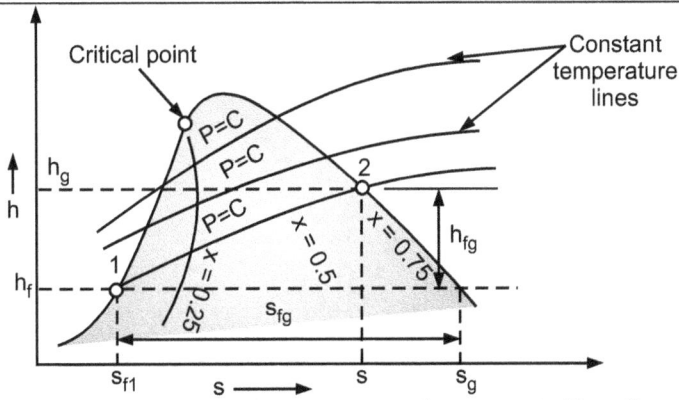

Fig. 2.11: Enthalpy-Entropy diagram of water (Mollier diagram)

Fig. 2.11 is the h-s or Mollier diagram indicating only the liquid and vapour phases. As the pressure increases, saturation temperature increases and also slope of the isobar increases. On this diagram, constant volume lines diverging in vapour region, is also shown. As the pressure increases, h_{fg} decreases and reduces to zero ($h_{fg} = 0$) at critical point.

2.3.4 T-s Diagram for Water

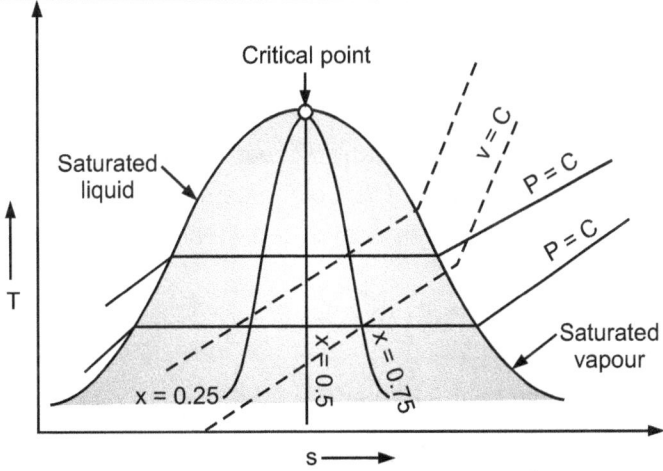

Fig. 2.12: Temperature-Entropy diagram for water

For reversible process, the change in entropy is given as:

$$ds = \frac{\partial Q}{T} = \int Tds = \int dQ$$

The area under the curve (T-s) for a process gives the heat transfer.

Fig. 2.12 shows T-s diagram for water. Constant pressure, constant specific volume and constant quality lines are also shown.

2.4 PROPERTIES OF STEAM

(a) Sensible Heat of Water or Enthalpy of Water: The quantity of heat absorbed by one kg of water to raise its temperature from the freezing point to the boiling point is known as sensible heat.

It is denoted by h_f and calculated as

$$h_f = c_p \, \Delta T \text{ for unit mass} \qquad \qquad ... (2.1)$$

where, c_p = Specific heat of water at constant pressure, kJ/kg·K

ΔT = Temperature rise, °C

h_f = Sensible heat, kJ/kg

The error resulted in the value of h_f, calculated by this formula increases as the temperature rises. Therefore, generally h_f is taken from Steam Table.

(b) Latent Heat (Enthalpy of Evaporation) (h_{fg}): It is the amount of heat required to convert one kg of water at a given saturated temperature T_s and pressure P into steam at the same temperature and pressure conditions. This varies with pressure.

For given temperature or pressure, it can be obtained from steam table.

Ex. (i) Find the enthalpy of evaporation at 3.5 kPa pressure.

Ans. Referring the steam table based on pressure, h_{fg} = 1753.7 kJ/kg at 3.5 kPa.

(ii)   Find enthalpy of evaporation at 150°C.

Ans. h_{fg} = 2114.3 kJ/kg at 150°C.

(c) Enthalpy or Total Heat: It is the amount of heat required to raise the temperature of one kg of water from freezing point to the boiling temperature, (corresponding to given pressure) and then to convert it into dry saturated steam at the same temperature and pressure.

It is denoted by h_g.

$$h_g = h_f + h_{fg} \qquad \qquad ... (2.2)$$

where, h_f = Sensible heat, kJ/kg and

h_{fg} = Latent heat, kJ/kg

(d) Wet Steam: It is a homogeneous mixture of vapour and fine water particles. This exists in the steam space of boiler.

The quality of wet steam depends on the amount of water particles present in the mixture. The quality of wet steam is defined by the dryness fraction.

The dryness fraction (x) is expressed by the ratio of mass of dry vapour (steam) to the total mass of the mixture of water and steam.

$$\therefore \qquad x = \frac{m_s}{m_w + m_s} \qquad \qquad ...(2.3)$$

where, x = Dryness fraction or quality of steam

m_s = Mass of dry steam, kg

m_w = Mass of liquid water in the mixture, kg

If dryness fraction of wet steam (x) = 0.8, then one kg of steam contains 0.2 kg of water (moisture) and 0.8 kg of dry steam.

(i)   Enthalpy of evaporation or Latent heat of 1 kg of wet steam

$$= x \cdot h_{fg} \text{ kJ/kg} \qquad \qquad ...(2.4)$$

(ii) Total heat or enthalpy of one kg of wet steam is equal to the sum of the enthalpy of saturated water + enthalpy of evaporation i.e.

$$h_g = h_f + x h_{fg} \text{ kJ/kg} \qquad \qquad ...(2.5)$$
$$= h_f + x (h_g - h_f)$$

(iii) Specific volume: Let us consider 1 kg of water heated at constant pressure (1.01325 bar). This heating process is shown in T-v diagram of Fig. 2.13.

Let point A be on the line 2–3 in vapour region having dryness fraction x. Therefore, each of mixture at 'A' contains x kg of vapour and (1 – x) kg of liquid water. At point 2, the water is at saturated liquid state completely (x = 0). At state point 3, the mixture is completely saturated steam (dry saturated state), therefore, x = 1.

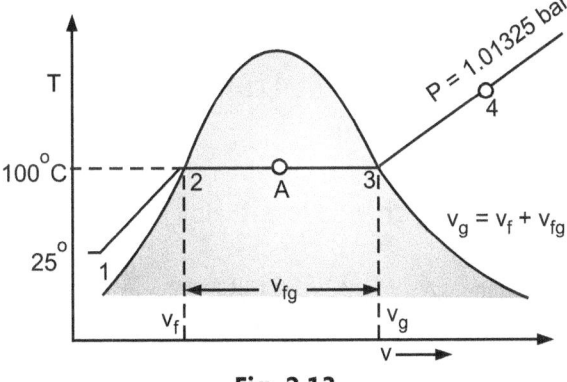

Fig. 2.13

If v_A is the specific volume at point A, then,

$$v_A = (1 - x) v_f + x \cdot v_g \qquad \qquad ...(2.6)$$

But $v_g = v_f + v_{fg}$

Put in equation (2.6) and simplify

$$v_A = v_f + x \cdot v_{fg} \text{ ...... m}^3\text{/kg} \qquad \qquad ...(2.7)$$

This is the specific volume of wet steam having dryness fraction x.

(e) The specific volume of superheated steam at superheat temperature T_{sup} is calculated by using Charle's law.

$$\frac{v_g}{T_s} = \frac{v_{sup}}{T_{sup}}$$

$\therefore \qquad v_{sup} = \frac{v_g}{T_s} \cdot T_{sup}$ ... (2.8)

where, v_g = Specific volume of dry saturated steam

         T_s = Temperature of dry saturated steam, K

         v_{sup} = Specific volume of superheated steam

(f) Superheated steam: When steam is heated out of contact with water, it will result in increase of temperature. Superheating of the steam occurs at constant pressure. The amount of superheating is measured by the rise in temperature of the steam above its saturation temperature (t_s). Greater superheating of the steam will help to acquire the properties of perfect gas.

     Enthalpy of superheat

$$= c_p (T_{sup} - T_{sat}) \text{ kJ/kg} \qquad ... (2.9)$$

where, c_p = Mean specific heat of superheated steam at constant temperature

The term ($T_{sup} - T_{sat}$) is known as degree of superheat.

The value of c_p ranges from 2 kJ/kg·K to 2.5 kJ/kg·K

The enthalpy (total heat) of one kg of superheated steam (H_{sup}) is

$$h_{sup} = h_f + h_{fg} + c_p (T_{sup} - T_{sat}) \text{ kJ/kg} \qquad ... (2.10)$$

$$= h_g + c_p (T_{sup} - T_{sat}) \qquad ... (2.11)$$

(g) Internal energy: We know that change in enthalpy is

$$dh = du + d(Pv)$$

$$h_2 - h_1 = u_2 - u_1 + (P_2v_2 - P_1v_1) \text{ for unit mass}$$

$\therefore \qquad u_2 - u_1 = (h_2 - h_1) - (P_2v_2 - P_1v_1) \text{ for } m = 1$ ... (2.12)

(i)   For wet steam,

     Let x_2 and x_1 be dryness fractions at conditions 2 and 1 respectively.

$\therefore \qquad h_2 = h_{f2} + x_2 \cdot h_{fg_2}$

and $v_2 = x_2 v_{g2}$

         $h_1 = h_{f_1} + x_1 \cdot h_{fg_1}$

and $v_1 = x_1 \cdot v_{g1}$

Then, change in internal energy,

$$(u_2 - u_1) = [(h_{f_2} + x_2 h_{fg_2}) - (h_{f_1} + x_1 h_{fg_1})] - \left[P_2 \cdot x_2 \cdot v_{g_2} - P_1 x_1 \cdot v_{g_1}\right] \qquad ... (2.13)$$

(ii)   Internal energy of superheated steam.

$$h_2 = h_{sup_2} = h_{g_2} + c_p \, (T_{sup_2} - T_{sat_1})$$

and $$v_2 = v_{sup_2} = \frac{v_{sat_2}}{T_{sat_2}} \times T_{sup_2}$$

∴ $$u_2 - u_1 = (h_{sup_2} - h_1) - (P_2 \, v_{sup_2} - P_1 v_1) \qquad \text{... (2.14)}$$

(h) Entropy (s): Entropy of a dry saturated steam can be obtained from steam table corresponding to a pressure or temperature of steam.

(i)   Entropy of wet steam

$$s = (1 - x) \, s_f + x \cdot s_g$$

or $$s = s_f + x \, s_{fg}$$

$$= s_f + x \, (s_g - s_f)$$

$$= s_f + x \, s_g \qquad \text{... (2.15)}$$

because $x s_f$ is very small.

(ii)   Entropy of superheated steam,

$$s_{sup} = s_g + \text{Entropy of superheat kJ/kg·K}$$

$$\text{Entropy of superheat} = c_p \, ln \left(\frac{T_{sup}}{T_{sat}} \right)$$

∴ $$s_{sup} = s_g + c_p \, ln \left(\frac{T_{sup}}{T_{sat}} \right) \qquad \text{kJ/kg·K for unit mass ... (2.16)}$$

SOLVED PROBLEMS

Problem 2.1: Obtain all the properties of steam in the following cases:

(i)   Steam is dry saturated at 11 bar.

(ii)   Steam has a pressure of 8 bar and dryness fraction 0.9.

(iii) Steam is superheated having pressure 15 bar and temperature 250°C. Assume c_p for superheated steam.

Solution: (i) Dry saturated steam at 11 bar

$$T_{sat} = 184.1°C \text{ from steam table}$$
$$v_g = 0.17739 \text{ m}^3/\text{kg}$$
$$v_f = 0.001133 \text{ m}^3/\text{kg}$$
$$h_f = 781.1 \text{ kJ/kg}$$
$$h_{fg} = 1998.6 \text{ kJ/kg}$$
$$h_g = h_f + h_{fg} = 2779.7 \text{ kJ/kg}$$
$$s_f = 2.179 \text{ kJ/kg·K}$$

$$s_{fg} = \frac{h_{fg}}{T_{sat}} = 4.371 \text{ kJ/kg·K}$$

$$s_g = s_f + s_{fg}$$

$$= 6.55 \text{ kJ/kg·K}$$

(ii)   Steam at 8 bar and 0.9 dryness fraction

→ Wet steam

$$T_{sat} \text{ at 8 bar} = 170.4°C \text{ from steam table}$$

$$v_f = 0.0011150 \text{ m}^3/\text{kg}$$

$$v_x = (1 - x)\, v_f + x \cdot v_g$$

$$= (1 - 0.9) \times 0.001115 + 0.9 \times 0.24026$$

$$= \mathbf{0.21635 \text{ m}^3/\text{kg}}$$

$$h_x = h_f + x h_{fg}$$

$$= 720.9 + 0.9 \times 2046.5$$

$$= \mathbf{2562.75 \text{ kJ/kg}}$$

$$s_f = 2.046 \text{ kJ/kg·K}$$

$$s_x = s_f + x \cdot s_{fg}$$

$$= 2.046 + 0.9 \times 4.614$$

$$= \mathbf{6.1986 \text{ kJ/kg·K}}$$

(iii)   Superheated steam at 15 bar and 250°C from steam table, $T_{sat} = 198.3°C$ at 15 bar.

$$v_{sup} = \frac{T_{sup}}{T_{sat}} \cdot v_g$$

$$= \left(\frac{250 + 273}{198.3 + 273}\right) \times 0.13167$$

$$= 0.14611 \text{ m}^3/\text{kg}$$

$$h_{sup} = h_g + c_p (T_{sup} - T_{sat})$$

$$= 2789.9 + 2.1 (250 - 198.3)$$

$$= \mathbf{2898.47 \text{ kJ/kg}}$$

$$s_{sup} = s_g + c_p \cdot \ln\left(\frac{T_{sup}}{T_{sat}}\right)$$

$$= 6.441 + 2.1 \ln\left(\frac{250 + 273}{198.3 + 273}\right)$$

$$= \mathbf{6.6596 \text{ kJ/kg}}$$

Problem 2.2: Estimate the condition of the steam in the following cases.

(i)   P = 20 bar,   h = 2797.2 kJ/kg

(ii)   P = 14 bar,   v = 0.13 m³/kg

(iii) P = 12 bar,   s = 6.70 kJ/kg·K

Solution:

(i)   For P = 20 bar, h_g = 2797.2 kJ/kg from steam table. Therefore, h_g = h.

∴   **Steam is dry and saturated.**
(**Note:** If h < h_g, it would be wet and if h > h_g, it would be superheated).

(ii)   P = 14 bar, v = 0.13 m³/kg,

From steam table, at p = 14 bar, v_g = 0.14073 m³/kg

Comparison of v and v_g:

v < v_g (0.13 < 0.14073)

∴   **Steam is wet.**

∴ $$v = v_x = x\, v_g$$

∴ $$x = \frac{v_x}{v_g} = \frac{0.13}{0.14073} = \mathbf{0.9237}$$

Note: The steam would have been dry saturated if v = v_g and would be superheated if v > v_g.

(iii)   P = 12 bar, s = 6.7 kJ/kg·K

Now s_g = 6.519 kJ/kg·K for dry saturated steam (from steam table).

Comparison of s and s_g:

s > s_g. Therefore steam is superheated.

(**Note:** It would be dry saturated if s = s_g and wet if s < s_g)

∴ $$s_{sup} = s_g + c_p \ln\left(\frac{T_{sup}}{T_{sat}}\right)$$

$$6.7 = 6.519 + 2.1 \ln\left(\frac{T_{sup}}{188 + 273}\right)$$

∴ $$T_{sup} = \mathbf{229.496°C}$$

2.5 THERMODYNAMIC PROCESSES

The general energy equations applicable to perfect gases are also applicable to vapours and the procedure for finding the change in internal energy is also same as was adopted in case of gases.

The different processes of expansion and compression of gases are also applicable to vapours but the results obtained may be different.

The equations for the work done by vapour are the same as those used for perfect gases.

2.5.1 Constant Volume Heating or Cooling

The process can be represented on P-v and T-s planes (See Fig. 2.14).

It is assumed that wet steam (state 1) is heated at constant volume, till it reaches a superheat condition (state 2).

$$v_1 = v_2 \text{ (for constant volume process)}$$

$$x_1 \cdot v_{g_1} = v_{sup_2}$$

$$x_1 v_{g_1} = \frac{T_{sup_2}}{T_{sup_2}} \cdot v_{sat_2} \qquad \qquad \text{... (2.17)}$$

(a) Work done,

$$W_{1-2} = \int_1^2 P \, dv = 0 \text{ , as dv = 0}$$

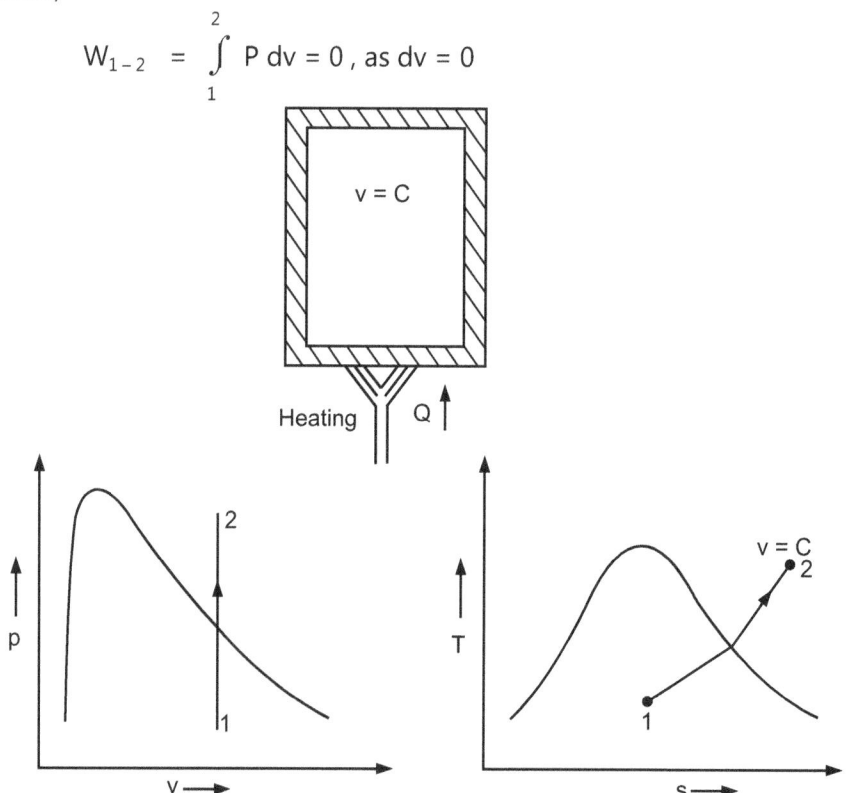

Fig. 2.14: Heating of vapour at constant volume (assuming state 2 superheated)

(b) Heat transferred by first law,

$$\delta Q = du + Pdx$$

$$Q_{1-2} = (u_2 - u_1) \text{ as Pdv = 0}$$

$$= (h_2 - p_2 v_2) - (h_1 - P_1 v_1) \qquad \qquad \text{... (2.18)}$$

where, $\quad h_2 = h_{sup_2}$

$$= h_g + c_p (T_{sup_2} - T_{sat_2}) \text{ kJ/kg}$$

$$P_2 = \text{Pressure at 2 kPa,}$$

$$v_2 = v_{sup_2}, \text{ m}^3\text{/kg}$$

$$h_1 = h_{x_1} = h_{f_1} + x \cdot h_{fg_1} \text{ kJ/kg}$$

$$P_1 = \text{Pressure at 1, kPa}$$

$$v_1 = vx_1$$
$$= v_{f_1} + x \cdot v_{fg_1} \text{ m}^3/\text{kg}$$

Similar equations are considered if the condition of steam at state 2 is wet.

SOLVED PROBLEMS

Problem 2.3: Constant volume: A vessel contains 4 kg of steam at 10 bar and 220°C. Find the volume of the vessel. If the vessel is cooled till the steam pressure drops to 3 bar, find the final condition of steam and the heat transfer during cooling.

Solution:

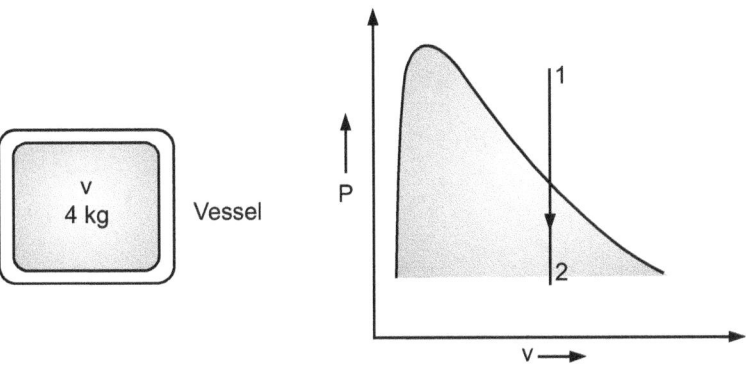

Fig. 2.15

Given: P_1 = 10 bar, m = 4 kg, T_1 = 220°C and P_2 = 3 bar.

For P_1 = 10 bar, T_{sat_1} = 179.9°C from steam table.

$T_1 > T_{sat_1}$, hence steam is super-heated.

$$v_{sup_1} = \frac{T_{sup_1}}{T_{sat_1}} \times v_{g_1} \text{ m}^3/\text{kg}$$

$$= \frac{(220 + 273)}{(179.9 + 273)} \times 0.1943$$

$$= \textbf{0.2115 m}^3\textbf{/kg}$$

∴ Volume of vessel,

$$V = m \times v_{sup_1}$$

$$= 4 \times 0.2115$$

$$= \textbf{0.846 m}^3$$

The steam undergoes a non-flow constant volume cooling process. If V_2 is the final specific volume of steam,

Volume of vessel $= v = m \cdot v_2$

∴ $$v_2 = \frac{v}{m} = \frac{0.846}{4} = \textbf{0.2115 m}^3\textbf{/kg}$$

Final condition of steam is found by comparing v_2 with v_{g_2} at 3 bar.

$\therefore \qquad v_{g_2} = 0.60553$ m³/kg from steam table

$\qquad\qquad v_2 < v_{g_2}$, the steam is wet having dryness fraction x_2

$\qquad\qquad v_2 = x_2 \cdot v_{g_2}$

$\qquad 0.2115 = x_2 \times 0.60553$

$\therefore \qquad\quad x_2 = \mathbf{0.3493}$

The heat transferred during the non-flow constant volume process can be found from the following equation

$$Q = \Delta u + W_{1-2}$$

$$W_{1-2} = \int_1^2 P dv = 0, \text{ Since } dv = 0$$

$$Q = \Delta u$$

$$= m (u_2 - u_1)$$

$$= m \left[\left(h_2 - P_2 v_2\right) - \left(h_1 - P_1 v_1\right) \right] \text{ kJ}$$

$$= m \left[\left(h_2 - h_1\right) - v_1 \left(P_2 - P_1\right) \right] \text{ kJ}$$

$\therefore \qquad h_2 = h_{f_2} + x_2 \cdot h_{fg_2}$

$$= 561.4 + 0.3493 \times 2163.2$$

$$= \mathbf{1316.96 \text{ kJ/kg}}$$

$\qquad h_1 = h_{g_1} + c_p (T_{sup_1} - T_{sat_1})$

$$= 2776.2 + 2.1 (220 - 179.9)$$

$$= \mathbf{2860.4 \text{ kJ/kg}}$$

$\therefore \qquad Q = \text{Heat transfer}$

$$= 4 \left[(1316.96 - 2860.4) - 0.2115 (3 - 10) \times 100 \right]$$

$$= \mathbf{-5581.58 \text{ kJ rejected.}}$$

Problem 2.4: A closed vessel of 0.75 m³ capacity contains dry saturated steam at 0.35 MPa. The vessel is cooled until the pressure is reduced to 0.2 MPa. Calculate

(i)   Mass of steam in the vessel.

(ii) The final dryness fraction of steam.

(iii) The amount of heat transferred during the cooling process.

Extract from steam table

Pressure in MPa	T_s (°C)	v_f (m³/kg)	v_g (m³/kg)	h_f (kJ/kg)	h_{fg} (kJ/kg)	h_g (kJ/kg)
0.18	116.9	0.001057	0.978	491	2211	2702
0.20	120.2	0.001061	0.886	505	2202	2702
0.3	133.5	0.001073	0.605	561	2163	2724
0.35	138.9	0.001078	0.524	584	2148	2732
0.40	143.6	0.001084	0.462	605	2134	2739

Solution: Given: Volume of vessel, $v = 0.75$ m³, $P_1 = 0.35$ MPa.

At this pressure, specific volume, $v_{g_1} = 0.524$ m³/kg.

(i)   Mass of steam in the vessel

$$= \frac{v}{v_{g_1}} = \frac{0.75}{0.524} = \textbf{1.431 kg}$$

(ii) The volume of vessel, $v = m \cdot v_2$

$$v_2 = \frac{v}{m} = \frac{0.75}{1.431} = \textbf{0.524 m³/kg}$$

At pressure $P_2 = 0.2$ MPa, volume of steam (dry saturated) $= v_{g_2} = 0.8860$.

$v_2 < v_{g_2}$. Therefore it is a wet steam.

∴ $x_2 \, v_{g_2} = v_2$

∴ $x_2 = \dfrac{v_2}{v_{g_2}} = \dfrac{0.524}{0.886} = 0.589$

(iii) Heat transfer,

$$Q = \Delta u + \int_{1}^{2} Pdv \text{ where } \int_{1}^{2} Pdv = 0$$

∴ $Q = \Delta u$

$= m [(h_2 - P_2 v_2) - (h_1 - P_1 v_1)]$

$h_2 = h_{f_2} + x \cdot h_{fg_2}$

$\quad = 505 + 0.589 \times 2202 = \textbf{1801.9 kJ/kg}$

$V_2 = x \cdot v_{g_2} = 0.589 \times 0.886$

$\quad = \textbf{0.524 m³/kg}$

$P_2 = 0.2 \text{ MPa} = 200 \text{ kPa}$

$h_1 = h_{g_1} = 2732 \text{ kJ/kg}$

$P_1 = \textbf{350 kPa}$

$V_1 = v_{g_1} = 0.524$

$Q = 1.431 [(1801.9 - 200 \times 0.524) - (2732 - 350 \times 0.524)]$

$\quad = 1.431 [1697.1 - 2548.6]$

$\quad = \textbf{– 1218.5 kJ}$

2.5.2 Constant Pressure Process

The process is represented on P-v and T-s planes (See Fig. 2.16).

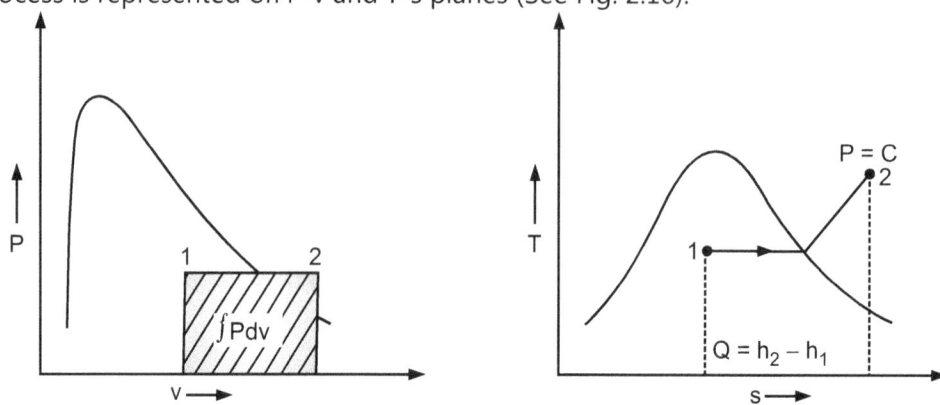

Fig. 2.16: Constant pressure process on p–v and T–s planes

(a) Work done:

$$W_{1-2} = \int P dv = P \int dv$$
$$= P (v_2 - v_1) \text{ kJ/kg} \qquad \qquad \text{... (2.19)}$$

P is in kN/m² and v in m³/kg

$$v_2 = v_{sup_2}$$

$$= \frac{T_{sup}}{T_{sat}} \times v_g \qquad \qquad \text{... (2.20)}$$

$v_1 = x_1 \cdot v_{g_1}$ at pressure p_1 and dryness fraction x_1

(b) Heat transfer:

$$Q_{1-2} = (u_2 - u_1) + \int_1^2 P dv$$

$$= (u_2 - u_1) + P (v_2 - v_1) \text{ kJ/kg}$$

where p is in kN/m² and v in m³/kg

$$P = P_1 = P_2$$

∴ $\qquad \qquad Q_{1-2} = h_2 - h_1 \qquad \qquad \text{... (2.21)}$

(c) Change in internal energy:

$$u_2 - u_1 = (h_2 - h_1) - (Pv_2 - Pv_1) \text{ kJ/kg} \qquad \qquad \text{... (2.22)}$$
$$= (h_2 - h_1) - P (v_2 - v_1) \text{ kJ/kg} \qquad \qquad \text{... (2.23)}$$

v_2 and v_1 are to be determined depending upon the condition.

Problem 2.5: Constant Pressure Process: Steam at 10 bar and 230°C is cooled under constant pressure until the quality of steam becomes 80% dry. Find (a) the work done, (b) change in enthalpy and heat transfer, if the process is non-flow.

Solution:

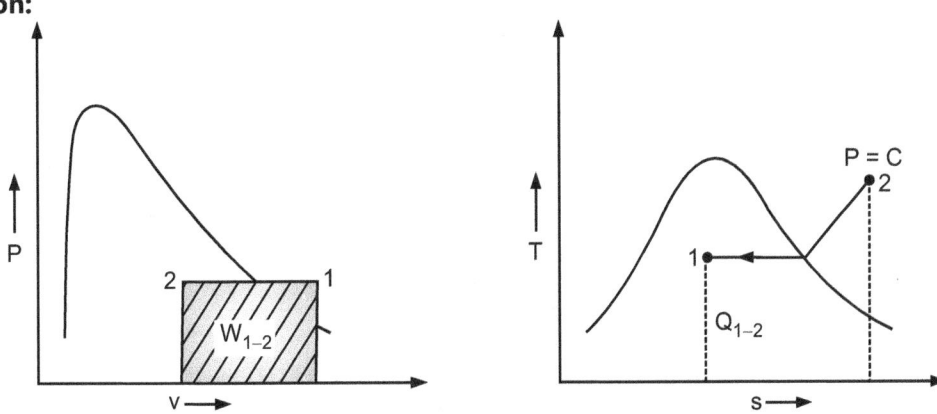

Fig. 2.17: P-v and T-s diagrams

For 10 bar pressure,
T_s = 179.9°C, v_f = 0.001127 m³/kg, v_g = 0.194,
h_f = 763 kJ/kg, h_{fg} = 2015 kJ/kg

(i) Work done,

$$W_{1-2} = \int_{1}^{2} pdv$$

$$W_{1-2} = P\,(v_2 - v_1) \text{ for m = 1}$$

As T_s = 179.9°C, but given temperature at state 1 is 230°C. Therefore steam is superheated at state 1.

$$\therefore \qquad v_{sup_1} = \frac{v_{sup_1}}{v_{sat_1}} \times v_{sat_1}$$

$$= \frac{(230 + 273)}{(179.9 + 273)} \times 0.194$$

$$= \mathbf{0.2154 \ m^3/kg}$$

Therefore, steam is in wet condition at state 2.
Therefore $v_2 = x_2 \cdot v_{g_2}$

$$= 0.8 \times 0.198$$

$$= \mathbf{0.1584 \ m^3/kg}$$

$$W_{1-2} = \frac{10 \times 10^5}{10^5} \times (0.1584 - 0.2154)$$

$$= \mathbf{-\ 57 \ kJ/kg}$$

Negative sign indicates that work is done on the steam.

(ii) Change in enthalpy = Heat transfer

$$= h_2 - h_1$$

$$= \left(h_{f_2} + x_2\,h_{fg_2}\right) - \left(h_{f_1} + h_{fg_1} + c_p\,(T_{sup_1} - T_{sat_1})\right)$$

But $\qquad h_{f_2} = h_{f_1}$

$\therefore$ Change in enthalpy $= (x_2 - 1) h_{fg_1} + c_p (T_{sup_1} - T_{sat_1})$

$$= (0.8 - 1) \times 2015 + 2.1 (230 - 179.9)$$
$$= -297.8 \text{ kJ/kg}$$

Negative sign indicates that heat is lost by the steam (system).

2.5.3 Constant Temperature (Isothermal) Process

For wet steam, a constant temperature process is also a constant pressure process. As soon as the steam becomes superheated, it behaves as a perfect gas and follows isothermal process. This is shown on P-v and T-s planes (See Fig. 2.18).

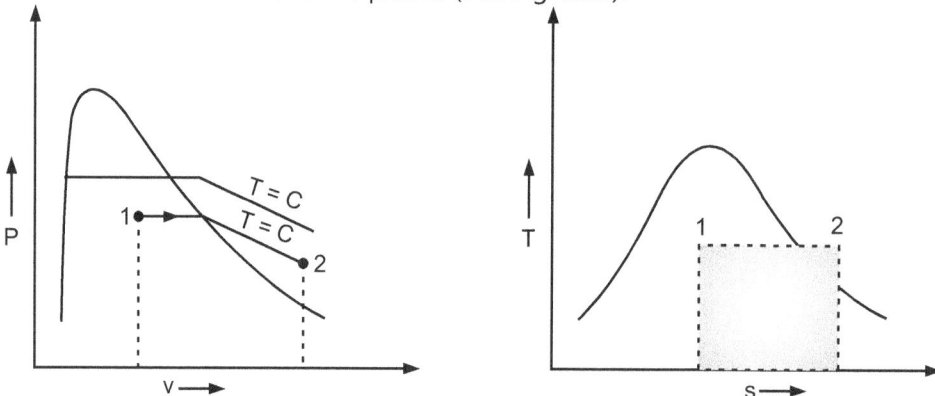

Fig. 2.18: Isothermal process

(a) Isothermal law can be applied to the process 1-2 as,

$$P_1 v_1 = P_2 v_2$$

i.e. $\qquad P_1 \cdot (x_1 v_{g_1}) = P_2 (v_{sup_2}) \qquad \qquad ... (2.24)$

because of the condition that steam is wet at state 1 and it is superheated at state 2 (See Fig. 2.18).

$\therefore$ From above equation, x_1 is determined. The state 2 may not be necessarily superheated, but may be wet also.

It follows that,

$h_1 = h_{f_1} + x_1 h_{fg_1}$

$h_2 = h_{f_2} + x_2 h_{fg_2}$ if final condition of steam is wet.

$h_2 = h_{f_2} + h_{fg_1} + k_p (T_{sup_2} - T_{sat_2})$ if steam is superheated at point 2.

(b) Work done: By first law

$$Q_{1-2} = \Delta u + W_{1-2}$$
$\therefore \qquad \qquad W_{1-2} = Q_{1-2} - \Delta u$

$$= Q_{1-2} - (u_2 - u_1)$$
$$= Q_{1-2} - (u_1 - u_2) \qquad \text{for unit mass ... (2.25)}$$

This W_{1-2} can also be obtained by

$$W_{1-2} = P_1 v_1 \, ln \left(\frac{v_2}{v_1} \right)$$

$$\therefore \qquad \frac{v_2}{v_1} = r = \frac{P_1}{P_2}$$

$$= P_1 \left(x_1 \cdot V_{g_1} \right) ln \, r \qquad \qquad \text{... (2.26)}$$

(c) Heat transfer

$$Q_{1-2} = W_{1-2} + (u_2 - u_1)$$
$$= P_1 \cdot x_1 \, V_{g_1} \, log_e \, r + (u_2 - u_1) \text{ per unit mass.} \qquad \text{... (2.27)}$$

SOLVED PROBLEM

Problem 2.6: A reciprocating steam engine receives dry saturated steam at 14 bar. Expansion takes place hyperbolically to a pressure of 4 bar. Calculate the final condition of steam at the end of expansion and the work done per kg of steam during expansion.

Solution: Let us represent the process on P-v and T-s diagrams.

The expansion is being hyperbolic, $P_1 v_1 = P_2 v_2$. The volume of dry saturated steam at 14 bar pressure is $v_{g_1} = 0.1633 \text{ m}^3/\text{kg}$.

The specific volume of dry saturated steam at pressure of 4 bar is $v_{g_2} = 0.4625 \text{ m}^3$.

$$\therefore \qquad P_1 v_1 = P_2 v_2$$

$$\therefore \qquad v_2 = \frac{P_1 v_1}{P_2} = \frac{14}{4} \times 0.1633 = \mathbf{0.49 \ m^3/kg}$$

$$\therefore \qquad v_2 > v_{g_2}$$

$\therefore$ Steam is superheated state at point 2.

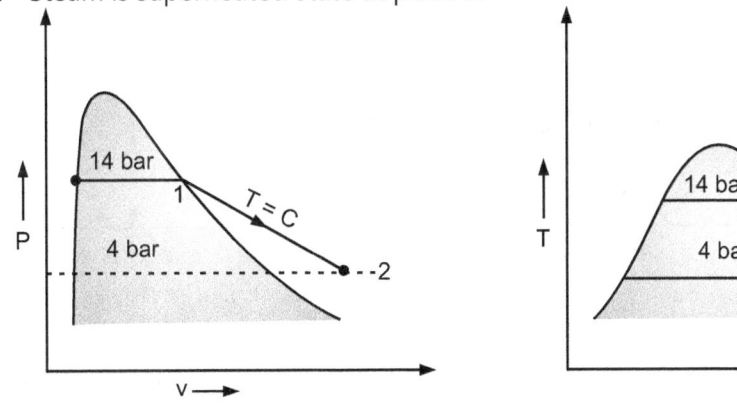

Fig. 2.19: P-v and T-s diagrams

Work done, $W_{1-2} = P_1 v_{g_1} \, ln\left(\dfrac{v_2}{v_1}\right) = P_1 v_{g_1} ln\left(\dfrac{P_1}{P_2}\right)$

$$= \dfrac{14 \times 10^5}{1000} \times 0.1633 \times log\,\dfrac{12}{4}$$

$$= \textbf{251.1 kJ/kg}$$

2.5.4 Polytropic Process

This process is stated by the law $Pv^n = c$, where n = polytropic index. For different values of 'n', each process discussed earlier can be obtained. But for vapour, Pv = RT does not apply. The process is shown in Fig. 2.20.

In Fig. 2.20, state 1 is assumed as superheated state and state 2 as wet condition.

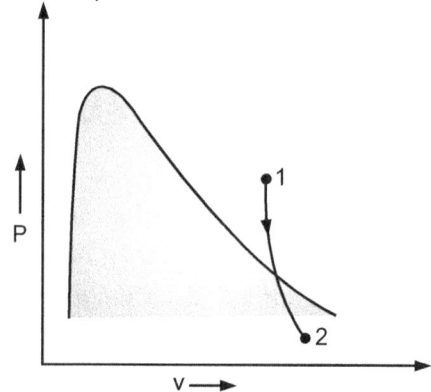

Fig. 2.20: Polytropic process on P-v plane

(a) Work done for non-flow process,

$$W_{1-2} = \int_{1}^{2} Pdv = \dfrac{P_1 v_1 - P_2 v_2}{n-1} \qquad\qquad \text{... (2.28)}$$

(b) Heat transfer during the non-flow process.

$$Q_{1-2} = (u_2 - u_1) + \dfrac{P_1 v_1 - P_2 v_2}{n-1}$$

v_1 and v_2 are calculated for the steam depending upon its state.

SOLVED PROBLEM

Problem 2.7: Steam at a pressure of 14 bar with 50°C superheat expands according to $Pv^{1.25} = C$ to a pressure of 4 bar in a cylinder-piston arrangement. Determine (1) work done per kg of steam, (2) heat transferred.

Solution: At pressure of 14 bar, the properties of dry saturated steam are: T_{sat} = 195.04°C, v_{g_1}= 0.14072 m³/kg, h_{f_1} = 830 kJ/kg, h_{fg_1} = 1957.7 kJ/kg, h_{g_1} = 2787.8 kJ/kg.

Similarly, at 4 bar pressure,

v_{g_2} = 0.46222 m³/kg, h_{f_2} = 604.67 m³/kg, h_{fg_2} = 2133 kJ/kg, h_{f_2} = 2737.6 kJ/kg.

T_1 = 195.04 + 50 = 244.04°C.

As the steam is superheated by 50°C,

$$v_{sup_1} = \frac{T_{sup_1}}{T_{sat_1}} \times v_{sat_1}$$

$$= \frac{(244.04 + 273)}{(195.04 + 273)} \times 0.14072$$

$$= \textbf{0.15545 m}^3\textbf{/kg}$$

(a) $$W_{1-2} = \frac{P_1 v_1 - P_2 v_2}{n - 1}$$

$$= \frac{P_1 v_1}{n - 1}\left[1 - \left(\frac{p_2}{p_1}\right)^{\frac{n-1}{n}}\right]$$

$$= \frac{14 \times 10^5}{1000} \times \frac{0.15545}{(1.25 - 1)}\left[1 - \left(\frac{4}{14}\right)^{\frac{1.25-1}{1.25}}\right]$$

$$= \textbf{192.9 kJ/kg}$$

The work done can also be calculated as

$$W_{1-2} = 100\frac{P_1 v_1 - P_2 v_2}{n - 1}; \text{ p in bar}$$

$$192.9 = 100 \times \frac{(14 \times 0.15545 - 4 \times v_2)}{1.25 - 1}$$

$$v_2 = 0.423 \text{ m}^3\text{/kg}$$

but $$v_{g_2} = 0.4622$$

∴ $$v_{g_1} > v_2 \therefore \text{ Steam is wet.}$$

Dryness fraction x_2 = ?

$$P_1 v_1^{\frac{1}{1}} = P_2 v_2^{n}$$

$$14 \times (0.15545) = 4 \times (x_2 \cdot v_{g_2})^n$$

∴ $$(x_2)^n = \frac{14}{4} \times \left(\frac{0.15545}{0.4622}\right)^n$$

$$x_2 = \left(\frac{14}{4}\right)^{\frac{1}{n}} \times \frac{0.15545}{0.4622} = \textbf{0.916}$$

(b) Heat transferred,

$$Q_{1-2} = (u_2 - u_1) + W_{1-2}$$

$$u_1 = h_1 - 100 \, P_1 v_1 \text{ at 14 bar, } P_1 \text{ in bar}$$

$$h_1 = h_{g_1} + c_p \log \left(\frac{T_{sup_1}}{T_{sat_1}} \right)$$

$$= 2787.8 + 2.1 \log (50)$$

$$= \mathbf{2796 \ kJ/kg}$$

$$u_1 = 2796 - 100 \times 14 \times 0.15545$$

$$= \mathbf{2578.3 \ kJ/kg}$$

$$u_2 = (h_2 - 100 \ P_2 v_2)$$

$$u_2 = h_{f_2} + x_2 \cdot h_{f_2} - 100 \times P_2 v_2$$

where $v_2 = x_2 \cdot v_{g_2}$

$\therefore$ $u_2 = (604.04 + 0.916 \times 2133) - 100 \times 4 \times (0.916 \times 0.4622)$

$$u_2 = 2388.8 \ kJ/kg$$

$$W_{1-2} = 192.9$$

$\therefore$ $Q_{1-2} = (2388.8 - 2578.3) + 192.9$

$$= \mathbf{2.97 \ kJ/kg}$$

2.5.5 Adiabatic Process

Reversible adiabatic process is an isentropic process. The process is stated by the law $PV^\gamma = c$, where γ = adiabatic index. This is represented on T-s and h-s planes.

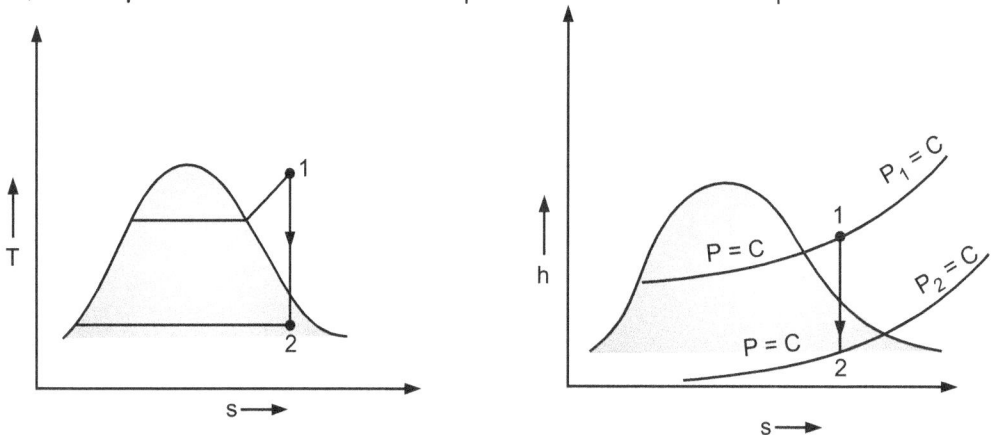

Fig. 2.21: Adiabatic process on T-s and h-s planes

(a) Work done $Q_{1-2} = u_2 - u_1 + W_{1-2}$

    For reversible adiabatic process,

        Heat transfer, $Q_{1-2} = 0$

$\therefore$ $W_{1-2} = -(u_2 - u_1)$

SOLVED PROBLEM

Problem 2.8: Steam initially at 1.5 MPa and 300°C expands reversibly and adiabatically in a steam engine to 40°C. Determine (a) condition of steam after expansion, (b) work done/kg of steam.

Solution: The reversible adiabatic expansion of steam in a turbine is a steady flow isentropic process.

Data: p_1 = 15 bar, T_1 = 300°C, T_2 = 40°C, $P_2 = P_{sat}$ at 40°C and $s_2 = s_1$.

Now,
$$s_1 = s_{g_1} + c_p \ln\left(\frac{T_1}{T_{sat}}\right) \text{ kJ/kg·K}$$

$$= 6.441 + 2.1 \ln\left(\frac{300 + 273}{198.3 + 273}\right)$$

$$= \mathbf{6.85732 \text{ kJ/kg·K}} = s_2 \text{ at } P_2$$

From steam table,

$$p_2 = 0.07375 \text{ bar at } T_2 = 40°C.$$

and
$$s_{g_2} = 8.258 \text{ kJ/kg·K at } 40°C$$

$$s_2 < s_{g_2}$$

Therefore steam after expansion is wet.

$$s_2 = 6.85132$$

$$= s_{x_2}$$

$$= s_{f_2} + x_2 \cdot s_{fg_2}$$

$$6.85732 = 0.572 + x_2 \times 7.686$$

$$\therefore \quad x_2 = \mathbf{0.81698}$$

Adiabatic expansion process is represented on h-s diagram (See Fig. 2.22).

(b) Work done (W_{1-2}):

By first law,

$$Q_{1-2} = u_2 - u_1 + W_{1-2}$$

$$Q_{1-2} = 0 \text{ for adiabatic process}$$

$$\therefore \quad W_{1-2} = u_1 - u_2$$

$$= (h_1 - h_2) - (P_1v_1 - P_2v_2) \qquad \qquad \text{... (1)}$$

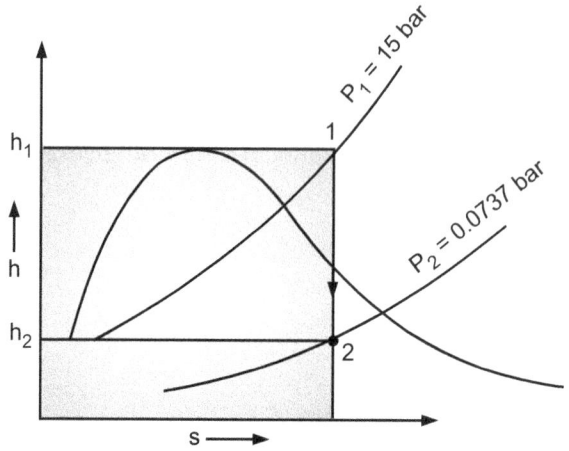

Fig. 2.22: h-s diagram

Now,
$$h_1 = h_{g_1} + c_p \cdot \ln\left(\frac{T_{sup_1}}{T_{sat_1}}\right)$$

$$= 2789.9 + 2.1 \, \ln\left(\frac{300 + 273}{198.1 + 273}\right)$$

$$= \textbf{2790.3 kJ/kg}$$

$$h_2 = h_{f_2} + x_2 h_{fg_2}$$

$$= 167.45 + 0.81698 \times 2406.9$$

$$= \textbf{2133.8 kJ/kg}$$

$$v_1 = v_{sup_1} = \frac{T_{sup_1}}{T_{sat_1}} \times v_{sat_1}$$

$$= \frac{(300 + 273)}{(198.1 + 273)} \times 0.13166$$

$$= \textbf{0.160 m}^3\textbf{/kg}$$

$$v_2 = v_{x_2} = v_{f_2} + x_2 v_{g_2}$$

$$= 0.0010078 + 0.81698 \times 19.546$$

$$= \textbf{15.9697 m}^3\textbf{/kg}$$

Put all these in equation (1)
$$W_{1-2} = (2790.3 - 2133.8) - (15 \times 100 \times 0.160 - 0.07375 \times 100 \times 15.9697)$$

$$= \textbf{533.0 kJ/kg}$$

∴ **Work is obtained**.

2.5.6 Throttling Process

When a fluid passes through small aperture (opening), it is said to be throttled and enthalpy of the fluid remains constant during throttling.

Throttling is a steady flow process, therefore, apply steady flow energy equation.

$$Q = \Delta h + \Delta KE + \Delta PE + W$$

Since $Q = 0$, $W = 0$. If ΔPE and ΔKE are neglected, then $\Delta h = 0$ i.e. $h_1 = h_2$.

It is represented on T-s and h-s planes (See Fig. 2.23). Throttling is an irreversible process. Hence shown by dotted lines.

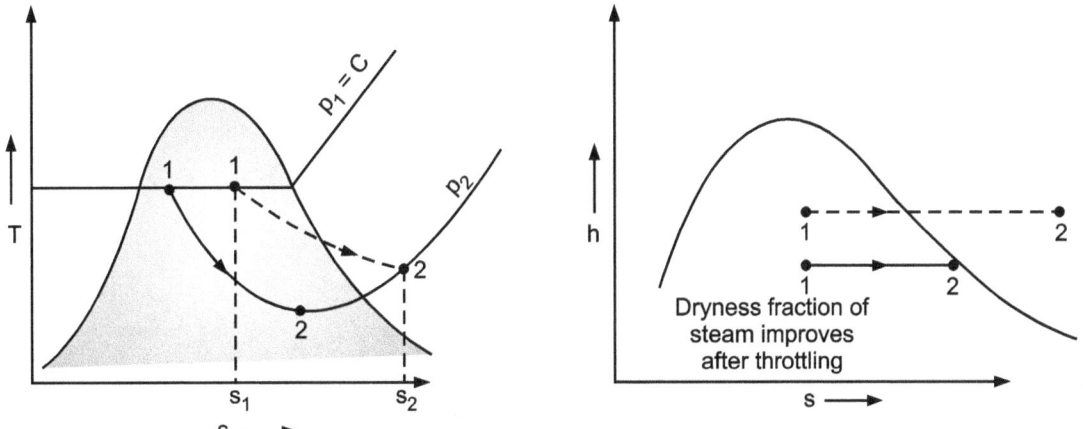

Fig. 2.23: Throttling process

SOLVED PROBLEM

Problem 2.9: Steam is throttled from 6 bar and 0.98 dryness fraction to a final pressure at 1 bar. Find the final condition of steam.

Solution: Throttling is irreversible and constant enthalpy process,

$$h_1 = h_{x_1} = h_{f_1} + x_1 h_{fg_1}$$

$$= 670.4 + 0.98 \times 2085$$

$$= 2713.7 \text{ kJ/kg}$$

$$= h_2 \text{ kJ/kg}$$

Now $h_{g_2} = 2675.4$ kJ/kg at 1 bar.

$h_2 > h_{g_2}$, hence steam after throttling is superheated

$$h_2 = h_{sup_2} = 2713.7$$

$$h_{sup_2} = h_{g_2} + c_p (T_{sup_2} - T_{sat_2})$$

$$2713.7 = 2675.4 + 2.1 (T_{sup_2} - 99.63)$$

$\therefore$ $T_{sup_2} = \mathbf{117.87}$

The final condition of steam after throttling can also be found from Mollier diagram shown below.

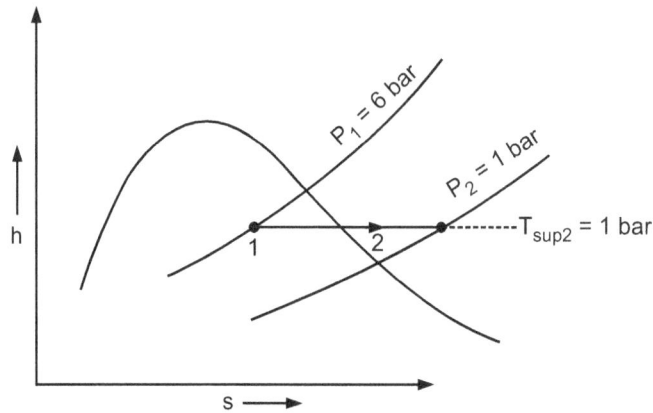

Fig. 2.24: h-s diagram

If the steam is expanded from state 1 (wet condition) to state 2 (wet condition)

$$\therefore \qquad h_{f_1} + x_1 h_{fg_1} \;=\; h_{f_2} + x_2 h_{fg_2} \qquad\qquad \dots (2.29)$$

If the steam becomes superheated after throttling as shown by dotted line 1-2, then

$$h_{f_1} + x_1 h_{fg_1} \;=\; h_{f_2} + x_2 h_{fg_2} + c_{ps}\,(T_{sup2} - T_{s_2})$$

$$\qquad\qquad\qquad = h_g + c_{ps}\,(T_{sup_2} - T_{s_2}) \qquad\qquad \dots (2.30)$$

During throttling, the pressure always falls.

$$\therefore \qquad\qquad\qquad p_2 \;<\; p_1$$

$$\therefore \qquad\qquad h_{f_1} > h_{f_2} \quad \text{and} \quad h_{fg_1} < h_{fg_2}$$

If the sensible heat difference $(h_{f_1} - h_{f_2}) = h_1$ is greater than $(h_{fg_1} - h_{fg_2}) = h_2$ then the heat $(h_1 - h_2)$ is utilized to dry out the steam or to even superheat which depends upon the initial condition of steam (x_1) and final pressure after throttling. The throttling process is used for:

- determining the dryness fraction of steam,
- controlling the speed of the engine and turbine,
- in refrigeration system to reduce the pressure and temperature of the liquid refrigerant from the condenser condition to the evaporator condition.

VAPOUR POWER CYCLES

Introduction

Thermal power plants use fossil fuels to generate the power. The steam power plant is one of the most successful thermal power plants for the conversion of heat energy into mechanical work. The sequences of various processes that occur in steam power plant are as listed below.

- Heat energy released by the combustion of fuel or by atomic fission is utilized to vapourize water into steam.

- The steam thus produced is expanded in a steam engine or turbine to obtain useful work or power.

- The vapour leaving the turbine is normally condensed and pumped back to its initial state constituting a cycle.

- Thus, the working fluid changes from liquid to vapour and back to its original state.

- This succession of processes is designated as vapour cycle to recognize the state of the working substance during the work output process.

Steam turbine power plants from 1 MW upto 1000 MW units resulting in about 35% to 38% overall thermal efficiency are in current use all over the world. Now-a-days, combined (gas and steam turbine) cycle plant is gaining popularity as it yields about 55 to 60% overall thermal efficiency.

The power developed from steam turbine plant is costlier than hydel-power plant. But one cannot meet the power demand only through hydel power plants, therefore, it is necessary to go for this plant. Also it takes a short time to set up (three to four years) as compared to the hydel which takes nearly ten years and needs a lot of preparatory work in the selection of site.

Carnot vapour cycle is the ideal cycle and which consists of the various ideal processes involved to generate the power from thermal energy.

2.6 THE CARNOT VAPOUR CYCLE

The Carnot vapour cycle consists of four fundamental elements namely:

(i)   Boiler (Steam generator),

(ii) Turbine,

(iii) Condenser,

(iv) Feed pump handling a two phase mixture-water and its vapour.

Fig. 2.25 shows a steam power plant operating on the Carnot cycle. The processes of the working fluid (steam, i.e. water) are represented on p-v and T-s diagrams as shown in Fig. 2.26.

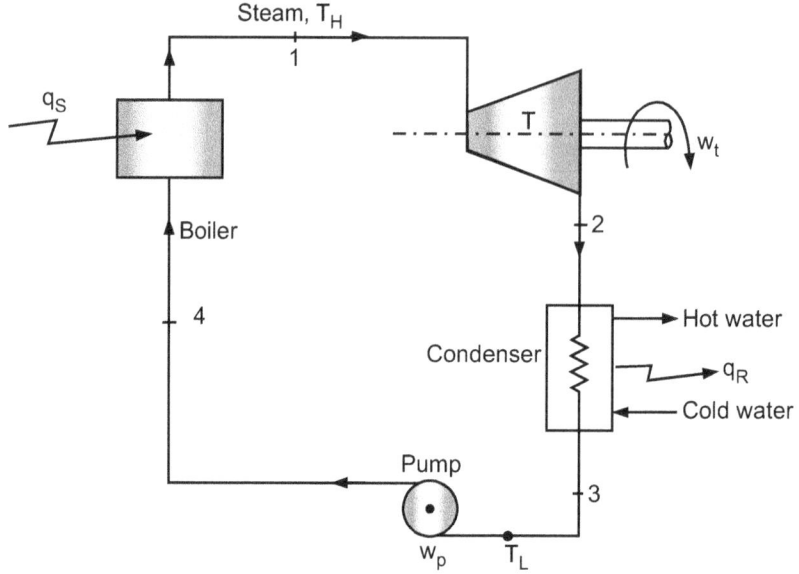

Fig. 2.25: A steam power plant operating on Carnot cycle

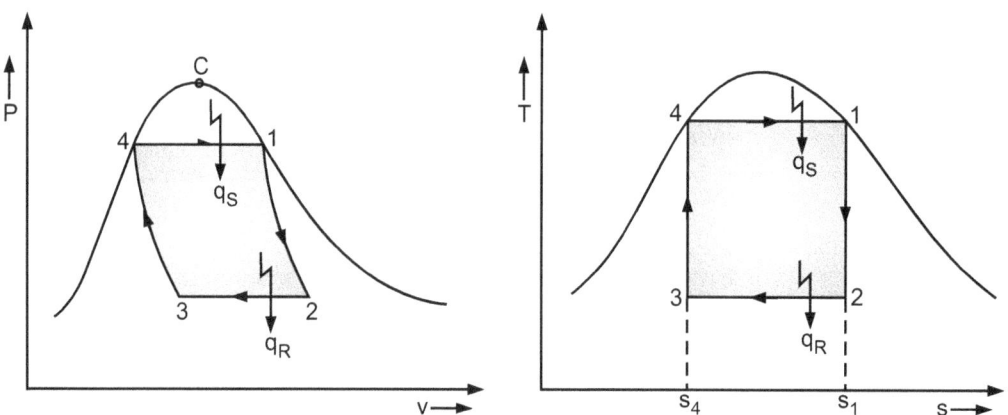

Fig. 2.26: Carnot vapour cycle on p-v and T-s diagrams

Water is heated at constant pressure in the boiler to produce steam. It means heat (q_s) is supplied to the boiler. The condition of steam at the outlet of boiler is at saturated state (represented by point 1 on P-v and T-s diagrams) in Carnot cycle. However, in practice the condition of steam may be superheated one. It is assumed that the condition of water at the outlet of condenser is at point 3. It means a mixture of water and vapour. The mixture is pressurized in the pump such that the condition of water is saturated (point 4). This saturated water is converted to steam in the boiler where it gains (receiver) heat from the burnt gases.

The analysis of Carnot cycle is given below assuming a unit mass of working substance.

Heat supplied in the boiler, $q_s = h_1 - h_{f_4}$

Heat rejected in the condenser, $q_R = h_2 - h_3$.

Work is obtained through turbine, where steam expands from its pressure p_1 to pressure p_2.

$$\text{Work, } w_1 = h_1 - h_2$$

$$\text{Work obtained} = \text{Heat supplied} - \text{Heat rejected}$$

$$= (h_1 - h_{f_4}) - (h_2 - h_3)$$

$$\text{Thermal efficiency, } \eta_{th} = \frac{\text{Work done}}{\text{Heat supplied}}$$

$$= \frac{(h_1 - h_{f_4}) - (h_2 - h_3)}{h_1 - h_{f_4}} \qquad \dots (2.31)$$

Thermal efficiency may also be obtained from turbine and pump work.

For turbine, $w_t = h_1 - h_2$

For pump, $w_p = w_{3-4} = h_{f_4} - h_3$

$$w_{net} = w_t - w_p = (h_1 - h_2) - (h_{f_4} - h_3)$$

$$= (h_1 - h_{f_4}) - (h_2 - h_3)$$

$\therefore$ $$\eta_{th} = \frac{w_{net}}{h_1 - h_{f_4}}$$

Thermal efficiency of a Carnot cycle may be expressed in terms of temperature.
    Referring T-s diagram,
        Heat supplied, $q_s = T_H (s_1 - s_4)$
        Heat rejected, $q_R = T_L (s_1 - s_4) = T_L (s_2 - s_3)$

$\therefore$ $$\eta_{th} = \frac{q_s - q_R}{q_s} = \frac{T_H - T_L}{T_H} \qquad \dots (2.32)$$

Limitations of Carnot Vapour Cycle:

(i) The condition of working substance at the outlet of condenser is a wet steam. It is a mixture of water and water vapour. The condition of this mixture from state point 3 (P-v and T-s diagram) is to be changed to state 4 (P-v and T-s diagram). This process is carried out through a pump. There is not pump which would handle a mixture of water and water vapour. Therefore, a complete condensation of water vapour in the condenser is desirable.

Further, the pump has to work in such a way that the condition of water at the outlet of pump is saturated (point 4 in P-v and T-s plots). This is also difficult to achieve in practice.

(ii) The saturated steam is expanded in the turbine. The quality of steam decreases while passing through the turbine, therefore, it is also difficult to carry out the expansion of wet steam in the turbine.

2.7 RANKINE CYCLE

Carnot cycle is not a theoretical cycle for steam power plant because it is difficult to build a pump which can pump a mixture of water and vapour and deliver it at a saturated condition. This difficulty is overcome in the Rankine cycle with complete condensation of steam in the condenser. Rankine cycle is the theoretical cycle for steam power plant.

A diagrammatic of Rankine cycle steam turbine power plant is shown in Fig. 2.27. The power plant consists of four basic elements: (i) boiler, (ii) steam turbine, (iii) condenser and (iv) feed pump.

(i) Boiler: In the boiler, steam is produced from water at the operating pressure. Fuel is burnt, the heat released is supplied to the water at constant pressure.

(ii) Steam turbine: Here, the steam from the boiler pressure expands and thus performs mechanical work.

(iii) Condenser: In the condenser, the exhaust steam from the turbine gives up heat to the cooling water which otherwise cannot be converted into work and is rejected. The condenser enables the exhaust steam to be used as a working fluid of the boiler again. There is a cooling system for condenser consisting of cooling tower and cooling pump. This is not shown in Fig. 2.27.

(iv) Feed pump: The feed pump is used to pump the condensate from the hot-well (in which the condensate is collected) to the boiler at the boiler pressure.

The various processes of the Rankine cycle on P-v, T-s and h-s diagrams are shown in Figs. 2.28, 2.29 and 2.30 respectively. The various processes are:

Process 3-4: The water which is at low pressure p_2 is pumped isentropically into the boiler at high pressure p_1.

Process 4-5: Water is first heated upto the saturation temperature or evaporation temperature T_1 in the boiler and during this process the state point moves along the curve 4-5 called the sensible heating. The heat supplied during the process is $(h_{f_5} - h_{f_4})$ and is represented by the area L-3-4-5-M on T-s diagram, i.e., the sensible heat of water. Many times point 5 is not shown in power plants because it is the intermediate point in steam generation.

Process 5-1: At constant pressure P_1 and temperature T_1, water is completely vapourized into steam. The heat added in this process is equal to $(h_1 - h_{f_5})$ and is represented by M-5-1-N on T-s diagram, i.e. the latent heat of vapourization. The state point 1 shows the dry and saturated condition of steam.

Process 1-2: It is an isentropic expansion of steam in turbine from pressure P_1 to P_2.

Process 2-3: At constant pressure P_2 and temperature T_2, the exhaust steam is condensed in the condenser giving latent heat to cooling water.

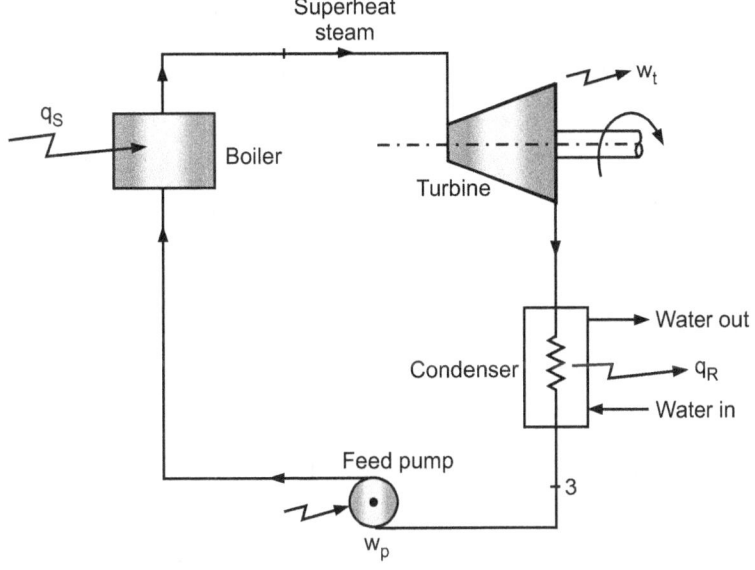

Fig. 2.27: Rankine cycle steam power plant

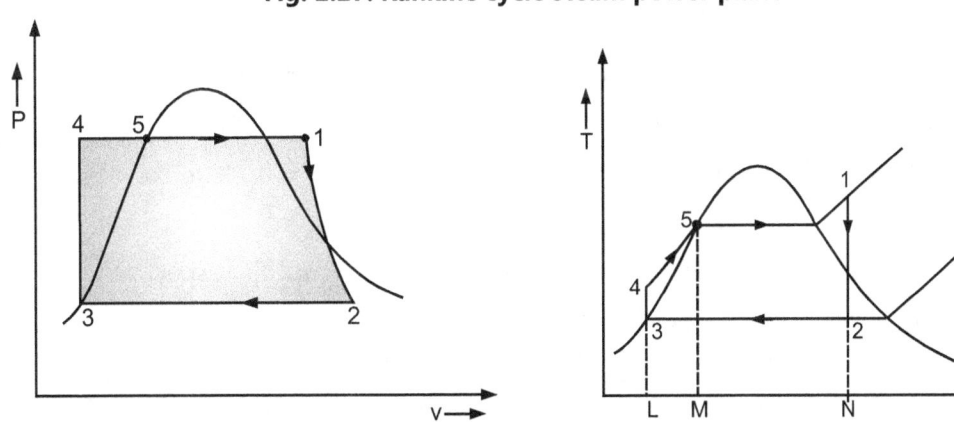

Fig. 2.28: Rankine cycle on P-v diagram   **Fig. 2.29: Rankine cycle on T-s diagram**

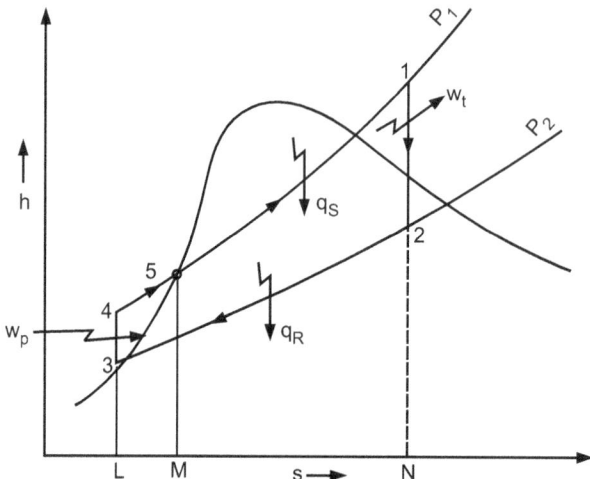

Fig. 2.30: Rankine cycle on h-s diagram

It is possible that steam leaving the boiler may be dry and saturated, wet or superheated. To obtain thermal efficiency of the Rankine cycle, the assumptions made are:

- Steady flow.

- Negligible kinetic and potential energy changes.

- One kg of working fluid flows through the various elements of the cycle.

First law of thermodynamics is applied separately to each of the four components of the Rankine cycle. Let us assume that, from **first law**, $\delta q - \delta u = dh$ or $q - w = \Delta h$.

Heat supplied in the boiler, process 4-1, $\qquad q_{4-1} = q_s = q_1 - h_{f_4}$

Heat rejected in the condenser, process 2-3, $\qquad q_{2-3} = q_R = h_2 - h_{f_3}$

Work obtained through turbine, 1-2, $\qquad w_{1-2} = w_t = h_1 - h_2$

Work supplied to the pump, 3-4, $\qquad w_{3-4} = w_p = h_{f_4} - h_{f_3}$

Pump work, w_p is also given by, $\qquad w_p = h_{f_4} - h_{f_3} = v_{f_3} (P_1 - P_3)$

$$= v_{f_2} (P_1 - P_2)$$

where h_{f_2} and h_{f_4} are the enthalpies of water at pressures P_2 and P_1 respectively. v_{f_2} is the specific volume of water in m^3/kg at final pressure P_2.

The net work $=$ Turbine work $-$ Pump work

or $\qquad w_{net} = w_t - w_p = (h_1 - h_2) - (h_{f_4} - h_{f_3}) \; kJ/kg$

or $\qquad w_{net} = (h_1 - h_2) - v_{f_2} (P_1 - P_2) \; kJ/kg$

While determining the net work from the plant, the work at the pump is to be subtracted from the turbine work output.

$$\eta_{th} = \frac{\text{Net work}}{\text{Head added}} = \frac{W_{net}}{q_A} = \frac{(h_1 - h_2) - (h_{f_4} - h_{f_3})}{(h_1 - h_{f_4})} \qquad \ldots (2.33)$$

Thermal efficiency may also be calculated from heat supplied q_A and heat rejected q_R.

$$W_{net} = q_s - q_R = (h_1 - h_{f_4}) - (h_2 - h_{f_2}) - (h_1 - h_2) - (h_{f_4} - h_{f_3})$$

$$\therefore \qquad \eta_{th} = \frac{W_{net}}{q_A} = \frac{(h_1 - h_2) - (h_{f_4} - h_{f_3})}{(h_1 - h_{f_4})}$$

or $\qquad \eta_{th} = \dfrac{(h_1 - h_2) - (h_{f_4} - h_{f_3})}{(h_1 - h_{f_3}) - (h_{f_4} - h_{f_3})} = \dfrac{(h_1 - h_2) - w_p}{(h_1 - h_{f2}) - w_p} \qquad \ldots (2.34)$

Many times the capacity of steam power plant is expressed in terms of **steam rate**. **Steam rate** is the rate of steam flow (kg/hr) required to produce unit shaft power (1 kW). Therefore,

$$\text{Steam rate} = \frac{1}{w_t - w_p} \times \frac{kg}{kJ} \times \frac{1 \text{ kJ/sec}}{1 \text{ kW}}$$

$$= \frac{1}{w_t - w_p} \cdot \frac{kg}{kW \text{ sec}} = \frac{3600}{w_t - w_p} \cdot \frac{kJ}{kWh}$$

Cycle efficiency is expressed many times as heat rate which is the rate of heat input (Q_s) required to produce work output (1 kW).

$$\text{Heat rate} = \frac{3600 \, Q_s}{w_t - w_p} = \frac{3600 \text{ kJ}}{\eta_{cycle} \cdot kWh}$$

Compared to turbine work, pump work is infinitesimally small and it may be neglected because the specific volume of water is very small. Here, we have

$$w_p = 0 \text{ or } h_{f_4} = h_{f_3} = h_{f_2}$$

$$\therefore \qquad \eta_{th} = \frac{h_1 - h_2}{h_1 - h_{f_3}} = \frac{h_1 - h_2}{h_1 - h_{f_2}} \qquad \ldots (2.35)$$

The thermal efficiency of the Rankine cycle may also be expressed in terms of areas on T-s diagram. Referring to Fig. 2.31,

$$\eta_{th} = \frac{\text{area } 123451}{\text{area L3451NL}} \text{ and neglecting pump work,}$$

$$\eta_{th} = \frac{\text{area } 123451}{\text{area L351NL}}$$

The overall thermal efficiency of a steam power plant varies from 35% to 38%.

In the above analysis, it is assumed that heat additions and rejection take place reversibly. This is, however, not possible in actual power plants. A substantial temperature difference exists between the hot flue gases and working fluid. But the irreversibility associated with this difference is reduced and the thermal efficiency of the cycle is increased by operating a steam generator at a pressure above the critical.

The efficiency of the Rankine cycle is shown on T-s plot in Fig. 2.31.

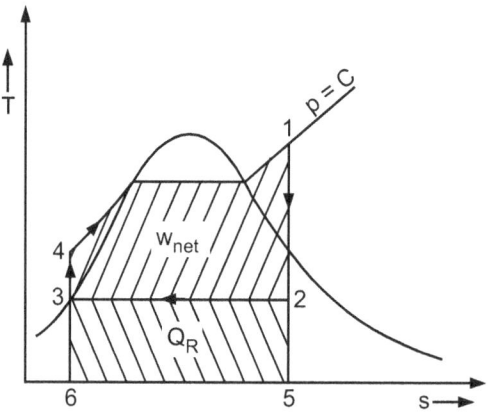

Fig. 2.31: w_{net} and Q_R are proportional to areas

The heat supplied Q_s is proportional to area 1-5-6-4-1, w_{net} is proportional to area 1-2-3-4-1 and the heat rejection Q_s is proportional to area 2-5-6-3-2.

2.8 COMPARISON OF RANKINE AND CARNOT CYCLES

Carnot cycle has the maximum possible efficiency operating between the limits of temperature. But it is not suitable in steam power plant. Carnot cycle and Rankine cycle are shown in Fig. 2.32 and Fig. 2.33 respectively with the help of T-s plots.

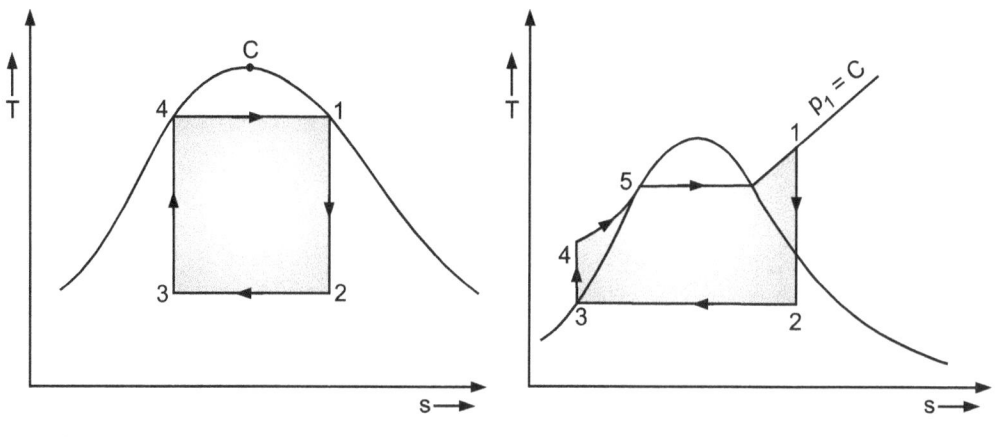

Fig. 2.32: Carnot cycle   **Fig. 2.33: Rankine cycle**

The reversible adiabatic expansion in the turbine, the constant temperature heat rejection in the condenser, and the reversible adiabatic compression in the pump are similar characteristic features of both Rankine and Carnot cycles.

1. The reversible heat addition takes place at constant temperature (process 4-1) in Carnot cycle; while it is at constant pressure (process 4-5-1) in Rankine cycle.

2. The heat supplied per kg of water is more in Rankine cycle than that in Carnot cycle. The heat rejection in condenser of both the cycles is same per unit mass operating between the same temperature limits. Therefore, thermal efficiency of Rankine cycle is less than that of Carnot cycle.

3. In Carnot cycle, it is difficult to control the quality of steam to state 3, so that at the end of isentropic compression, it reaches saturated liquid state. But there is a complete condensation of steam in Rankine cycle.

2.9 IMPROVING THE EFFICIENCY OF THE RANKINE CYCLE

Steam power plants are responsible for the production of most of the electric power in the world. A small increase in the thermal efficiency will lead to a large saving in the fuel requirement. Therefore, every effort is made to improve the efficiency of the cycle on which steam power plants operate.

Thermal efficiency of a power cycle would be increased by two ways:

(i) Increase the average temperature at which heat is transferred to the working fluid in the boiler, or

(ii) Decrease the average temperature at which heat is rejected from the working fluid in the condenser.

Next we discuss three ways of accomplishing this for the simple ideal Rankine cycle.

2.9.1 Lowering the Condenser Pressure (Lowers $T_{low, av}$)

Lowering the operating pressure of the condenser automatically lowers the temperature of the steam and thus the temperature at which heat is rejected. Steam exists as a saturated mixture in the condenser at the saturation temperature corresponding to the pressure inside.

• The effect of lowering the condenser pressure on the Rankine cycle efficiency is illustrated on T-s diagram in Fig. 2.34.

• For comparison purposes, the turbine inlet state is maintained the same.

- The coloured area on this diagram represents the increase in net work output as a result of lowering the condenser pressure from P_4 to P_4'.

- The increase in the input requirements is represented by the area under curve 2'-2, but this increase is very small. Thus, the overall effect of lowering the condenser pressure is an increase in the thermal efficiency of the cycle.

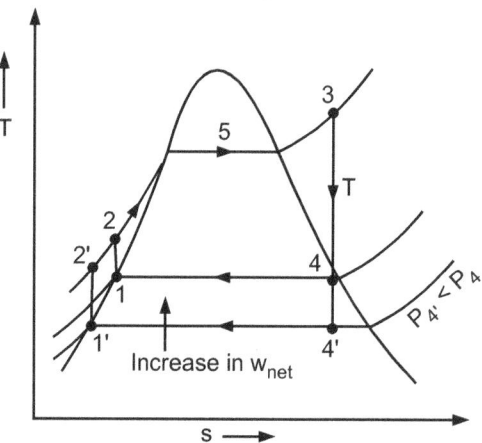

Fig. 2.34: The effect of lower condenser pressure on Rankine cycle

The condensers of steam power plants usually operate well below the atmospheric pressure which increases the efficiency. Vapour power cycles operate in a closed loop therefore, the vacuum pressure in the condenser does not present a major problem. However, there is a lower limit on the condenser pressure that can be used. It cannot be lower than the saturation pressure corresponding to the temperature of the cooling medium. Let us take an example of a condenser to be cooled by water at 15°C. Allowing a temperature difference of 8°C for effective heat transfer, the steam temperature in the condenser must be above 23°C, thus the condenser pressure must be above 3.5 kPa, which is the saturation pressure at 23°C.

Lowering the condenser pressure, it creates the problem of air leakage into the condenser. More importantly, it increases the moisture content of the steam at the last stages of the turbine, as highly undesirable in turbines because it decreases the turbine efficiency and erodes the turbine blades.

2.9.2 Superheating the Steam to High Temperature (Increases $T_{high, av}$)

The average temperature at which heat is added to the steam can be increased without increasing the boiler by superheating the steam to high temperatures.

- The effect of superheating on the performance of vapour power cycles is illustrated on a T-s diagram in Fig. 2.35.

- The coloured area on this diagram represents the increase in the heat input.

- Thus both the net work and heat input increase as a result of superheating the steam to a higher temperature.

- The overall effect is an increase in thermal efficiency, however, since the average temperature at which heat is added increases.

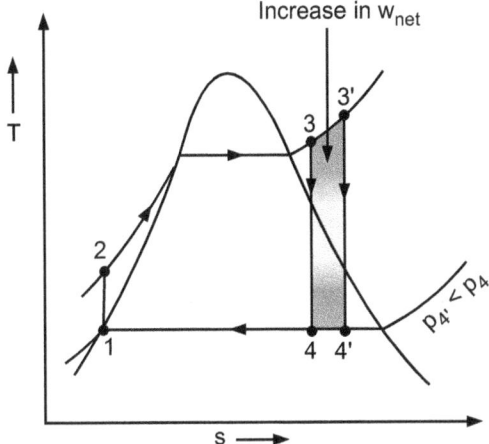

Fig. 2.35: The effect of superheating the steam to higher temperature on the ideal Rankine cycle

Superheating the steam to higher temperature decreases the moisture content of the steam at the turbine exit, as can be seen from the T-s diagram (the quality at state 4' is higher than that at state 4). This is desirable effect.

The temperature to which steam can be superheated is limited. However, by metallurgical considerations, presently, the highest steam temperature allowed at the turbine inlet is about 620°C. This value depends on improving the present materials or finding new ones that can withstand higher temperatures. Ceramics are very promising in this regard.

2.9.3 Increasing the Boiler Pressure (Increases $T_{high,\ av}$)

Another way of increasing the average temperature during the heat addition process is to increase the operating pressure of the boiler. This, in turn, raises the average temperature at which heat is added to the steam and thus raises the thermal efficiency of the cycle.

- The effect of increasing the boiler pressure on the performance of vapour B power cycles is illustrated on a T-s diagram in Fig. 2.36.

- For a fixed turbine inlet temperature, the cycle shifts to the left and the moisture content of steam at the turbine exit increases.

- This undesirable side effect can be corrected, however, by reheating the steam, as discussed in the next section.

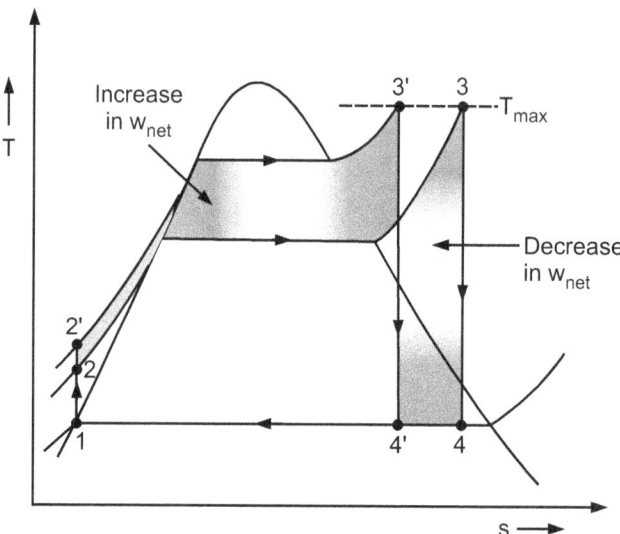

Fig. 2.36: Effect of increasing boiler pressure on ideal Rankine cycle

Operating pressures of boilers have gradually increase over the years from about 2-7 bar in 1922 to over to 300 bar today. Today many modern steam power plants operate at supercritical pressures (P > 22.09 MPa) and have thermal efficiencies of about 40% for fossil-fuel plants and 34% for nuclear power plants is due to the lower maximum temperatures used in those plants for safety reasons.

2.10 THE IDEAL REHEAT RANKINE CYCLE

Increasing the boiler pressure increases the thermal efficiency of the Rankine cycle, but it also increases the moisture content of the steam to unacceptable levels.

To resolve the issue, two possibilities come to mind:

1. It is desirable solution to superheat the steam to very high temperatures before it enters the turbine thus increasing the cycle efficiency. This also increases the temperature of the boiler material. This is not a viable solution, however, since it will require raising the steam temperature to metallurgically unsafe levels.

2. Expand the steam in the turbine in two stages, and reheat it in between. In other words, modify the simple ideal Rankine cycle with a reheat process. Reheating is a

practical solution to the excessive moisture problem in turbines, and it is used frequently in modern steam power plants.

- The T-s diagram of the ideal reheat Rankine cycle and the schematic of the power plant operating on this cycle are shown in Fig. 2.37.

- The ideal reheat Rankine cycle differs from the simple ideal Rankine cycle in that the expansion process takes place in two stages.

- In the first stage (the high-pressure turbine), steam is expanded isentropically to an intermediate pressure and sent back to the boiler where it is reheated at constant pressure, usually to the inlet temperature of the first turbine stage.

- Steam then expands isentropically in the second stage (low-pressure turbine) to the condenser pressure.

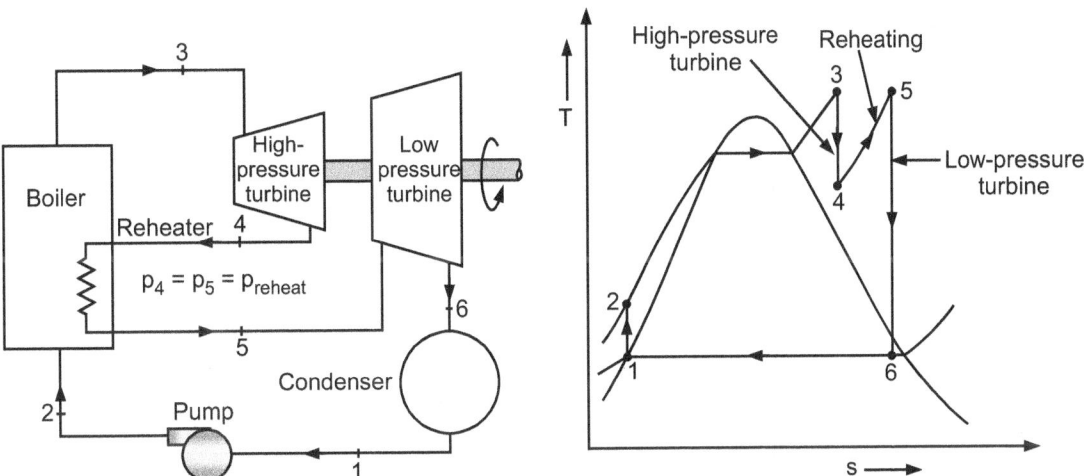

Fig. 2.37: Ideal reheat cycle (Block diagram and T-s diagram)

Thus, the total heat input and the total turbine work output for a reheat cycle become,

$$q_{in} = q_{primary} + q_{reheat} = (h_3 - h_2) + (h_5 - h_4) \text{ (kJ/kg)}$$

and

$$w_{turb, \, out} = w_{turb, \, II} = (h_3 - h_4) + (h_5 - h_6) \text{ (kJ/kg)}$$

- The cycle efficiency is not influenced greatly by the reheating process because the reheating process, in general, does not significantly change the average temperature at which heat is added.

- The efficiency of the Rankine cycle may increase or decrease somewhat as a result of reheating, depending on the average temperature at which heat is added during the reheat process.

- This temperature should be maintained as high as possible (without allowing excessive moisture) to prevent any decrease in the cycle efficiency.

- The average temperature during the reheat process can be increased by increasing the number of expansion and reheat stages.

- As the number of stages is increased, the expansion and reheat processes approach an isothermal process at the maximum temperature, as shown in Fig. 2.38.

- The optimum number is determined by economical considerations. The use of more than one or two reheat stages, in general, cannot be justified economically even in large power plants because the savings resulting from increased efficiency are more than offset by the increased cost.

- Remember that the sole purpose of the reheat cycle is to reduce the moisture content of the steam at the final stages of the expansion process. If we had materials that could withstand sufficiently high temperatures, there would be no need for the reheat cycle.

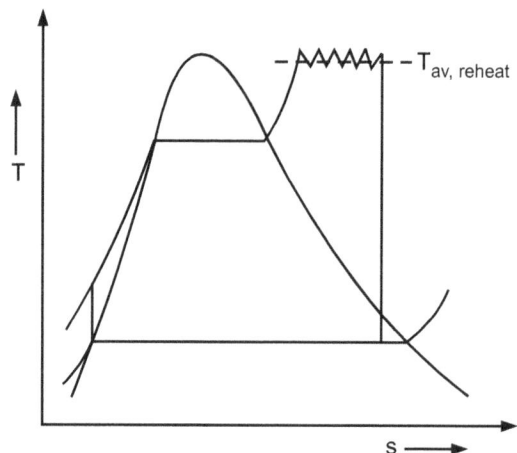

Fig. 2.38: The average temperature at which heat is added during reheating increases, as the number of reheat stages is increased

2.11 THE IDEAL REGENERATIVE RANKINE CYCLE

The Rankine cycle shown on T-s diagram in Fig. 2.39 shows that heat is added to the working fluid during process 2-2' at a relatively low temperature. This lowers the cycle efficiency.

To overcome this shortcoming, there are two ways:

1. To raise the temperature of the liquid (called the feedwater) leaving the pump before it enters the boiler. One such possibility is to raise the pressure of feed-water isentropically to a high temperature, as the Carnot cycle. This, however, would involve extremely high pressures and is therefore impractical.

2.   Another possibility is to transfer heat to the feedwater from the expanding steam in a counterflow heat exchanger built into the turbine, that is, to use regeneration. This solution is also impractical.

A practical regeneration process in steam power plants is accomplished by extracting, or "bleeding", steam from the turbine at various points. This steam bled from turbine is used to heat the feedwater. The device where the feedwater is heated by regeneration is called a regenerator, or a feedwater heater.

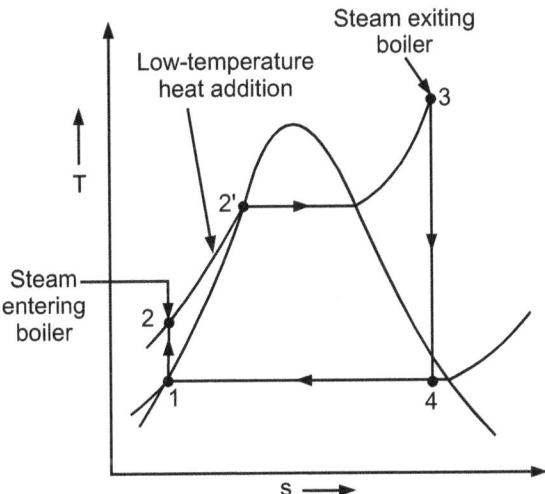

Fig. 2.39: Part of heat addition in the boiler takes place at relatively low temperature

Regeneration is beneficial in three ways:

1.   It improves cycle efficiency.

2.   It also provides a convenient means of deaerating the feedwater (removing the air that leaks in at the condenser) to prevent corrosion in the boiler.

3.   It also helps control the large volume flow rate of the steam at the final stages of the turbine (due to the large specific volumes at low pressures). Therefore, regeneration is used in all modern steam power plants.

A feedwater heater is basically a heat exchanger where heat is transferred from the steam to the feedwater either by mixing the two fluid streams (open feedwater heaters) or without mixing them (closed feedwater heaters). Regeneration with both types of feedwater heaters is discussed below.

Open Feedwater Heaters:

The steam power plant with one open feedwater heater (also called single-stage regenerative cycle) and the T-s diagram of the cycle are shown in Fig. 2.40.

An open (or direct-contact) feedwater heater is basically a mixing chamber, where the steam extracted from the turbine mixes with the feedwater exiting the pump. Ideally, the mixture leaves the heater as a saturated liquid at the heater pressure.

Refer an ideal regenerative Rankine cycle as shown in Fig. 2.39.

- Steam enters the turbine at the boiler pressure (state 5) and expands isentropically to an intermediate pressure (state 6).
- Some steam is extracted at this state and routed to the feedwater heater, while the remaining steam continues to expand isentropically to the condenser pressure (state 7).
- This steam leaves the condenser as a saturated liquid at the condenser pressure (state 1). The condensed water, which is also called the feedwater, then enters an isentropic pump, where it is compressed to the feedwater heater pressure (state 2) and is routed to the feedwater heater where it mixes with the steam extracted from the turbine.
- The fraction of the steam extracted is such that the mixture leaves the heater as a saturated liquid at the heater pressure (state 3).
- A second pump raises the pressure of the water to the boiler pressure (state 4). The cycle is completed by heating the water in the boiler to the turbine inlet state (state 5).

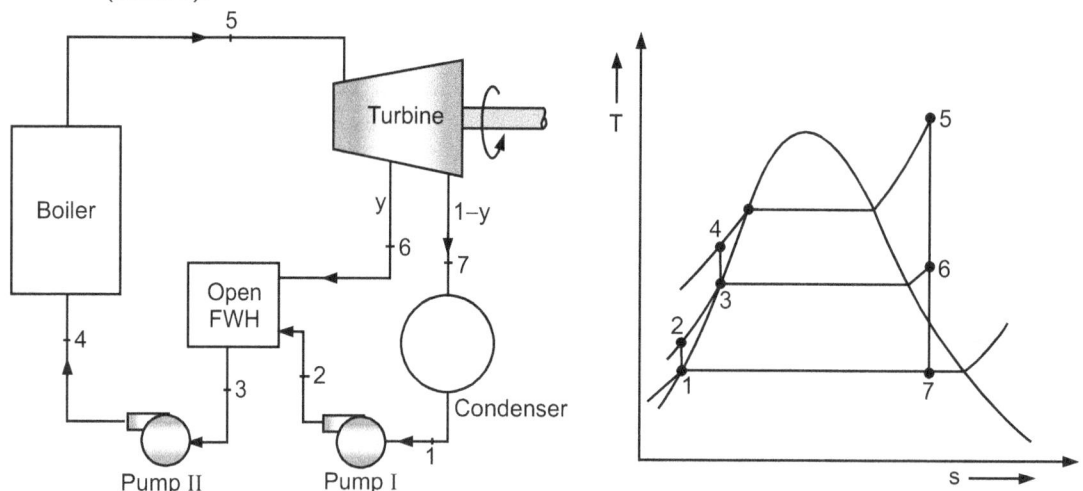

Fig. 2.40: An ideal regenerative Rankine cycle with an open feedwater heater

In the analysis of steam power plants, it is more convenient to work with quantities expressed per unit mass of the steam flowing through the boiler. For each 1 kg of steam leaving the boiler, y kg expands partially in the turbine and is extracted at state 6. The remaining (1 – y) kg expands completely to the condenser pressure. Therefore, the mass flow rates are different in different components. If the mass flow rate through the boiler is

m, for example, it will be (1 – y) $\dot{m}$ through the condenser.

1.   The thermal efficiency of the Rankine cycle increases as a result of regeneration. This is because regeneration raises the average temperature at which heat is added to the steam in the boiler by raising the temperature of the water before it enters the boiler.

2.   The cycle efficiency increases further as the number of feedwater heaters is increased.

Closed Feedwater Heaters :

The schematic of a steam power plant with one closed feedwater heater and the T-s diagram of the cycle are shown in Fig. 2.41.

- In the closed feedwater heater, heat is transferred from the extracted steam to the feedwater without any mixing taking place.

- The two streams now can be at different pressures, since they do not mix. In an ideal closed feedwater heater, the feedwater is heated to the exit temperature of the extracted steam, which ideally leaves the heater as a saturated liquid at the extraction pressure.

- In actual power plants, the feedwater leaves the heater below the exit temperature of the extracted steam because a temperature difference of at least a few degrees is required for any effective heat transfer to take place.

- The condensed steam is then either pumped to the feedwater line or routed to another heater or to the condenser through a device called a trap.

- A trap allows the liquid to be throttled to a lower pressure region but traps the vapour. The enthalpy of steam remains constant during this throttling process.

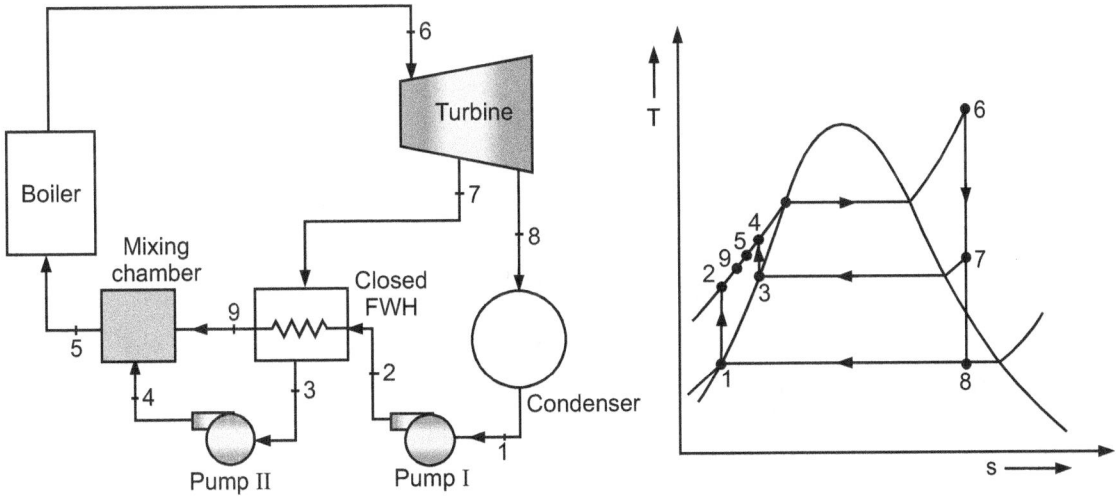

Fig. 2.41: The ideal regenerative Rankine cycle with a closed feedwater heater

Comparison of the Open and Closed Feedwater Heaters:

- Open feedwaters are simple and inexpensive and have good heat transfer characteristics. They also bring the feedwater to the saturation state. But for each heater, a pump is required to handle the feedwater.
- The closed feedwater heaters are more complex because of the internal piping network, and thus they are more expensive. Heat transfer in closed feedwater heaters is also less effective since the two streams are not allowed to be separate pump for each heater since the two streams are not allowed to be in direct contact. However, closed feedwater heaters do not require a separate pump for each heater since the extracted steam and the feedwater can be at different pressures.

SOLVED PROBLEMS

Problem 2.10: A simple Rankine cycle works between pressure of 25 bar and 0.05 bar. The initial condition of steam is dry saturated. Calculate the cycle efficiency, work ratio and specific steam consumption.

Sat. Temp. (°C)	Sat. Pr. (bar)	v_f (m³/kg)	v_g (m³/kg)	h_f (kJ/kg)	h_g (kJ/kg)	s_f (kJ/kg·K)	s_g (kJ/kg·K)
223.9	25	0.001197	0.0799	961.9	2800.9	2.554	6.254
32.9	0.05	0.001005	28.195	137.8	2561.6	0.476	8.396

Solution: The cycle is represented on T-s diagram as shown in Fig. 2.42.

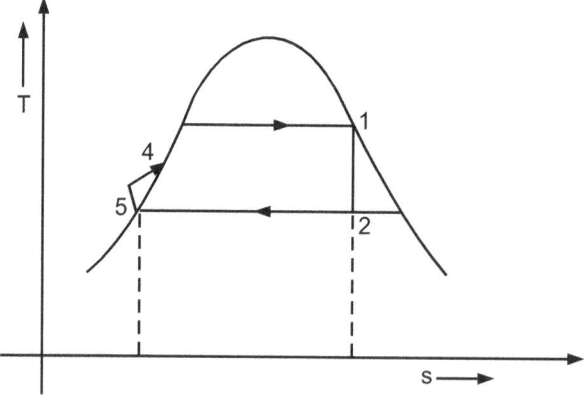

Fig. 2.42

The turbine process being 1-2

From tables,

$$h_1 = 2800.9 \text{ kJ/kg}$$

$$s_1 = 6.254 \text{ kJ/kg·K}$$

$$\text{The pump work} = v_f [P_4 - P_3]$$

$$= 0.001197 \, [25 + 0.05] \times 10^5 \, J = 5.9 \, kJ/kg$$

As $\qquad s_1 = s_2 = s_{f_2} + x_2 \, (s_{g_2} - s_{f_2})$

$\therefore \qquad\qquad x_2 = \dfrac{6.254 - 0.476}{8.396} = 0.6881$

$\therefore \qquad h_2 = h_{f_2} + x h_{fg_2} = 137.8 + 0.688 \times 2561.1 = 1812.15 \, kJ/kg$

$\therefore \qquad$ Turbine work $= 2800.9 - 1812.15 = 988.75 \, kJ/kg$

$\qquad$ Cycle efficiency $= \dfrac{(h_1 - h_2) + (h_4 - h_3)}{(h_1 - h_{f_4})} = \dfrac{988.75 - 5.9}{2800.9 - (137.8 + 5.9)}$

$$= \mathbf{0.3698 \ or \ 36.98\%}$$

$\qquad$ Work ratio $= \dfrac{\text{Net work}}{\text{Turbine work}} = \dfrac{982.85}{988.75} = \mathbf{0.994}$

$\qquad$ Specific steam consumption $= \dfrac{1}{W} \times 3600 = \dfrac{3600}{988.75} = \mathbf{3.64 \ kg/kWh}$

Problem 2.11: A steam power plant based on simple Rankine cycle works between 50 bar and 0.1 bar. If the steam supplied is dry saturated find (a) Cycle efficiency, and (b) Specific steam consumption.

Solution: The Rankine cycle is shown in Fig. 2.43. The following values are taken from steam tables.

P (sat) (bar)	T (°C)	v_f (m³/kg)	v_g (m³/kg)	h_f (kJ/kg)	h_g (kJ/kg)	s_f (kJ/kg·K)	s_g (kJ/kg·K)
50	263.9	0.001286	0.039	1154.4	2794.2	2.921	5.974
0.1	45.83	0.00101	14.67	191.8	2584.8	0.649	8.151

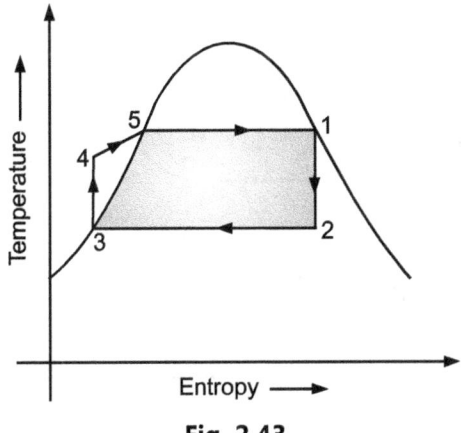

Fig. 2.43

As process 1-2 is isentropic expansion,

$$s_1 = s_2$$
$$\therefore \quad s_{f_1} + s_{fg_1} = s_{f_2} + x s_{fg_2}$$
$$2.921 + 3.053 = 0.649 + x_2 \times 7.502$$
$$\therefore \quad x_2 = 0.706$$
$$h_{g_1} = h_{f_1} + h_{fg_1}$$
$$= 1087 + 1713 = 2794.2 \text{ kJ/kg}$$
$$\therefore \quad h_{g_2} = h_{f_2} + x_2 h_{fg_2}$$
$$= 191.8 + 0.906 \times 2392.9 = 1881.19 \text{ kJ/kg}$$

Work done by the pump, $w_p = v_{sw_1}(p_4 - p_3)$

$$= \frac{0.00101\,(50 - 0.1) \times 10^5}{1000} = \textbf{5.014 kJ/kg}$$

Net work done per kg of steam

$$w_n = h_{g_1} - h_{g_2} - w_p = 2794.2 - 1881.19 - 5.014 = 907.996 \text{ kJ/kg}$$
$$\eta_{rankine} = w_n/(h_{g_1} - h_{f_4}) = 907.9/[2794.2 - (191.8 + 5.014)]$$
$$= \textbf{34.8\%}$$

Specific steam consumption = 1 kW – hr/[w_{net}] kJ/kg = 3600/907.9

$$= \textbf{3.965 kg/kW-hr.}$$

Problem 2.11: In a Rankine cycle, the steam at inlet to turbine is saturated at a pressure of 25 bar and the exhaust pressure is 0.1 bar. Determine: (i) The pump work, (ii) Turbine power, (iii) The Rankine efficiency, (iv) The condenser heat flow and (v) The dryness at the end of expansion. Assume flow rate of 10 kg/s.

Solution: From the steam tables:

P (sat) (bar)	T (sat) (°C)	v_f (m³/kg)	v_g (m³/kg)	h_f (kJ/kg	h_g (kJ/kg)	s_f (kJ/kg·K)	s_g (kJ/kg·K)	v_f (m³/kg)	v_g (m³/kg)
25	223.9	0.001197	0.0799	961.9	1839	2800.9	2.554	3.699	6.254
0.1	45.83	0.00101	14.67	191.8	2392.9	2584.8	0.649	7.502	8.151

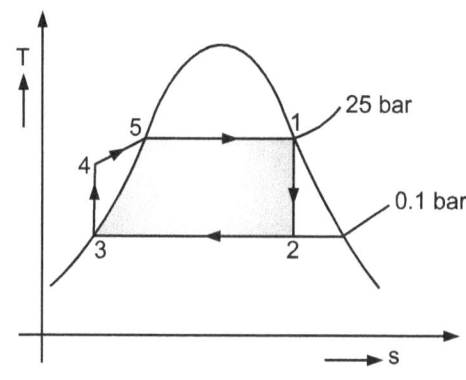

Fig. 2.44

$$h_1 = h_{g_1} = 2800.9 \text{ kJ/kg}$$

$$h_3 = h_{f_3} \text{ at 0.1 bar} = \textbf{191.8 kJ/kg}$$

(i)   The pump work $= m(p_4 - p_3)v_f$

$$= 1 \times 10^5 (25 - 0.1) \times 0.00101$$

$$= 2.514 \text{ kJ}$$

As v_f at 0.1 bar $= 0.00101 \text{ m}^3/\text{kg}$

$$h_4 = h_3 + 3 \text{ kJ/kg}$$

$$= 191.8 + 2.514 \text{ kJ/kg}$$

The power required for the pump $= \dfrac{10 \times 2.514 \text{ kJ}}{\text{sec}} = \dfrac{25.14 \text{ kJ}}{\text{sec}} = \textbf{25.14 kW}$

(ii)   The isentropic enthalpy drop is found using

$\therefore$ $s_1 = s_2 = s_{f_2} + x_2(s_{g_2} + s_{f_2})$

From steam tables,

$$s_1 = 6.254 \text{ kJ/kg·K}$$

$$s_{f_2} = 0.649 \text{ kJ/kg·K}$$

$$s_{g_2} = 8.151 \text{ kJ/kg·K}$$

$\therefore$ Dryness at the outlet of expansion process

$$x_2 = \frac{s_1 - s_{f_2}}{s_{g_2} - s_{f_2}} = \frac{6.254 - 0.649}{8.151 - 0.649} = 0.747$$

$\therefore$ $h_2 = h_{f_2} + x_2 h_{fg_2} = 1979.2 \text{ kJ/kg}$

$\therefore$ Turbine power $= m(h_1 - h_2)$

$$= 10(2800.9 - 1979.2) \text{ kJ/s}$$

$$= \textbf{8127 kW}$$

Compared to this, the pumping power of 30 kW is very small.

(iii)   Rankine efficiency: $= \dfrac{(h_1 - h_2) - (h_4 - h_3)}{(h_1 - h_4)}$

$$= \frac{(2800.9 - 1979.2) - (191.8 - 189.3)}{(2800.9 - 191.8)}$$

$$= 0.3139 \text{ or } \textbf{31.39\%}$$

(iv)   The heat flow in the condenser $= m(h_2 - h_3) = 10(1979.2 - 189.3)$

$$= \textbf{17899 kW}$$

(v)   Dryness at the end of expansion $= \textbf{0.747 or 74.7\%}$

Problem 2.13: A steam power plant operating on ideal Carnot cycle uses steam at 5 bar and 90% dryness at the end of the isothermal expansion process. The pressure during isothermal compression is 3 bar. Find the thermal efficiency of the cycle.

Also find the power developed by the engine if the engine uses 1 kg of steam per cycle and makes 200 cycles/min. Assume that the liquid is saturated at the beginning of isothermal expansion (evaporation).

Solution: The cycle is shown on T-s diagram as shown in Fig. 2.45. From steam table, T_1 and T_2 are obtained.

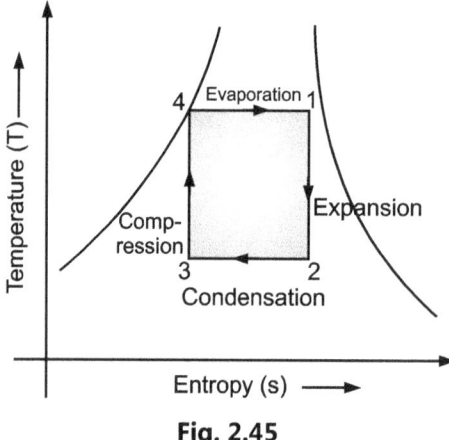

Fig. 2.45

Saturated temperature, T_1 at 5 bar = 151.9°C = 424.9 K

Saturated temperature, T_2 at 3 bar = 133.5°C = 406.5 K

$$\eta_{th} = \frac{T_1 - T_2}{T_1} = \frac{424.9 - 406.5}{424.9} \times 100 = 4.3\%$$

Input during the isothermal expansion per cycle = $m_s \cdot x h_{fg}$

where, m_s = Mass of steam per cycle

                          x = Dryness fraction of steam at 10 bar

                          h_{fg} = Latent heat of steam at 10 bar

∴   Input = $1 \times 0.9 \times 2163.2$ = 1446.8 kJ/cycle

where, h_{fg} = 2163.2 kJ

∴   Output/cycle = 906×0.043 = 83.715

∴   Output per minute = 83.715×200 = **16743.168 kJ/m**

∴   Power = $\dfrac{16743.168}{60}$ = **279.05 kW**

Problem 2.14: A steam turbine operates on ideal Carnot cycles using dry saturated steam at 15 bar. The exhaust takes place at 0.05 bar into a condenser. Assume that the expansion and compression are isentropic and liquid enters the boiler as saturated liquid. Find the (a) Power developed by the turbine if the steam consumption is 20 kg/min. and (b) The efficiency of the operating cycle.

Solution: h_1 = Enthalpy of dry saturated steam at 15 bar (from steam tables).

Sat. temp (°C)	v_f (m³/kg)	v_g (m³/kg)	h_f (kJ/kg)	h_g (kJ/kg)	s_f (kJ/kg·K)	s_g (kJ/kg·K)	v_f (m³/kg)
198.3	15 bar	0.001154	0.13167	144.6	2789.9	2.314	6.441
32.90	0.05 bar	0.001005	28.194	137.8	2561.6	0.476	8.396

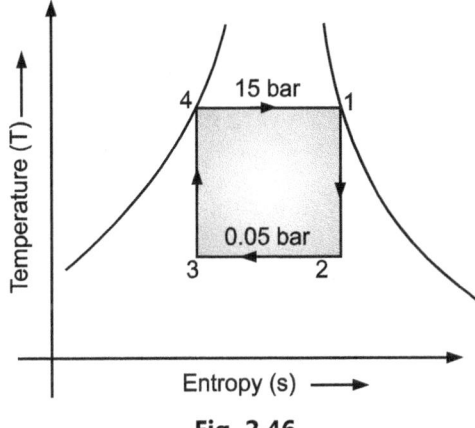

Fig. 2.46

$$h_1 = h_g = 2789.9 \text{ kJ/kg}$$

The expansion 1-2 is isentropic.

$$s_1 = s_2$$
$$s_1 = s_{g_1} = s_{f_2} + x_2\, s_{fg}$$

Substituting the values from steam tables,

$$6.441 = 0.476 + x_2\,(7.92)$$

∴
$$x_2 = 0.753$$
$$h_2 = h_{f_2} + x_2\, h_{fg_2}$$

∴   (at 0.05 bar) $= 137.8 + 0.753 \times 2561.6 = $ **2066.68 kJ/kg**

For isentropic compression process 3-4,

∴
$$s_3 = s_4 = s_{f_4} \text{ as point 4 is on saturated liquid line}$$

$$s_3 = s_{f_3} + x_3\, s_{fg_3}$$

Substituting the values from steam tables,

$$0.476 + x_3 (7.920) = 2.314$$

$\therefore$ $\qquad\qquad\qquad\qquad x_3 = 0.232$

$$h_3 = h_{f_3} + x_3\, h_{fg_3} = 137.8 + 0.232 \times 2423.8 = \mathbf{700.12\ kJ/kg}$$

Work of expansion is given by,

$$w_e = h_1 - h_2 = 2789.9 - 2066.68 = \mathbf{723.22\ kJ}$$

Work of compression is given by,

$$w_c = h_4 - h_3 = h_{f_4} - h_3$$

$$= 844.6 - 700.12 = \mathbf{144.48\ kJ/kg}$$

$$w_n \text{ (Net work done)} = w_e - w_c$$

$$= 723.22 - 144.48 = \mathbf{578.74\ kJ/kg}$$

$\therefore$ Work done per minute $= 578.74 \times 20 = \mathbf{11574.8\ kJ/min}$

$\therefore$ Power developed by the engine $= \dfrac{11574.8}{60} = \mathbf{192.91\ kW}$

$$\text{Heat supplied} = h_1 - h_4 = h_1 - h_{f_4}$$

$$= 2789.9 - 844.6 = \mathbf{1945.3\ kJ/kg}$$

$\therefore$ $\qquad$ Cycle efficiency $= \dfrac{578.74}{1945.3} = 0.2975 = \mathbf{29.75\%}$

The Carnot efficiency is also given by

$$= \frac{T_1 - T_2}{T_1}$$

where, T_1 saturation temperature of steam at 15 bar = (273 + 198.3) K and T_2 (saturation temperature of steam at 0.05 bar = 273 + 33) K.

$\therefore$ $\qquad$ Carnot efficiency $= \dfrac{(198.3 + 273) - (33 + 273)}{(198.3)} = \dfrac{165.3}{471.3}$

$$= 0.3507 \text{ or } \mathbf{35.07\%}$$

Problem 2.15: A boiler feed pump works on the (full admission) non-expansive cycle. Steam is supplied at 12 bar and dry saturated condition. The exhaust takes place at 1 bar. Draw the cycle of operation on p-v and T-s diagrams and find:

(a) The steam consumption per kW-hour

(b) Theoretical efficiency of the cycle.

(c) Heat removed in the condenser per kg of steam.

(d) If the feed pump supplies 50 kg of water per minute to the boiler, find the power required to run the pump.

Solution: Non-expansive cycle means that there is no expansion of the steam in the cylinder, and high pressure steam is admitted throughout the stroke.

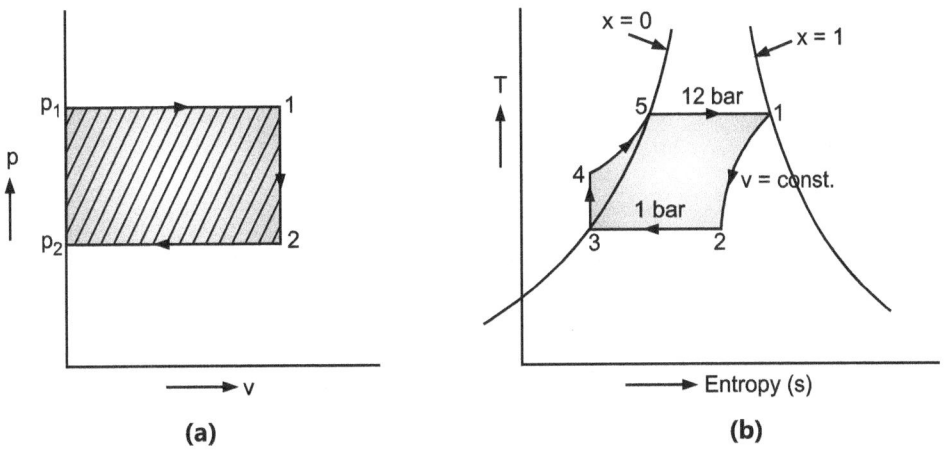

(a)　　　　　　　　　　　　　　　　(b)

Fig. 2.47

(a) Work done per kg of steam:

$$w = \frac{(P_1 - P_2)\, v_1}{J}$$

where,　　　　　　　$v_1 = v_{s_1}$ (as dry steam is supplied)

$$= \frac{[(12 - 1) \times 10^5] \times 0.16321}{1000} = \textbf{179.53 kJ/kg}$$

Pump work per kg of steam:

$$w_p = \frac{v_s\, (P_1 - P_2)}{J}$$

where, v_s is the specific volume of saturated water at 1 bar.

$$\therefore \qquad\qquad w_p = \frac{0.001043\, (12 - 1) \times 10^5}{1000} = \textbf{1.1473 kJ/kg}$$

Net work available is,

$$w_n = 179.53 - 1.1473 \ = \ 178.38 \text{ kJ/kg}$$

$$\text{Steam consumption per kWh} = \frac{3600}{178.38} = \textbf{20.18 kg/kWh}$$

(b) Heat supplied per kg of steam is

$$h_s = h_1 - h_{f4}$$

$$= h_1 - (h_{f_3} + w_p)$$

$$h_1 = 2782.7$$

$\therefore$ $\qquad$ $h_2 = 2782.7 - (417.5 + 1.1473) = 2364.05$ kJ/kg

The cycle efficiency $= \dfrac{178.38}{2364.05} \times 100 = \textbf{7.54\%}$

(c) Heat removed in the condenser per kg of steam

$$= h_2 - h_{f_3} = (h_1 - w_n) - h_{f_3}$$

$$= 2782.7 - 178.38 - 417.5 = \textbf{2186.82 kJ/kg}$$

(d) Power required to run the feed pump $= \left(\dfrac{100}{60}\right) \times w_p = \left(\dfrac{100}{60}\right) \times 1.1473 = \textbf{1.912 kW}$

Problem 2.16: Dry saturated steam at 12 bar is supplied to a steam turbine. The exhaust takes at 1 bar. Determine the following: (a) Rankine efficiency, (b) Steam consumption per kWh if the efficiency ratio is 0.65, (c) Carnot efficiency for the given pressure limit using steam as a working fluid. (d) If the exhaust pressure is reduced to 0.1 bar by introducing a jet condenser, find the percentage increase in Rankine efficiency and percentage decrease in specific steam consumption. Neglect the pump work.

Solution: Enthalpy of dry saturated steam at 12 bar.

From steam table, $h_g = 2782.7$ kJ/kg.

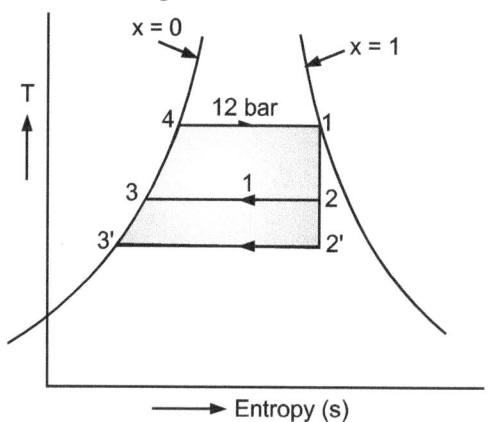

Fig. 2.48

The isentropic expansion from 12 bar to 1 bar is represented by 1-2.

$\therefore$ $\qquad$ $s_{g_1} = s_{f_2} + x_2 \, s_{fg_2}$

$\therefore$ $\qquad$ $6.519 = 1.303 + x_2 \times 6.057$

$\therefore$ $\qquad$ $x_2 = 0.8611$

Similarly, for exhaust pressure 0.1 bar, the process is 1-2.

$$\therefore \qquad\qquad s_{g1} = s'_{f_2} + x'_2 \times s'_{fg_2}$$

$$\therefore \qquad\qquad 6.519 = 0.649 + x'_2 \times 7.502$$

$$\therefore \qquad\qquad x'_2 = 0.7824$$

The enthalpies at 2 and 2' are calculated as,

$$h_2 = h_{f_2} + x_2 h_{fg_2} = 417.5 + 0.8611 \times 2257.9 = 2361.77 \text{ kJ/kg}$$

$$h'_2 = h'_{f_2} + x'_2 h'_{fg_2} = 191.8 + 0.7824 \times 2392.9 = 2064.0 \text{ kJ/kg}$$

(a) Rankine efficiency when exhaust pressure is 1 bar is,

$$\eta_r = \frac{h_1 - h_2}{h_1 - h_{f_2}} = \frac{2782.7 - 2361.77}{2782.7 - 417.5} = \frac{420.93}{2365.2} = 0.1779 = 17.79\%$$

Rankine efficiency when exhaust pressure is 0.1 bar is,

$$\frac{h_1 - h'_2}{h_1 - h'_{f_2}} = \frac{2782.7 - 2064}{2782.7 - 191.8} = \frac{718.7}{2590.9} = 0.2773 = 27.73\%$$

(b) Efficiency ratio $= \dfrac{\text{Indicated thermal efficiency}}{\text{Rankine efficiency}}$

(i) When exhaust pressure is 1 bar

Indicated thermal efficiency, $\eta_i = 0.1779 \times 0.65 = 0.115635$

Indicated thermal efficiency, $\eta_i = \dfrac{3600}{m_s (h_1 - h_{f_2})}$

where, m_s is specific steam consumption in kg/kWh.

$$0.115635 = \frac{3600}{m_s (2782.7 - 417.5)}$$

$$\therefore \qquad\qquad m_s = \frac{3600}{0.115635 \times 2365.2} = 13.08 \text{ kg/kWh}$$

(ii) When the exhaust pressure is 0.1 bar, then η_i (indicated thermal efficiency)

$$= 0.2773 \times 0.65 = 0.18024$$

$$\therefore \qquad\qquad m_s = \frac{3600}{\eta'_i (h_1 - h'_{f_2})} = \frac{3600}{0.18024 (2782.7 - 191.8)}$$

$$= 7.709 \text{ kg/kWh}$$

$\therefore$ Percentage decrease in specific steam consumption

$$= \frac{13.08 - 7.709}{13.08} \times 100 = 41.06\%$$

(c) Carnot efficiency when exhaust pressure is 1 bar

$$= \frac{T_1 - T_2}{T_1} = \frac{188 - 100}{188 + 273} = \frac{88}{461.0}$$

$$= 0.190 = 19.08\%$$

Carnot efficiency when exhaust pressure is 0.1 bar

$$= \frac{T_1 - T_2}{T_1} = \frac{188 - 46}{188 + 273}$$

$$= \frac{142}{461} = 0.3080 = 30.80\%$$

Percentage increase in Carnot efficiency

$$= \frac{30.80 - 19.8}{19.8} = 0.3571 = 35.71\%$$

Exhaust pressure	Carnot efficiency	Rankine efficiency
1 bar	19.08	17.79
0.1 bar	30.80	27.73

Problem 2.17: In a Rankine engine, the specific steam consumption is 6 kg/kWh. The enthalpy of steam supplied is 2000 kJ/kg and condensate is at a temperature of 60°C. Find thermal efficiency of the engine.

Solution: The Rankine engine working on Rankine cycle is shown in Fig. 2.49.

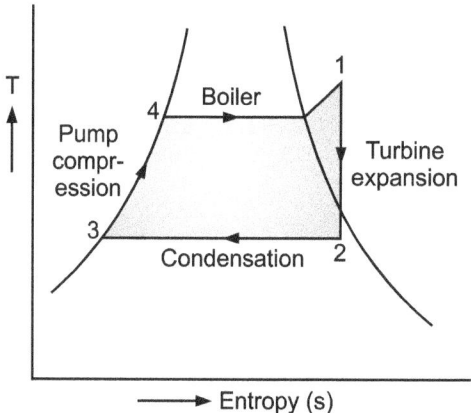

Fig. 2.49

$$h_1 = 2500 \text{ kJ/kg}$$

$$h_{f_3} = 4.2 \times (60 - 0) = 252 \text{ kJ/kg}$$

The thermal efficiency is given by,

$$\eta = \frac{kW}{m'_s (h_1 - h_{f_3})}$$

where, h_1 and h_{f_3} are in kJ and m'_s is steam consumption per second.

$$\therefore \quad \eta \ = \ \frac{kW \times 3600}{3600 \ m'_s \ (h_1 - h_{f_3})} = \frac{kW \times 3600}{m_s \ (h_1 - h_{f_3})}$$

where, m_s is steam consumption per hour.

$$\eta \ = \ \frac{3600}{\dfrac{m_s}{kW} \ (h_1 - h_{f_3})} = \frac{3600}{\dot{m} \ (h_1 - h_{f_3})}$$

where, $\dot{m}_s$ is the steam consumption per kW per hour which is known as specific steam consumption.

$$\therefore \quad \eta \ = \ \frac{3600}{6 \ (2000 - 252)} = 0.34 = \textbf{34\%}$$

Problem 2.18: Dry saturated steam is supplied to a turbine at 16 bar. The isentropic expansion continues to 1.1 bar. Determine (i) The Rankine efficiency, (ii) How is the Rankine efficiency affected if the exhaust is sent to condenser where pressure is maintained at 0.3 bar?

Solution: Refer to Fig. 2.50.

(i) The Rankine efficiency is,

$$\eta_r \ = \ \frac{h_1 - h_2}{h_1 - h_{f_2}}, h_1 = h_g = 2791$$

$$h_1 \ = \ 2791.7 \ kJ/kg$$

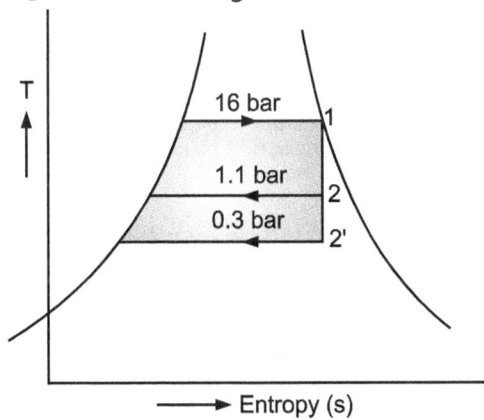

Fig. 2.50

As expansion 1-2 is isentropic,

$$\therefore \qquad\qquad s_1 \ = \ s_2$$

$$s_{g_1} \ = \ s_{f_2} + x_2 \ s_{fg_2} \qquad\qquad \text{(values are taken from steam table)}$$

$$\therefore \qquad 6.418 \ = \ 1.33 + x_2 \times 5.9947$$

$$\therefore \qquad\qquad x_2 \ = \ 0.8482$$

∴ $\qquad\qquad h_2 = h_{f_2} + x_2\, h_{fg_2} = 428.84 + 1 + 2250.8 = 2680.64$ kJ/kg

$$\eta_r = \frac{2791.7 - 2346.5}{2791.7 - 428.84} = 0.1884 = \textbf{18.8\%}$$

(ii) When the expansion is continued to 0.3 bar, then,

$$s_1 = s_2' = s_{f_2}' + x_2' \, h_{fg_2}'$$

∴ $\qquad\qquad 6.44 = 0.944 + x_2' \times 6.825$

∴ $\qquad\qquad x_2' = 0.805$

∴ $\qquad\qquad h_2' = h_{f_2}' + x_2' \cdot h_{fg_2}' = 289.3 + 0.805 \times 2336.1 = 2169.86$ kJ/kg

∴ $\qquad\qquad \eta_r' = \dfrac{h_1 - h_2'}{h_1 - h_{f_2}'} = \dfrac{2791.7 - 2169.86}{2791.7 - 289.3} = \dfrac{621.84}{2502.4} = 0.248 = \textbf{24.84\%}$

Alternately, h_2 and h_2' can also be directly obtained from h-s chart after drawing vertical line from point '1' and making the points 2 and 2' which is more easy than this method.

Problem 2.19: The enthalpy of steam at inlet to a turbine of a power plant is 3000 kJ/kg and enthalpy of steam leaving the turbine is 2600 kJ/kg.

    (a)   If the temperature of saturated condensate is 50°C, find (i) Rankine efficiency and (ii) Specific steam consumption.

    (b)   If the highest temperature of steam supplied in the above power plant is 400°C, what would be the maximum possible efficiency of the plant?

    (c)   If the mass flow rate of steam in the above power plant is 1 kg/sec. find

(i) Power developed by the turbine, (ii) Heat transfer in the condenser, (iii) Work required for the feed pump if the boiler pressure is 10 bar, (iv) Heat supplied in the boiler.

Solution: Refer to Fig. 2.51.

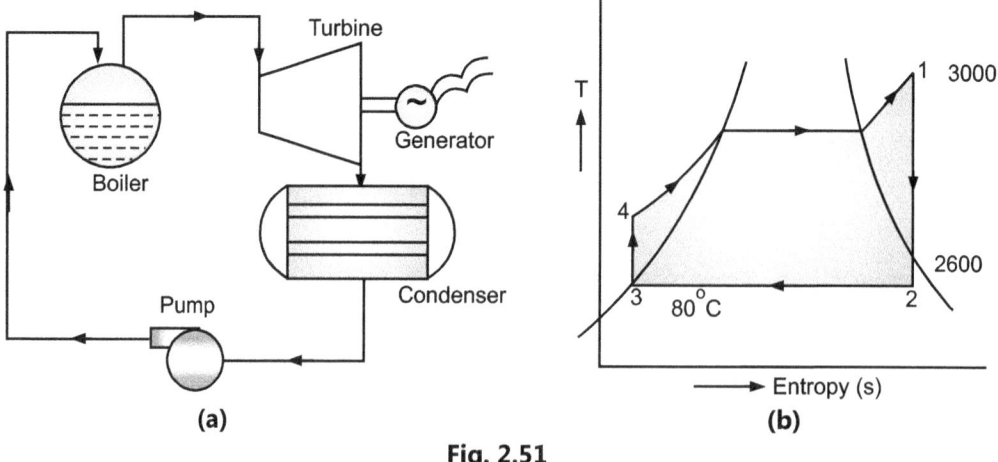

Fig. 2.51

Rankine efficiency is given by,

$$\eta_r = \frac{h_1 - h_2}{h_1 - h_{f_2}} = \frac{3000 - 2600}{3000 - 50} = \frac{400}{2950} = 0.1355 = 13.55\%$$

$$\eta_r = \frac{3000}{\dot{m}_s (h_1 - h_{f_3})} = \frac{3000}{\dot{m}_s (3000 - 50)} \quad \text{where, } \dot{m}_s \text{ is in kg/kW-hr.}$$

$$\dot{m}_s = \frac{3000}{0.1355 \times 2950} = 7.505 \text{ kg/kW-hr}$$

(b) The highest possible efficiency is as per Carnot efficiency

$$\therefore \qquad \eta_c = \frac{T_1 - T_2}{T_1} = \frac{400 - 50}{400 + 273} = \frac{350}{673} = 0.52 = \textbf{52\%}$$

(c) (i) Power developed by the turbine $= 1 \times (3000 - 2600) = 400$ kW

(ii) Heat transfer in the condenser per kg of steam

$$= h_2 - h_{f_2} = 2600 - 50 = \textbf{2550 kJ/kg}$$

(iii) Work required to run pump $= (v_w \cdot dP) m_w$

where, v_w is specific volume of saturated water at 50°C

$$= \frac{0.001012 \times (10 - 0.12335) \times 10^5 \times (1)}{10^3} \text{ kW} = \textbf{1 kW}$$

(iv) Heat supplied in the boiler per kg of steam

$$= h_2 - h_{f_3} = 3000 - 50 = \textbf{2950 kJ/kg}$$

Problem 2.20: A steam turbine plant operates on the Rankine cycle. Steam is delivered from the boiler to the turbine at a pressure of 3.5 MN/m^2 and with a temperature of 350°C. Steam from the turbine exhausts into a condenser at a pressure of 10 kN/m^2 condensate from the condenser is returned to the boiler by means of a feed pump.
Determine:

(i) The dryness fraction of the steam entering the condenser.

(ii) Rankine efficiency.   **(Dec. 2004)**

Draw T-s diagram.

Solution: Given Data: Rankine cycle

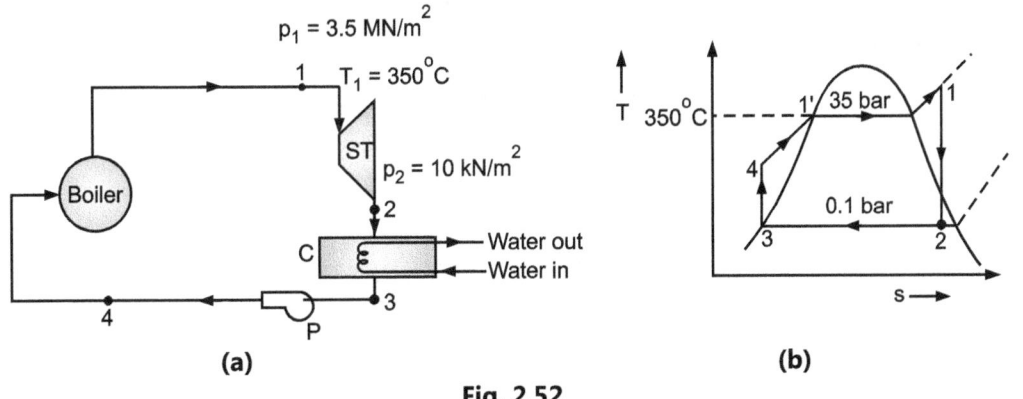

Fig. 2.52

Determine:

    (i) Dryness fraction of steam at point 2.

    (ii) Rankine efficiency.

At 35 bar and 350°C from steam table (superheated),

$$h_1 = 3106.45 \text{ kJ/kg}$$

$$s_1 = 6.663 \text{ kJ/kg·K}$$

To find h_2, from isentropic expansion process 1-2,

$$s_1 = s_2$$

$$= s_{f_2} + x_2 \cdot s_{fg_2}$$

∴ $6.663 = 0.649 + x_2 \times 7.502$ … (at 0.1 bar)

∴ $x_2 = \dfrac{6.663 - 0.649}{7.502} = 0.8016$

Now, $h_2 = h_{f_2} + x_2 \cdot h_{fg_2}$

                $= 191.8 + 0.8016 \times 2392.9$ … (at 0.1 bar)

             $h_2 = 2110.075 \text{ kJ/kg}$

From steam table, at 0.1 bar,

$$h_3 = h_{f_2} = 191.8 \text{ kJ/kg}$$

Also,   Pump (w_p) work $= v_4 (p_4 - p_3)$

                $= 0.001010 \times (35 - 0.1) \times 10^2 \text{ kJ/kg}$

                $= 3.5249 \text{ kJ/kg}$

∴ $h_4 - h_3 = 3.5249$

∴ $h_4 = h_3 + 3.5249$

               $= 191.8 + 3.5249$

             $h_4 = 195.3249 \text{ kJ/kg}$

Now, Rankine cycle efficiency (η_R):

$$= \frac{\text{Turbine work} - \text{Pump work}}{\text{Heat supplied}}$$

$$= \frac{(h_1 - h_2) - w_p}{h_1 - h_4}$$

$$= \frac{(3106.45 - 2110.075) - 3.5249}{(3106.45 - 195.3249)}$$

$$= \frac{992.85}{2911.1251} = 0.341 \text{ or } \textbf{34.1\%}$$

Problem 2.21: The feed water to a boiler enters an economiser at 32°C and leaves at 120°C, being fed into the boiler at this temperature. The steam leaves the boiler 0.95 dry at 2 MPa and passes through a superheater where its temperature is raised to 250°C without change of pressure. The steam output is 8.2 kg/kg of coal burned and the calorific value of the coal is 28000 kJ/kg. Determine the energy received per kilogram of water and steam in: (i) The economiser, (ii) The boiler, (iii) The superheater expressing the answers as percentages of the energy supplied by the coal.   **(P.U. Dec. 2004)**

Solution:

Heat released per kg of coal = Q = 28000 kJ/kg

Energy received per kg of water in economiser = Q_1

$$= c_{pw} (T_{w_2} - T_{w_1}) = 4.18 \times (120 - 32) = 367.84 \text{ kJ/kg}$$

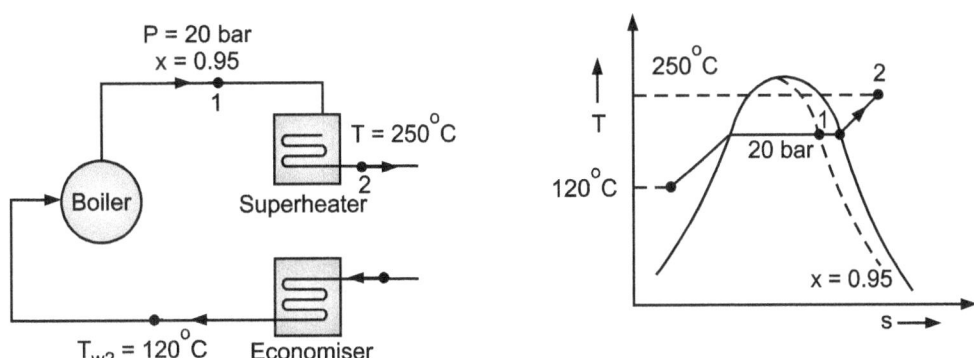

Fig. 2.53

Energy received per kg of water in boiler = Q_2

$$= h_1 - h_{f \text{ (at 120°C)}}$$
$$= (h_{f_1} + x h_{fg_1}) - h_{f \text{ (at 120°C)}}$$
$$= (908.6 + 0.95 \times 1888.6) - 504.1$$
$$= \textbf{2198.67 kJ/kg} \qquad\qquad ... (7.85\% \text{ of } Q)$$

Energy received per kg of steam in superheater = Q_3

$$= (h_2 - h_1) = (2902.4 - 2702.77)$$
$$= \textbf{199.63 kJ/kg} \qquad\qquad ... (0.713\% \text{ of } Q)$$

Problem 2.22: A steam power plant is operated at a boiler pressure of 7 MPa and the condenser pressure of 20 kPa. Calculate:

(i) Pump work

(ii) Turbine work

(iii) Heat added

(iv) Rankine cycle efficiency

(v) Net power produced in MW if the steam is produced at the rate of 37.8 kg/sec and at 550°C.   **(P.U. May 2005)**

Solution: Rankine cycle:

Steam pressure at inlet to turbine = P_1 = 7 MPa = 70 bar

Steam temperature at inlet to turbine = T_2 = 550°C

Steam pressure at exit of turbine = P_2 = 20 kPa = 0.2 bar

Mass flow rate of steam = m_s = 37.8 kg/sec

Calculate:

(i) Pump work = w_p, (ii) Turbine work = w_T, (iii) Heat added = Q_A, (iv) Rankine cycle efficiency = η_{cycle}, (v) Net power produced in MW.

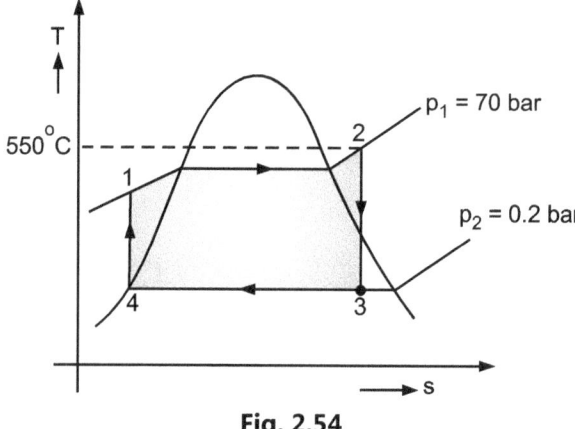

Fig. 2.54

The following properties are taken from superheat steam table.

At p_1 = 70 bar and T_1 = 550°C.

Enthalpy of steam at point 2 = h_2 = 3530.9 kJ/kg.

Entropy of steam at point 2 = s_2 = 6.9486 kJ/kg·K

From saturated steam table,

At p_3 = 0.2 bar,

Entropy of steam at point 3 = $s_3 = s_{f_3} + x_3 \cdot s_{fg_3}$

$$= 0.8320 + x_3 \cdot (7.0766)$$

For, isentropic expansion (2-3) process,

$$s_2 = s_3$$

∴ $$6.9486 = 0.8320 + x_3 \cdot (7.0766)$$

∴ $$x_3 = 0.864$$

Now, Enthalpy of steam at exit of turbine = $h_3 = h_{f_3} + x_3 \cdot h_{fg_3}$

$$= 251.4 + 0.864 \times 2358.3$$

$$= 2288.96 \text{ kJ/kg}$$

Enthalpy at point 4 = $h_4 = h_{f_3}$ = 251.4 kJ/kg

For finding 'h_1',

Pump work = $w_p = v_f \cdot (P_1 - P_2)$

∴ $h_1 - h_4 = v_f (P_1 - P_2)$

∴ $h_1 = v_f (P_1 - P_2) + h_4$

$= (0.001017) (70 - 0.2) \times 10^2 + 251.4$

h_1 = 258.881 kJ/kg

(i)   Pump work = $w_p = v_f (P_1 - P_2)$

$= 0.001017 \times (70 - 0.2) \times 10^2 =$ **7.48256 kJ/kg**

(ii)   Turbine work = $w_T = h_2 - h_3$

$= 3530.9 - 2288.97 =$ **1241.93 kJ/kg**

(iii)   Heat supplied = $Q_s = h_2 - h_1$

$= 3530.9 - 258.88 =$ **3272.02 kJ/kg**

(iv)   Rankine cycle efficiency = η_{cycle}

$= \dfrac{w_T - w_p}{Q_A}$

$= \dfrac{1241.93 - 7.48256}{3272.02} =$ **0.3773 or 37.73%**

(v) Net power developed:

Net work done = $w_T - w_p$

$= 1241.93 - 7.48256 =$ **1234.45 kJ/kg**

Given that,

Steam flow rate = m_s = 37.8 kg/sec

∴   Net power developed = Net work done $\times m_s$

$= 1234.45 \times 37.8$

$= 46662.113$ kJ/sec or kW = **46.66 kW**

Problem 2.23: A steam power plant operates between boiler pressure of 30 bar and condenser pressure of 0.04 bar with dry saturated steam supplied at inlet to the turbine. Calculate:

(i) The cycle efficiency

(ii) Specific steam consumption

(iii) Work ratio

(iv) Plot the cycle on T-s diagram.   **(P.U. May 2005)**

Solution: Given:

Boiler pressure, P_1 = 30 bar

Condenser pressure, P_2 = 0.04 bar

At inlet to turbine, dry saturated steam.

Calculate:

(i) The cycle efficiency = η_{cycle}

(ii) Specific steam consumption = S.S.C.

(iii) Work ratio

(iv) Plot the cycle on T-s diagram.

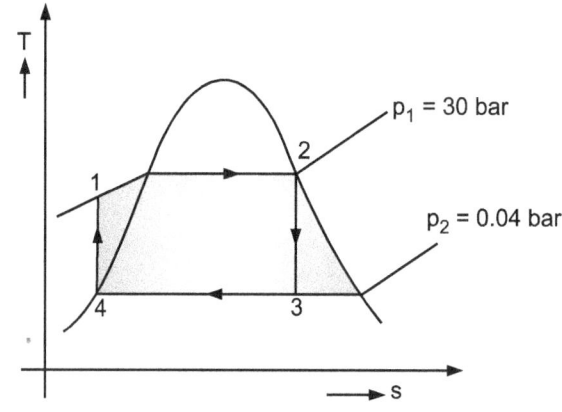

Fig. 2.55

At pressure, p_1 = 30 bar

Enthalpy at inlet of turbine = h_2 = h_g = 2804.2 kJ/kg

Entropy at inlet of turbine = s_2 = s_g = 6.1869 kJ/kg

For process 2-3:

$$s_2 = s_3$$

$$\text{at 30 bar} = \text{at 0.04 bar}$$

∴ $$s_2 = s_{f_3} + x_3 \cdot s_{fg_3}$$

∴ $$6.1869 = 0.4226 + x_3 \times 8.0520$$

$$x_3 = 0.7159$$

Now,

Enthalpy at point 3 = h_3 = $h_{f_3} + x_3 \cdot h_{fg_3}$

$$= 121.46 + 0.7159 \times 2432.9 = 1863.1 \text{ kJ/kg}$$

Enthalpy at point 4 = h_4 = h_{f_3} = 121.46 kJ/kg

For finding h_1:

$$\text{Pump work} = w_p = h_1 - h_4$$

$\therefore$ $\qquad\qquad v_f (P_1 - P_4) = h_1 - h_4$ $\qquad\qquad\qquad\qquad\qquad$ ... (1)

At 0.04 bar, $\qquad\qquad\qquad v_f = 0.001004 \text{ m}^3/\text{kg}$

Then equation (1) becomes,

$$(0.001004) \times (30 - 0.04) \times 10^2 = h_1 - 121.46$$

$\therefore$ $\qquad\qquad\qquad\qquad h_1 = 124.47 \text{ kJ/kg}$

(i) $\qquad$ Rankine cycle efficiency $= \eta_{cycle} = \dfrac{(h_2 - h_3) - (h_1 - h_4)}{(h_2 - h_1)}$

$$= (2804.2 - 1863.135) - \dfrac{(124.47 - 121.46)}{(2804.2 - 124.47)}$$

$$= \dfrac{(941.065 - 3.01)}{2679.73} = \mathbf{0.35 \text{ or } 35\%}$$

(ii) Specific steam consumption (SSC):

$$\text{SSC} = \dfrac{3600}{w_{net}} \text{ kg/kW-hr.}$$

$$= \dfrac{3600}{(w_T - w_p)}$$

$$= \dfrac{3600}{(h_2 - h_3) - (h_1 - h_4)}$$

$$= \dfrac{3600}{(941.065 - 3.01)} = \mathbf{3.84}$$

(iii) Work Ratio (WR):

$$\text{WR} = \dfrac{w_{net}}{w_T}$$

$$= \dfrac{(h_2 - h_3) - (h_1 - h_4)}{(h_2 - h_3)}$$

$$= \dfrac{941.065 - 3.01}{941.065} = \mathbf{0.997}$$

(iv) Cycle on T-s diagram is shown in Fig. 2.55.

Problem 2.24: A steam turbine receives superheated steam at 100 bar and 600°C. It is exhausted at 2 bar and then used for process of humidity control. If the steam flow rate is 7200 kg/hr, find the ideal cycle efficiency of the plant. Also find the input in kW and specific steam consumption. $\qquad\qquad$ **(P.U. Dec. 2005)**

Solution: Given Data: P_2 = 100 bar, T_2 = 600°C, P_3 = 2 bar, m_s = 7200 kg/hr

From steam table,
    At 100 bar, T_2 = 600°C

$$h_2 = 3622.7 \text{ kJ/kg}$$
$$s_2 = 6.9013 \text{ kJ/kg·K}$$

At 2 bar,

$$s_f = 1.5301$$
$$s_{fg} = 5.5967 \text{ kJ/kg·K}$$

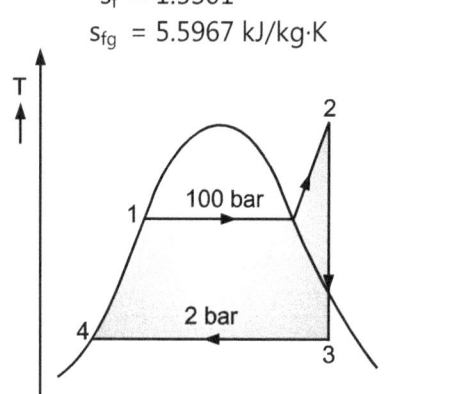

Fig. 2.56

Adiabatic expansion 2-3,

$$s_2 = s_3$$
$$6.9013 = s_f + x_3\, s_{fg}$$
$$6.9013 = 1.5301 + x_3 \times 5.5967$$
$$x_3 = 0.9591$$

The enthalpy of steam at point '3'

$$h_3 = h_f + x_3\, h_{fg} \text{ at 2 bar}$$
$$= 504.7 + 0.9591 \times 2201.6 = 2617.59 \text{ kJ/kg}$$

$$\text{Heat supplied} = h_2 - h_1$$
$$= 3622.7 - 1408.04 = 2214.66 \text{ kJ/kg}$$

$$\text{Turbine work} = h_2 - h_3$$
$$= 3622.7 - 2617.59 = 1005.11 \text{ kJ/kg}$$

$$\text{Ideal cycle efficiency} = \frac{\text{Turbine work}}{\text{Heat supplied}}$$
$$= \frac{1005.11}{2214.66} = \textbf{45.38\%}$$

$$\text{Output in kW} = 1005.11 \times \frac{7200}{3600} = \textbf{0.2010.2 kW}$$
$$= \textbf{2010.22 kW}$$

$$\text{Specific steam consumption} = \frac{7200}{2010.22} = \textbf{3.582 kg/kW-h}$$

Problem 2.25: Steam of mass 10 kg and pressure 1000 kPa, 0.85 dry, is heated at constant pressure till the volume is doubled. Determine:

(i) Final quality of steam.

(ii) Heat added.

(iii) Change in internal energy.   **(P.U. May 2006)**

Solution: Given Data: $m = 10$ kg, $P_1 = 1000$ kPa, $x = 0.85$, $v_2 = 2v_1$

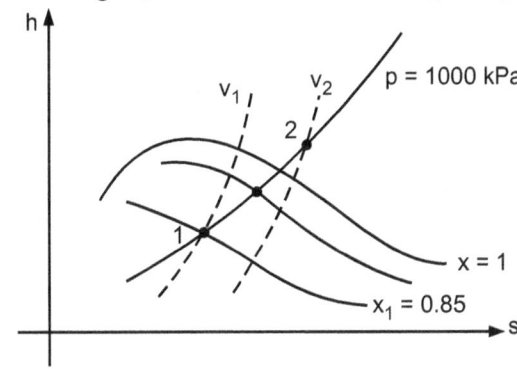

Fig. 2.57

At 10 bar pressure,

$$v_g = 0.19429 \text{ m}^3/\text{kg}$$

$$T_s = 179.88°C$$

$$v_1 = x \times 0.19429$$

$$= 0.85 \times 0.19429$$

$$v_1 = \mathbf{0.1651465}$$

The specific volume at point 2 (after heating),

$$v_2 = 2 \times v_1 = 2 \times 0.1651465$$

$$= 0.3303 \text{ m}^3/\text{kg}$$

But, $v_2 > v_g$ at 10 bar pressure.

Therefore, steam is in superheat state.

∴ Final quality of steam is **superheated**.

From superheat steam table,

At $v_2 = 0.3303$ m³/kg, $p_2 = 1000$ kPa

$$T_2 = 450.11°C$$

Now, $$h_1 = h_{f_1} + xh_{fg}$$

$$= 762.61 + 0.85 \times 2013.6 = 2474.17 \text{ kJ/kg}$$

(∵ at 10 bar)

and $h_2 = 3371.35$ kJ/kg   ... ($\because$ at $T_2 = 450.11°C$)

Heat added $= h_2 - h_1 = 3371.35 - 2475.17$
$$= 897.18 \text{ kJ/kg}$$
$$= 897.18 \times 10 \text{ kJ} = \textbf{8971.8 kJ}$$

Change in internal energy,
$$u_2 - u_1 = (h_2 - h_1) + (P_1 v_1 - P_2 v_2)$$
$$= 8971.8 + 10 \times 1000 \times (0.1651465 - 0.3303)$$
$$= \textbf{7320.335 kJ}$$

(i)   Final quality of steam = Superheated steam with temperature 450.11°C.
(ii) Heat added = 8971.8 kJ.
(iii) Change in IE = 7320.335 kJ.

Problem 2.26: A Carnot steam cycle operates between a source temperature of 311.06°C for a boiler pressure of 10 MPa and a sink temperature of 32.88°C (condenser pressure 5 kPa). Determine the ratio of net work to turbine work and the thermal efficiency of the cycle when all processes are reversible. Also determine specific steam consumption.

(P.U. May 2006)

Solution: Given Data: Carnot cycle

$T_1 = 311.06°C = 311.06 + 273 = 584.06$ K
$T_2 = 32.88°C = 32.88 + 273 = 305.88$ K
$P_1 = 10$ MPa $= 100$ bar
$P_2 = 5$ kPa $= 0.05$ bar

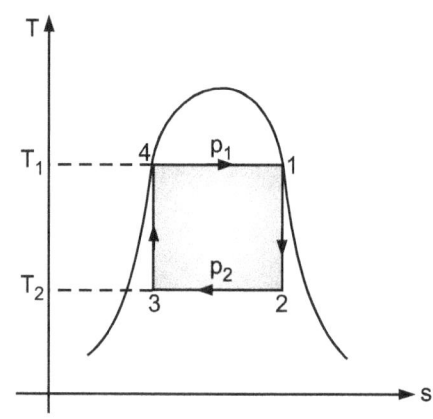

Fig. 2.58

At 100 bar pressure, from steam table,
$$T_s = 310.96°C$$
$$h_1 = h_g = 2727.70 \text{ kJ/kg}$$
$$h_4 = h_f = 1407.04 \text{ kJ/kg}$$
$$s_1 = s_g = 5.6198 \text{ kJ/kg·K}$$
$$s_4 = s_f = 3.3605 \text{ kJ/kg·K}$$

At 0.05 bar pressure,

$$T_s = 32.898°C, h_f = 137.77 \text{ kJ/kg}$$
$$h_{fg} = 2423.8 \text{ kJ/kg}$$
$$s_f = 0.4763 \text{ kJ/kg·K}$$
$$s_{fg} = 7.9197 \text{ kJ/kg·K}$$

To find dryness fraction at point 2, equate entropies at point 1 and point 2.

$$s_1 = s_{f_2} + x_2 s_{fg_2}$$
$$5.6198 = 0.4763 + x_2 \times 7.9197$$
$$x_2 = 0.64945$$
$$h_2 = h_{f_2} + x_2 h_{fg_2}$$
$$= 137.77 + 0.64945 \times 2423.8 = 1711.9 \text{ kJ/kg}$$

To find dryness fraction at point '3', equate entropies at point 4 and point 3.

$$s_4 = s_{f_3} + x_3 s_{fg_3}$$

$\therefore$
$$3.3605 = 0.4763 + x_3 \times 7.9197$$

$\therefore$
$$x_3 = 0.3642$$

$\therefore$
$$h_3 = h_{f_3} + x_3 h_{fg_3}$$
$$= 137.77 + 0.3642 \times 2423.8 = 1020.7 \text{ kJ/kg}$$

$$\text{Turbine work} = w_T = h_1 - h_2 = 2727.70 - 1711.92 = 1015.78 \text{ kJ/kg}$$
$$\text{Pump work} = w_p = h_4 - h_3 = 1408.04 - 1020.67 = 387.37 \text{ kJ/kg}$$
$$\text{Heat supplied} = Q_s = h_1 - h_4 = 2727.70 - 1408.04 = 1319.66 \text{ kJ/kg}$$
$$\text{Net work} = w_{net} = w_T - w_p = 1015.78 - 387.37 = 628.41 \text{ kJ/kg}$$
$$\text{Work ratio} = \frac{w_T - w_p}{w_T} = \frac{w_{net}}{w_T} = \frac{628.41}{1015.78} = \mathbf{0.6186}$$
$$\text{Thermal efficiency} = \eta_{th} = \frac{w_{net}}{Q_s} = \frac{628.41}{1319.66} = \mathbf{0.4762 \text{ or } 47.62\%}$$
$$\text{Specific steam consumption} = \frac{3600}{w_{net}} = \frac{3600}{628.41} = \mathbf{5.729 \text{ kg/kW-hr}}$$

Problem 2.27: A steam power plant operating on Rankine cycle receives steam from a boiler at 3.5 MPa and 350°C. It is exhausted to condenser at 10 kPa. Calculate:

   (i) Energy supplied per kg of steam generated in a boiler.

   (ii) Quality of steam entering the condenser.

   (iii) Rankine cycle efficiency considering feed pump work.

   (iv) Specific steam consumption.   **(P.U. Dec. 2006)**

Solution: Given: P_1 = 3.5 MPa = 35 bar

T_1 = 350°C

P_2 = 10 kPa = 0.1 bar

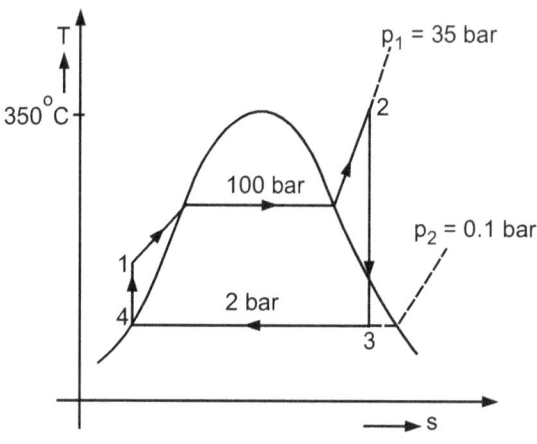

Fig. 2.59

From steam table, at 0.1 bar,

$$h_4 = h_f = 191.8 \text{ kJ/kg}$$

$$w_p = \frac{P_1 - P_2}{10} = 3.49 \text{ kJ/kg} = h_1 - h_4$$

∴ h_1 = 195.29 kJ/kg

and h_2 corresponding to 35 bar and 350°C = 3106.45 kJ/kg

For isentropic process, $s_2 = s_3$

$$s_2 = s_{f_3} + x_3 \, s_{fg_3}$$

s_2 at 35 bar and 350°C = 6.663 kJ/kg by interpolation.

∴   6.663 = 0.649 + $x_3 \times$ 7.502

∴ x_3 = 0.8016

and $h_3 = h_{f_3} + x_3 \, h_{fg_3}$

$$= 191.8 + 0.8016 \times 2392.9 = 2110.075$$

$$= 2110.075 \text{ kJ/kg}$$

∴   Heat supplied = $h_2 - h_1$ = 2911.16 kJ/kg

Work of turbine = w_T = $h_2 - h_3$

$$= 3106.45 - 2110.075 = \textbf{996.375 kJ/kg}$$

$$\text{Rankine efficiency} = \eta_{rankine} = \frac{W_T - W_p}{\text{Heat supplied}}$$

$$= \frac{996.375 - 3.49}{2911.6} = \textbf{0.3410 or 34.10\%}$$

$$\text{Specific steam consumption} = 55 = \frac{3600}{W_{net}} = \frac{3600}{992.88} = \textbf{3.63 kg/kW-hr}$$

Problem 2.28: A steam plant using Rankine cycle generated steam at 10 bar and 380°C. Condensation occurs at 0.06 bar. Find out Rankine efficiency. What will be Carnot efficiency? Neglect feed pump work. **(P.U. May 2007)**

Solution: Rankine cycle,

$$p_1 = 10 \text{ bar, } T_{sup_3} = 380°C,$$

$$p_b = 0.06 \text{ bar}$$

Neglecting pump work,

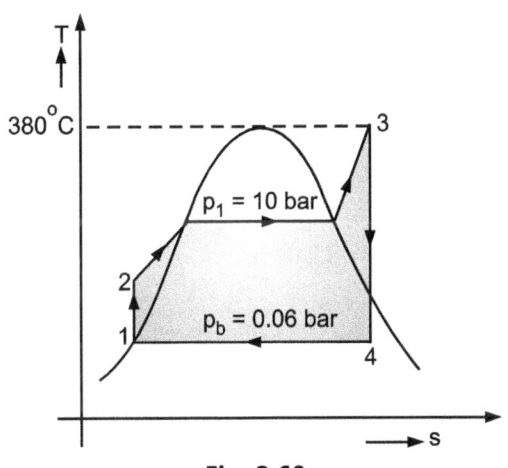

Fig. 2.60

At $P_1 = 10$ bar, $T_{sup_3} = 380°C$ from steam table,

$$h_3 = 3240 \text{ kJ/kg}$$
$$s_3 = 7.4 \text{ kJ/kg·K}$$
$$T_{s_3} = 179.88°C$$

At $P_b = 0.06$ bar,

$$h_1 = h_{f_4} = 151.50 \text{ kJ/kg}$$
$$h_{fg_4} = 2416 \text{ kJ/kg}$$
$$s_{f_4} = 0.5209 \text{ kJ/kg}$$
$$s_{fg_4} = 7.8103 \text{ kJ/kg}$$
$$T_{s_4} = 36.183°C$$

For isentropic process 3-4,

$$s_3 = s_4$$

$$s_3 = s_4$$

∴ $$7.4 = s_{f_4} + x_4 \, s_{fg_4}$$

∴ $$7.4 = 0.5209 + x_4 \times 7.8103$$

∴ $$x_4 = 0.881$$

∴ $$h_4 = h_{f_4} + x_4 \cdot h_{fg_4}$$

$$= 151.50 + 0.881 \times 2416$$

$$h_4 = 2279.996 \text{ kJ/kg}$$

Turbine work $= w_T = h_3 - h_4$

$$= 3240 - 2279.996$$

$$= \mathbf{960 \ kJ/kg}$$

Heat supplied $= Q_s = h_3 - h_1$

$$= 3240 - 151.50$$

$$= \mathbf{3088.5 \ kJ/kg}$$

Rankine efficiency $= \dfrac{w_T}{Q_s} = \dfrac{960}{3088.5}$

$$= 0.3108$$

$$= \mathbf{31.08\%}$$

Carnot efficiency $= \dfrac{T_1 - T_2}{T_1}$

$$= \dfrac{T_{s_3} - T_{s_4}}{T_{s_3}}$$

$$= \dfrac{179.88 - 36.183}{179.88}$$

$$= 0.7988$$

$$= \mathbf{79.88\%}$$

Problem 2.29: In a Rankine cycle, the steam at inlet to turbine is saturated at a pressure of 35 bar and the exhaust pressure is 0.2 bar.
Determine:
   (i) Pump work
   (ii) Turbine work
   (iii) Rankine efficiency
   (iv) Condenser heat flow
   (v) Dryness at the end of expansion.
Assume flow rate of 9.5 kg/s.

Solution: Pressure and conditions of steam, at inlet to the turbine,

$$P_1 = 35 \text{ bar}$$

$$x = 1$$

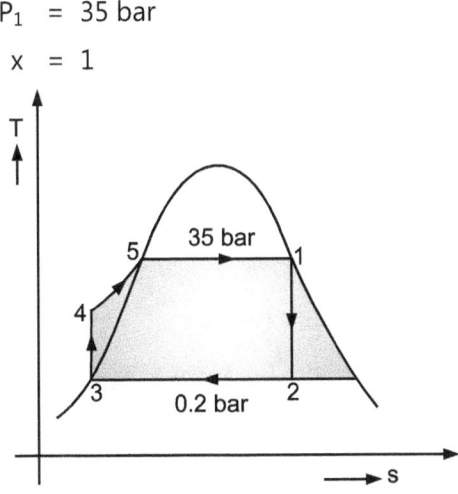

Fig. 2.61

Exhaust pressure, $P_2 = 0.2$ bar

Flow rate, $\dot{m} = 9.5$ kg/sec

From steam table,

At 35 bar, $h_1 = h_{g_1} = 2802$ kJ/kg

$$c_{g_1} = 6.1228 \text{ kJ/kg·K}$$

At 0.2 bar, $h_f = 251.5$ kJ/kg

$$h_{fg} = 2358.4 \text{ kJ/kg}$$

$$v_f = 0.001017 \text{ m}^3/\text{kg}$$

$$s_f = 0.8312 \text{ kJ/kg·K}$$

$$s_{fg} = 7.0773 \text{ kJ/kg·K}$$

(i) The pump work: Pump work $= (P_4 - P_3) \, v_f = (35 - 0.2) \times 10^5 \times 0.001017$

$$= 3.54 \text{ kJ/kg}$$

$\therefore$ Power required to drive the pump $= 9.5 \times 3.54$ kJ/sec

$$= 33.63 \text{ kW}$$

(ii) The turbine work: $s_1 = s_2 = s_{f2} + x_2 \cdot s_{fg_2}$

$$6.1228 = 0.8321 + x_2 \times 7.0773$$

$$x_2 = 0.747$$

$\therefore$ $h_4 = h_{f_2} + x_2 \cdot h_{fg_2}$

$$= 251.5 + 0.747 \times 2358.4$$

$$= 2013 \text{ kJ/kg}$$

∴   Turbine work $= \dot{m}\,(h_1 - h_2) = 9.5 \times (2802 - 2013)$

$$= \textbf{7495.5 kW}$$

(iii) Rankine efficiency: $\eta_{Rankine} = \dfrac{h_1 - h_2}{h_1 - h_{f_2}} = \dfrac{2802 - 2013}{2802 - 251.5}$

$$= \frac{789}{2550.5} = \textbf{0.3093 or 30.93\%}$$

(iv) Condenser heat flow:

The condenser heat flow $= \dot{m}\,(h_2 - h_{f_3})$

$$= 9.5 \times [(2013) - 251.5]$$

$$= \textbf{16734.25 kW}$$

(v) The dryness at the end of expansion, x_2:

$$x_2 = 0.747 \text{ or } 74.7\%$$

Problem 2.30: Steam at 20 bar and 360° expands in a steam turbine to 0.08 bar. It is then condensed in a condenser to saturated water. The pump feeds back the water to the boiler. Assume ideal Rankine cycle and determine:

(i)   The net work done per kg of steam.

(ii)   The Rankine efficiency.   **(P.U. May 2008)**

Solution:

Given Data: P_1 = 20 bar

                                    T_1 = 360°C

                                    P_b = 0.08 bar

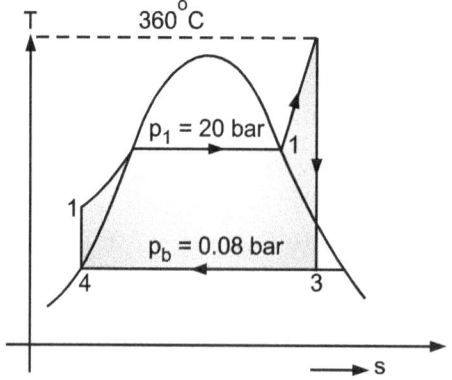

Fig. 2.62

From steam tables corresponding to condenser pressure of 8 bar,

$$h_4 = h_f = 173.86 \text{ kJ/kg}$$

We have,

$$w_p = \left[\frac{P_1 - P_b}{10}\right] \text{kJ/kg} = h_1 - h_4$$

$$= \frac{20 - 0.08}{10} = 1.992 \text{ kJ/kg} = h_1 - h_4$$

∴
$$h_1 = w_p + h_4 = 1.992 + 173.86$$

$$h_1 = 175.852 \text{ kJ/kg}$$

∴ h_2 corresponding to 20 bar and 360°C = 3160.62 kJ/kg

At 350°C = 3138.6 kJ/kg and at 400°C = 3248.7 kJ/kg

$$\text{Difference is } \frac{110.1}{50°C} = 2.202 \text{ kJ/kg}$$

∴
$$2.202 \times 10 = 22.02 \text{ kJ/kg}$$

∴
$$\text{At } 360°C = 3138.6 + 22.02 = 3160.62 \text{ kJ/kg}$$

Now, for isentropic process 2-3:

Entropy before expansion s_2 = Entropy after expansion s_3

To find s_2 = 7.1296 at 400°C

6.9596 at 350°C $\frac{0.17}{50} = 0.0034 \text{ kJ/kg·K}$

$$0.0034 \times 10 = 0.034 \text{ kJ/kg·K}$$

$$6.9596 + 0.034 = 6.9936 \text{ kJ/kg·K}$$

∴
$$6.9936 = s_{f_3} + x_3 \cdot s_{fg_3} \text{ at condenser pressure}$$

$$= 0.5925 + x_3 \times 7.6371$$

∴
$$x_3 = 0.8382$$

$$h_3 = h_{f_3} + x_3 \cdot h_{fg_3} \text{ at condenser pressure}$$

$$= 173.86 + 0.8382 \times 2403.2$$

$$= 2188.15 \text{ kJ/kg}$$

∴ Work done $= w_s = w_T - w_p = (h_2 - h_3) - w_p$

$$= (3160.62 - 2188.15) - 1.992$$

$$= 970.478 \text{ kJ/kg}$$

and
$$\eta_{Rankine} = \frac{w_s}{q_i} = \frac{970.478}{h_2 - h_1}$$

$$= \frac{970.478}{3160.62 - 175.852} = \textbf{32.51\%}$$

CONDENSERS

Introduction

In any heat engine the amount of work done per kg of working fluid depends on the range of temperature of the fluid in the engine, being greater the greater the range.

We know that the thermal efficiency of a closed cycle power developing plant using steam as the working fluid and working on Carnot cycle is given by an expression $\left(\dfrac{T_1 - T_2}{T_1}\right)$ where T_1 is the maximum temperature in the cycle and T_2 is the lowest temperature reached in the cycle. This efficiency expression shows that an efficiency increases as T_1 increases and T_2 decreases. We understand that the maximum temperature T_1 of the steam supplied to the steam prime-mover is limited by the material of the turbine blades used. Similarly, the temperature T_2 at which the heat is rejected, is limited by the atmospheric conditions. Pressure of steam corresponding to atmospheric temperature will be very much less than atmospheric pressure. (For example: at atm-temperature of 27°C, the saturation pressure is 0.03564 bar.)

Stated in another way, when the work done is greater, the greater amount of fluid is expanded. In any heat engine, it is a more or less simple matter to expand the working fluid to a small absolute pressure, but the difficulty is to get rid of the fluid after it has expanded to a pressure less than atmospheric pressure. In internal combustion engine, the working fluid cannot be used over again, and it has therefore to be discharged into the atmosphere, and the pressure of the atmosphere, therefore, fixes the lower limit of expansion. When steam is the working fluid, however, it may be returned to the boiler and used over again and this can be done most conveniently and most economically by first condensing it and then pumping the resulting water into the boiler.

It is not the condensation of the steam in a condenser which causes the low pressure of the steam as it enters the condenser should, for greatest thermodynamic efficiency, be the same as that in the condenser, and condensing it need not lower its pressure of atmosphere. But by condensing the steam, it may then be more economically removed to make way for more steam from the engine. The heat taken from the steam in condensing it is generally entirely lost.

2.12 NECESSITY OF CONDENSERS

Condenser is, basically, a vacuum vessel in which steam is condensed by abstracting the heat and the pressure is maintained below atmospheric pressure.

The primary object of condensing exhaust steam is to make it possible to remove it economically at a pressure less than that of the atmosphere after it has done its work in the prime-mover, and therefore to enable the steam to expand to a greater extent and do more work.

A secondary object is the obtaining of hot feed-water for the boiler.

The amount of heat available for conversion into work, with different back pressures and different initial pressures, is given in the table below. The amounts of heat given are the enthalpy drops due to isentropic expansions. The specific volumes of the steam at the back pressures are also given. The steam is assumed to be initially dry and saturated, but it will of course be wet after expansion.

Abs. initial press (bar)	Abs. back press (bar)	*Vacuum mm of Hg	Available heat/kg steam (kJ)	Sp. vol. at back pre (cu-m)
20	1.0	00	505	1.3888
20	0.15	647.50	750	7.7678
20	0.07	707.50	827	15.3161
10	1.0	00	381	1.4786
10	0.15	647.50	645	8.0585
.10	0.07	707.50	720	16.1168
1	0.15	647.50	295	9.1209
1	0.07	707.50	380	18.2110
* Vacuum referred to 760 mm of Hg.				

It will be seen from the table that, the advantage due to lowering the back pressure, it is made possible by condensing the exhaust steam, is relatively greater the lower the initial pressure. Also the gain per bar reduction in back pressure is greater, the lower the back pressure.

Although the thermodynamic efficiency is greater, the lower the back pressure, the ultimate efficiency may be reduced when the back pressure is reduced beyond a limit depending on the cost of producing and utilizing that back pressure. In reciprocating engines there is generally no saving by increasing the vacuum beyond 690 mm of Hg and 664 mm of Hg is often taken as the limit, but in steam turbines, the vacuum may with advantage be 715 mm of Hg and in special cases it may exceed 740 mm of Hg.

2.13 VACUUM MEASUREMENT

The measure of a vacuum in a vessel is the difference between the atmospheric pressure and the absolute pressure in the vessel. To make this measurement definite it must be converted to correspond with a standard atmospheric pressure. The standard atmospheric pressure generally taken in connection with vacuum measurement is the barometric pressure of 760 mm of Hg which corresponds to 1.01325 bar.

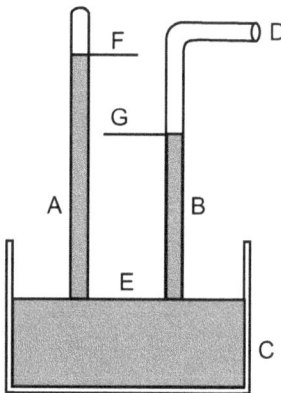

Fig. 2.63: Barometer

The conversion of a vacuum gauge reading to standard will be best understood by referring to Fig. 2.63. A is a mercury barometer and B a mercury vacuum gauge, both dipping into an open basin of mercury C. The vacuum gauge is connected at D to the condenser or other vessel, the vacuum in which is to be measured. The column of mercury EF in A balances the pressure of the atmosphere acting on the surface of the mercury in C. The column of mercury EG in B plus the absolute pressure P in the vessel connected to B at D acting on the top of the column EG also balances the pressure of the atmosphere, therefore, the height GF measures the absolute pressure p above the mercury in B. But the pressure p is independent of the pressure of the atmosphere. Hence, if the reading of the vacuum gauge, corrected to standard, is Z

$$760 - Z = EF - EG \text{ or } Z = 760 - EF + EG$$

For example, if the gauge shows a vacuum of 710 mm of Hg when the barometer shows 750 mm of Hg, the vacuum corrected to standard is 760 − 750 + 710 = 720 mm of Hg.

The vacuum gauge reading, corrected to standard, is sometimes expressed as a percentage of the standard barometric height, thus, in the above example 720 mm is 94.74% of 760 mm. A vacuum so expressed must not, however, be confused with vacuum efficiency as defined in this chapter.

The vacuum gauges used in practice are similar to pressure gauges and are of the Bourdon type, but the dials are graduated either to read centimeters or millimetre of mercury.

2.14 ELEMENTS OF A CONDENSING PLANT

For the purpose of maintaining a vacuum by the condensation and removal of the exhaust steam, the principal requirements are:

(a) A condenser in which the steam is condensed.

(b) A supply of injection or cooling water.

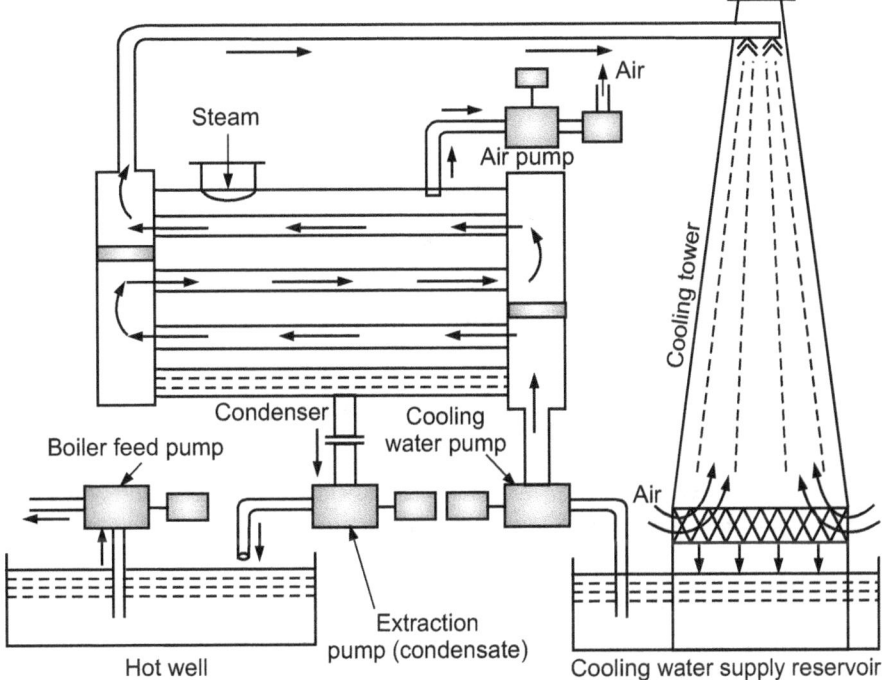

Fig. 2.64

(a) A pump to circulate the cooling water when a surface condenser is used.

(b) A pump, called the air pump, for removing the condensed steam and the air and uncondensed water vapour from the condenser. [Separate pumps may be used for (a) the condensed steam and (b) the air and uncondensed water vapour].

(c) A reservoir or a receptacle for the condensed steam discharged by the air pump, called the hot-well, from which the boiler feed is taken.

(d) Arrangement for retooling the cooling water of a surface condenser or the excess injection water not required for boiler feed, in cases where the water is to be used over and over again for cooling or injection purposes.

The condensing plant incorporating these elements is as shown in Fig. 2.64.

2.15 TYPES OF CONDENSERS

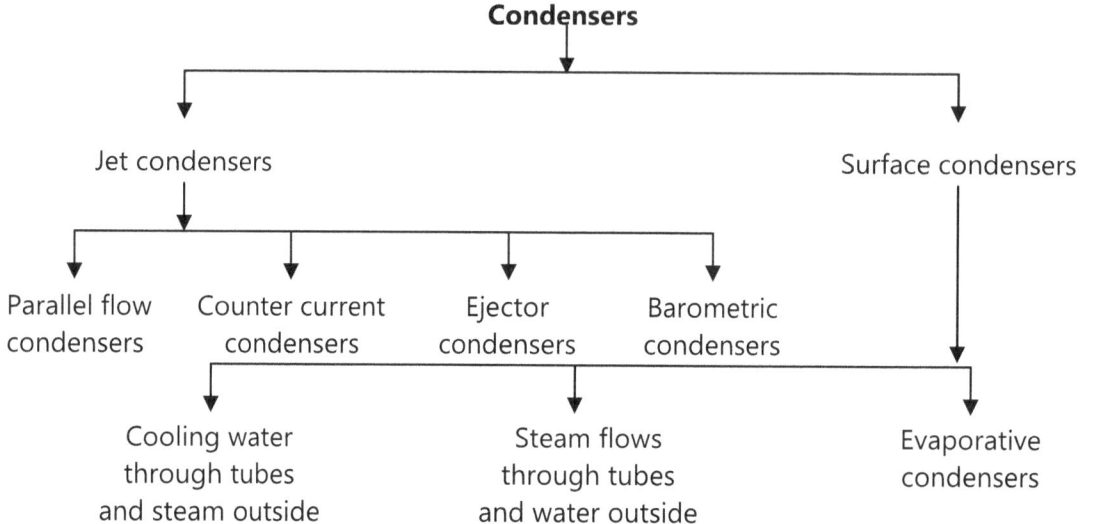

There are two main classes of condensers.

1. **Jet condensers:** In this case, the water for the condensation of the steam mixes with the steam and
2. **Surface condensers:** Here the steam is condensed by contact with metal tubes kept comparatively cool by water which does not mix with the steam.

The first class may be subdivided into -

(a) **Parallel flow condensers** in which the jet or spray of water and the steam enter the condenser at the top and fall together to the bottom.

(b) **Counter current or flow condensers** in which the steam flows upwards through the condenser, meeting the water which streams downwards from the top. The air is removed at the top and the water, separately, at the bottom.

(c) **Ejector condensers** in which the steam and water mix in a series of combining cones and the kinetic energy of the steam is utilized to assist in moving water through condenser into the hot-well against the pressure of the atmosphere.

(d) **Barometric condensers** in which a jet condenser at a high level is provided with a long vertical discharge pipe delivering the hot water into a sump at the bottom without the aid of a pump, but an air pump is required to remove the air at the top.

The second class may be subdivided into –

(a) **Surface condensers** in which the steam flows through tubes while the steam flows around them.

(b) **Surface condensers** in which the steam flows through the tubes while the cooling water flows around them.

(c) **Evaporative condensers** in which the steam flows through the tubes which are comparatively cool by water trickling over them, the cooling water being evaporated and taking its latent heat of vaporisation from the tubes.

Jet condensers are only used when the supply of condensing water is resonably pure because it goes with the condensed steam to the hot-well from which the boiler feed water is taken.

In modern condensing plants, the most common types of condensers are, the counter current jet condenser and the surface condenser in which the cooling water flows through the tubes and the steam flows around them.

2.15.1 Parallel-flow Jet Condensers

In this jet condenser, the water and steam are flowing or passing through the condenser in the same direction and thus water and steam come in contacted with each other. Steam is condensed and both cooling water and condensate is collected at the bottom of the condenser and is admitted to the condensate extraction pump and air is removed with the help of air pump.

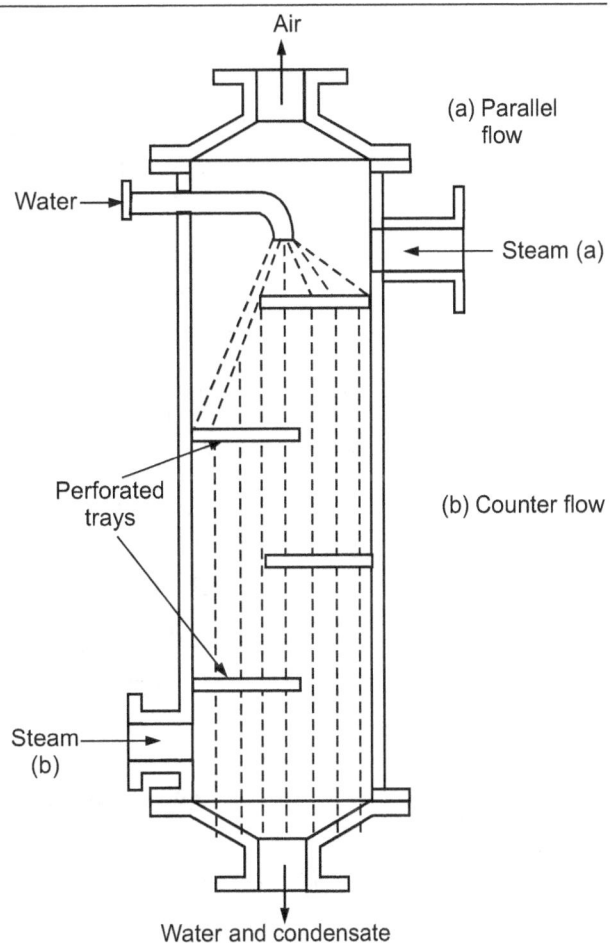

Fig. 2.65 (a) and (b): Parallel flow jet condenser

A schematic diagram of parallel flow jet condenser is shown in Fig. 2.65 where dotted lines are shown for steam admission in case of a parallel flow jet condenser. The condensate falls to the bottom of the condenser and flows to the condensate extraction pump which removes it to the hot well and air is taken at the top by an air pump as shown.

2.15.2 Counter-flow Type Condenser

In this counter-flow type condenser, water and steam, flow in the direction opposite to each other. The schematic diagram of such a condenser is shown in Fig. 2.65 (b). A vertical section of another counter-flow jet condenser is shown in Fig. 2.66.

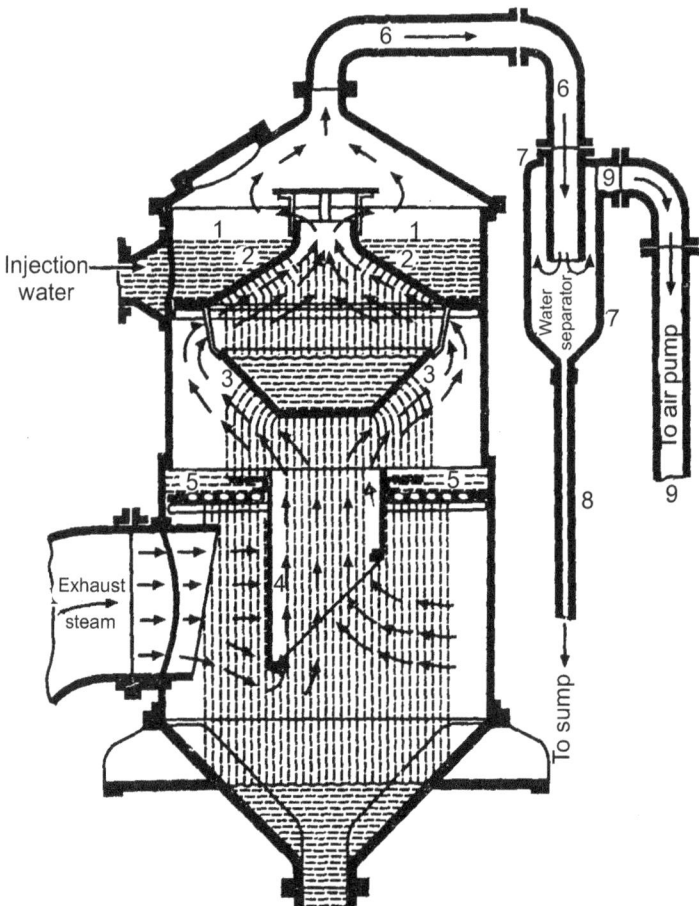

Fig. 2.66: Counter flow condenser

The main parts of this type of condenser are as –

1. Water entry compartment.
2. Perforated conical shaped plate for water to flow in number of jets.
3. Tray.
4. Short pipe through which water jets flows to the bottom of condenser.
5. Collection tray from where water jets also come to the bottom of condenser.
6. The air and uncondensed water vapour are led further through pipe 6.
7. The separator where water vapour drops suspendender are separator.
8. Pipe through which separated water particles are taken to the sump.
9. Pipe 9 leads the moist air to the air pump.

If the condenser is a low-level one, when it is placed near the level of the engine or turbine (generally it will be slightly below the level of turbine or engine-nearly 5-6 ft or 1.5 to 2 metres), the water is taken from a tank or reservoir below it by a pump, generally of the centrifugal type. This low-level condensers are further divided into two categories as low-vacuum and high-vacuum jet condensers.

In these condensers, the air pump has only to deal with the moist air.

2.15.3 Ejector Condensers

The main principle of this condenser is that the momentum of flowing water removes the mixture of condensate and cooling water against the atmospheric pressure. The water enters at the top, and flows through a number of nozzles (co-axial) fixed in a tube in which there are steam ports leading into the spaces between the nozzles. The exhaust steam enters at the top and surrounds the cones through which cooling water flows at high velocity. Steam is drawn into it due to the vacuum produced by this flow of water, thereby condensing the steam. The mass of condensate, cooling water and air is discharged out of the condenser, due to this velocity, against the atmospheric pressure.

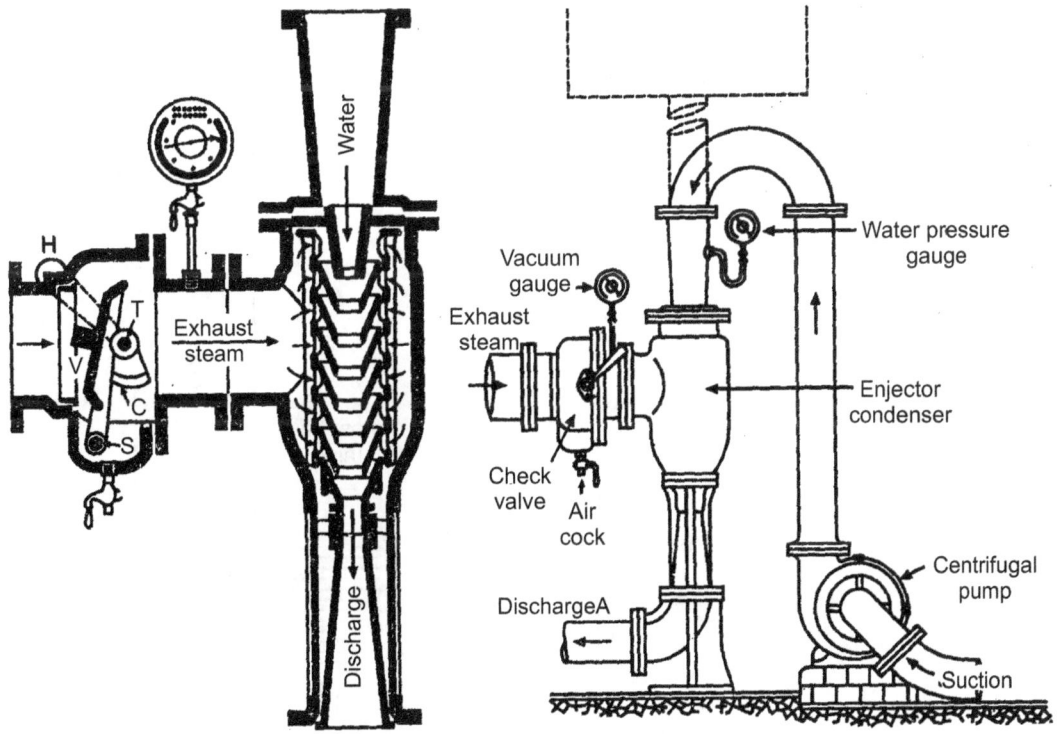

Fig. 2.67: Ejector condenser

Ledward's well known ejector condenser is shown in Fig. 2.66.

It is usual to fit a check valve V in the exhaust pipe near to the condenser. This is a non-return valve hinged on a spindle S. The use of this valve is to prevent the backward rush of water from the discharge tank to the engine which would follow a sudden failure of the water supply to the condenser. Such a backward rush of water would close the check valve. An addition to the check valve is a can C attached to a spindle T operated by a handle H by which means the check valve may be locked in its closed position.

The ejector condenser is small in comparison with other types of condensers and there being no air pump, the first cost is low. It is also simple and reliable, but it is generally used for comparatively small engines. The vacuum obtained is generally about 60 cm of Hg.

2.15.4 Barometric or High-level Jet Condenser

In this condenser, the condensing chamber is elevated above 34-35 feet or 10.36 – 10.5 metres above the level of the water in the collecting tank or sump, and the condenser is self discharging so far as the water is concerned. But a pump is necessary to force the injection water up to the condenser. From condenser.

This is shown in Fig. 2.68. The condenser itself is generally counter-flow type.

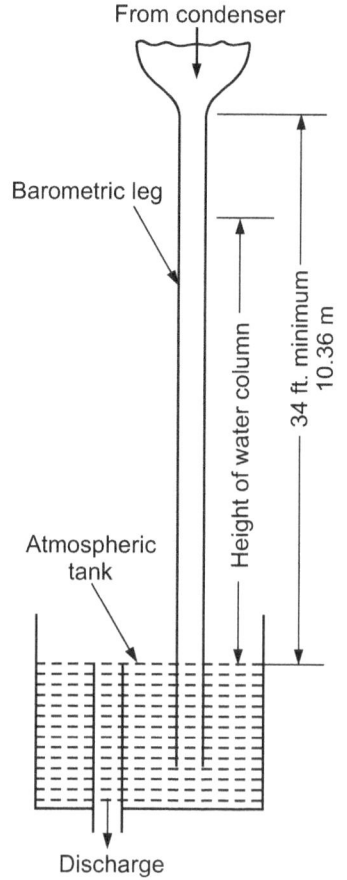

Fig. 2.68: Jet condenser

2.15.5 Surface Condensers

Surface condenser has a great advantage over the jet condenser as the condensate does not mix with the cooling water; the whole of the condensate can, therefore, be reused in the boiler. This is very necessary in ships which can carry only a limited amount of fresh water for the boilers, and use sea water for cooling water. With land installations, the cooling water can be allowed to cool again after use and thus be reused continuously through the condenser; this reduces the water consumption of the plant. The necessary high vacuum pressure in the condenser is maintained by the extraction pump and air pump too. Sometimes an ejector is used for this purpose in place of a pump.

We have before classified surface condenser depending upon the relative positions of steam and cooling water with respect to tubes.

   (a)   Standard Surface Condensers: In standard surface condensers, the steam to be condensed is made to flow over the outside of tubes, while the cooling or circulating water is made to flow inside the tubes. This flow pattern is used because the clean steam does not contaminate the outside of the tubes.

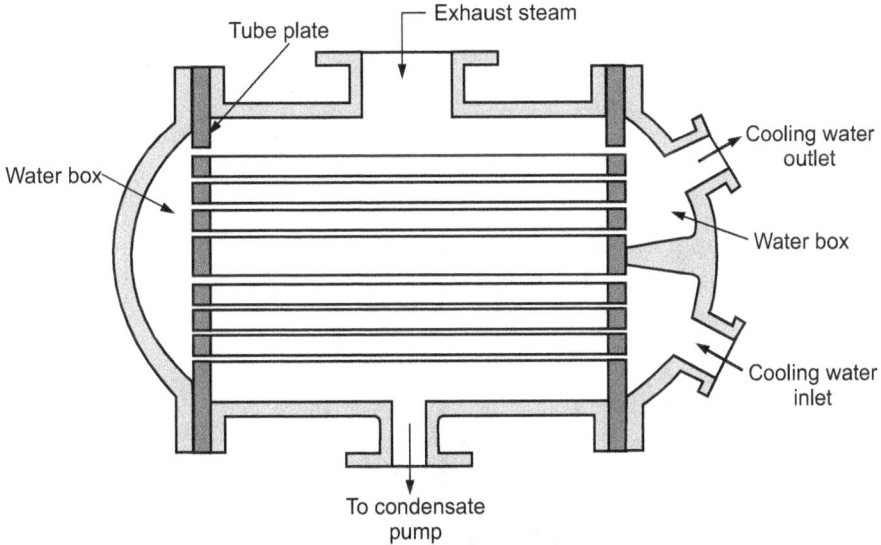

Fig. 2.69 (a): Surface condenser

This type of the surface condenser may be further classified as single-pass or multi-pass condensers.

In single-pass condensers, the water flows in one direction only through all the tubes or it traverses the length of the tubes only once. In multi-pass condensers, the water flows or travels the lengths of tubes many times (twice in case of a two-pass condenser or four times in case of a four pass condensers).

Fig. 2.69 (a) shows one form of standard type of surface condenser having two passes. The steam enters at the top of surface condenser and passing downwards over the tubes, through which cooling water is flowing, is condensed and the condensate is removed at the bottom by means of an extraction pump. The cooling water enters at one end of the tubes situated in the bottom half of the condenser and after passing to the other end returns back through the tubes situated in the top half of the condenser.

This condenser is also called as Down flow type condenser.

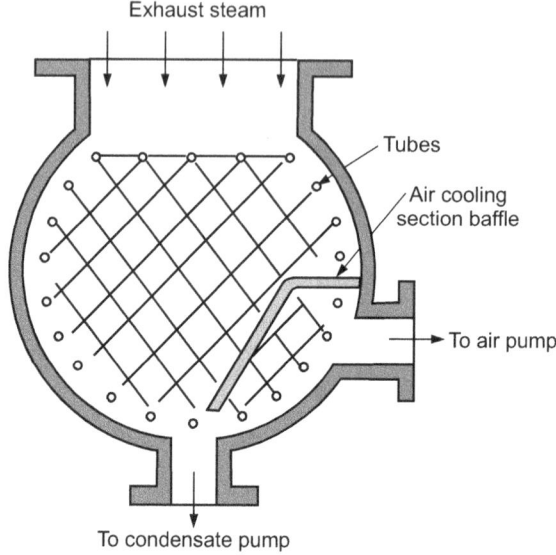

Fig. 2.69 (b): Down flow type

The salient features of the modern trend in the design of the condenser is to shield the air exit from the downstream of condensate by means of a baffle and thus air is extracted with only a comparatively small amount of water vapour. A section of tubes is screened by the baffle to form an air cooling section as shown in Fig. 2.68 (b). The air cooling section reduces the required capacity of the air pump and the weight of the steam removal by the air pump. See an illustrated example for this.

(b) Central flow type surface condenser: In this type of condenser, the suction pipe of the air extraction pump is placed in the centre of the tube nest as shown in Fig. 2.70.

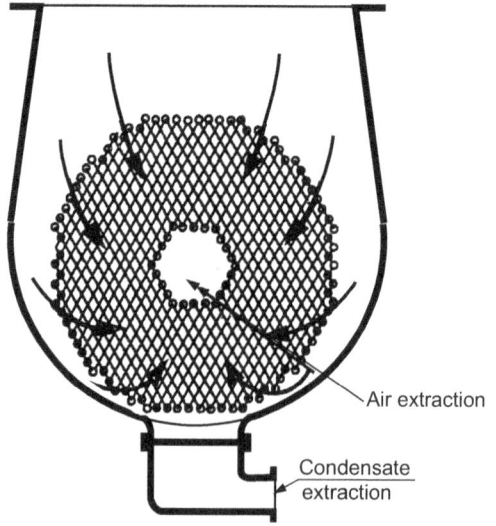

Fig. 2.70: Central flow surface condenser

This causes the condensate to flow radially towards the centre of the tube nest. It then leaves at the bottom where the condensate extraction pump is situated. This method is an improvement on the downward flow type as the steam is directed radially inwards by a volute casing around the tube nest. It has thus access to the whole periphery of the tubes.

(c) **Inverted type of surface condenser:** Inverted type of surface condenser has the air suction at the top. The steam enters near the bottom and flows outwards; it then returns to the bottom of the condenser by flowing near the outer surface. The condensate extraction pump is at the bottom.

(d) **Regenerative type of surface condenser:** This term is applied to condensers adopting a regenerative method of heating of condensate. After leaving the tube banks the condensate is passed through the entering exhaust steam from the engine or turbine, thus the temperature of the condensate is raised and is used as feed water for the boilers.

2.15.6 Evaporative Condenser

The principle of the evaporative condenser may be explained as shown in Fig. 2.71.

The steam to be condensed enters at the top of series of tubes around which a spray of cold water is falling. At the same time a current of air circulates over the water film formed on the surface of tubes. A natural or forced air current causes rapid evaporation of the water film with the result that the steam flowing through the tubes gets condensed. The vapour of the cooling water passes off with the heated air. The remainder of the cooling water at increased temperature is collected and used again after its temperature is restored to the original value by the addition of the requisite quantity of cold make-up water.

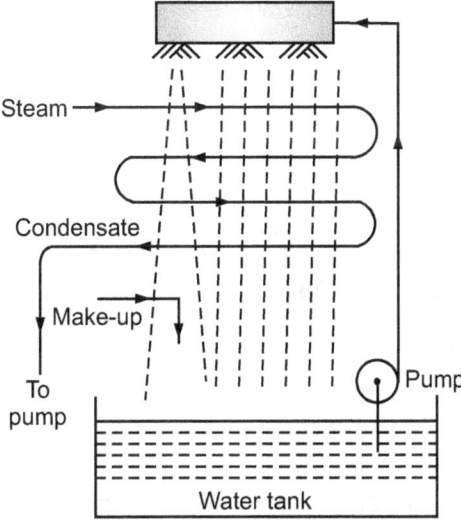

Fig. 2.71: Evaporative condenser

This type of the condenser is restricted to small powers on account of nuisance which would result from the production of cloud in a populated area. It can take overload for a short period without seriously affecting the vacuum.

2.15.7 Comparison of Jet and Surface Condensers

I. Surface Condensers:

(a) Advantages:

1. Vacuum obtained is comparatively high with consequent higher plant efficiency.
2. As cooling water does not mix with steam, any water can be used with treating the water.
3. Condensate being very pure, it can be used as boiler feed.
4. It is more suitable for high power capacity plants.

(b) Disadvantages:

1. It requires more space.
2. Maintenance is costly.

II. Jet Condensers:

(a) Advantages:

1. Mixing of steam and cooling water is more perfect.
2. Requires comparatively less quantity of cooling water.
3. The condensing plant is simple and less costly.
4. Maintenance is easy and less.
5. Condensate extraction pump is eliminated in case of high-level or barometric condensers.

(b) Disadvantages:

1. If condensate is to be used, the cooling water should be clean and pure so that it can be used directly in the boiler.
2. If water is not pure, condensate is wasted.
3. The power required for extraction pumps is comparatively high.
4. The high level or barometric condenser has a long pipe and is costly.
5. Vacuum in jet condenser seldom exceeds 650 mm of Hg due to liberation of dissolved gases in the cooling water.

2.16 DALTON's LAW OF PARTIAL PRESSURES AND MIXTURE OF AIR AND WATER VAPOUR

Dalton (1766-1844) demonstrated experimentally the following laws which were known as Dalton's Law of partial pressure. These laws were afterwards verified by Gay-Lussac. The laws are

1. The pressure, and, consequently, the quantity, of vapour which saturates a given space are the same for the same temperature, whether there is or is not any other gaseous substance in the space.

2. The pressure of the mixture of a gas and a vapour is equal to the sum of the pressures which each would exert if it occupied the same space, and same temperature, alone.

Here the second law is a consequence of the first and is known as the law of partial pressures.

The application of the above laws to condenser and air pump problems is illustrated by the following examples.

SOLVED PROBLEMS

Problem 2.31: The vacuum in a condenser is found to be 71.12 cm of Hg (barometer 76 cm of Hg) and the temperature is 30°C. To find the weight of air present per kg of uncondensed steam.

Solution: From the steam tables, 1 kg of steam at 30°C will exert a pressure of 0.04242 bar and have a volume of 32.939 cu.m. The air present per kg of steam will, by Dalton's first law, have a volume of 32.939 cu.m.

The combined pressure of air and steam is 76 − 71.12 = 4.88 cm of Hg or $\dfrac{4.88 \times 1.01325}{76}$

0.0651 bar. By Dalton's second law, the pressure of the air is 0.06510 − 0.04242 = 0.02268 bar.

For air, $\qquad 10^5 \, pv = m \, R \, T$

∴   Mass of air associated with 1 kg of steam is given by

$$m = \frac{10^5 \times 0.02268 \times 32.939}{287 \times 303}$$

$$= \mathbf{0.8591 \ kg} \qquad\qquad\qquad \textbf{... Ans.}$$

Problem 2.32: A surface condenser deals with 5000 kg of steam per hour and the air leakage amounts to 2 kg per hour. The temperature of the air pump suction is 35°C and the vacuum is 68.58 cm of Hg (barometer 76 cm of Hg). To determine the discharging capacity of the air pump in cu.m. per minute to remove the air and condensed steam. Assume volumetric efficiency of the air pump to be 80%.

Solution: At 35°C, the pressure of steam is 0.05622 bar.

The combined pressure of air and steam is

(76 − 68.58 = 7.42 cm of Hg = 0.09893 bar.)

$\qquad\qquad$ Partial pressure of air = 0.09893 − 0.05622

$\qquad\qquad\qquad\qquad\qquad\qquad$ = 0.04271 bar

$\qquad$ Weight of air per minute $= \dfrac{2}{60}$ bar

∴ $\qquad$ Volume of air per minute = v

We have, $\qquad\qquad 10^6 \, p_a v_a = m_a R_a T_a$

$$10^5 \times 0.04271 \times v = \frac{2}{60} \times 287 \times 308$$

∴ $\qquad\qquad\qquad\qquad v = \dfrac{2}{60} \times \dfrac{287 \times 308}{0.04271 \times 10^5}$

$$= \mathbf{0.69 \ cu.m./min}$$

Again weight of steam condensed per minute $= \dfrac{5000}{60}$ kg

∴   Volume of condensate per minute

$$= \dfrac{5000}{60} \times \dfrac{1}{1000} = \dfrac{5}{60} = \dfrac{1}{12}$$

$$= 0.0833 \text{ m}^3/\text{min}$$

∴   Theoretical capacity of the air pump

= Volume of condensate + Volume of air

= 0.69 + 0.0833

= 0.7733 cu.m/min

As the volumetric efficiency of the air pump is 80%, the effective capacity of the air pump

$$= \dfrac{\text{Theoretical capacity}}{\text{Volumetric efficiency}}$$

$$= \dfrac{0.7733}{0.8}$$

= 0.9667 cu.m./min.   **... Ans.**

EXERCISE

1. Explain with neat sketch formation of steam from ice at −10°C at atmospheric pressure.
2. Define:
    (a) Sensible heat, (b) Latent heat of vapourisation, (c) Degree of superheating, (d) Dryness fraction.
3. Explain critical point.
4. Explain the following processes of steam on T-s and h-s diagram.
    (a) Adiabatic process, (b) Throttling process.
5. What are the four basic components of a steam power plant?
6. What is the reversible cycle that represents the simple steam power plant? Draw the flow rate, p-v, T-s and h-s diagrams of this cycle.
7. What do you understand by steam rate and heat rate? What are their units?
8. Why is Carnot cycle not practicable for a steam power plant?
9. What do you understand by the mean temperature of heat addition?
10. For a given T_2, show how the Rankine cycle efficiency depends on the mean temperature of heat addition.
11. What is metallurgical limit?
12. Explain how the quality at turbine exhaust gets restricted.

13. How are the maximum temperature and maximum pressure in the Rankine cycle fixed?

14. When is reheating of steam recommended in a steam power plant? How does the reheat pressure get optimized?

15. What is the effect of reheat on (a) the specific output, (b) the cycle efficiency, (c) steam rate, and (d) heat rate, of a steam power plant?

16. Give the flow and T-s diagrams of the ideal regenerative cycle. Why is the efficiency of this cycle equal to Carnot efficiency? Why is this cycle not practicable?

17. What is the effect of regeneration on the (a) specific output, (b) mean temperature of heat addition, (c) cycle efficiency, (d) steam rate and (e) heat rate of a steam power plant?

18. How does the regeneration of steam carnotite the Rankine cycle?

19. What are open and closed heaters? Mention their merits and demerits.

20. Why is one open and one closed heaters are used in a steam plant? What is it called?

21. How are the number of heaters and the degree of regeneration get optimized?

22. Draw the T-s diagram of an ideal working fluid in a vapour power cycle.

23. Discuss the desirable characteristics of working fluid in a vapour power cycle.

24. Mention a few working fluids suitable in the high temperature range of a vapour power cycle.

25. What is a binary vapour cycle?

26. What are topping and bottoming cycles?

27. Show that the overall efficiency of two cycles coupled in series equals the sum of the individual cycle efficiencies minus their product.

28. What is a back pressure turbine? What are its applications?

29. What is a cogeneration plant? What are the thermodynamic advantages of such a plant?

30. What is the biggest loss in a steam plant? How can this loss be reduced?

31. What is a pass-out turbine? When is it used?

32. Express the overall efficiency of a steam plant as the product of boiler, turbine, generator and cycle efficiencies.

33. Explain the necessity of condenser for steam power plant.

34. Classify the different types of condenser.

35. Compare jet condensers and surface condenser.

36. Explain with neat sketch:

(a) Ejector condenser, (b) Down flow condenser, (c) Evapourator condenser, (d) Barometric jet condenser.

UNIT III

COMPRESSIBLE FLUID FLOW AND STEAM NOZZLES

3.1 INTRODUCTION STATIC AND STAGNATION PROPERTIES

To define the flow, the properties of the system must be known. It should be remembered that the flow properties of a system which define the state of the system are the static properties, and are those which are determined by measuring devices which have velocities of zero with respect to the flow system. It means that the measuring instruments must be moving with the velocity equal to that of the flowing fluid.

Properties like pressure, temperature, enthalpy, internal energy etc. of the fluid at rest (not flowing) are called *stagnation properties*. If the thermometer is used for measuring the temperature of the moving or flowing fluid by inserting the thermometer in the fluid flow, the velocity of the fluid near the thermometer bulb will be brought to zero and the fluid near the bulb get compressed adiabatically so that the temperature of the gases increases and the thermometer reads the temperature called the *stagnation temperature*. Stagnation properties are denoted by the suffix 'o', so that stagnation temperature is given by t_o, pressure p_o and so on viz. h_o, U_o etc. Static properties are those which are determined by measuring devices which are moving with the velocity equal to the velocity of flow i.e. zero relative velocities between flow and device.

3.2 ONE DIMENSIONAL FLOW

The compression or expansion of a gas can take place in numerous ways, the most important of which will be considered here. In fluid dynamics, it is often useful to designate flow according to a dimensionless parameter-the Reynolds number. This is a useful criterion in gas dynamics as well. However, the Reynolds number, defined as the ratio of the inertia forces to the viscous forces, is a mechanical concept and does not consider the thermal effects so important in any study of gas dynamics. Accordingly, it is necessary to employ other approaches when both fluid dynamics and thermodynamic factors are present.

One significant approach is to classify the flow of gases on the basis of the change of entropy accompanying the process. A flow process is *isentropic* if it proceeds reversibly and adiabatically (Q = 0). A different type of flow is one which proceeds without frictional losses, but during the flow the gas exchanges heat with its surroundings. Such a reversible flow is called *diabatic flow*. During diabatic flow, the entropy may increase or decrease depending on the direction of heat exchange between the gas and the surroundings.

A flow process is said to be irreversible if events take place which reduce the total available energy of the system and the surroundings. Such flows are accompanied by losses of the type associated with friction or shock waves. If irreversible processes take place adiabatically, the second law specifies that the entropy must increase.

3.3 ACOUSTIC VELOCITY

The speed of sound is called acoustic or sonic speed. Since sound is a small pressure wave, some medium is essential for its transmission.

The acoustic velocity or the velocity of sound in a fluid medium, is by definition the speed with which a small disturbance is transmitted through the fluid.

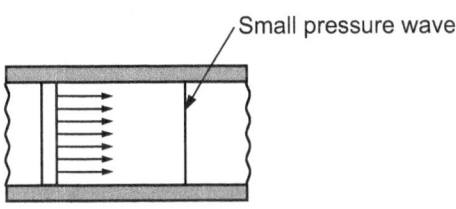

Small pressure wave

Fig. 3.1

Consider a piston which may slide without friction in a tube shown in Fig. 3.1 and assume that the piston and gas in the tube are at rest originally. Let p be the pressure of the gas uniform throughout. If the small impulse is given to the piston, the gas immediately adjacent to the piston will experience a slight rise in pressure or, in other words, it will be compressed. The change in density takes place because the gas is compressible and there is, therefore, a lapse of time between the motion of the piston and the time this is observed at the far end of the tube. Thus it will take the pulse a certain time to reach the far end of the tube or, in other words, there is a finite velocity of propagation which by definition is the acoustic velocity.

Let the change in pressure be denoted by dp, and let the change of density of gas, due to compression of the latter be dρ.

The bulk modulus E is defined by

$$E = \rho \cdot \frac{dp}{d\rho} \qquad \qquad \text{... (3.1)}$$

Dimensionally, $\sqrt{\dfrac{E}{\rho}}$ is a velocity and it can be shown that this is also the acoustic velocity.

$$\therefore \qquad a = \sqrt{E/\rho} \qquad \qquad \text{... (3.2)}$$

$$= \sqrt{\frac{dp}{d\rho}} \qquad \qquad \text{... (3.3)}$$

Equation (3.3) shows that the velocity with which a small pressure wave is propagated, that the velocity of sound, are related to the compressibility of the gas medium. It can be seen from equation (3.3) that greater the compressibility of gas, lower will be the speed of sound. The velocity of the pressure wave cannot always be defined by equation (3.3) as this is valid only when the pressure and velocity increments across the wave are so small that they can be approximated by their differentials. If the variations in pressure, velocity and temperature are vanishingly small, it can be concluded that the process takes place reversibly. Also, the process takes place very rapidly and no drastic temperature gradients are involved, so that the process is essentially adiabatic and a sound wave can be treated as an isentropic phenomenon.

Hence the derivative in equation (3.3) must be taken along an isentropic process. It is, therefore, more correct to use partial differential notation, namely

$$a = \sqrt{\left(\frac{\partial p}{\partial \rho}\right)_s} \qquad \qquad \text{... (3.4)}$$

We have for perfect or ideal gas,

$$pv^K = \text{const or } \frac{p}{\rho^K} = \text{const.} \qquad \qquad \text{... (3.5)}$$

$$\therefore \qquad \frac{\partial p}{\partial \rho} = \text{const.} \times K \cdot \rho^{K-1} = \frac{C \times K \cdot \rho^K}{\rho}$$

$$= \frac{K}{\rho}(C \times \rho^K) = \frac{K \cdot p}{\rho}$$

$$= K \cdot RT$$

$$\therefore \qquad \boxed{\frac{\partial p}{\partial \rho} = KRT}$$

∴   For a perfect gas, the acoustic or sonic velocity is given by

$$a = \sqrt{\left(\frac{\partial p}{\partial \rho}\right)_s}$$

$$= \sqrt{KRT} \qquad \qquad \qquad ... (3.6)$$

$$= \sqrt{\frac{Kp}{\rho}} \qquad \qquad \qquad ... (3.7)$$

∴ $$\boxed{a = \sqrt{KRT}} \qquad \qquad \qquad ... (3.8)$$

The acoustic velocity was defined as the speed with which a small disturbance propagates under isentropic conditions. The following question may be asked. Can a pressure wave move faster than the speed of sound in the medium ? This question can be answered by a simple derivation outlined by *Binder*. Which makes use of the equations of the conservation of mass, of energy and momentum. As before, consider a volume of a gas within a piston cylinder arrangement to be subjected to the force exerted by the piston as shown in Fig. 3.2 (a).

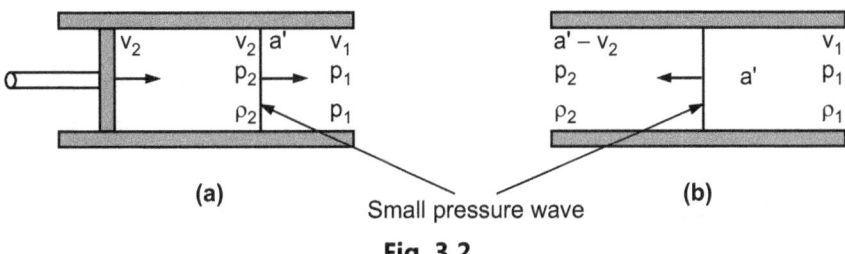

(a)   Small pressure wave   (b)

Fig. 3.2

Assume that the system is adiabatic, the frictionless piston and then one dimensional flow analysis is applicable.

Let the piston and gas be at rest at start with $V_1 = 0$ and the pressure throughout gas p_1. When the piston is pushed into the tube with some velocity V_2, the static pressure in the immediate vicinity of the piston will no longer be p_1, but will rise to some value p_2. The pressure in the whole system does not become p_2 immediately because each portion of gas remains as pressure p_1 until the pressure wave has travelled downstream with some velocity a'. As soon as the disturbance arrives at each point, the fluid there will be set into motion, thereby acquiring a velocity V_2 and a pressure p_2. The pressure wave is then a discontinuity across which the velocity, the pressure and the density are different. Across this discontinuity one may apply the equations of continuity, momentum and energy. To the conditions of each side of the discontinuity an acoustic velocity will correspond. The equations can be applied most conveniently by assuming that the observer travels with the disturbance as shown in Fig. 3.2 (b).

By the continuity equation, we have,

$$a'\rho_1 = (a' - V_2)\,\rho_2 \qquad\qquad \text{... (3.8 (a))}$$

The momentum equation gives

$$p + \rho_1 a'^2 = p_2 + \rho_2\,(a' - V_2)^2 \qquad\qquad \text{... (3.9)}$$

and energy equation gives

$$\frac{K}{K-1}\left(\frac{p_2}{\rho_2} - \frac{p_1}{\rho_1}\right) = \frac{a'^2 - (a' - V_2)^2}{2} \qquad\qquad \text{... (3.10)}$$

The acoustic velocity corresponding to the initial state is given by

$$a_1 = \sqrt{\frac{K \cdot p_1}{\rho_1}}$$

Combining these four equations and eliminating ρ_1, ρ_2, V_2 and solving for ratio $\dfrac{a'}{a_1}$, we get,

$$\frac{a}{a_1} = \sqrt{\frac{1}{2K}\left[K - 1 + (K + 1)\,\frac{p_2}{p_1}\right]} \qquad\qquad \text{... (3.11)}$$

When $p_1 = p_2$, $a' = a_1$ or when the pressure change across the wave is infinitesimal, $a' = a_1$.

When $\dfrac{p_2}{p_1}$ is appreciably greater than unity, the velocity of the pressure wave will be supersonic, and the process will no longer be isentropic. In conclusion, it may be said that the acoustic velocity is the lowest velocity with which a compression wave may travel.

Newton computed the acoustic velocity with the assumption that the temperature remains constant in the condensation and rarefactions accompanying the transmission of sound.

$$\therefore \qquad\qquad \frac{p}{\rho} = RT \text{ or } p = \rho\,RT$$

$$\text{or} \qquad\qquad \frac{dp}{d\rho} = RT$$

$$\therefore \qquad\qquad \boxed{a = \sqrt{RT}} \qquad\qquad \text{... (3.12)}$$

This equation is the definition of Newton's acoustic velocity. The Newton's equation and equation (3.6) differ by the ratio $\sqrt{K}$, and this is called, in honour of Laplace, Laplace's correction. It should be remembered that in isothermal flow, or even when the flow is adiabatic, a sound wave propagates isentropically.

Velocity of sound as defined by equations (3.6) and (3.7) is in reasonable agreement with the experimental data. Nevertheless the equation is developed on the premise that the gas under consideration obeys perfect gas laws.

The NACA standard velocity at 15°C is 340.7 m/sec. In comparison, the speed of sound in steel is 4944 m/s and in water it is 1438.2 m/s at NTP.

For air,
$$a = \sqrt{KRT}$$
$$= \sqrt{1.4 \times 287\ T}$$
$$= 20.045\ \sqrt{T} \qquad \ldots (3.13)$$

where
$$a = \text{Sonic velocity}$$
$$T = \text{Temperature in °K.}$$

3.4 MACH NUMBER, MACH LINE AND MACH ANGLE

A parameter that is fundamental in compressible flow theory is the speed of sound 'a'. In a flowing fluid, the speed of sound is a significant measure of the effects of compressibility only when it is compared to the speed of the flow. This introduces a dimensionless parameter which is called the *mach number* denoted by M.

$$\boxed{M = \frac{V}{a} = \frac{V}{\sqrt{KRT}}}$$

It is the most important parameter in compressible flow theory.

It is evident that M will vary from point to point in a given flow, not only because V changes but also because 'a' depends on the local conditions.

Flow may be classified according to the value of the existing mach number as -

Mach Number	Classification
M < 1	Subsonic flow
M = 1	Sonic flow
M > 1	Supersonic flow
M > 5	Hypersonic flow

Mach number is based on velocity and not on frequency. In acoustical work, the term *ultrasonic* is used in referring to the frequencies above the audible range. This usage has no place in Gas Dynamics.

It is often desirable to define variations of the mach number in terms of changes in velocity and temperature.

$$M = \frac{V}{\sqrt{KRT}} \text{ or } M^2 = \frac{V^2}{KRT} \qquad \ldots (3.15)$$

$$\therefore \qquad 2\,M \cdot dM = \frac{2V \cdot dV}{KRT} - \frac{V^2}{KR} \times \frac{1}{T^2} \cdot dT$$

$$M \cdot dM = \frac{V \cdot dV}{KRT} - \frac{V^2 \cdot dT}{2\, KRT^2}$$

Dividing by M^2 or $\dfrac{V^2}{KRT}$, we get

$$\frac{dM}{M} = \frac{dV}{V} - \frac{dT}{2T} \qquad \qquad \dots (3.16)$$

This equation (3.16) is particularly useful in isothermal analysis.

Consider a stationary object emitting small pressure impulses as a fluid moves over it with various velocities or, in other words, in the stationary fluid the object is moving with various velocities.

Fig. 3.3 (a) shows the situation with the fluid moving very slowly or not at all. In this the pressure impulses spread uniformly in all the directions. This is the case for any fluid with a very large sonic velocity, i.e. incompressible fluid. When the mach number is small, either the velocity may be very small or the acoustic velocity may be large, and for either case the fluid may be considered to be incompressible for many calculations.

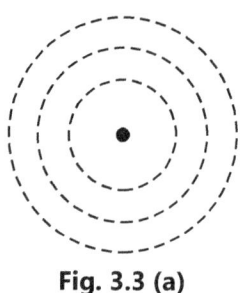

Fig. 3.3 (a)

Fig. 3.3 (b) indicates that for mach number is less than unity, but not negligible, the pressure impulses are felt in all directions but the intensity is not symmetrical.

Consider a point source travelling with a velocity V < a as shown in Fig. 3.3 (b). At reference time zero the point disturbance is assumed to be at A. At unit time later (1 t), the point source will have moved to B, a distance Vt. At 2 time units later, 2T, the source will have moved to C, a distance 2 Vt. Mean while, the spherical pressure wavefront which started out from A will have grown after time 2 t to a radius 2 at, and the wavefront from B which could not start until the source reached B will have grown to a radius at. At time 2 t, the source will have just reached point C. This step-by-step analysis of a point source moving with subsonic velocity indicates that each succeeding wavefront will always be contained within the initial or preceding wavefront.

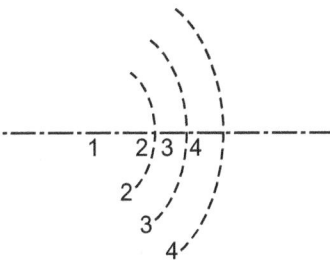

Fig. 3.3 (b)

If the point source moves at a speed V such that V > a, the wavefront circles will no longer contain the source. The condition is shown in Fig. 3.3 (c). The envelope to this family of circles is a straight line, known as *Mach line*. It is easy to see from Fig. 3.3 (c).

$$\sin \alpha = \frac{a}{V} = \frac{1}{M}$$

or

$$\alpha = \sin^{-1}\frac{1}{M}$$

Fig. 3.3 (c)

The angle between the Mach line and the direction of flow is known as *Mach angle*.

The Mach line constitutes a demarcation. It is easy to see that the fluid outside the Mach line will not receive any signal from the source because the disturbances travel with a speed equal to that of sound. Von Karman has appropriately called this phenomenon "*the rule of forbidden signals*". Further, he called the region ahead of the mach lines "*the zone of silence*" and the region inside the mach lines "*the zone of action*".

Based on figures above, and on the assumption that disturbances in the fluid are small i.e. acoustic waves, Von Karman postulated the following three rules

(a) The rule of forbidden - signals:
It is evident that slight pressure changes, produced in the moving fluid by a stationary source, cannot reach points upstream of the body if the velocity of flow is greater than the speed of sound. Similarly, if the fluid is stagnant and the body moving with a velocity greater than the sound, the pressure fluctuation cannot reach points ahead of the body. In this respect, there is a fundamental contrast between subsonic and supersonic flow.

(b) The zone of action and the zone of silence:

A small source in a stream of fluid with supersonic velocity produces effects only on points that lie on or inside the Mach cone extending downstream from the source. Similarly, in a stagnant fluid, conditions at an arbitrary point can be influenced by disturbances which are moving with supersonic speed only if the disturbance is on or in a cone of the same vertex angle extending upstream from the chosen arbitrary point.

(c) The rule of concentrated action:

This rule concerns the distribution of the pressure effect in the fluid relative to the body. The distance between the circles (spheres in three-dimensions) which represent pressure impulses is an inverse measurement of the strength of the pressure disturbance in that region. The closer the circles are, the weaker the impulse becomes. For the case of incompressible flow (or stationary fluid and source), the field is symmetrical about the source. For subsonic flow, the field is unsymmetrical; and for supersonic flow, the pressure disturbance is concentrated in the viscinity of the Mach cone which bound the zone of action.

From Fig. 1.3 (c) we see that all the impulses are limited to a cone. The pressure signals cannot be observed upstream since the cone has its apex at the stationary source of the impulses and the orientation is such that the apex points into the flow. This cone is called the *Mach cone.*

The lines which bound the Mach cone, having an inclination of a with the direction of flow, are called *Mach lines*, and in some of the literature, *Mach waves*.

In a plane (two-dimensional) there are two lines emanating from any point in the flow. Each of the lines makes an angle a with the streamline and if we look down the streamline, it is evident that one line runs to the left and the other to the right. Consequently, it is possible to refer to left running Mach lines and right running Mach lines. These lines are *characteristics* of the flow, or of the mathematics describing the flow, and hence have been given the name characteristics.

3.5 THE FLOW SYSTEM

Essentially all the problems of gas dynamics may be considered to take place in a flow system which may be considered as represented in Fig. 3.4 below. This consists of an infinite reservoir and a flow section. The conditions in the reservoir are denoted by the subscript 0. The flow section may be of any shape. It may be a convergent section, a straight section or a convergent - divergent section. In the flow section there is a point where the Mach Number is equal to unit and this section is called the critical point. In a convergent- divergent flow section and with reversible adiabatic flow, the throat is always the critical section.

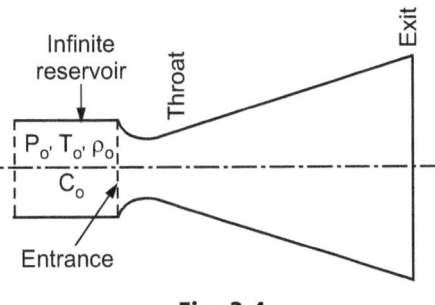

Fig. 3.4

At any section, we have,

$$h_o + \frac{V_o^2}{2} = h + \frac{V^2}{2}$$

or $$h_o = h + \frac{V^2}{2} \text{ as } V_o = 0$$

$\therefore$ $$(h_o - h) = \frac{V^2}{2} = C_p (T_o - T)$$

$$= \frac{KR}{K-1} (T_o - T) \text{ for ideal gas}$$

$\therefore$ $$dh = \frac{KR}{K-1} \cdot dT$$

$$= du + d (p \cdot v)$$

$$= du + d \left(\frac{p}{\rho}\right)$$

$$= du + \frac{dp}{\rho} - \frac{pd\rho}{\rho^2} \qquad \text{... (3.17)}$$

With isentropic flow, $W_{sf} = 0$, $Q = 0$ and with $\Delta P = 0$, we have

$$0 = \Delta K + \Delta h$$

$$= dK + dV$$

$$= V \cdot dh + C_p \, dT$$

$$= V \cdot dV + \frac{KR}{K-1} \cdot dT \qquad \text{... (3.18)}$$

This equation (3.18) is basic to most derivations involving isentropic flow. From this many equations can be obtained.

$$\therefore \qquad 0 = V \cdot dV + \frac{KR}{K-1} \cdot dT$$

$$= \frac{V \cdot dV}{KRT} + \frac{1}{K-1} \cdot \frac{dT}{T} \text{ dividing by KRT}$$

$$= \frac{V^2}{KRT} \cdot \frac{dV}{V} + \frac{1}{K-1} \cdot \frac{dT}{T}$$

$$= M^2 \cdot \frac{dV}{V} + \frac{1}{K-1} \frac{dT}{T}$$

$$\therefore \qquad 0 = \frac{dT}{T} + (K-1) M^2 \cdot \frac{dV}{V} \qquad \qquad \text{... (3.19)}$$

A relation between temperature, velocity and Mach number.

Flow Parameters:

We have, $$0 = V \, dV + \frac{KR}{K-1} \cdot dT$$

$$\therefore \qquad \text{Constant} = \int^V V \cdot dV + \frac{KR}{K-1} \int^T dT$$

$$= \frac{V^2}{2} + \frac{KR}{K-1} \cdot T$$

$$\therefore \qquad \frac{V_0^2}{2} + \frac{KR}{K-1} \cdot T_0 = \frac{V^2}{2} + \frac{KR}{K-1} \cdot T$$

$$\frac{KR}{K-1} T_0 = \frac{V^2}{2} + \frac{KRT}{K-1} \qquad \qquad (\because V_0 = 0)$$

$$\text{or} \qquad \frac{a_0^2}{K-1} = \frac{V^2}{2} + \frac{a^2}{K-1} \qquad \qquad \text{... (3.20)}$$

$$\text{or} \qquad T_0 = \frac{V^2}{2} + \frac{K-1}{KR} + T$$

This equation implies that in a reversible adiabatic expansion process, the acoustic velocity based on the reservoir conditions is greater than the local acoustic velocity at any point of the flow section. On the basis of temperature, this means that the reservoir temperature is higher than the local temperature at each subsequent point. This can easily be understood if it is remembered that a gas cooled when it is expanded reversibly and adiabatically.

Now, let the temperature at some point in the expansion section be reduced to absolute zero. (Theoretically).

$\therefore$ $\qquad$ $\dfrac{KR}{K-1} T \to 0$

$\therefore$ $\quad$ Local velocity V will be maximum.

$\therefore$ $\qquad$ $\dfrac{a_0^2}{K-1} = \dfrac{V_{max}^2}{2}$ or $V_{max}^2 = \dfrac{2a_0^2}{K-1}$

$$V_{max} = \sqrt{\dfrac{2a_0^2}{K-1}} \qquad \qquad \ldots (3.21)$$

$$= a_0 \sqrt{\dfrac{2}{K-1}}$$

For air, K = 1.4

$\therefore$ $\qquad$ $V_{max} = a_0 \sqrt{\dfrac{2}{0.4}} = 5$

$$= a_0 \sqrt{5}$$
$$= 2.24\, a_0$$
$$= 2.24\, \sqrt{KRT_0}$$
$$= 2.24\, \sqrt{1.4 \times 287\, T_0}$$

$$\boxed{V_{max} = 44.9\, \sqrt{T_0}} \qquad \qquad \ldots (3.22)$$

In practice V_{max} is never reached; nevertheless, equation (3.22) shows why the air entering supersonic wind tunnels must be heated if extremely high velocities such as those in hypersonic wind tunnels are desired in the test section. At V_{max}, $M \to \infty$.

Let us now consider subsonic flow and imagine a gradual increase of the local velocity until the acoustic velocity is approached at a particular location. The expansion and increase in velocity results in a lowering of temperature and this also lowers the local acoustic velocity. Thus, while the local velocity increases, the local acoustic- velocity decreases. With further expansion, the stream velocity could become equal to the acoustic velocity V = a. At this condition and this point is denoted by a*.

From equation (3.20), we have

$$\dfrac{a_0^2}{K-1} = \dfrac{a^2}{K-1} + \dfrac{V^2}{2} = \dfrac{a^{*2}}{K-1} + \dfrac{a^{*2}}{2}$$

$$= a^{*2}\left[\dfrac{1}{K-1} + \dfrac{1}{2}\right] = a^{*2}\left[\dfrac{2 + K - 1}{2(K-1)}\right]$$

$$= \dfrac{K+1}{2(K-1)}\, a^{*2}$$

or
$$a^{*2} = \frac{2(K-1)a_0^2}{(K+1)(K-1)} = \frac{2a_0^2}{K+1}$$
... (3.23)

For air, the critical acoustic velocity and the acoustic velocity in the reservoir are related by,

$$a^{*2} = \frac{2a_0^2}{1.4+1}$$

$$= \frac{2 \times a_0^2}{2.4} = \frac{1}{1.2}a_0^2$$

$$a^* = a_0\sqrt{1/1.2} = 0.93\,a_0$$

$$\boxed{a^* = 0.93\,a_0}$$
... (3.24)

It follows that for any particular reservouir, the maximum possible velocity is limited. However, it should not be inferred from this that the speed of the aircraft is limited by these same considerations. Theoretically, there is no limit on the maximum speed which air planes may reach.

The critical acoustic velocity serves a very useful purpose in defining a velocity ratio based on it, namely –

$$M^* = \frac{V}{V^*} = \frac{V}{a^*}$$
... (3.25)

Although this is in the form of a Mach number, it pertains to no particular local conditions, but constitutes a reference ratio. There are two advantages in defining M*. First it is a parameter which for any particular section is a function of the velocity only. Second, at extremely high speeds the acoustic velocity decreases while the velocity itself increases. Hence, the Mach number tends towards infinity, complicating its use in equations. Defining the Mach number M based on a* is solved this difficulty.

For stagnation temperature, we have -

$$C_p(T_0 - T) = \frac{V^2}{2}$$

or
$$T_0 = T + \frac{V^2}{2C_p \times 1000}$$

$$= T + \frac{V^2}{2010}$$

Also,
$$T_0 = T + \frac{V^2}{2C_p} = T + \frac{V^2}{2000 \times \frac{KR}{K-1}}$$

$$= T + \frac{(K-1)V^2}{2000 \times KR}$$

$$\therefore \qquad \frac{T_0}{T} = 1 + \frac{K - 1 \cdot V^2}{2000 \times KRT}$$

$$\boxed{\frac{T_0}{T} = 1 + \frac{K - 1}{2} \times M^2} \qquad \dots (3.26)$$

From this equation, we get,

$$\frac{T_0}{T_1} = 1 + \frac{K - 1}{2} M_1^2$$

$$\frac{T_0}{T_1} = 1 + \frac{K - 1}{2} M_2^2$$

$$\therefore \qquad \boxed{\frac{T_1}{T_2} = \frac{1 + \dfrac{K - 1}{2} M_2^2}{1 + \dfrac{K - 1}{2} \cdot M_1^2}}$$

For stagnation pressure, we have,

$$\frac{T_0}{T} = \left(\frac{p_0}{p}\right)^{\frac{K-1}{K}} = 1 + \frac{K - 1}{2} M^2$$

$$\therefore \qquad \boxed{\frac{p_0}{p} = \left\{1 + \frac{K - 1}{2} M^2\right\}^{\frac{K}{K-1}}} \qquad \dots (3.27)$$

The dynamic pressure q is defined by,

$$q = \frac{1}{2} \rho V^2$$

Also,

$$M = \frac{V}{\sqrt{KRT}} \text{ or } M^2 = \frac{V^2}{KRT}$$

$$\therefore \qquad V^2 = M^2 \cdot KRT = M^2 \cdot K \cdot \frac{p}{\rho}$$

$$\therefore \qquad q = \frac{1}{2} \cdot \rho \cdot \frac{M^2 Kp}{\rho}$$

$$\boxed{q = \frac{M^2 Kp}{2}} \qquad \dots (3.28)$$

Also, we have

$$p_0 = p\left\{1 + \frac{K - 1}{2} M^2\right\}^{\frac{K}{K-1}}$$

$$\therefore \qquad p_0 - p = \left[p\left\{1 + \frac{K - 1}{2} M^2\right\}^{\frac{K}{K-1}} - 1\right]$$

$$\therefore \qquad \frac{p_0 - p}{q} = p\left[\left\{1 + \frac{K-1}{2}M^2\right\}^{\frac{K}{K-1}} - 1\right]\frac{2}{Kp\,M^2}$$

$$= \frac{2}{KM^2}\left[\left\{1 + \frac{K-1}{2}M^2\right\}^{\frac{K}{K-1}} - 1\right]$$

$$= \frac{2}{KM^2}\left[1 + \frac{K}{2}M^2 + \frac{K}{8}M^4 + \frac{K}{48}(2-K)M^6 + \dots - 1\right]$$

$$\therefore \qquad p_0 - p = \frac{1}{2}\rho V^2 \frac{2}{KM^2}\left[\frac{K}{2}M^2 + \frac{K}{8}M^4 + \frac{K}{48}(2-K)M^6 + \dots\right]$$

$$\therefore \qquad p_0 = p + \frac{\rho V^2}{2}\left[\frac{2}{KM^2} + \frac{M^2}{4} + \frac{2-K}{12}\cdot\frac{M^4}{K} + \dots\right] \qquad \dots (3.29)$$

SOLVED EXAMPLES

Example 3.1:

Find the lowest speed of sound which may be encountered in the standard atmosphere.

Solution:

$$a = \text{Acoustic velocity} = \text{Sound velocity}$$

$$= \sqrt{KRT} = \sqrt{1.4 \times 287\,T}$$

$$= 20\sqrt{T} = 200 \times \sqrt{288} \text{ standard temperature } 15°C$$

$$= \textbf{339.4 m/sec} \qquad\qquad \textbf{... Ans.}$$

Example 3.2:

The speed of sound in air in kmph may be computed by the equation $a = c\sqrt{T}$. If T is given in °K, find the value and units of c.

Solution:

$$\text{For air, } a = \sqrt{KRT}$$

$$= 20\sqrt{T} \text{ m/s}$$

$$= 20\sqrt{T} \times \frac{3600}{1000} \text{ km/hr}$$

$$= 72\sqrt{T} = c\sqrt{T}$$

$$\therefore \qquad c = \textbf{72}\,\frac{\textbf{km}}{\textbf{hour}} \times \frac{\textbf{1}}{\textbf{°K}} \qquad\qquad \textbf{... Ans.}$$

Example 3.3:

A model is placed in a wind tunnel operating at a test section where M = 1.2.

(a) Find the velocity of air stream based on standard air.

(b) Find the Mach Angle α.

Solution:

(a) For standard air, a = 339.4 m/sec.

and
$$M = 1.2 = \frac{V}{a}$$

$$V = \text{Velocity of air stream}$$
$$= 1.2 \times 339.4$$
$$= \textbf{407.28 m/sec} \qquad \textbf{... Ans.}$$

(b) Mach angle is given by

$$\sin \alpha = \frac{1}{M} = \frac{1}{1.2} = 0.8333$$
$$\alpha = \text{Mach angle}$$
$$= \textbf{56°.27} \qquad \textbf{... Ans.}$$

Example 3.4:

What is the dynamic pressure at 4500 m ($\rho_w = 0.024$ kgf/m^3) when the velocity is 600 kmph?

Solution: Dynamic pressure $= \frac{1}{2}\rho V^2$ where, V = 600 kmph

$$= \frac{1}{2} \times 0.024 \times \frac{(500)^2}{9} \qquad = 600 \times \frac{1000}{3600} \text{ m/s}$$

$$= 0.012 \times \frac{250000}{9} \qquad = \frac{500}{3} \text{ m/sec}$$

$$= \textbf{0.0333 kg/cm}^2 \qquad \textbf{... Ans.}$$

Example 3.5:

For a hypersonic wind tunnel having a test section Mach number of 100, find:

(a) the pressure ratio $\dfrac{p_0}{p}$

(b) the temperature ratio $\dfrac{T_0}{T}$

Solution:

(a) Pressure ratio is given by

$$\frac{p_0}{p} = \left[1 + \frac{K-1}{2} \cdot M^2 \right]^{\frac{K}{K-1}}$$

$$= \left[1 + \frac{0.4}{2} \cdot 10^2 \right]^{\frac{1.4}{0.4}}$$

$$= (1 + 20)^{3.5}$$
$$= (21)^{3.5}$$
$$= \textbf{42430} \qquad \textbf{... Ans.}$$

(b) Temperature ratio is given by,

$$\frac{T_0}{T} = \left[1 + \frac{K-1}{2} M^2 \right]$$

$$= \left[1 + \frac{0.4 \times 100}{2} \right]$$

$$= \textbf{21} \qquad \textbf{... Ans.}$$

Example 3.6:

Standard air at zero velocity expands to M = 0.9. Find (a) the final density and (b) density change.

Solution:

(a) Temperature of standard air is 288° K and its density before expansion 1.222 kg/cu.m

Now, we have
$$-\frac{p_o}{p} = \left[1 + \frac{K-1}{2}M^2\right]^{\frac{K}{K-1}}$$

$$= \left[1 + \frac{0.4}{2} \times 0.81\right]^{3.5}$$

$$= (1.162)^{3.5} = \mathbf{1.695}$$

Also, we have
$$\frac{T_o}{T} = \left(1 + \frac{K-1}{2}M^2\right)$$

$$= \mathbf{1.162}$$

∴ We can write,
$$\frac{p_o}{\rho_o T_o} = \frac{p}{\rho T}$$

∴
$$\frac{\rho_o}{\rho} = \frac{p_o}{p} \times \frac{T}{T_o} \times \frac{1.695}{1.162}$$

$$= \mathbf{1.46}$$

$$\rho = \frac{1.222}{1.46} = \mathbf{0.837\ kgm/m^3} \qquad \qquad \text{... Ans.}$$

(b) Density change,
$$\Delta\rho = -(\rho_o - \rho)$$

$$= -(1.222 - 0.837)$$

$$= \mathbf{-0.385} \qquad \qquad \text{... Ans.}$$

Example 3.7:

Standard air at 48 kmph is accelerated isentropically in a nozzle to 800 kmph. Find:

    (a) the change in temperature,

    (b) the change in pressure,

    (c) change in density,

    (d) change in stagnation temperature,

    (e) the change in stagnation pressure.

Solution:

(a) Change in temperature:

$$48\ \text{kmph} = \frac{48 \times 1000}{3600} = \frac{40}{3}\ \text{m/s}$$

$$800\ \text{kmph} = \frac{800 \times 1000}{3600} = \frac{2000}{9}$$

For steady flow process and isentropic process,

$$0 = \Delta K + \Delta h \text{ as } Q = 0, W_{sf} = 0, \Delta P = 0$$

$$\therefore \qquad K_1 + h_1 = K_2 + h_2$$

$$h_1 - h_2 = \frac{V_2^2 - V_1^2}{2} \text{ or } Cp\,(t_1 - t_2) = \frac{\dfrac{2000^2}{81} - \dfrac{40^2}{9}}{2}$$

$$\therefore \qquad t_2 - t_1 = \text{Change in temperature}$$

$$= \frac{\left(\dfrac{1600}{9} - \dfrac{4 \times 10^6}{81}\right)}{2 \times 1000 \times 1.05} = \frac{14400 - 4000000}{81 \times 2 \times 1000 \times 1.05}$$

$$= \frac{-39856}{1620 \times 1.05}$$

$$= -24.45°C \qquad \qquad \text{... Ans.}$$

−ve sign indicates that the temperature decreases.

(b) Change in pressure:

Temperature of standard air = 15° = 288°K

$$\therefore \qquad\qquad T_2 = 288 - 24.45 = 263.55° \text{ K}$$

For isentropic flow,

$$\frac{T_2}{T_1} = \left(\frac{p_2}{p_1}\right)^{\frac{K-1}{K}} \text{ or } \frac{T_1}{T_2} = \left(\frac{p_1}{p_2}\right)^{\frac{K-1}{K}} = \frac{288}{263.55} = 1.135$$

$$\therefore \qquad 1.135 = \left(\frac{p_1}{p_2}\right)^{2/7} \qquad \therefore \quad \frac{p_1}{p_2} = 1.56$$

$$\therefore \qquad \frac{p_2}{p_1} = 0.64 \qquad \therefore \quad \frac{p_2 - p_1}{p_1} = \frac{p_2}{p_1} - 1 = 0.64 - 1 = 0.36$$

$$p_1 = \text{Standard pressure} = 1.01325 \text{ bar}$$

$$\therefore \qquad p_2 - p_1 = \text{Change in pressure} = -0.36 \times 1.01325$$

$$= -0.3648 \text{ bar} \qquad\qquad \text{... Ans.}$$

−ve sign indicates that the pressure decreases.

Change in density:

$$\text{Initial density } \rho_1 = 1.222 \text{ kg/m}^3$$

$$\text{For final density, } \frac{p_2}{\rho_2} = RT_2$$

$$\rho_2 \frac{p_2}{RT_a} = \frac{10^5\,(1.01325 - 0.3648)}{287 \times 263.55}$$

$$= \frac{0.64845 \times 10^5}{287 \times 263.55} = 0.8573 \text{ kg/m}^3$$

∴   Change of density $= 0.8573 - 1.2220$

$= \mathbf{-0.3657}$ **... Ans.**

$-$ ve sign indicates that the density decreases.

(d) Change in stagnation temperature:

Stagnation temperature is given by,

$$T_o = T + \frac{V^2}{2010}$$

∴ $$T_{o_1} = T_1 + \frac{V_1^2}{2010} = 15 + \frac{(40/3)^2}{2010}$$

$$= 15 + \frac{1600}{9 \times 2010} = 15 + 0.08825$$

$$= \mathbf{15.08825° \ C \ or \ 288.08825 \ °K}$$

Similarly, $$T_{o_2} = T_2 + \frac{V_2^2}{2010} = 263.55 + \frac{(2000/9)^2}{2010}$$

$$= 263.55 + \frac{4 \times 10^6}{81 \times 2010}$$

$$= 263.55 + 24.57$$

$$= \mathbf{288.12°K}$$

∴   Change in stagnation temperature

$$= T_{o_2} - T_{o_1} = 288.12 - 288.08825$$

$$= \mathbf{0.03175°K}$$ **... Ans.**

(e) Change in stagnation pressure:

We have, $$\left(\frac{p_{o_1}}{p_1}\right)^{\frac{K-1}{K}} = \frac{T_o}{T_1} = \frac{288.08825}{288}$$

$$\approx 1$$

∴ $$\frac{p_{o_1}}{p_1} = 1 \text{ or } p_o = p_1 = \mathbf{1.01325 \ bar}$$

Similarly, $$\left(\frac{p_{o_2}}{p_2}\right)^{\frac{K-1}{K}} = \frac{T_{o_2}}{T_2} = \frac{288.12}{263.55} = 1.093$$

∴ $$\frac{p_{o_2}}{p_2} = (1.093)^{1.4/0.4} = 1.093^{3.5}$$

$$= 1.366$$

∴ $$p_{o_2} = 1.366 \times (1.01325 - 0.3648)$$

$$= 1366 \times 0.64845$$

$$= \mathbf{0.886}$$

∴   Change in stagnation pressure

$$= p_{o_2} - p_{o_1} = 0.886 - 1.01325$$

$$= -0.12725 \text{ bar} \qquad \text{... Ans.}$$

Example 3.8:

It is desired to design a supersonic wind tunnel which will have in the test section standard air and a Mach number of 5. Find the conditions of the air in the reservoir.

Solution: For standard air, temperature = 288°K and p = 1.01325 bar.

$$\text{Sonic velocity} = 20\sqrt{T} = 20\sqrt{288}$$

$$= 339.4 \text{ m/s}$$

and

$$M = \frac{V}{a} \quad \therefore \quad 5 = \frac{V}{339.4}$$

$$V = 5 \times 339.4 = 1697 \text{ m/s}$$

Let, the reservoir conditions be p_o, T_o, and $V_o = 0$.

For isentropic flow –

$$T_o = T + \frac{V^2}{2010} = 288 + \frac{1697 \times 1697}{2010}$$

$$= 288 + 1432.74$$

$$= 1720.74°K \qquad \text{... Ans.}$$

Again

$$\frac{T_o}{T} = \left(\frac{p_o}{p}\right)^{\frac{K-1}{K}} = \frac{1720.74}{288} = 5.975$$

∴

$$\frac{p_o}{p} = (5.975)^{3.5} = 521.4$$

$$p_o = 521.4 \times 1.01325$$

$$= 528.26 \text{ bar} \qquad \text{... Ans.}$$

Example 3.9:

An aircraft at 4500 m altitude (275° K) has a true speed of 580 kmph.

Find: (a) the critical velocity, (b) the maximum possible velocity. Assume friction is negligible.

Solution: (a) Critical velocity:

$$580 \text{ kmph} = \frac{580 \times 1000}{3600}$$

$$= 161.11 \text{ m/s}$$

Acoustic velocity at 4500 altitude

$$= 20\sqrt{T} = 20\sqrt{275} = 331.66 \text{ m/s}$$

The point where the Mach number becomes unity, is called critical point and the velocity at that point is called critical velocity.

∴   Critical velocity = **331.6 m/s**   ... Ans.

(b) Maximum velocity:

We have,
$$C_p (T_o - T) = \frac{V^2}{2}$$

$$\frac{KR}{K - 1} T_o = \frac{KRT}{K - 1} + \frac{V^2}{2}$$

For maximum velocity, T = 0 and V = V_{max}

$$\therefore \qquad \frac{a_0^2}{K - 1} = \frac{V_{max}^2}{2}$$

$$\therefore \qquad V_{max}^2 = \frac{2a_0^2}{K - 1} \qquad\qquad \therefore \quad V_{max} = 44.8\sqrt{T_o}$$

$$V_{max} = 44.8 \times \sqrt{275}$$

$$= \textbf{742.92 m/s} \qquad\qquad\qquad \textbf{... Ans.}$$

Example 3.10:

During research test runs in the North Western University Gas dynamics Laboratory, a pitot-static tube indicated a static pressure of 0.67 bar (g). At the same conditions, manometer difference between stagnation and static pressures was 11.1 cm of Hg. The corrected barometric pressure was 75 cm of Hg and the stagnation temperature 35.2°C. Find the air velocity.

Solution: Barometric pressure = 75 cm. Hg

$$\therefore \qquad \text{Absolute static pressure} = 0.67 + \frac{75}{76} \times 1.01325$$

$$= 0.67 + 1$$

$$= \textbf{1.67 bar}$$

$$\therefore \qquad \text{Stagnation pressure} = 1.67 + \frac{11.1}{76} \times 1.01325$$

$$= 1.67 + 0.148$$

$$= \textbf{1.818 bar}$$

$$\text{Stagnation temperature} = 35.2 + 273$$

$$T_o = \textbf{308.2°K}$$

$$\therefore \qquad \frac{T_o}{T} = \left(\frac{p_o}{p}\right)^{\frac{K - 1}{K}} = \left(\frac{1.818}{1.69}\right)^{2/7} = 1.0211$$

$$\therefore \qquad T = \frac{T_o}{1.0211} = \frac{308.2}{1.0211} = \textbf{301.83°K}$$

$$\text{Isentropic enthalpy drop} = C_p (T_o - T) = \frac{KR}{K - 1}(T_o - T_1)$$

$$= \frac{1.4 \times 287}{0.4} \times \frac{(308.2 - 301.83)}{1000} \text{ kJ}$$

$$= 3.5 \times 2.87 \times 6.37$$

$$= \textbf{6.4 kJ}$$

$$= \frac{V^2}{2} = \frac{V_2^2}{2000}$$

$\therefore$
$$V = \sqrt{(6.4) \times 2000} = 44.72 \sqrt{6.4}$$

$$= \textbf{113.134 kJ/kg} \qquad \text{... Ans.}$$

OR

$$\frac{T_o}{T} = 1 + \frac{K - 1}{2} M^2 = 1 + 0.2\, M^2$$

$\therefore$
$$1.0211 = 1 + 0.2\, M^2$$

$$M^2 = \frac{0.0211}{0.2} = 0.1055 \quad \therefore \textbf{M = 0.325}$$

$$a = \text{Acoustic velocity} = 20\sqrt{T} = 20\sqrt{301.83}$$

$\therefore$
$$\text{Velocity of air} = aM$$

$$= 347.47 \times 0.325$$

$$= \textbf{113 m/sec} \qquad \text{... Ans.}$$

Example 3.11:

Air flows in a pipe having an internal diameter of 1.86 cm. The air entering the pipe is at 5.6 bar (gauge) and 38° C. The capacity of the compressor supplying the air is 42.75 cu.m./min. of free air. Find the stagnation temperature in the air stream, and the Mach No.

Solution:

Assuming atmospheric pressure to be 1.01325 bar, the absolute pressure of air entering the pipe is 5.6 + 1.01325 = **6.61325 bar**. Temperature of this air is (273 + 38) = **311°K.**

$$\text{Supply capacity} = 42.75 \text{ cu. m/min. of free air}$$

$$= \frac{42.75 \times 1.01325}{6.61325} \times \frac{311}{280}$$

$$= 7.275 \text{ cu.m/min.}$$

$$= \textbf{0.1212 cu.m/min.}$$

$\therefore$
$$0.1212 = \frac{\pi d^2}{4} \times V = \frac{\pi}{4} \times \left(\frac{1.86}{100}\right)^2 \times V$$

$\therefore$
$$\text{Velocity of air} = V = \frac{0.1212 \times 100 \times 100}{0.785 \times 1.86 \times 1.86}$$

$$= \textbf{446.3 m/sec.}$$

∴   Stagnation temperature,

$$T_o = T_1 + \frac{V^2}{2010} = 311 + \frac{446.3 \times 446.3}{2010}$$

$$= 311 + 99.1$$

$$= \mathbf{410.1°K} \qquad \text{... Ans.}$$

$$\text{Sonic velocity, } a = 20\sqrt{T} = 20\sqrt{311}$$

$$= \mathbf{352.7 \ m/s}$$

∴ $$M = \frac{V}{a} = \frac{446.3}{352.7}$$

$$= \mathbf{1.265} \qquad \text{... Ans.}$$

Example 3.12:

Air from a standard reservoir enters a De-Laval nozzle. It is observed that at a section where the Mach angle is 28°, the static pressure is 0.35 bar. Find -

(a)   Mach number at the section.

(b)   The temperature at the section and

(c)   The velocity at the section.

Solution: Standard reservoir, $T_o = 288°K$

$$p_o = 1.01325 \text{ bar}$$

(a) Mach number:

Mach angle = α = 28°   ∴ sin α = sin 28° = 0.4695

and $$\frac{1}{M} = \sin \alpha \text{ or } M = \frac{1}{\sin \alpha} = \frac{1}{0.4695}$$

$$= \mathbf{2.13} \qquad \text{... Ans.}$$

(b) Temperature at the section:

At the section, p = 0.35 bar

∴ $$\frac{T_o}{T} = \left(\frac{p_o}{p}\right)^{\frac{K-1}{K}} = \left(\frac{1.01325}{0.35}\right)^{0.286} = (2.895)^{0.286}$$

$$= 1.3553$$

∴ $$T = \text{Temperature at the section}$$

$$= \frac{288}{1.3553}$$

$$= \mathbf{212.5°K} \qquad \text{... Ans.}$$

(c) Velocity at the section:

$$T_o = T + \frac{V^2}{2010}$$

$$288 = 212.5 + \frac{V^2}{2010}$$

$$V^2 = (288 - 212.5) \times 2010$$
$$= 75.5 \times 2010$$

$\therefore$ $V = \textbf{389.56 m/sec.}$ **... Ans.**

$$= \text{Velocity at the section}$$

Example 3.13:

Show that isentropic flow,

$$V_{max} = \sqrt{V^2 + \frac{2a^2}{K-1}}$$

Solution: We know

$$\frac{KRT_o}{K-1} = \frac{KRT}{K-1} + \frac{V^2}{2}$$

$$\frac{a_0^2}{K-1} = \frac{a^2}{K-1} + \frac{V^2}{2}$$

$$a_0^2 = a^2 + \frac{V^2}{2} \times (K-1)$$

We know that, $\dfrac{a_0^2}{K-1} = \dfrac{V_{max}^2}{2}$

or $V_{max}^2 = \dfrac{2a_0^2}{K-1}$

$$= \frac{2}{K-1}\left[a^2 + \frac{V^2}{2}(K-1)\right]$$

$$= \frac{2a^2}{K-1} + V^2$$

$$\boxed{V_{max} = \sqrt{\frac{2a^2}{K-1} + V^2}}$$ **... Q.E.D.**

Example 3.14:

Show that for isentropic flow,

$$a^* = \sqrt{\frac{2a^2 + V^2(K-1)}{K+1}}$$

Solution: We have, $\dfrac{a_0^2}{K-1} = \dfrac{a^2}{K-1} + \dfrac{V^2}{2}$ When V = a, a = a*

$\therefore$ $\dfrac{a_0^2}{K-1} = \dfrac{a^2}{K-1} + \dfrac{V^2}{2} = \dfrac{a_0^2}{K-1} + \dfrac{a^2}{2}$

$$= \frac{2a^2 + a^2(K-1)}{2(K-1)} = \frac{2a^2 + a^2K - a^2}{2(K-1)}$$

$$= \frac{a^2 (1 + K)}{2 (K - 1)}$$

$\therefore$

$$a_0^2 = \frac{2a_0^2}{K + 1}$$

or

$$a^{*2} = \frac{2a_0^2}{K + 1}$$

$$= \frac{2}{K + 1} \left[\frac{a^2}{K - 1} + \frac{V^2}{2} \right] (K - 1)$$

$$= \frac{2a^2}{K + 1} + \frac{V^2(K - 1)}{K + 1}$$

$$= \frac{2a^2 + V^2 (K - 1)}{K + 1}$$

$\therefore$

$$\boxed{a^* = \sqrt{\frac{2a^2 + V^2 (K - 1)}{K + 1}}}$$

... Q.E.D

Example 3.15:

Show that

$$M^{*2} = \frac{\dfrac{M^2}{2} \times (K + 1)}{M^2 \left(\dfrac{K - 1}{2} \right) + 1}$$

Solution:

$$\text{R.H.S.} = \frac{\dfrac{M^2}{2} \times (K + 1)}{M^2 \left(\dfrac{K - 1}{2} \right) + 1}$$

$$= \frac{\dfrac{V^2}{2a^2} \cdot (K + 1)}{\dfrac{V^2}{a^2} \left(\dfrac{K - 1}{2} \right) + 1}$$

$$= \frac{\dfrac{(V^2 K + V^2)}{2a^2}}{\dfrac{V^2 (K - 1)}{2a^2/2a^2}}$$

$$= \frac{V^2 K + V^2}{2a^2 + V^2 (K - 1)}$$

$$= \frac{V^2 (K + 1)}{2a^2 + V^2 (K - 1)}$$

$$= \frac{V^2 (1)}{\dfrac{2a^2 + V^2 (K - 1)}{K + 1}}$$

$$= \frac{V^2}{a^{*2}}$$

$$= M^{*2}$$

$$= \text{L.H.S.} \qquad \qquad \text{... Q.E.D.}$$

Example 3.16:

For air undergoing an isentropic process, derive the equation $a^* = c\sqrt{T_o}$ and determine the numerical value of constant c when a^* is given in m/sec. and T_o, $^\circ$K.

Solution: We have for isentropic flow,

$$\frac{a_0^2}{K - 1} = \frac{a^2}{K - 1} + \frac{V^2}{2}$$

When $V = a$, $a = a^*$

$$\therefore \qquad \frac{a_0^2}{K - 1} = \frac{a^2}{K - 1} + \frac{a^2}{2} = \frac{2a^2 + a^2 (K - 1)}{2 (K - 1)}$$

$$= \frac{a^2 (K + 1)}{2 (K - 1)}$$

$$\therefore \qquad a_0^2 = \frac{a^2}{2} \times \frac{K + 1}{K - 1}$$

$$\therefore \qquad a_0^2 = \frac{a^{*2} (K + 1)}{2}$$

$$\therefore \qquad a^{*2} = \frac{2a_0^2}{K + 1}$$

$$\therefore \qquad a^* = \frac{a_0}{K + 1} \sqrt{\left(\frac{2}{K + 1}\right)} a_0$$

$$= 20 \sqrt{T_o} \times \sqrt{\frac{2}{K + 1}}$$

$$= 20 \sqrt{\frac{2}{2.4}} \times \sqrt{T_o}$$

$$= 20 \sqrt{\frac{1}{1.2}} \times \sqrt{T_o}$$

$$= 18.26 \sqrt{T_o}$$

$$= c\sqrt{T_o}$$

$$\therefore \qquad \boxed{c = 18.26} \qquad \qquad \text{... Ans.}$$

3.6 INTRODUCTION: NOZZLES

A nozzle is a device which serves two purposes

1.   To convert thermal energy into kinetic energy.

2.   To direct mass flow from it at a specified angle.

There are many applications which require high velocity jet of fluid.

Nozzles are used in steam and gas turbines, jet engines etc. The other applications of the nozzle are the injectors for pumping feed water into the boiler and the ejectors for removing air from the condensers.

Steam Turbine Layout:

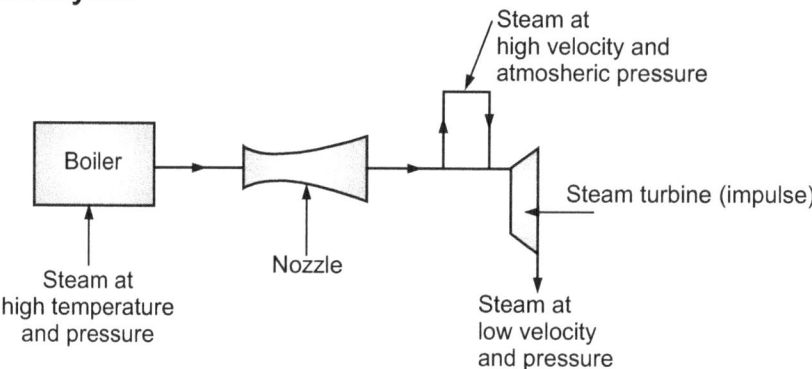

Fig. 3.5: Steam Turbine Layout

3.7 NOZZLE SHAPES

There are two types of nozzle shapes.

(i)   Convergent Nozzle:

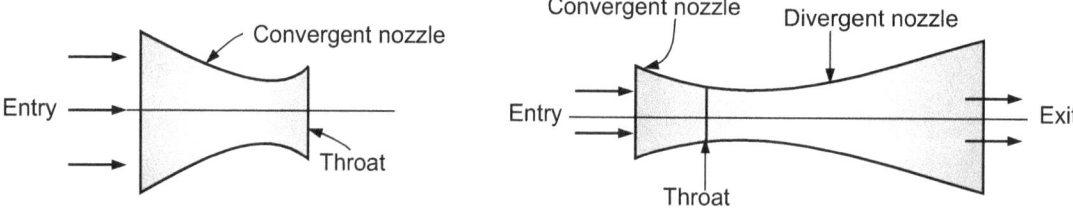

Fig. 3.6: Convergent Nozzle   **Fig. 3.7: Convergent divergent nozzle**

The cross-section of the nozzle can be circular, rectangular, square or elliptical.

3.8 NOZZLE FLOW CONDITIONS

The nozzle is an open system in which flow of fluid is a steady flow process.

Hence, the flow of fluid through the nozzle should satisfy following conditions:
1. Mass flow rate into and out of system are equal and do not vary with time.
2. State and energy of the fluid at entrance and exit should not vary with time.
3. The rates of heat and work transfer into and out of the system should not change with time.

We will derive relations for exit velocity and discharge for ideal gas flowing through the nozzle and apply these relations to steam by using suitable value of index 'n'.

3.9 FLOW OF AN IDEAL GAS THROUGH NOZZLE

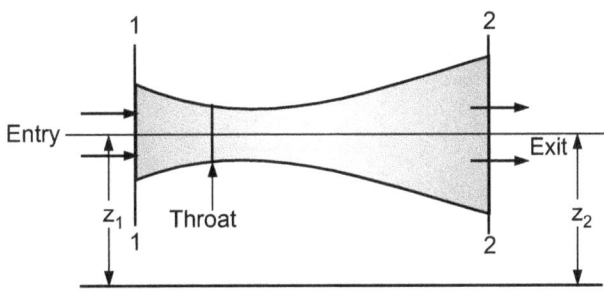

Fig. 3.8: Flow of gas through nozzle

Let, A_1, A_2 = Cross-sectional area of nozzle at entrance and exit respectively

$\dot{m}$ = Mass flow rate in kg/sec.

P_1, P_2 = Pressure absolute in N/m^2

v_1, v_2 = Specific volume in m^3/kg

u_1, u_2 = Specific internal energy in J/kg

c_1, c_2 = Velocity in meters/sec.

z_1, z_2 = Elevation above arbitrary datum in meter

q = Net rate of heat transfer in J/kg

w = Net rate of work transfer in J/kg

Applying steady state flow energy equation to nozzle

$$\frac{c_1^2}{2} + z_1 \cdot g + h_1 + q = \frac{c_2^2}{2} + z_2 \cdot g + h_2 + w \qquad \ldots (3.30)$$

Assumptions:
(i) Normally nozzle is horizontal $\therefore z_1 = z_2$
(ii) Flow is isentropic $\therefore q = 0$
(iii) No work is done $\therefore w = 0$

∴   Equation (3.30) reduces to,

$$\frac{c_1^2}{2} + h_1 = \frac{c_2^2}{2} + h_2$$

or $\qquad\qquad \dfrac{c_2^2 - c_1^2}{2} = h_1 - h_2$ ... (3.31)

Velocity of fluid when it enters the nozzle is known as velocity of approach (c_1). Normally, velocity of approach is very small as compared with exit velocity and hence can be neglected.

∴ $\qquad\qquad\qquad c_2 = \sqrt{h_1 - h_2}$

In the above equation, unit of every term is in J/kg. However, as the enthalpy for ideal gas is given in kJ/kg, the equation can be written with each term in kJ/kg.

∴ $\qquad\qquad\qquad \dfrac{c_2^2}{1000} = 2\,(h_1 - h_2)$ ... (3.32)

∴ $\qquad\qquad\qquad c_2^2 = 2000\,(h_1 - h_2)$

∴ $\qquad\qquad\qquad c_2 = 44.7\sqrt{h_1 - h_2}$ ... (3.33)

By using equation (3.33), exit velocity of the fluid can be found out when the enthalpy drop across the nozzle is known.

3.10 MASS FLOW RATE THROUGH THE NOZZLE

The change in kinetic energy of fluid flowing through the nozzle is given by the equation (3.31)

$$\frac{c_2^2 - c_1^2}{2} = h_1 - h_2$$

∴ $\qquad\qquad \dfrac{c_2^2 - c_1^2}{2} = u_1 + P_1 v_1 - u_2 - P_2 v_2$

∴ $\qquad\qquad \dfrac{c_2^2 - c_1^2}{2} = (P_1 v_1 - P_2 v_2) + (u_1 - u_2)$

$$\qquad\qquad\qquad\quad = (P_1 v_1 - P_2 v_2) + c_v\,(T_1 - T_2)$$

$$(\because\ du = c_v\,dt)$$

For ideal gas $\qquad\quad P_1 v_1 = RT_1$ per kg and $c_p - c_v = R$

∴ $\qquad\qquad \dfrac{c_2^2 - c_1^2}{2} = (P_1 v_1 - P_2 v_2) + \dfrac{c_v \cdot R}{R}\,(T_1 - T_2)$

∴ $\qquad\qquad \dfrac{c_2^2 - c_1^2}{2} = (P_1 v_1 - P_2 v_2) + \dfrac{c_v}{c_p - c_v}\,(RT_1 - RT_2)$

∴ $\qquad\qquad \dfrac{c_2^2 - c_1^2}{2} = (P_1 v_1 - P_2 v_2) + \dfrac{1}{r - 1}\,(P_1 v_1 - P_2 v_2)$

Chp 3 | 3.29

(In expression $\dfrac{c_v}{c_p - c_v}$, dividing numerator and denominator by c_v).

$\therefore$
$$\frac{c_2^2 - c_1^2}{2} = (P_1v_1 - P_2v_2)\left[1 - \frac{1}{\gamma - 1}\right]$$

$\therefore$
$$\frac{c_2^2 - c_1^2}{2} = (P_1v_1 - P_2v_2)\left(\frac{\gamma}{\gamma - 1}\right)$$

If the velocity of approach c_1 is neglected,

$$\frac{c_2^2}{2} = (P_1v_1 - P_2v_2)\frac{\gamma}{\gamma - 1}$$

$\therefore$
$$c_2 = \sqrt{\frac{2 \cdot \gamma}{\gamma - 1}(P_1v_1 - P_2v_2)}$$

$\therefore$
$$c_2 = \sqrt{2 \cdot \frac{\gamma}{\gamma - 1} \cdot P_1v_1\left(1 - \frac{P_2v_2}{P_1v_1}\right)}$$

As
$$P_1v_1^\gamma = P_2v_2^\gamma$$

$\therefore$
$$\frac{v_2}{v_1} = \left(\frac{P_2}{P_1}\right)^{-1/\gamma}$$

Substituting for $\dfrac{v_2}{v_1}$,

We get,
$$c_2 = \sqrt{2 \cdot \frac{\gamma}{\gamma - 1}P_1v_1\left\{1 - \left(\frac{P_2}{P_1}\right)^{\frac{\gamma - 1}{\gamma}}\right\}} \qquad \text{... (3.34)}$$

$$\text{Mass flow rate in kg/sec.} = \frac{\text{Area} \times \text{Velocity}}{\text{Specific volume}}$$

Hence, the mass flow rate in kg/sec. when the fluid flows through cross-sectional area A_2 and where specific volume of fluid is v_2 is given by,

$$m = \sqrt{2\frac{\gamma}{\gamma - 1}P_1v_1\left\{1 - \left(\frac{P_2}{P_1}\right)^{\frac{\gamma - 1}{\gamma}}\right\}} \qquad \text{... (3.35)}$$

We will convert this expression in terms of P_1v_1, A_2 and ratio $\dfrac{P_1}{P_2}$ which are known *quantities*.

Now,
$$P_1v_1^\gamma = P_2v_2^\gamma$$

$\therefore$
$$\left(\frac{v_2}{v_1}\right)^\gamma = \frac{P_1}{P_2}$$

$\therefore$
$$\frac{v_2}{v_1} = \left(\frac{P_1}{P_2}\right)^{1/\gamma}$$

$$\therefore \qquad v_2 = v_1 \left(\frac{P_1}{P_2}\right)^{1/\gamma} = v_1 \left(\frac{P_1}{P_2}\right)^{-1/\gamma}$$

Substituting this value of v_2 in equation (3.35), we get,

$$m = \frac{A_2}{v_1}\left(\frac{P_1}{P_2}\right)^{1/\gamma} \sqrt{2 \cdot \frac{\gamma}{\gamma - 1} P_1 v_1 \left\{1 - \left(\frac{P_2}{P_1}\right)^{\frac{\gamma-1}{\gamma}}\right\}}$$

$$= A_2 \sqrt{2 \cdot \frac{\gamma}{\gamma - 1} \cdot P_1 v_1 \left(\frac{P_2}{P_1}\right)^{\frac{2}{\gamma}} \cdot \frac{1}{v_1^2}\left\{1 - \left(\frac{P_2}{P_1}\right)^{\frac{\gamma-1}{\gamma}}\right\}}$$

$$= A_2 \sqrt{2 \cdot \frac{P_1}{v_1} \cdot \frac{\gamma}{\gamma - 1} \left\{\left(\frac{P_2}{P_1}\right)^{\frac{2}{\gamma}} - \left(\frac{P_2}{P_1}\right)^{\frac{\gamma+1}{\gamma}}\right\}} \qquad \text{... (3.36)}$$

This is a very important relation which gives mass flow rate in kg/sec. in terms of known quantities P_1, P_2, v_1 and A_2.

3.11 CONDITIONS FOR MAXIMUM DISCHARGE THROUGH NOZZLE

Nozzles are always designed for maximum discharge conditions. The maximum discharge condition determines the pressure at throat and area at throat. The pressure and volume at entry are constant and, considering maximum discharge conditions, pressure and volume at throat are determined.

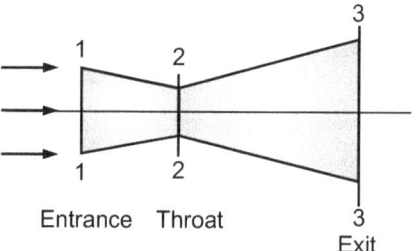

Fig. 3.9: Nozzle

In the expression, $\qquad m = A_2 \sqrt{\dfrac{P_1}{v_1}\dfrac{\gamma}{\gamma - 1}\left\{\left(\dfrac{P_2}{P_1}\right)^{\frac{2}{\gamma}} - \left(\dfrac{P_2}{P_1}\right)^{\frac{\gamma+1}{\gamma}}\right\}}$

P_1, v_1 and γ are all constants so the mass flow rate per unit area is dependent on ratio $\dfrac{P_2}{P_1}$ where, P_2 is the pressure at throat and P_1 is pressure at entrance.

Hence there is only one value of $\dfrac{P_2}{P_1}$ which will give maximum discharge.

Hence differentiating the term $\left\{\left(\dfrac{P_2}{P_1}\right)^{\frac{2}{\gamma}} - \left(\dfrac{P_2}{P_1}\right)^{\frac{\gamma+1}{\gamma}}\right\}$ with respect to $\dfrac{P_2}{P_1}$ and equating it to zero

will give the value of $\dfrac{P_2}{P_1}$ at which discharge will be maximum.

$$\therefore \qquad \frac{d}{d\left(\dfrac{P_2}{P_1}\right)}\left\{\left(\frac{P_2}{P_1}\right)^{\frac{2}{\gamma}} - \left(\frac{P_2}{P_1}\right)^{\frac{\gamma+1}{\gamma}}\right\} = 0$$

$$\therefore \qquad \frac{2}{\gamma}\left(\frac{P_2}{P_1}\right)^{\frac{2}{\gamma}-1} - \frac{\gamma+1}{\gamma}\left(\frac{P_2}{P_1}\right)^{\frac{\gamma+1}{\gamma}} = 0$$

$\therefore$ Simplifying, $\dfrac{P_c}{P_1} = \dfrac{P_2}{P_1} = \left(\dfrac{2}{\gamma+1}\right)^{\frac{\gamma}{\gamma-1}}$ ... (3.37)

$$\therefore \qquad P_2 = P_1\left(\frac{2}{\gamma+1}\right)^{\frac{\gamma}{\gamma-1}} = P_c \qquad\qquad \text{... (3.38)}$$

This is known as critical pressure which gives maximum discharge and $\dfrac{P_c}{P_1} = \left(\dfrac{2}{\gamma+1}\right)^{\frac{\gamma}{\gamma-1}}$ is

called critical pressure ratio.

3.12 CRITICAL TEMPERATURE RATIO

This is the ratio of temperature at throat and at entrance for maximum discharge condition.
Let T_c be the temperature at throat and T_1 be the temperature at entrance.

For maximum discharge, $\dfrac{P_c}{P_1} = \left(\dfrac{2}{\gamma+1}\right)^{\frac{\gamma}{\gamma-1}}$

Now, general relation between pressure and temperature for an ideal gas is,

$$\frac{T_c}{T_1} = \left(\frac{P_c}{P_1}\right)^{\frac{\gamma}{\gamma-1}}$$

Substituting $\dfrac{P_c}{P_1} = \left(\dfrac{2}{\gamma+1}\right)^{\frac{\gamma}{\gamma-1}}$ in the above equation, we get,

$$\frac{T_c}{T_1} = \left[\left(\frac{2}{\gamma+1}\right)^{\frac{\gamma}{\gamma-1}}\right]^{\frac{\gamma-1}{\gamma}} = \frac{2}{\gamma+1} \qquad\qquad \text{... (3.39)}$$

The ratio $\dfrac{T_c}{T_1}$ is called *critical temperature ratio*.

3.13 FLOW OF STEAM THROUGH NOZZLE

The expression for critical pressure and maximum discharge derived earlier apply to perfect gas and not vapours. This is due to the fact that in case of vapours the exponent of expansion is no longer constant but depends upon initial and final states of vapour.

Close approximation is achieved for expansion of steam through nozzle if the expansion is assumed to follow the law $Pv^n = C$.

1. For steam initially superheated, $n = 1.3$.
2. For steam initially dry saturated, $n = 1.135$.
3. For steam initially wet with dryness fraction 'X', $n^* = 1.035 + X(0.10)$

    * This is known as Zeuner's equation.

Using these values of n, we can write expression of critical pressure ratios as under:

1. For superheated steam,

$$\frac{P_c}{P_1} = \left(\frac{2}{1.3 + 1}\right)^{\frac{1.3}{0.3}} = 0.546 \qquad\qquad \ldots (3.40)$$

2. For dry saturated steam,

$$\frac{P_c}{P_1} = \left(\frac{2}{1.135 + 1}\right)^{\frac{1.135}{1.135 - 1}} = 0.578$$

3. For wet steam, $\qquad\qquad n = 1.035 + (0.6)(0.1)$

$$\left(\begin{array}{c}\text{Say with dryness}\\ \text{fraction} = 0.6\end{array}\right) = 1.095$$

$$\frac{P_c}{P_1} = \left(\frac{2}{1.095 + 1}\right)^{\frac{1.095}{1.095 - 1}} = (0.9546)^{11.52} = 0.585$$

3.14 EFFECT OF FRICTION ON NOZZLE EFFICIENCY

When the steam expands through the nozzle, there is friction present which will increase entropy and process cannot be expressed by a vertical line on enthalpy-entropy diagram.

The friction is between steam and inner surface of the nozzle.

Consider expansion of steam. The expansion without friction is expressed by AB and expansion with friction is expressed by AB'. During expansion AB', entropy increases.

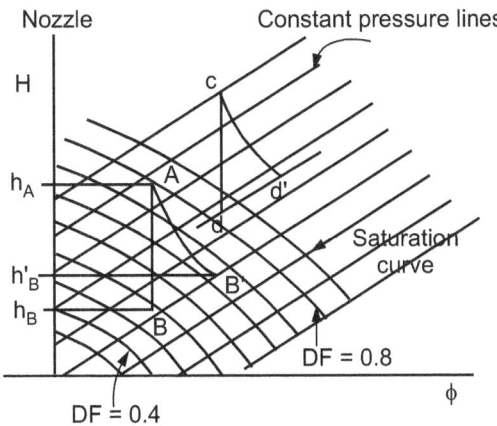

Fig. 3.10: Flow with friction

3.15 EFFECTS OF FRICTIONAL LOSSES

(I)   During expansion with friction from A to B',

Enthalpy drop $= h_A - h_B'$

During expansion without friction from A to B,

Enthalpy drop $= h_A - h_B$

Hence reduction in enthalpy drop due to friction $= h_{B'} - h_B$.

(II) When the expansion takes place with friction, the heat due to friction is utilized in heating the steam. As such steam which is wet, its dryness fraction improves. Steam which is dry saturated gets superheated and for superheated steam its temperature increases.

(III) When steam expands with friction its dryness fraction improves which in turn increases its volume as compared with volume during expansion without friction. All these observations can be better understood with the help of H-S or Mollier chart.

3.16 NOZZLE EFFICIENCY

The nozzle efficiency can be explained as, it is the efficiency with which pressure energy can be converted into kinetic energy.

$$\text{Nozzle efficiency (Referring to Fig. 3.10)} = \frac{\text{Actual enthalpy drop}}{\text{Theoretical enthalpy drop}}$$

$$H_A = \frac{h_A - h_{B'}}{h_A - h_B} \qquad \dots (3.42)$$

3.17 VELOCITY COEFFICIENT

It is defined as the ratio of actual exit velocity to *isentropic velocity for the same pressure drop.*

$$\therefore \qquad \text{Velocity coefficient} = \frac{\text{Actual velocity}}{\text{Isentropic velocity}} = \frac{44.7\sqrt{h_A - h_B{'}}}{44.7\sqrt{h_A - h_B}} = \sqrt{\frac{h_A - h_B{'}}{h_A - h_B}}$$

But $\dfrac{h_A - h_B{'}}{h_A - h_B}$ is nozzle efficiency.

$$\therefore \qquad \text{Velocity coefficient} = \sqrt{\text{Nozzle efficiency}}$$

3.18 COEFFICIENT OF DISCHARGE

It is defined as *actual discharge in kg per second divided by discharge in kg/sec. when the expansion is isentropic.*

$$\text{Coefficient of discharge} = \frac{m_{actual}}{m_{isentropic}} \qquad\qquad \text{... (3.44)}$$

3.19 VARIATION OF VELOCITY, AREA AND SPECIFIC VOLUME

We can plot the graph of nozzle length versus specific volume, velocity, nozzle area in the following manner.

Assumptions:

(i)   The inlet conditions are fixed.

(ii)   The process of expansion of fluid is known.

From this we can find enthalpy with the help of Mollier chart or using process equations. Then specific volume of the fluid can be calculated at any section.

As you know discharge and specific volume, cross-sectional area of the nozzle at any section can be calculated.

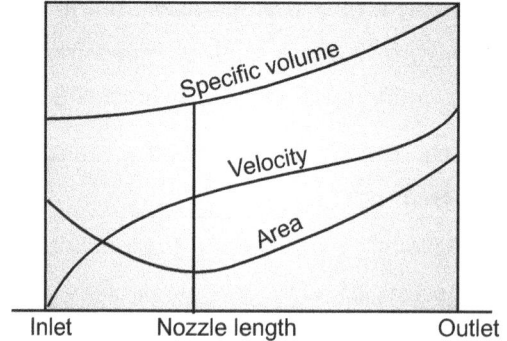

Fig. 3.11: Nozzle length Vs. Specific volume, area and velocity

The velocity can be calculated by using equation (3.33).

Area and specific volume can be calculated as described above.

Hence, we can plot graphs of nozzle length versus specific volume, velocity, area.

Important Observations:
1. Velocity increases continuously from inlet to outlet. This is obvious as pressure energy is converted into kinetic energy.
2. The rate of increase of specific volume is gradual.

3.20 CHOCKING OF NOZZLES AND GENERAL COMMENTS

The application of nozzle is to convert pressure energy into kinetic energy and we require flow of steam to attain supersonic velocity as it enters the turbine. The initial velocity of steam as it comes out from the boiler is subsonic.

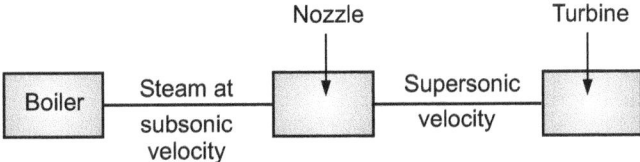

Fig. 3.12: Steam plant layout

We will study how to get this change by using nozzle. Let us consider any flow passage of varying sectional area in the direction of flow.

It is a duct with varying cross-sectional area which gives increase in velocity.

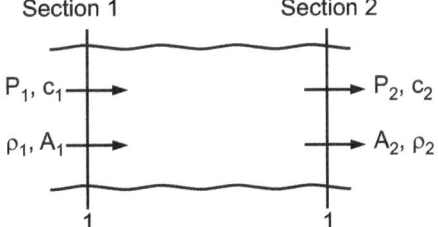

Fig. 3.13: Flow through duct

Consider section 1-1 and section 2-2 and applying continuity equation and using usual notation for P_1, c_1, ρ_1 and A_1, we get,

$$\rho_1 A_1 c_1 = \rho_2 A_2 c_2$$

Similarly, applying energy equation (3.30) to this flow,

$$\frac{c_1^2}{2} + z_1 \cdot g + h_1 + q = \frac{c_2^2}{2} + z_2 \cdot g + h_2 + w$$

As $z_1 = z_2$, and since no work is done, $w = 0$.

We get, $$\frac{c_1^2}{2} + h_1 + q = \frac{c_2^2}{2} + h_2$$

$\therefore$ $$q = \frac{c_2^2}{2} - \frac{c_1^2}{2} + h_2 - h_1$$

$\therefore$ $$dq = dK + dh$$

where, $$\frac{c_2^2}{2} - \frac{c_1^2}{2} = dK \text{ and } h_2 - h_1 = dh$$

$\therefore$ $$dq = dK + du + d\,(Pv)$$

$\therefore$ $$dq = dK + du + Pdv + vdP$$

But $$dq = du + Pdv$$

$\therefore$ $$du + Pdv = dK + du + Pdv + vdP$$

$\therefore$ $$0 = dK + vdP$$

$$\left(\text{Change in kinetic energy} = \frac{c_2^2}{2} \text{ neglecting } \frac{c_1^2}{2} \right)$$

The differential form, $$dK = \frac{2c}{2} \cdot dc = c\,dc$$

$\therefore$ $$0 = c\,dc + v\,dP$$

$\therefore$ $$c\,dc = -v\,dP \qquad\qquad \text{... (3.45 A)}$$

Now, consider continuity equation which is

$$\rho_1 A_1 c_1 = \rho_2 A_2 c_2 = \rho A C = \text{constant}$$

where, $$\rho = \text{Density, kg/m}^3$$
$$A = \text{Area, m}^2$$
$$c = \text{Velocity in m/sec.}$$

By partial differentiation, we get,

$$0 = \frac{1}{v} \cdot A\,dc + \frac{c}{v}\,dA - A\frac{c}{v^2} \cdot dv$$

Dividing both sides of this equation by $\dfrac{Ac}{v}$, we get,

$$0 = \frac{A\,dc}{v \cdot Ac} v + \frac{c}{v}\,dA \cdot \frac{v}{Ac} - \frac{Ac}{v^2} \cdot dv \cdot \frac{v}{Ac}$$

$$0 = \frac{dc}{c} + \frac{dA}{A} - \frac{dv}{v} \qquad\qquad \text{... (3.45 B)}$$

Now, substituting the value of dc from equation (3.45 B), we get,

$$0 = -\frac{v\,dP}{c} \cdot \frac{1}{c} + \frac{dA}{A} - \frac{dv}{v}$$

$\therefore$
$$0 = -\frac{v\,dP}{c^2} + \frac{dA}{A} - \frac{dv}{v}$$

$\therefore$
$$\frac{dA}{A} = \frac{dv}{v} + \frac{vdP}{c^2} = \frac{vdP}{c^2}\left[\frac{dv}{v}\cdot\frac{c^2}{vdP} + 1\right]$$

But
$$\frac{dv}{v^2 - dP} = -\frac{1}{(\text{sonic velocity})^2}$$

$$= -\frac{1}{a^2}\,(\text{From sonic velocity derivation})$$

where, a is the sonic velocity.

$\therefore$
$$\frac{dA}{A} = \frac{vdP}{c^2}\left[-\frac{c^2}{a^2} + 1\right]$$

$$= \frac{vdP}{c^2}\,[1 - M^2]$$

Substituting for vdP from equation (3.45 C), we get,

This is an important relation between velocity, area and acoustic velocity at any particular case.

Now,
$$M = \frac{\text{Velocity}}{\text{Velocity of sound}} = \text{Mach Number} = \frac{c}{a}$$

Case I:

If
$$M < 1 \text{ i.e. velocity is less than one mach number}$$
$$M^2 < 1 \text{ and } M^2 - 1 \text{ is negative.}$$

i.e.
$$\frac{dA}{A} = \frac{dc}{c}\,(\text{-ve quantity})$$

$\therefore$
$$\frac{dc}{c} = -\frac{dA}{A}$$

Now, if we want velocity to increase, $\frac{dc}{c}$ will be +ve and $\frac{dA}{A}$ will be negative. Therefore sectional area is decreasing in the direction of flow. Such a flow passage is called nozzle and the velocity is then sonic velocity, the nozzle is called subsonic nozzle.

In the subsonic nozzle the flow is accelerated while the area is reducing and the limit is that the velocity equal velocity of sound when M = 1.

Case II:

If
$$M > 1, \text{ i.e. the velocity is greater than sonic velocity}$$
$$M^2 > 1 \text{ and } M^2 - 1 \text{ is positive.}$$

i.e.
$$\frac{dA}{A} = \frac{dc}{c}\,(\text{+ve quantity})$$

$\therefore$
$$\frac{dc}{c} = +\frac{dA}{A}$$

Now, if we want velocity to increase, $\frac{dc}{c}$ will be +ve and $\frac{dA}{A}$ will be positive. Therefore sectional area is increasing in the direction of flow and such a passage is called diverging nozzle. Here supersonic flow is further accelerated and the nozzle is called supersonic nozzle.

Therefore subsonic nozzle will be accelerated to sonic velocity and it will be further accelerated to supersonic velocity. Thus, if a fluid with subsonic velocity enters convergent-divergent nozzle we will get supersonic velocity at the outlet.

Hence, following conclusions can be drawn,
1. For subsonic velocities (M < 1) dA and dc must be opposite in sign i.e. an increase of cross-sectional area causes a reduction of velocity and vice versa.
2. For supersonic velocities (M > 1) dA and dc are of same sign. An increase of cross-sectional area then causes an increase of velocity and vice versa.
3. When M = 1, dA must be zero and since the second derivative is positive, A must be minimum. Thus, if the velocity of flow equals the sonic velocity anywhere, it must be at minimum area which is throat.

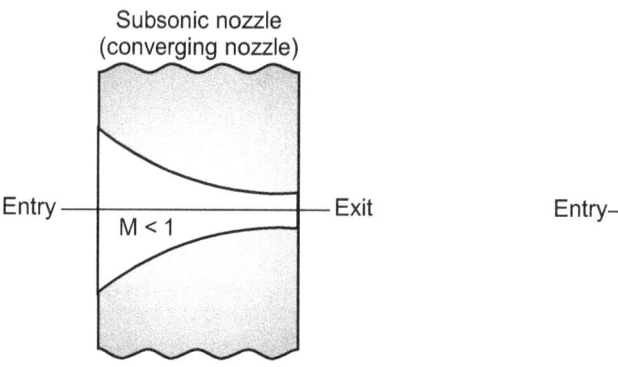

Fig. 3.14: Subsonic nozzle

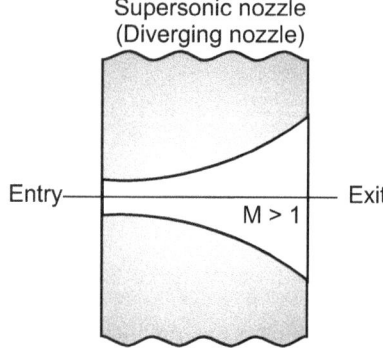

Fig. 3.15: Supersonic nozzle

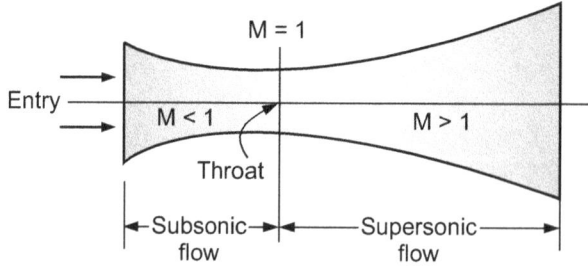

Fig. 3.16: Convergent-divergent nozzle

Nozzles are used for increasing the velocity of steam. At the exit of the boiler, velocity is negligible. Then steam passes through subsonic nozzle and its velocity increases to sonic velocity (M = 1) and it reaches throat. We still want higher velocity, hence divergent nozzle has to be used.

3.21 FLOW CHARACTERISTIC OF A NOZZLE AND CHOCKING OF NOZZLE

$$m = \text{Mass flow rate} = \frac{\text{Area} \times \text{Velocity}}{\text{Specific volume}} = \frac{Ac}{v}$$

Now,

$$\text{Velocity, } c = M \times a$$
$$= M \sqrt{\gamma \cdot R \cdot T}$$

and

$$\frac{1}{v} = \frac{P}{RT}$$

We get,

$$m = \frac{APM}{\sqrt{T}} \sqrt{\frac{\gamma}{R}}$$

For sonic velocity M = 1, pressure and temperature at the throat will have critical values. The critical values are

$$P_c = \left(\frac{2}{\gamma + 1}\right)^{\frac{\gamma}{\gamma - 1}} \cdot P_1$$

and

$$T_c = \left(\frac{2}{\gamma + 1}\right) T_1$$

Substituting these values in the above equation,

$$m = \frac{A \cdot \left(\dfrac{2}{\gamma + 1}\right)^{\frac{\gamma}{\gamma - 1}} \cdot P_1}{\sqrt{\dfrac{2}{\gamma + 1} \cdot T_1}} \sqrt{\frac{\gamma}{R}}$$

If R and y are fixed for a gas, mass flow is a function of upstream pressure and temperature only.

The mass flow rate increases as ratio $\dfrac{P_c}{P_1}$ increases. At throat $\dfrac{P_c}{P_1}$ = 0.528 for perfect gas, 0.546 for superheated steam, and 0.578 for dry saturated steam. When this ratio increases beyond this value, the mass flow starts decreasing and when this ratio is 1, i.e. when throat pressure is equal to inlet pressure the discharge is zero.

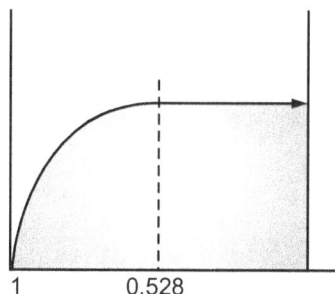

Fig. 3.17: Pressure ratio, $\dfrac{P_c}{P_1}$

The nozzles are always designed for maximum discharge and the discharge at point B is maximum and at this point the nozzle is said to be chocked. The discharge of nozzle cannot be more than this value.

3.22 BEHAVIOUR OF THE NOZZLE WHEN NOT OPERATING AT DESIGNED PRESSURE OR EFFECT OF CHANGE IN BACK PRESSURE ON NOZZLE PERFORMANCE

The nozzles are always designed for maximum discharge. When nozzle is used in an impulse turbine, inlet pressure is high. (Range 100 – 200 bar). The throat pressure for maximum discharge is critical pressure.

(P_c/P_1 = 0.546 or 0.578 etc.) The discharge pressure is condenser pressure of the turbine which is 0.1 to 0.5 bar. So the steam expands from 200 Bar to 0.1 Bar in a convergent-divergent nozzle.

It is interesting to know what happens to the flow of steam if exit/back pressure is not the designed pressure.

To study this, nozzle is connected to a very large reservouir at one end and to a vacuum pump at the other end. By means of vacuum pump, back pressure can be changed.

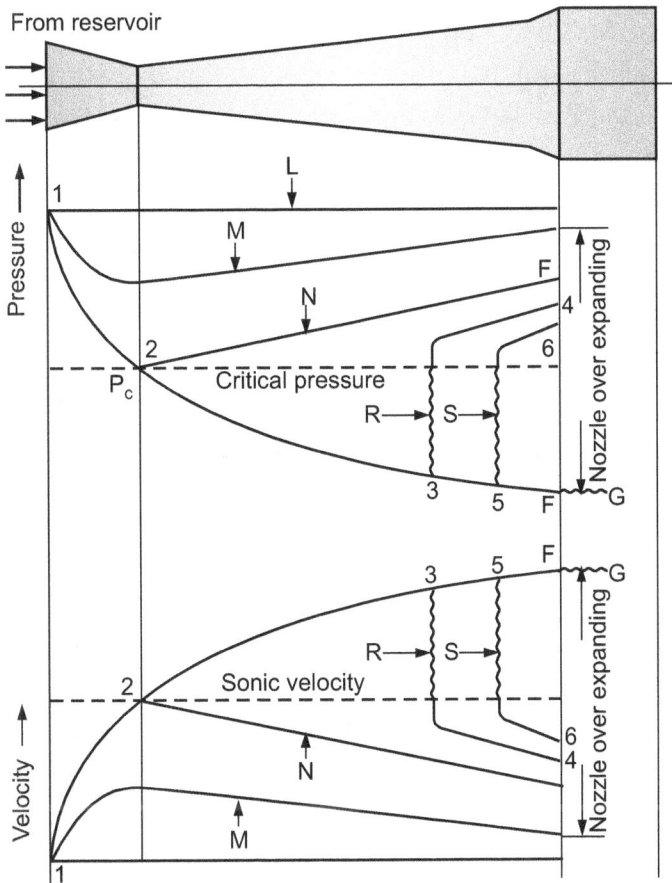

Fig. 3.18: Effect of back pressure on nozzle performance

1. **Condition L:** When the back pressure is equal to inlet pressure there will not be flow of steam.

2. **Condition M:** The discharge pressure is reduced to such a value that throat pressure is above critical pressure, the flow is entirely subsonic. The convergent-divergent nozzle performs like a venturi.

3. **Condition N:** Discharge pressure is such that, at throat velocity of steam is sonic and remains subsonic in divergent portion. Hence, in the convergent portion there is isentropic expansion to critical pressure and in divergent portion there is isentropic diffusion.

4. **Design Condition:** When the discharge pressure is equal to nozzle designed outlet pressure, there is steady acceleration in the entire passage. The velocity is subsonic in convergent portion and supersonic in divergent portion and pressure diagram is 1 – 2 – F and velocity diagram is 1 – 2 – F. This is an ideal condition.

5. **Condition R and S:** When due to any condition back pressure is above designed pressure, the expansion will be as shown in curve R and S and expansion takes place inside the nozzle. This is called over expanding nozzle. The expansion is with turbulence. The expansion curves are 1234 or 1256.

When due to any reason back pressure is below designed pressure, the expansion takes place as 1 FG and it is under expanding nozzle. The expansion takes place outside the nozzle in the passage connecting end of nozzle and intake of turbine and expansion is with turbulence.

The ideal expansion is as shown by curve 1 -- 2 – F.

3.23 SUPER SATURATED FLOW THROUGH STEAM NOZZLES

Consider expansion of steam in a nozzle from condition a to condition c. At a the steam is superheated at pressure P_1 and temperature T_a. As the steam expands from a to b the steam is cooled and at point b it is saturated. When steam expands from b to c, the temperature of steam drops down from T_b to T_c and steam becomes wet with a certain dryness fraction.

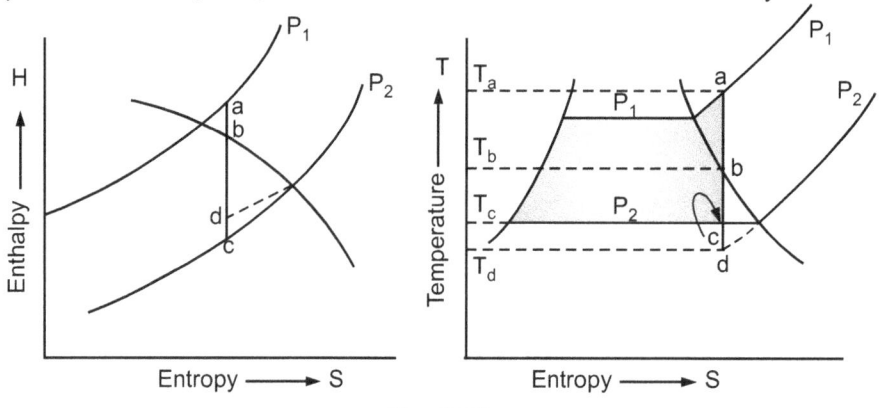

Fig. 3.19

The expansion of steam from A to B to C is expansion under thermal equilibrium.

However, in actual practice, the condensation of steam from b to c does not take place as steam has extremely less time available for condensation. If we consider that steam expands from point a to c, the time available is as small as $\frac{1}{10000}$th of a second and this time is not sufficient for steam to condense. Hence, instead of following the path abc, it follows the path abd. d is the point of intersection of ac and pressure line P_2 extended. At point V steam is not wet but in a gaseous form. Hence, it is not in equilibrium condition because at that temperature it should be partly wet.

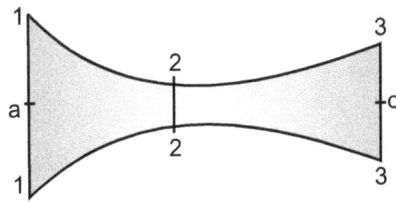

Fig. 3.20

Hence the expansion abd is non-equilibrium or metastable or supersaturated flow.
The temperature of steam will be T_d instead of T_c. As T_d is less than T_c, the steam is undercooled or supercooled.

Degree of undercooling: It is defined as difference between the saturation temperature corresponding to pressure P_2 and the actual temperature of the supersaturated vapour at point 'd'. $T_c - T_d$ is called degree of undercooling.
Degree of supersaturation: It is defined as the *ratio of actual pressure P_2 and the saturation pressure corresponding to actual temperature of the supersaturated vapour at point 'd'.*
These definitions will be clear when we solve a problem on supersaturated flow.

3.24 WILSON LINE

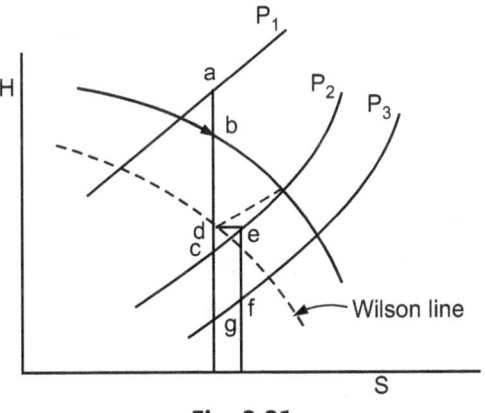

Fig. 3.21

There is however limit to the degree of undercooling and the limit of supersaturated flow is represented by WILSON LINE. That is supersaturated flow cannot continue beyond point d. At point 'd' the steam immediately comes back to pressure P_2 following the path de. Further expansion of the steam takes place like ef.
Hence supersaturated flow will be a b d e f.

Flow under thermal equilibrium will be abcg.

I.   Hence loss in heat drop = $H_f - H_g$

II.   Increase in entropy = $S_f - S_g$

During supersaturated adiabatic expansion of steam (bd), the steam vapour expands according to the law $Pv^{1.3}$ = constant i.e. as superheated steam.

SOLVED EXAMPLES

Example 3.17:

Steam enters a convergent-divergent nozzle at pressure of 22 bar and temperature of 300°C. the exit pressure is 4 bar. Steam flow rate is 11 kg/sec. Find (a) velocity of steam at throat and exit. (b) Area of nozzle at throat and exit in mm^2.

Solution:

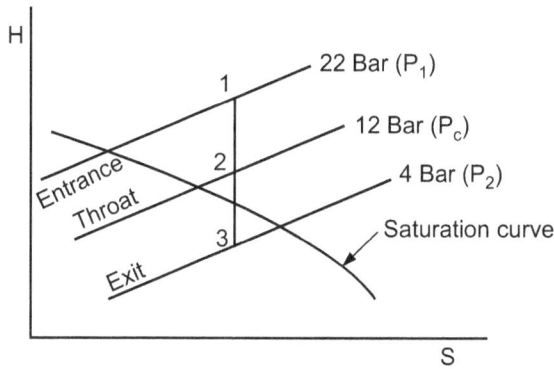

Fig. 3.22

From steam tables at pressure of 22 Bar, saturation temperature is 217.24°C. As the temperature of steam is 300°C, it is superheated.

Nozzles are always designed for maximum discharge and throat pressure P_c for superheated steam of maximum discharge will be $P_c = 0.546 \cdot P_1$.

$$\therefore \qquad P_c = (0.546)(22)$$
$$= 12.012 \text{ Bar}$$

From Mollier chart, $h_1 = 3019$ kJ/kg

$h_2 = 2890$ kJ/kg, Temp. 225°C

$h_3 = 2675$ kJ/kg, dryness fraction 0.97

1.   Velocity of throat $= 44.7 \sqrt{h_1 - h_2} = 44.7 \sqrt{3019 - 2890}$

$$= 507.69 \text{ m/sec.} \qquad \textbf{... Ans.}$$

2.   Velocity at exit $= 44.7 \sqrt{h_1 - h_3} = 44.7 \sqrt{3019 - 2675}$

$= 829.06$ m/sec.   ... **Ans.**

3.   Rate of discharge in kg/sec. $= \dfrac{Area \times Velocity}{Specific\ volume}$

At throat steam is superheated at 12 Bar pressure and 225°C temperature.

Specific volume in m³/kg $= v_{sup} = v_{sat} \dfrac{T_{sup}}{T_{sat}}$

$= (0.1632) \left(\dfrac{225 + 273}{187.96 + 273} \right)$

$= (0.1632)\ (1.080)$

$= 0.1763$ m³/kg

Discharge $= \dfrac{Area \times Velocity}{Specific\ volume}$

∴   Area $= \dfrac{Discharge \times Specific\ volume}{Velocity}$

$= \dfrac{(11)\ (0.1763)}{507.69}$ m²

$= 38198.85$ mm²   ... **Ans.**

At exit steam is wet at a pressure of 4 Bar and dryness fraction 0.97.

Specific volume in m³/kg $= (X\ v_g) = (0.97 \times 0.4622)$

$= 0.4483$ m³/kg

$= 0.4483$ m³/kg

Area at exit $\dfrac{(11)\ (0.4483)}{829.06} = 5948.06$ mm²   ... **Ans.**

Example 3.18:

Steam which is at a pressure of 3 Bar and dry saturated expands in a convergent nozzle to a pressure of 2 Bar. The area of throat is 3 cm². Neglecting approach velocity, calculate the exit velocity and mass flow rate if

(a) Equilibrium flow is assumed

(b) Supersaturated flow is assumed.

Also calculate degree of supersaturation.

Solution: (a) Equilibrium flow:

Note: Remember that nozzle is convergent and as throat pressure is 0.66 times initial pressure, maximum discharge conditions do not apply.

From steam tables, $h_1 = 2724.7$ kJ/kg

$S_1 = S_g = 6.9909$ kJ/kg/K

As flow is isentropic to 2 Bar,

$$S_1 = S_2 = 6.9909 = S_f + X (S_{fg}) = 1.5301 + X_2 (5.597)$$

$$\therefore \qquad X_2 = 0.9756$$

$$h_2 = h_f + X_2 (h_{fg})$$

$$= 504.7 + (0.9756) (2201.6)$$

$$= 2652.58 \text{ kJ/kg}$$

$$v_2 = X_2 v_g = (0.9756) (0.8854) = 0.8637 \text{ m}^3/\text{kg}$$

$$c_2 = 44.7 \sqrt{(h_1 - h_2)} = 44.7 \sqrt{(2724.7 - 2652.58)}$$

$$= 379.6 \text{ m/sec}$$

$$\text{Mass flow rate in kg/sec.} = \frac{\text{Area} \times \text{Velocity}}{\text{Specific volume}} = \frac{3 \times 10^{-4} \times 379.6}{0.8637}$$

$$= 0.1318 \text{ kg/sec.} \qquad \qquad \textbf{... Ans.}$$

(b) Supersaturated flow:

For supersaturated flow the fluid behave like gas and expansion takes place as per law

$$(P_1 v_1^{1.3}) = (P_2 v_2^{1.3})$$

$$\therefore \qquad [(3 \times 100) (0.6055)^{1.3}] = [(2 \times 100) (v_2)^{1.3}]$$

$$\therefore \qquad v_2 = 0.6055 \left(\frac{3}{2}\right)^{\frac{1}{1.3}} = (0.6055) (1.5)^{0.7692}$$

$$= 0.8271 \text{ m}^3/\text{kg}$$

$$\therefore \qquad c_2 = \sqrt{2 \cdot \frac{n}{n-1} P_1 v_1 \left\{ 1 - \left(\frac{P_2}{P_1}\right)^{\frac{n-1}{n}} \right\}}$$

$$= \sqrt{2 \times \frac{1.3}{1.3 - 1} \times 3 \times 10^5 \times 0.6055 \times \left\{ 1 - \left(\frac{2}{3}\right)^{\frac{0.3}{1.3}} \right\}}$$

$$= \sqrt{15.7 \times 10^5 (1 - 0.910)} = 373.8 \text{ m/sec.}$$

$$\text{Mass flow rate, m} = \frac{A_2 c_2}{v_2} = \frac{(3) (10)^{-4} (373.8)}{0.8271} = 0.135 \text{ kg/sec.}$$

From the steam tables saturation temperature at 3 Bar is 133.54°C and as steam expands as per law $Pv^{1.3} = c$,

$$T_2 = T_1 \left(\frac{P_2}{P_1}\right)^{\frac{1.3-1}{1.3}} = (133.54 + 273) \left(\frac{2}{3}\right)^{\frac{0.3}{1.3}}$$

$$= 369.95 \text{ K} = 96.95°C$$

From the steam tables at 96.95°C, saturation pressure is 0.9094 Bar (Use temperature tables).

$$\text{Degree of supersaturation} = \frac{2}{0.9094} = 2.199 \qquad \qquad \textbf{... Ans.}$$

Example 3.19:

Steam nozzle supplied with pressure of 7 Bar and 275°C discharges steam at 1 Bar. If the diverging portion of the nozzle is 60 mm long and the throat diameter is 5 mm, determine the cone angle of the divergent portion. Assume 10% of the total available enthalpy drop to be lost in friction in the divergent portion. Also determine the velocity and temperature of steam at the throat.

Solution:

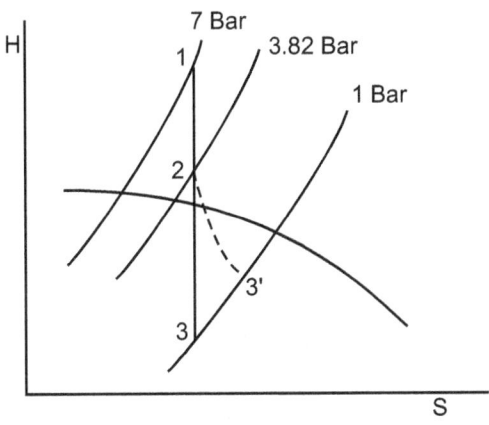

Fig. 3.23

The steam is initially superheated.

Throat pressure for maximum discharge = $P_c = 0.546\ P_1$

$$= (0.546)\ (7)$$

$$= 3.82\ \text{Bar}$$

From Moiller chart, $h_1 = 3000\ \text{kJ/kg}$

$h_2 = 2850\ \text{kJ/kg}$

$T_2 = 195°C$

∴ $h_1 - h_2 = 3000 - 2850 = 150\ \text{kJ/kg}$

At point 2, $V_{sup} = V_{sat} \dfrac{T_{sup}}{T_{sat}} = 0.485 \times \dfrac{195 + 273}{141.78 + 273}$

$$= 0.485 \times \dfrac{468}{414.78} = 0.5472\ \text{m}^3/\text{kg}$$

Velocity at throat = $c_2 = 44.7\ \sqrt{h_1 - h_2}$

$$= 44.7\ \sqrt{150}\ \text{m/sec}$$

$$= 547.46\ \text{m/sec.}$$ **... Ans.**

From Moiller chart, $h_3 = 2615\ \text{kJ/kg}$

$X_3 = 0.972$

Velocity at exit = $c_3 = 44.7\ \sqrt{(h_1 - h_3)\ (0.9)}$

$$= 44.7 \sqrt{(3000 - 2615)\,(0.9)}$$

$$= 831.86 \text{ m/sec.} \qquad \qquad \text{... Ans.}$$

[**Note:** When results are obtained by using Moiller chart, error will be about ± 5 percent]

Now, $\qquad$ Mass flow rate $= \dfrac{\text{Area} \times \text{Velocity}}{\text{Specific volume}}$

$$= \frac{\frac{\pi}{4} \cdot d^2 \times (547.46)}{0.5472} = \frac{(0.7854)\left(\frac{5}{1000}\right)^2 (547.46)}{0.5472}$$

$$= 0.01964 \text{ kg/sec.}$$

From this information we can calculate diameter at exit.

$$\text{Mass flow rate} = 0.01964 = \frac{\frac{\pi}{4} \cdot D^2 \times 831.86}{1.6937 \times 0.972}$$

$$\therefore \qquad \qquad 0.01964 = \frac{(0.7854)\,(D^2)\,(831.86)}{1.6937 \times 0.972}$$

$$\therefore \qquad \qquad D_3^2 = 4.948836 \times 10^{-5} \text{ m}^2$$

$$= 4.948836 \times 10^{-5} \times 10^6 \text{ mm}^2$$

$$= 49.448 \text{ mm}^2$$

$$\therefore \qquad \qquad D_3 = 7.034 \text{ mm}$$

$$\tan \theta = \frac{\dfrac{(7.034 - 5)}{2}}{60} = 0.01695$$

$$\therefore \qquad \qquad \theta = 0.97°$$

$$\therefore \qquad \text{Cone angle} = 2\theta = 0.97 \times 2 = 1.94° \qquad \qquad \text{... Ans.}$$

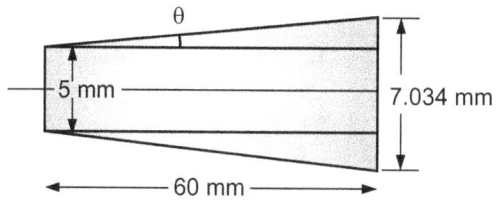

Fig. 3.24

Example 3.20:

Steam at a pressure of 10 Bar and 200°C expands in a convergent-divergent nozzle to a pressure of 0.1 Bar. The flow rate is 5 kg/min. The expansion is supersaturated upto throat and in the thermal equilibrium afterwards. Calculate (a) Diameter of nozzle at exit, (b) Degree of supersaturation, (c) Degree of undercooling at throat.

Solution:

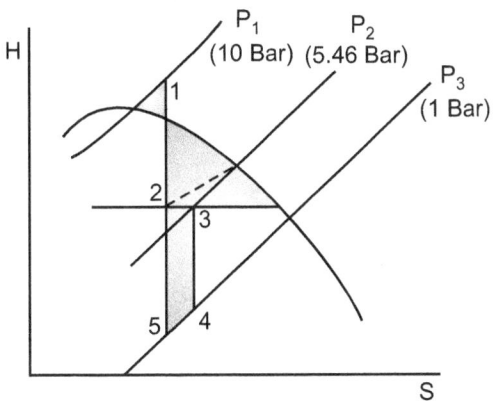

Fig. 3.25

The supersaturated expansion upto throat is 1 – 2.

The expansion in thermal equilibrium is 34.

From superheated steam tables at 10 Bar and 200°C,

$h_1 = 2826.8; v_1 = 0.2059$

Expansion 1 – 2 is as per law,

$$P_1 v_1^{1.3} = P_2 v_2^{1.3}$$

$$h_1 - h_2 = \frac{n}{n-1} \cdot P_1 v_1 \left[1 - \left(\frac{P_2}{P_1} \right)^{\frac{n-1}{n}} \right], \text{ take } n = 1.3.$$

$$= \frac{1.3}{1.3 - 1} \times 10 \times 100 \times 0.2059 \left[1 - \left(\frac{5.46}{10} \right)^{\frac{1.3-1}{1.3}} \right]$$

$$= 4.33 \times 1000 \times 0.2059 \, [1 - (0.546)^{0.23}]$$

$$= 4.33 \times 1000 \times 0.2059 \, (0.13) \text{ kJ/kg}$$

$$= 115.9 \text{ kJ/kg}$$

∴ $\qquad\qquad h_2 = 2826.8 - 115.9 = 2710.9$ kJ/kg

From Moiller chart, $\qquad h_4 = 2120$ kJ/kg, $X_4 = 0.807$

$$v_4 = v_g \times 0.807 = {}^*14.675 \times 0.807 = 11.84 \text{ m}^3/\text{kg}$$

(* This value is taken from steam tables).

$$\text{Velocity at exit} = c_4 = 44.7 \sqrt{h_1 - h_4}$$

$$= 44.7 \sqrt{2826.8 - 2120}$$

$$= 1188.12 \text{ m/sec.}$$

Now, for calculating diameter at exit, we will have to calculate area at exit.

$$\text{Mass flow rate in kg/sec.} = \frac{\text{Area} \times \text{Velocity}}{\text{Specific volume}}$$

$$\therefore \qquad \frac{5}{60} = \frac{\text{Area} \times 1188.12}{11.84}$$

$$\therefore \qquad \text{Area} = \frac{5 \times 11.84}{1188.12 \times 60} \, m^2 = 830.443 \, mm^2$$

$$\therefore \qquad d^2 = \frac{830.443}{0.7854} = 1057.35 \, mm^2 \qquad \text{... Ans.}$$

$$d = 32.51 \, mm$$

As 1-2 is supersaturated expansion, it follows the law $Pv^{1.3} = c$

$$\therefore \qquad \frac{T_2}{T_1} = \left(\frac{P_2}{P_1}\right)^{\frac{1.3-1}{1.3}}$$

$$\therefore \qquad T_2 = (200 + 273) \left(\frac{5.46}{10}\right)^{\frac{0.3}{1.3}} = (473)(0.87)$$

$$= 411.5°K = 138.54°C$$

The saturation temperature corresponding to pressure of 5.46 Bar is 154.76°C. (This value is taken from steam tables for pressure of 5.4 Bar).

$$\therefore \qquad \text{Degree of undercooling} = 154.76 - 138.54$$

$$= 16.22°C \qquad \text{... Ans.}$$

Degree of Supersaturation:

The pressure corresponding to temperature of 138.54°C is 3.45 Bar by interpolation (rough estimate).

$$\therefore \qquad \text{Degree of supersaturation} = \frac{\text{Pressure } P_2}{\text{Pressure corresponding to saturation temperature}}$$

$$= \frac{5.46}{3.45} = 1.582 \qquad \text{... Ans.}$$

(**Note:** As values are taken from Moiller diagram and exact values from steam tables are difficult to evaluate, approximation is ± 5%).

Example 3.21:

Steam is supplied through a group of six nozzles at 35 Bar and 300°C. The exit pressure is 3 Bar. The mass flow rate is 5.2 kg/sec. The flow is supersaturated. Determine:

1. Exit area and diameter for circular cross-section.

2. Enthalpy loss due to supersaturation.

3. Mass flow rate increase due to supersaturation.

Solution:

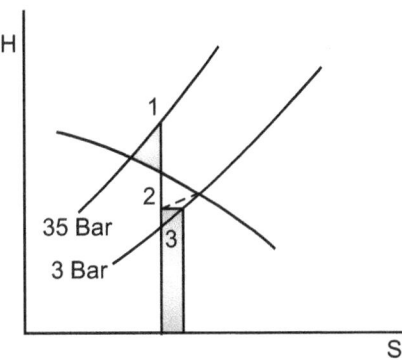

Fig. 3.26

$$P_1 = 35 \text{ bar, } t_1 = 300°C$$
$$P_2 = 3 \text{ bar}$$

From steam tables,

$$h_1 = 2978.9 \text{ kJ/kg}$$
$$v_1 = 0.06848 \text{ m}^3/\text{kg}$$
$$s_1 = 6.4492 \text{ kJ/kgK}$$

The expansion 1-2 is supersaturated flow according to the law $P_1 v_1^{1.3} = P_2 v_2^{1.3}$

$$\therefore \qquad \frac{v_2}{v_1} = \left(\frac{P_1}{P_2}\right)^{1/n}$$

$$\therefore \qquad \frac{v_2}{v_1} = \left(\frac{35}{3}\right)^{1/1.3} = (11.66)^{0.7692} = 6.6146$$

$$\therefore \qquad v_2 = v_1 \times 6.6146 = (0.06849 \times 6.6146)$$

$$= 0.453 \text{ m}^3/\text{kg}$$

$$h_1 - h_2 = \frac{n}{n-1}[P_1 v_1 - P_2 v_2]$$

$$= \frac{1.3}{1.3-1}[35 \times 100 \times 0.06849 - 3 \times 100 \times 0.453]$$

$$= 4.33 [239.715 - 135.9]$$

$$= 449.518 \text{ kJ/kg}$$

$$c_2 = 44.7 \sqrt{449.518} = 947.64 \text{ m/sec.}$$

$$\text{Mass flow rate} = \frac{A_2 c_2}{v_2} = \frac{A_2 \times 947.64}{0.453} = \frac{5.2}{6}$$

$\therefore$ $\qquad$ $A_2 = \dfrac{(5.2)\,(0.453)}{(6)\,(947.64)}\ m^2 = 414.29\ mm^2$

$\therefore$ $\qquad$ $\dfrac{\pi}{4} D_2^2 = 414.29$

$\therefore$ $\qquad$ $D_2 = 22.97\ mm$ $\qquad\qquad\qquad$ **... Ans.**

When the flow is in equilibrium by using Moiller chart,

$\qquad\qquad$ $h_3 = 2505\ kJ/kg$

and $\qquad\qquad$ $h_2 = h_1 - 449.518 = 2529.38\ kJ/kg$

Loss of enthalpy due to supersaturation

$\qquad\qquad$ $= h_2 - h_3 = 2529.38 - 2505$

$\qquad\qquad$ $= 24.38\ kJ/kg$ $\qquad\qquad\qquad$ **... Ans.**

Increase in mass flow rate due to supersaturation:

Mass flow rate under equilibrium condition has to be calculated.

$\qquad$ $\dfrac{\text{Mass flow rate}}{\text{(Equilibrium condition)}} = \dfrac{\text{Area} \times \text{Velocity}}{\text{Specfic volume}}$ $\qquad$ Here $A_3 = A_2$

$\qquad\qquad$ $= \dfrac{414.29 \times 10^{-6} \times 44.7\,\sqrt{2978.9 - 2505}}{0.9 \times 0.60556}$

(Dryness fraction from Mollier chart, specific volume of dry saturated steam is from steam tables).

$\qquad\qquad$ $= \dfrac{414.29 \times 10^{-6} \times 44.7 \times 21.76}{0.545}\ kg/sec.$

$\dfrac{\text{Mass flow rate}}{\text{(Equilibrium condition)}} = 0.7393\ kg/sec.$

$\dfrac{\text{Mass flow ratw}}{\text{(Supersaturated condition)}} = \dfrac{5.2}{6} = 0.8666\ kg/sec.$

$\therefore$ $\qquad\qquad$ % increase $= \dfrac{0.8666 - 0.7393}{0.7393} \times 100 = 17.21\%$ $\qquad$ **... Ans.**

Example 3.22:

Dry saturated steam is expanded in a nozzle from a pressure of 10 Bar to a pressure of 4 Bar. If the expansion is supersaturated, find:

1.　The degree of undercooling

2.　The degree of supersaturation

Solution:

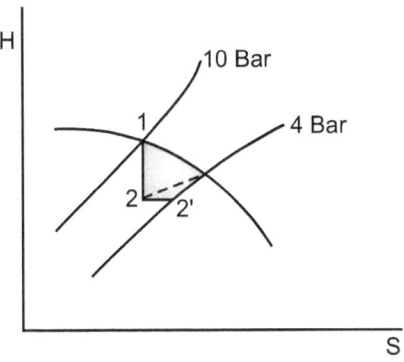

Fig. 3.27

The expansion 1-2 is supersaturated, hence it is according to the equation

$$Pv^{1.3} = \text{Constant}$$

$$\therefore \qquad P_1 v_1^{1.3} = P_2 v_2^{1.3}$$

$$\therefore \qquad \frac{T_1}{T_2} = \left(\frac{P_1}{P_2}\right)^{\frac{1.3-1}{1.3}}$$

$$= \left(\frac{10}{4}\right)^{0.23}$$

$$= 1.234$$

$$\therefore \qquad T_2 = \frac{T_1}{1.234} = \frac{179.88 + 273}{1.234} = 367K = 94°C$$

$$\therefore \qquad \text{Degree of undercooling} = \frac{\text{Saturation temperature}}{\text{corresponding to pressure 4 Bar}} - \frac{\text{Actual}}{\text{temperature}}$$

$$= 143.62 - 94 = 49.62°C \qquad \qquad \text{... Ans.}$$

Now, saturation pressure corresponding to temperature of 94°C is 0.8146 Bar.

$$\therefore \qquad \text{Degree of supersaturation} = \frac{\text{Actual pressure}}{\substack{\text{Saturation pressure corresponding} \\ \text{to actual temperature}}}$$

$$= \frac{4}{0.8146} = 4.91 \qquad \qquad \text{... Ans.}$$

Example 3.23:

Steam enters the nozzle of an impulse turbine at 10 Bar and 250°C and leaves at 1 Bar. The turbine develops 225 kW with specific steam consumption of 16. If the throat diameter is 8 mm find the number of nozzles and the exit diameter, assuming that 10% of the total enthalpy drop is lost in overcoming friction in the divergent portion only. Neglect velocity of approach.

Solution:

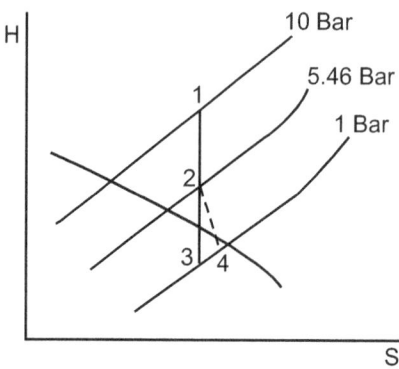

Fig. 3.28

The steam is initially superheated. Hence, assuming maximum discharge condition,
$$P_2 = 0.546, P_1 = 5.46 \text{ Bar}$$
From steam tables, for 10 Bar and 250°C temperature,
$$h_1 = 2943 \text{ kJ/kg}$$
$$s_1 = 6.9259 \text{ kJ/kgK}$$

$$s_1 = s_2 = s_g + c_p ln \frac{T_{sup}}{T_{sup}}$$

$$6.9259 = 6.7870 + 2.1 \, ln \frac{T_{sup}}{155.46 + 273}$$

∴ $$\frac{0.1389}{2.1} = ln \frac{T_{sup}}{155.46 + 273} = ln \frac{T_{sup}}{428.46}$$

∴ $$0.06614 = ln \frac{T_{sup}}{428.46}$$

∴ $$1.06837 = \frac{T_{sup}}{428.46}$$

∴ $$T_{sup} = 457.75K = T_2 = 184.75°C$$

Enthalpy at point 2 $$= h_2 = 2751.7 + 2.1 (184.75 - 155.46)$$
$$= 2813.2 \text{ kJ/kg}$$

Now,   velocity at 2 $$= c_2 = 44.7 \sqrt{h_1 - h_2} = 44.7 \sqrt{2943 - 2813.2}$$
$$= 509.13 \text{ m/sec.}$$

Specific volume at point 2 $$= v_2 = v_{sat} \cdot \frac{T_{sup}}{T_{sat}} = 0.3425 \times \frac{457.75}{428.46}$$
$$= 0.3659 \text{ m}^3/\text{kg}$$

Flow through the nozzle $$= \frac{\text{Area} \times \text{Velocity}}{\text{Specific volume}} = \frac{\frac{\pi}{4} \times (0.008)^2 \times 509.13}{0.3659} \text{ kg/sec.}$$
$$= 0.0699 \text{ kg/sec.}$$

The actual discharge $$= \frac{225 \times 16}{3600} \text{ kg/s} = 1 \text{ kg/sec.}$$

$$\text{Number of nozzles} = \frac{\text{Actual discharge in kg/sec.}}{\text{Discharge per nozzle/sec.}} = \frac{1}{0.0699} = 14.306$$

$$= 15 \text{ nozzles are required}$$

From steam tables,

$$s_3 = s_f + X s_{f_g}$$

$$s_3 = 1.3027 + X (6.0571)$$

But $\quad s_1 = s_2 = s_3 = 6.9259$

$\therefore \quad 6.9259 = 1.3027 + X (6.0571)$

$\therefore \quad X = \dfrac{6.9259 - 1.3027}{6.0571} = 0.928$

$\therefore \quad$ Enthalpy at point 3 $= h_f + X \cdot h_{f_g}$

$$= 417.51 + (0.928)(2257.9)$$

$$= 2512.84 \text{ kJ/kg}$$

Enthalpy drop in friction $= (0.1)(h_1 - h_3) = (0.1)(2943 - 2512.84)$

$$= 43.016 \text{ kJ/kg}$$

$\therefore \quad h_4 = h_3 + 43.016 = 2555.8 \text{ kJ/kg}$

$\therefore \quad$ Velocity at exit $= 44.7 \sqrt{h_1 - h_4} = 44.7 \sqrt{2943 - 2555.8}$

$$= 879.24 \text{ m/sec}$$

Now, $\quad$ Discharge per nozzle $= \dfrac{\text{Area} \times \text{Velocity}}{\text{Specific volume}}$

We will have to find condition of steam at point 4.

$$h_4 = 2555.8 = h_f + X h_{f_g} = 417.51 + X (2257.9)$$

$\therefore \quad X = \dfrac{2555.8 - 417.51}{2257.9} = 0.948$

$\therefore \quad 0.0699 = \dfrac{\text{Area} \times 879.24}{0.948}$

$\therefore \quad \text{Area} = \dfrac{(0.0699)(0.948)}{879.24} = 753.66 \text{ mm}^2 = \dfrac{\pi}{4} \cdot D_{exit}^2$

$\therefore \quad$ Diameter at exit $= 30.98 \text{ mm}$ $\qquad$ **... Ans.**

Example 3.24:

A steam nozzle admits steam at 7 bar and 275°C. The throat diameter is 5 mm. Expansion of steam upto throat is frictionless. The velocity at throat and exit are 533 m/sec. and 838 m/sec. respectively. The steam leaves the nozzle at 1 Bar. Determine:

1. Throat pressure
2. Exit diameter.

Solution: From Mollier diagram,

$$h_1 = 3010 \text{ kJ/kg}$$

Velocity at throat $= c_2 = 44.7 \sqrt{h_1 - h_2} = 533$

$\therefore \quad 533 = 44.7 \sqrt{3010 - h_2}$

$\therefore$ $\sqrt{3010 - h_2} = 11.92$

$\therefore$ $3010 - h_2 = 142$

$\therefore$ $h_2 = 3010 - 142 = 2868$ kJ/kg

$\therefore$ From Mollier chart, throat pressure = 4.1 Bar   **... Ans.**

Condition of steam at throat is superheated at 200°C.

$\therefore$

$$v_2 = v_{sat} \cdot \frac{T_{sup}}{T_{sat}}$$

$$= 0.45162 \times \frac{200 + 273}{144.52 + 273}$$

$$= 0.5112 \text{ m}^3\text{/kg}$$

Now, $c_3 = 44.7 \sqrt{h_1 - h_3}$

$\therefore$ $838 = 44.7 \sqrt{3010 - h_3}$

$\therefore$ $\dfrac{838}{44.7} = \sqrt{3010 - h_3} = 18.74$

$\therefore$ $3010 - h_3 = 351.18$

$\therefore$ $h_3 = 3010 - 351.18 = \mathbf{2658.82 \text{ kJ/kg}}$

Now, for 7 Bar and 275°C temperature, entropy of steam from steam tables = 7.2031 kJ/kgK

$\therefore$ $s_1 = 7.2031 = s_3 = s_f + X s_{f_g}$

$\therefore$ $7.2031 = 1.3027 + X \cdot 6.0571$

$\therefore$ $X = 0.974$

$\therefore$ $v_3 = X \cdot v_g = (0.974)(1.6937) = 1.649$ m^3/kg

For steady flow, $\dfrac{A_2 c_2}{v_2} = \dfrac{A_3 c_3}{v_3}$

$\therefore$

$$A_3 = \frac{A_2 c_2}{v_2} \cdot \frac{v_3}{c_3}$$

$$= \frac{\left(\frac{\pi}{4}\right)(0.005)^2 \times 533 \times 1.649}{0.5112 \times 838} \times 10^6$$

$$A_3 = 40.28 \text{ mm}^2 = \frac{\pi}{4} d_3^2$$

$\therefore$ $d_3 = 7.16$ mm   **... Ans.**

EXERCISE

1. What are static and stagnation properties? Explain.
2. Define acoustic velocity and derive the relation for acousting velocity in terms of absolute temperature and adiabatic index.
3. Explain with sketches the following:
   (a) Mach line, (b) Mach angle, (c) Mach cone and (d) Mach wave
4. What do you understand by 'the zone of silence' and 'zone of action'?

5. With usual notations derive the following relation for adiabatic flow

$$p_0 = p + \frac{\rho V^2}{2}\left[\frac{2}{KM^2} + \frac{M^2}{4} + \frac{2-K}{12} \cdot M^4 + \ldots\right]$$

EXAMPLES FOR PRACTICE

1. Steam at a pressure of 3 bar and 10°C superheat is passed through a convergent nozzle. The velocity of steam before entering the nozzle is 100 m/sec. The back pressure is 1.5 Bar. Assuming nozzle efficiency of 92% and specific heat of superheated steam as 2.3 kJ/kg. K, determine the area of nozzle at throat for a discharge of 0.45 kg/sec.

    [**Ans.** 10.509 cm^2]

2. Steam enters a group of convergent-divergent nozzles at a pressure of 2.2 MN/m^2 and with a temperature of 260°C, Equilibrium expansion through the nozzles to an exit pressure of 0.4 MN/m^2 takes place. Upto the throat of the nozzles the flow can be considered frictionless. From the throat to exit, however, there is an efficiency of expansion of 85%. The rate of steam flow through the nozzle is 11 kg/sec. Using enthalpy-entropy chart for steam, determine:
    (a) The throat and exit velocities.
    (b) The throat and exit areas.

    [**Ans.** 547.7 m/sec, 799.97 m/sec., 3210 mm^2, 6050 mm^2]

3. Steam expands through a convergent-divergent nozzle from 5 bar and dry saturated to a back pressure of 0.2 bar. Mass flow is 2 kg/sec. Calculate the exit and throat areas when the friction loss in the divergent part is 10% of the total heat drop. Neglect approach velocity.

    [**Ans.** Throat area = 33.74 cm^2, Exit area = 142.8 cm^2]

4. Dry saturated steam is expanded in a nozzle from a pressure of 10 Bar to a pressure of 5 Bar. If the expansion is supersaturated, find the degree of (i) undercooling, (ii) super-saturation.   [**Ans.** 39.8°C, 3.2]

5. Compare the mass of discharge from a CD nozzle expanding from 8 bar and 250°C to 2 bar absolute when (i) the expansion takes place under thermal equilibrium, (ii) metastable expansion.   [**Ans.** 2.37%]

6. The nozzles in the stage of an impulse turbine receive steam at 12 bar, superheat 62°C. The pressure in the wheel chamber is 4 bar. State whether the nozzle is convergent, divergent or convergent-divergent. Assuming negligible approach velocity and 10% frictional loss, suggest suitable number of nozzles to be used for a flow rate of 450 kg/min approximately with the exit area of 2.4 cm^2. Also find rate of discharge through the nozzles.

    [**Ans.** Convergent-divergent, number of nozzles = 24, 0.3125 kg/sec/nozzle]

UNIT IV

RECIPROCATING AIR COMPRESSOR

INTRODUCTION

An air compressor is a machine to compress the air and to raise its pressure. The air compressor sucks the air from the atmosphere, compresses it and then delivers the high pressure air to a storage vessel. From the storage vessel, it may be conveyed by the pipe line to a place where the supply of compressed air is required. Since process of compressing the air requires some work to be done on it, therefore, compressor must be driven by some prime mover.

The general arrangement of the compressor and prime mover used to run the compressor is shown in Fig. 4.1.

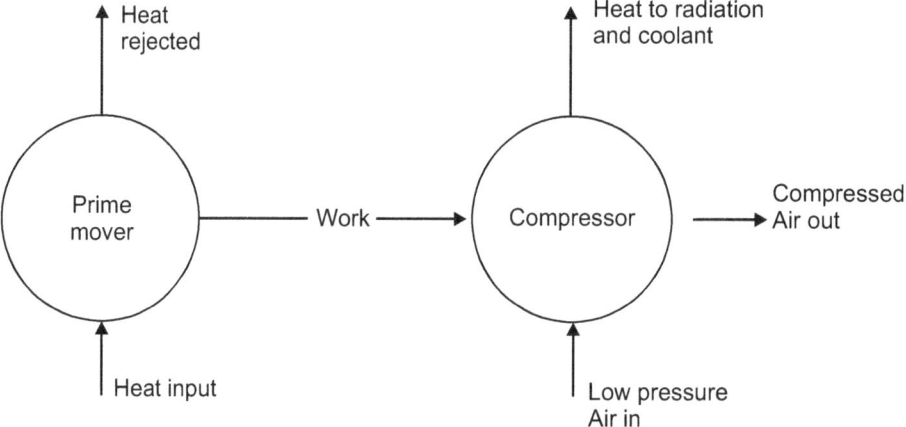

Fig. 4.1: General arrangement of prime mover and compressor

Part of the heat supplied to the prime mover (I.C. engine, steam engine is converted into work to drive the compressor. Some part of the work supplied to the compressor is lost in friction, heat radiation and to the coolant used to cool the compressor and the remaining is used to increase the pressure of the air. The compressor must be designed to use the maximum work supplied to increase the pressure of the air.

Uses of Compressed Air:

The compressed air has wide applications in industry as well as in commercial equipments, as listed below:

- In industry, it is used to blast sand and to clean the jobs in foundry.
- To operate revetting tools in aircraft industry,

- Spray painting,
- For starting and supercharging of I.C. engines, in gas turbine plants, jet engines and air motors,
- For driving pneumatic tools and air-operated controlling equipments etc.
- Chemical industries like fertilizer plant,
- In refrigeration systems, air conditioning, drying and ventilation fields.

Classification of Air Compressors:

The air compressors are classified into two main types:

1. Reciprocating compressors and
2. Rotary compressors.

4.1 SINGLE-STAGE RECIPROCATING COMPRESSOR

4.1.1 Working of Single-stage Reciprocating Compressor

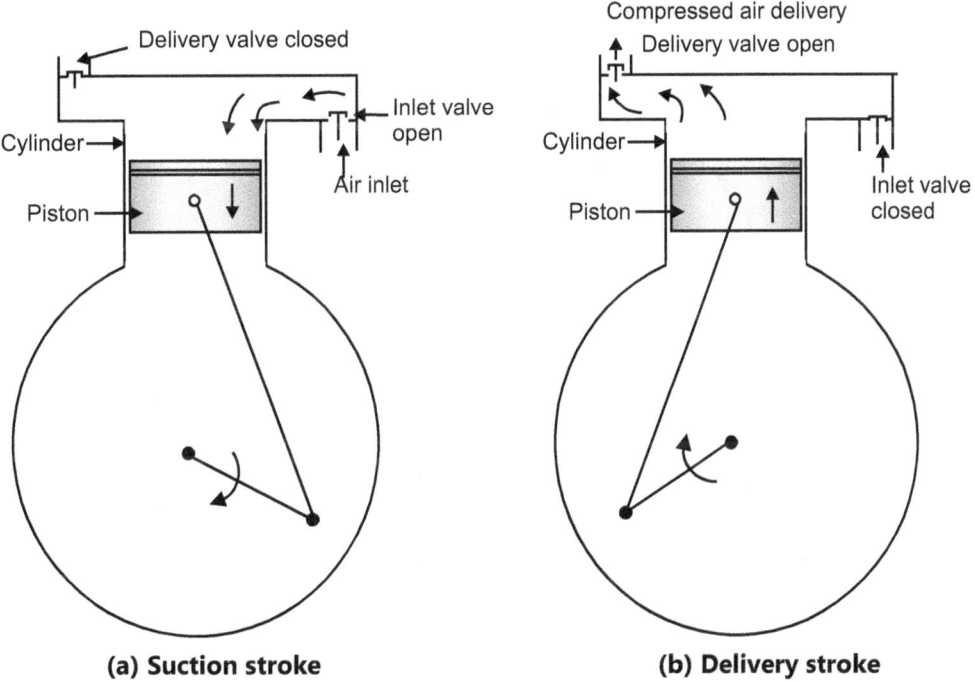

(a) Suction stroke   **(b) Delivery stroke**

Fig. 4.2: Single-stage reciprocating air compressor

- The single-stage reciprocating air compressor consists of a piston which reciprocates in a cylinder, driven through a connecting rod and crank mounted in a crank case.

- There are inlet and delivery valves mounted in the head of the cylinder. These valves are usually of the pressure differential type, operates as a result of the pressure difference across the valve.
- As shown in Fig. 4.2 (a), the downward movement of piston in the cylinder causes pressure drop in the cylinder below the atmospheric pressure. The inlet valve is opened due to pressure difference. The air is taken into the cylinder until the piston reaches bottom dead centre position.
- As shown in Fig. 4.2 (b), the piston is now moving upwards. A slight increase in cylinder pressure will close the inlet valve. The pressure starts increasing continuously until the pressure inside the cylinder is above the pressure of the delivery side which is connected to the receiver. Then the delivery valve opens and compressed air is delivered during the remaining upward motion of the piston to the receiver.
- At the end of delivery stroke, small volume of high pressure air is left in the clearance space. This air expands as the piston starts moving downwards and pressure of the air falls until it is just below the atmospheric pressure. This causes opening of inlet valve and entry of atmospheric air in the cylinder and the cycle is repeated. The suction, compression and delivery of the air take place within two strokes of the piston or one revolution of the crank.
- There is intermittent flow of air in a reciprocating air compressor.

4.1.2 Computation of Work Done (Neglecting Clearance)

Fig. 4.3 shows a theoretical p-V diagram for a single-stage reciprocating compressor neglecting clearance.

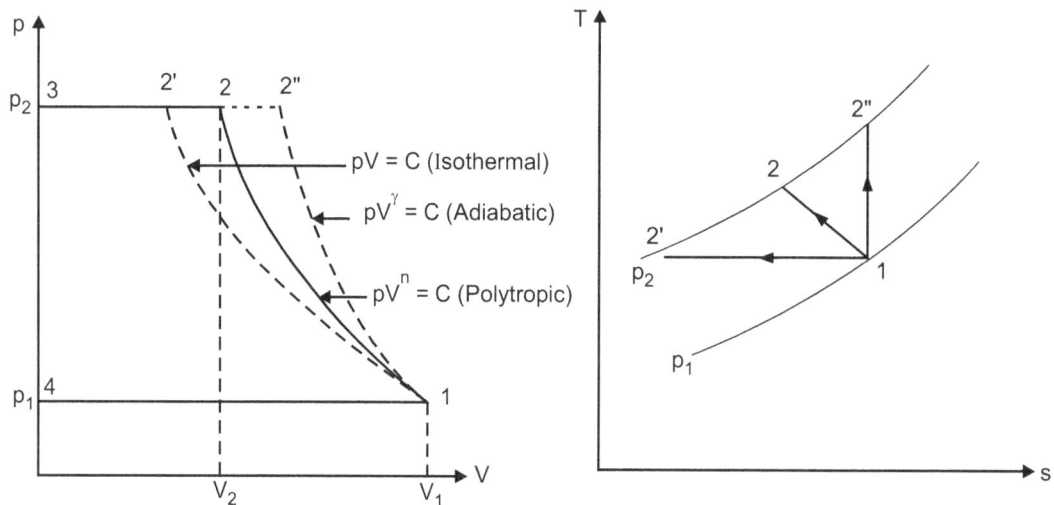

Fig. 4.3: Theoretical p-V and T-s diagrams for a single-stage reciprocating air compressor

Three different operations of the compressors viz. suction, compression and delivery, are shown in Fig. 4.3.

4-1 (Suction)   :   Air of volume V_1 enters into compressor at pressure p_1 and temperature T_1.

1-2 (Compression)   :   Air compressed according to the law $pV^n = C$, from pressure p_1 to p_2. Volume decreases from V_1 to V_2. Temperature increases from T_1 to T_2.

2-3 (Delivery)   :   Compressed air of volume V_2 delivered from compressor at pressure p_2 and temperature T_2.

1.   **Work Done during polytropic compression ($pV^n = C$):**

The area 4-1-2-3-4 represents the work done per cycle,

$$W = p_2V_2 + \frac{p_2V_2 - p_1V_1}{n - 1} - p_1V_1$$

$$= (p_2V_2 - p_1V_1) + \frac{p_2V_2 - p_1V_1}{n - 1}$$

$$= (p_2V_2 - p_1V_1)\left[1 + \frac{1}{n - 1}\right]$$

$$= \frac{n}{n - 1}(p_2V_2 - p_1V_1) \qquad\qquad \text{... (4.1)}$$

$$= \frac{n}{n - 1}p_1V_1\left[\frac{p_2V_2}{p_1V_1} - 1\right] \qquad\qquad \text{... (4.2)}$$

But, $p_1V_1^n = p_2V_2$

∴ $\dfrac{V_2}{V_1} = \left(\dfrac{p_1}{p_2}\right)^{\frac{1}{n}} = \left(\dfrac{p_2}{p_1}\right)^{-\frac{1}{n}}$

Substituting this in equation (4.2), we have,

$$W = \frac{n}{n - 1}p_1V_1\left[\frac{p_2}{p_1}\cdot\left(\frac{p_2}{p_1}\right)^{-\frac{1}{n}} - 1\right]$$

$$= \frac{n}{n - 1}p_1V_1\left[\left(\frac{p_2}{p_1}\right)^{1 - \frac{1}{n}} - 1\right]$$

$$W = \frac{n}{n - 1}p_1V_1\left[\left(\frac{p_2}{p_1}\right)^{\frac{n - 1}{n}} - 1\right] \qquad\qquad \text{... (4.3)}$$

$$= \frac{n}{n - 1}mRT_1\left[\left(\frac{p_2}{p_1}\right)^{\frac{n - 1}{n}} - 1\right] \qquad (\because p_1V_1 = mRT_1) \text{... (4.4)}$$

Work done per kg of air delivered $= \dfrac{n}{n-1} RT_1 \left[\left(\dfrac{p_2}{p_1} \right)^{\frac{n-1}{n}} - 1 \right]$ ... (4.5)

The air delivery temperature T_2 can be obtained by using equation,

$$\dfrac{T_2}{T_1} = \left(\dfrac{p_2}{p_1} \right)^{\frac{n-1}{n}}$$

2. Work done during isothermal compression (pV = C):

The area 4-1-2'-3-4 represents work done per cycle if compression process is isothermal,

$$W' = p_2 V_2' + p_1 V_1 \, ln \left(\dfrac{V_1}{V_2'} \right) - p_1 V_1$$

But, $p_1 V_1 = p_2 V_2$ is the required condition for isothermal process

$\therefore$ $W' = p_1 V_1 \, ln \left(\dfrac{V_1}{V_2'} \right) = p_1 V_1 \, ln \left(\dfrac{p_2}{p_1} \right) = p_1 V_1 \, ln \, r \left(r = \dfrac{p_2}{p_1} \right)$ ... (4.6)

$$= mRT_1 \, ln \left(\dfrac{p_2}{p_1} \right)$$

3. Work done during isentropic (Adiabatic) compression ($pV^\gamma = C$):

The area 4-1-2"-3-4 represents work done per cycle when compression is isentropic.

$$W'' = \dfrac{\gamma}{\gamma-1} p_1 V_1 \left[\left(\dfrac{p_2}{p_1} \right)^{\frac{\gamma-1}{\gamma}} - 1 \right]$$ ... (4.7)

4.2 ISOTHERMAL EFFICIENCY

- Inspection of p-V diagram (Fig. 4.3 (a)) shows that, the work required to run the compressor becomes minimum if the compression follows isothermal process (minimum area under isothermal process) than actual compression ($pV^n = C$).

- Isothermal compression cannot be achieved in practice but an attempt is made to approach the isothermal case by cooling the compressor either by addition of cooling fins or a water jacket to a compressor cylinder.

- For a reciprocating compressor, a comparison between the actual work done during compression and ideal isothermal work done is made by means of the isothermal efficiency.

This is defined as,

$$\text{Isothermal efficiency} = \dfrac{\text{Isothermal work done}}{\text{Actual work done}}$$

Thus, higher the isothermal efficiency, the more nearly has the actual compression approached the ideal isothermal compression (when point 2 moves towards 2', the area under the curve i.e. actual work done decreases and isothermal efficiency increases).

$$\eta_i = \frac{W'}{W}$$

Substituting W and W' from equations (4.3) and (4.6), above equations becomes,

$$\eta_i = \frac{p_1 V_1 \ln\left(\frac{p_2}{p_1}\right)}{\frac{n}{n-1} p_1 V_1 \left[\left(\frac{p_2}{p_1}\right)^{\frac{n-1}{n}} - 1\right]} \qquad \ldots (4.8)$$

4.2.1 Methods for Improving Isothermal Efficiency

The following practical methods are used to achieve nearly isothermal compression (n little above one) for high speed compressors. The object of all these methods is to reduce the final temperature T_2 during compression so that actual work approaches more closely to the isothermal compression. These methods are as follows:

1. **External Fins:**

Effective cooling can be achieved for small capacity air compressor with the use of fins on the external surface of the compressor.

2. **Spray Injection:**

The water supply injection into compressor cylinder towards the end of compression stroke used some years ago, has following disadvantages.

(a)   Needs special gear for injection.

(b)   Injected water mixes with cylinder lubrication and attacks cylinder walls and valves.

(c)   The water mixed with air should be separated before using air.

3. **Water Jacketing:**

In this method, the water is circulated around the cylinder through the water jacket which helps to cool the air during compression. Now-a-days, this is commonly used method.

4. **Inter-cooling:**

Water jacketing is not much effective when the speed of compressor is high and pressure ratio required is also high with single-stage compression. Inter-cooling is used in addition to water jacketing by dividing the compression process into two or more stages. The air compressed in first stage is cooled in a heat exchanger known as inter-cooler to its original temperature before it is taken to the second stage.

5. By a suitable choice of cylinder proportions:

By providing short stroke and a large bore in conjunction with sleeve valves, a much greater surface is available for cooling, and the surface of the cylinder head is far more effective in this respect than the surface of the barrel. Because the periodic motion of the piston does not allow the barrel to be exposed to the air for a sufficient time for heat to flow away. Moreover the air is compressed against the cylinder cover.

4.3 SINGLE-STAGE COMPRESSORS WITH CLEARANCE VOLUME

- The clearance volume is the volume within the cylinder between cylinder head and piston, at the end of inward stroke.
- The effect of clearance volume is to reduce the volume actually aspirated. Therefore, clearance volume should be as small as possible.
- It is not possible to reduce clearance volume to zero, for mechanical reason. Moreover, it is not desirable to allow the piston head to come in contact with the cylinder head.
- In addition to this, the passage leading to the inlet and outlet valves always contribute to clearance volume.

As shown in Fig. 4.4, at point 1, the cylinder is full of intake air, volume V_1 and the piston is about to start its compression stroke. The air is compressed polytropically ($pV^n = C$) to delivery pressure p_2 and volume V_2. At point 2, delivery valve theoretically opens and compressed air is delivered till the piston reaches at 3. At this stage, there will be some air (equal to clearance volume) left in the clearance space of the cylinder at pressure p_2. Then the piston begins intake stroke and the expansion of residual air takes place polytropically to the pressure p_1 and volume V_4. At point 4, inlet valve opens to take fresh air charge in. For remainder of intake stroke (4 to 1) fresh charge is taken into the cylinder. This volume ($V_1 - V_4$) is the effective swept volume.

Work done per cycle,

$$W = \text{Net area 1-2-3-4-1}$$
$$= \text{Area 1-2-6-5-1} - \text{Area 3-4-5-6-3}$$

Assuming polytropic compression and clearance expansion,

$$W = \frac{n}{n-1} p_1 V_1 \left[\left(\frac{p_2}{p_1}\right)^{\frac{n-1}{n}} - 1 \right] - \frac{n}{n-1} p_4 V_4 \left[\left(\frac{p_3}{p_4}\right)^{\frac{n-1}{n}} - 1 \right]$$

$$\dots (4.9)$$

But $p_4 = p_1$ and $p_3 = p_2$, then equation (4.9) becomes,

$$W = \frac{n}{n-1} p_1 V_1 \left[\left(\frac{p_2}{p_1}\right)^{\frac{n-1}{n}} - 1 \right] - \frac{n}{n-1} p_1 V_4 \left[\left(\frac{p_2}{p_1}\right)^{\frac{n-1}{n}} - 1 \right]$$

$$= \frac{n}{n-1} p_1 (V_1 - V_4) \left[\left(\frac{p_2}{p_1} \right)^{\frac{n-1}{n}} - 1 \right] \qquad ...(4.10)$$

$$= \frac{n}{n-1} p_1 V_a \left[\left(\frac{p_2}{p_1} \right)^{\frac{n-1}{n}} - 1 \right] \qquad ... (4.11)$$

where, $V_a = V_1 - V_4$ is the actual volume of free air delivered per cycle.

$$W = \frac{n}{n-1} m_1 R T_1 \left[\left(\frac{p_2}{p_1} \right)^{\frac{n-1}{n}} - 1 \right] \qquad ... (4.12)$$

where, m_1 is the actual mass of the air delivered per cycle.

∴   Work done per kg of air delivered

$$= \frac{n}{n-1} R T_1 \left[\left(\frac{p_2}{p_1} \right)^{\frac{n-1}{n}} - 1 \right] \qquad ... (4.13)$$

From equations (4.5) and (4.13), it is clear that, the clearance volume does not affect the work of compression per kg of air.

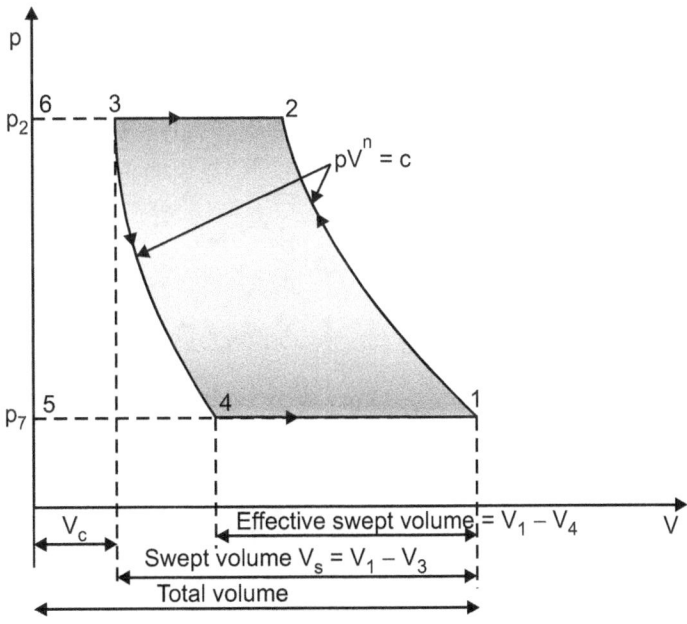

Fig. 4.4: p-V diagram for single stage-compressor with clearance volume

•   The clearance volume of the compressor is given as a percentage of the stroke volume.

4.4 VOLUMETRIC EFFICIENCY

- The volumetric efficiency of a compressor is the ratio of free air delivered to the displacement of compressor. It is also expressed as the ratio of effective stroke volume to the stroke volume.

$$\text{Volumetric efficiency} = \frac{\text{Effective stroke volume}}{\text{Stroke volume}}$$

$$\eta_{vol} = \frac{V_1 - V_4}{V_1 - V_3} \qquad \dots (4.14)$$

- Because of the presence of clearance volume, volumetric efficiency is always less than unity. As a percentage, it usually varies from 60% to 85%.
- Volumetric efficiency can be expressed in terms of clearance ratio C and pressure ratio (p_2/p_1).

  The clearance ratio,

$$C = \frac{\text{Clearance volume}}{\text{Stroke volume}} = \frac{V_3}{V_1 - V_3} = \frac{V_c}{V_s} \qquad \dots (4.15)$$

The C is expressed as percentage of stroke volume and in general it is between 4% and 10% of the stroke volume.

From equation (4.15),

$$V_3 = (V_1 - V_3) \cdot C \qquad \dots (4.16)$$

From relation

$$p_3 V_3^n = p_4 V_4^n$$

$$V_4 = V_3 \cdot \left(\frac{p_3}{p_4}\right)^{\frac{1}{n}}$$

Substituting V_3 from equation (4.16), we get,

$$V_4 = C \cdot (V_1 - V_3) \left(\frac{p_3}{p_4}\right)^{\frac{1}{n}}$$

Also, $p_1 = p_4$ and $p_3 = p_2$

$$\therefore \qquad V_4 = C (V_1 - V_3) \left(\frac{p_2}{p_1}\right)^{\frac{1}{n}}$$

$$= C \cdot V_s \cdot \left(\frac{p_2}{p_1}\right)^{\frac{1}{n}}$$

Now,

$$\eta_{vol} = \frac{V_1 - V_4}{V_1 - V_3} = \frac{V_1 - V_4}{V_s}$$

But,

$$V_1 = V_c + V_s = C \cdot V_s + V_s$$

$$\therefore \qquad \eta_{vol} = \frac{C \cdot V_s + V_s - C \cdot V_s \left(\frac{p_2}{p_1}\right)^{\frac{1}{n}}}{V_s}$$

$$\therefore \qquad \eta_{vol} = 1 + C - C \left(\frac{p_2}{p_1}\right)^{\frac{1}{n}}$$

$$= 1 - C \left[\left(\frac{p_2}{p_1}\right)^{\frac{1}{n}} - 1\right] \qquad \qquad \ldots (4.17)$$

Fig. 4.5 is the plot of equation (4.17).

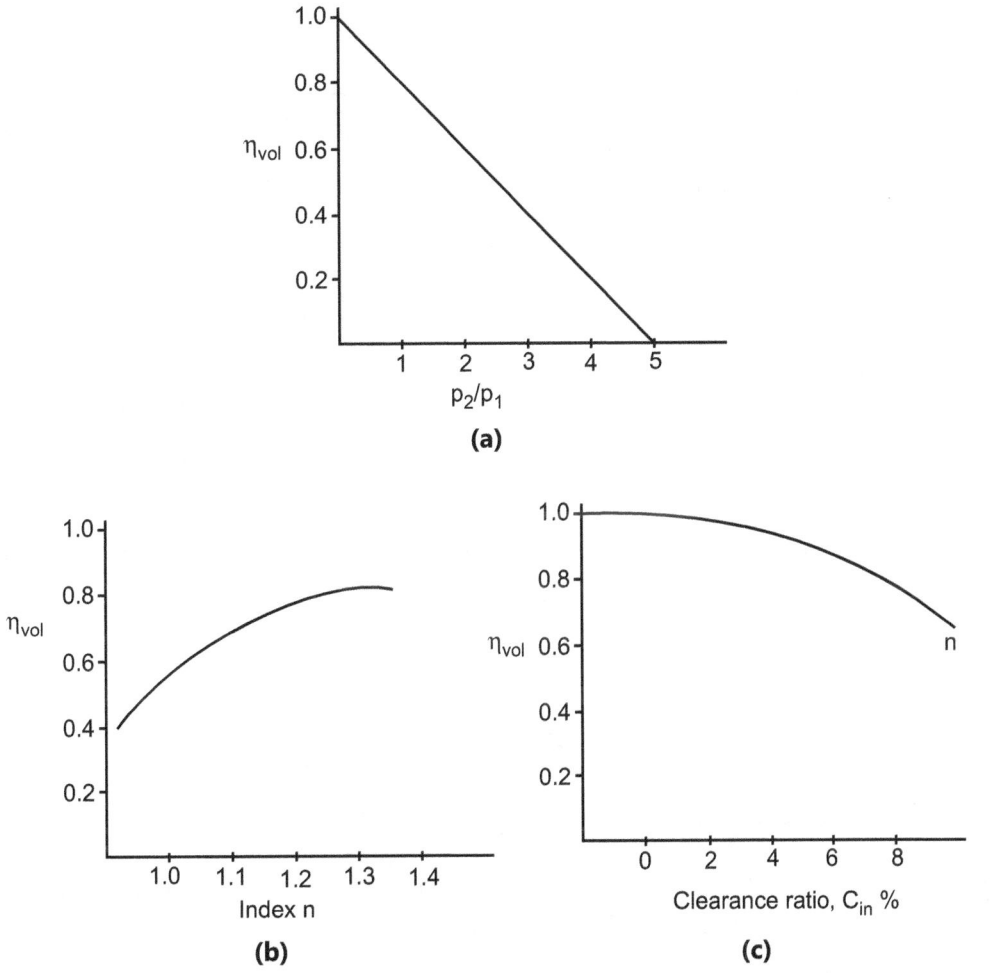

Fig. 4.5: Effect of clearance ratio, pressure ratio and index n on volumetric efficiency

From the plot, it is observed that,

For $p_2 = p_1$, there is no compression and η_{vol} = 100%.

Volumetric efficiency decreases with increase in delivery pressure p_2 and clearance ratio C.

Volumetric efficiency increases with increase in index n.

The volumetric efficiency is lowered by any one of the following conditions:

    (i)   Very high speed.

    (ii)   Leakage past the piston.

    (iii) Obstruction at inlet valves.

    (iv) Overheating of air by contact with hot cylinder walls.

    (v)   Inertia effect of air in suction pipe.

By paying careful attention in the design of the compressor to these causes of loss, an improvement in volumetric efficiency can be obtained.

4.5 POWER OF A SINGLE-STAGE COMPRESSOR

The power required to drive the compressor can be obtained from the relation,

$$p = \frac{W \cdot N_w}{60} \text{ watts}$$

If N is the speed of the compressor in r.p.m., then number of working strokes per minute (N_w),

$$N_w = N \qquad \qquad \text{... (For single-acting compressor)}$$
$$= 2N \qquad \qquad \text{... (For double-acting compressor)}$$

Since the compression takes place in three different ways, therefore, power obtained from different work done will be different and given as,

$$\text{Isothermal power} = \frac{W' N_w}{60} \text{ watts}$$

$$\text{Indicated power} = \frac{W N_w}{60} \text{ watts}$$

$$\text{Isentropic/Adiabatic power} = \frac{W'' N_w}{60} \text{ watts}$$

where,   W', W, W" = Isothermal, Polytropic, Isentropic work done respectively

4.6 MECHANICAL EFFICIENCY

The mechanical efficiency of the compressor is the ratio of indicated power to the brake power (shaft power).

$$\eta_{mech} = \frac{\text{Indicated power}}{\text{Brake power}}$$

4.7 Mean Effective Pressure

In practice, air pressure on the compressor piston keeps on changing with movement of piston in the cylinder. The mean effective pressure (p_m) of the compressor can be determined mathematically by dividing the work done per cycle to the stroke volume.

$$p_m = \frac{\text{Work done}}{\text{Stroke volume}}$$

Work done per cycle,

$$W = \frac{n}{n-1} p_1 (V_1 - V_4) \left[\left(\frac{p_2}{p_1}\right)^{\frac{n-1}{n}} - 1 \right]$$

$$\therefore \qquad p_m V_s = \frac{n}{n-1} p_1 \cdot V_a \left[\left(\frac{p_2}{p_1}\right)^{\frac{n-1}{n}} - 1 \right] \qquad \left(\because p_m = \frac{W}{V_s} \right)$$

$$\therefore \qquad p_m = \frac{n}{n-1} p_1 \frac{V_a}{V_s} \left[\left(\frac{p_2}{p_1}\right)^{\frac{n-1}{n}} - 1 \right]$$

$$\therefore \qquad p_m = \frac{n}{n-1} p_1 \cdot \eta_{vol} \left[\left(\frac{p_2}{p_1}\right)^{\frac{n-1}{n}} - 1 \right] \qquad \left(\because \eta_{vol} = \frac{V_a}{V_s} \right)$$

4.8 FREE AIR DELIVERY

The Free Air Delivered (F.A.D) is the actual volume delivered at the stated pressure reduced to intake temperature and pressure. It is expressed in m^3/min. The displacement is actual volume in m^3/min swept out.

The free air delivered per minute is less than the displacement of the compressor because of the following reasons:

1. The fluid resistance through the air intake, and valves prevents the cylinder being fully charged with air at atmospheric conditions.
2. On entering the hot cylinder, the air expands, so that the mass of the air present (compared with that at atmospheric temperature) is reduced.
3. The high pressure air tapped in the clearance space, must expand to a pressure below atmospheric before the automatic suction valves can open; a portion of the suction stroke is therefore wasted in effecting this expansion.
4. A certain loss is caused by the leakage.

4.9 ACTUAL p-V (INDICATOR) DIAGRAM FOR SINGLE-STAGE COMPRESSOR

The actual p-V diagram for a single-stage compressor is shown in Fig. 4.6.

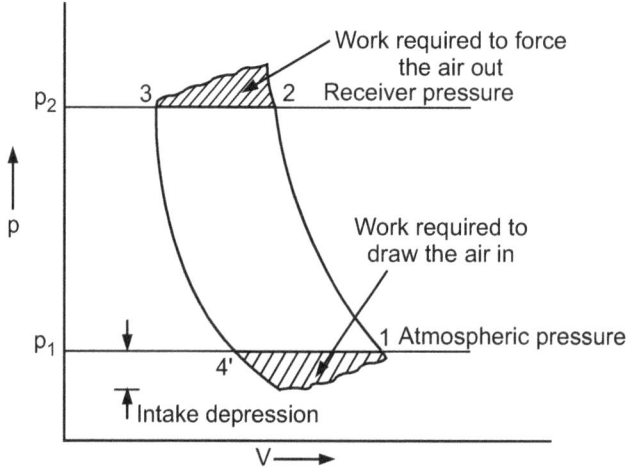

Fig. 4.6: Actual p-V (indicator) diagram for a single-stage compressor

The actual diagram differs from the theoretical as there are intake and discharge losses. The intake losses include:

- the friction loss in pipe,
- friction loss in inlet valve
- valve inertia loss.

- Theoretically, the inlet valve should open at 4, but in actual practice it will not open. This is because of inlet valve inertia and pressure difference required to open the valve. Thus, the pressure drops below atmospheric pressure until the valve is closed (i.e. point 1). The oscillating part of the curve indicates valve bounce or valve flutter due to vibration of valve. This negative pressure is known as intake depression.

- Similar situation occurs on the delivery side also. Theoretically, discharge valve should open at 2, but actually it opens afterwards at pressure more than delivery pressure with bounce or flutter.

- The effect of these added shaded areas is to increase the work required per kg of air delivered to the receiver. Therefore, the actual work required to compress the air will be greater than the theoretical work.

SOLVED PROBLEMS ON SINGLE-STAGE COMPRESSOR

Problem 4.1: A single-stage, single-acting air compressor delivers 15 m^3/min of free air from 1 bar to 8 bar at 300 r.p.m. The clearance volume is 6.25% of the stroke volume and compression and expansion follow the law $pV^{1.3}$ = C. Find the diameter and stroke of the compressor. Take L/D = 1.5. The temperature and pressure of air at suction are same as that of free air. Also determine indicated power of the compressor.

Solution:

Given: F.A.D. = 15 m^3/min, p_1 = 1 bar, p_2 = 8 bar, N = 300 r.p.m., n = 1.3, C = 0.0625, L/D = 1.5.

Diameter and Stroke:

$$\text{Free air delivery per cycle} = V_a = \frac{F.A.D/min}{N} = \frac{15}{300}$$

$$V_a = 0.05 \text{ m}^3/\text{cycle}$$

Volumetric efficiency is given by,

$$\eta_{vol} = 1 - C\left[\left(\frac{p_2}{p_1}\right)^{\frac{1}{n}} - 1\right]$$

$$= 1 - 0.0625\left[\left(\frac{8}{1}\right)^{\frac{1}{1.3}} - 1\right]$$

$$= 0.753 = \textbf{75.306\%}$$

Volumetric efficiency is also written as,

$$\eta_{vol} = \frac{V_a}{V_s}$$

$\therefore$ $\quad$ Stroke volume, $V_s = \dfrac{V_a}{\eta_{vol}}$

$$= \frac{0.05}{0.753}$$

$$= 0.06639 \text{ m}^3$$

But, $\qquad\qquad V_s = \dfrac{\pi}{4} D^2 \cdot L = \textbf{0.06639}$

$\therefore$ $\qquad\qquad \dfrac{\pi}{4} D^2 \times 1.5 \, D = \textbf{0.06639}$

$$D^3 = \frac{0.06639 \times 4}{1.5 \, \pi} = 0.05635$$

$\therefore$ $\qquad\qquad$ D = 0.383 m = 383 mm

and $\qquad\qquad$ L = 1.5 × D = 1.5 × 0.383 = 0.575 m = **575 mm**

Indicated power:

The work done per cycle,

$$W = \frac{n}{n-1} p_1 V_a \left[\left(\frac{p_2}{p_1} \right)^{\frac{n-1}{n}} - 1 \right]$$

$$= \frac{1.3}{1.3-1} \times 1 \times 10^5 \times 0.05 \left[\left(\frac{8}{1} \right)^{\frac{1.3-1}{1.3}} - 1 \right]$$

$$= 13344 \text{ J/cycle} = 13.344 \text{ kJ/cycle}$$

Indicated power,

$$P = \frac{W \cdot N_w}{60}$$

$$= \frac{13344 \times 300}{60 \times 1000}$$

$$= \mathbf{66.72 \text{ kW}}$$

Problem 4.2: A single-stage, single-acting reciprocating air compressor takes in air at 1 bar, 27°C and delivers at 7 bar, volume of air entering the compressor is 5 m^3/min.

Air is compressed according to $pV^{1.3}$ = C. Calculate isothermal efficiency, power required to drive the compressor, neglecting clearance volume.   **(P.U. December 2005)**

Solution: Given: p_1 = 1 bar, T_1 = 27°C, p_2 = 7 bar, V_1 = 5 m^3/min, n = 1.3.

Isothermal efficiency:

$$\eta_i = \frac{W'}{W} = \frac{p_1 V_1 \ln \left(\frac{p_2}{p_1} \right)}{\frac{n}{n-1} p_1 V_1 \left[\left(\frac{p_2}{p_1} \right)^{\frac{n-1}{n}} - 1 \right]}$$

$$= \frac{\ln \left(\frac{7}{1} \right)}{\frac{1.3}{0.3} \left[(7)^{\frac{0.3}{1.3}} - 1 \right]}$$

$$\eta_i = 0.7922$$

Isothermal efficiency, η_i = **79.22%**

Power:

Power required to drive the compressor is nothing but work done per second.

Work done per cycle is given by,

$$W = \frac{n}{n-1} p_1 V_1 \left[\left(\frac{p_2}{p_1} \right)^{\frac{n-1}{n}} - 1 \right] \qquad (V_1 \text{ in } m^3)$$

In above equation, V_1 is in m^3. When V_1 is taken as m^3/sec, we get power required to drive the compressor.

$$\therefore \quad Power = \frac{n}{n-1} p_1 V_1 \left[\left(\frac{p_2}{p_1} \right)^{\frac{n-1}{n}} - 1 \right] \qquad \left(V_1 \text{ in } \frac{m^3}{sec} \right)$$

$$= \frac{1.3}{0.3} \times 1 \times 10^5 \times \frac{5}{60} \times \left[\left(\frac{7}{1} \right)^{\frac{0.3}{1.3}} - 1 \right]$$

$$= 20468.86 \text{ W}$$

$$= \textbf{20.468 kW}$$

Power required to drive the compressor neglecting clearance volume = 20.468 kW.

Problem 4.3: A single-stage, single-acting air compressor works between 01 bar and 16 bar by the compression law $pV^{1.3} = C$ at 350 mm. Piston speed is 200 m/min. Indicated power is 30 kW. Determine cylinder dimensions, if the volumetric efficiency of the compressor is 85%.

Solution:

Given: $p_1 = 1$ bar, $p_2 = 16$ bar, $n = 1.3$, $N = 350$ r.p.m., Piston speed = 200 m/min, $p_{ind} = 30$ kW, $\eta_{vol} = 0.85$.

Power of single-stage compressor,

$$p = \frac{W \cdot N}{60} \text{ watts}$$

$$30 \times 10^3 = \frac{W \times 350}{60}$$

$$\therefore \qquad W = 5142.857 \text{ N·m/cycle}$$

Work done per cycle,

$$W = \frac{n}{n-1} p_1 V_a \left[\left(\frac{p_2}{p_1} \right)^{\frac{n-1}{n}} - 1 \right]$$

$$5142.857 = \frac{1.3}{0.3} \times 1 \times 10^5 \times V_a \times \left[\left(\frac{16}{1} \right)^{\frac{0.3}{1.3}} - 1 \right]$$

$$V_a = \textbf{0.01324 m}^3$$

Volumetric efficiency,

$$\eta_{vol} = \frac{V_a}{V_s}$$

$$\therefore \qquad V_s = \frac{V_a}{\eta_{vol}}$$

$$= \frac{0.01324}{0.85}$$

$$V_s = \textbf{0.01558 m}^3$$

Piston speed/min $= 2 LN$

$$200 = 2L \times 350$$

$$L = \frac{200}{2 \times 350}$$

$$= \mathbf{0.2857 \ m}$$

Stroke volume, $V_s = \frac{\pi}{4} \times D^2 \times L$

$$0.01558 = \frac{\pi}{4} \times D^2 \times 0.2857$$

$$D = 0.2635 \ m$$

Length of piston stroke = **285 mm**

Diameter of cylinder = **264 mm**

Problem 4.4: A single-acting air compressor has a cylinder bore of 15 cm and piston stroke of 25 cm. The crankshaft is rotating at 600 r.p.m. Air is taken from atmosphere at pressure 1.013 bar and 27°C and delivered at 11 bar. Assume compression takes place polytropically by law $pV^{1.25} = C$. The clearance volume is 5% of the stroke volume. Mechanical efficiency of the compressor is 80%.   **(P.U. May 2005)**

Determine:

    (i)   Power required to drive the compressor,

    (ii) Volumetric efficiency,

    (iii) Delivery temperature,

    (iv) Time required to deliver air of volume 1 m^3.

Solution:

Given: $D = 0.15$ m, $L = 0.25$ m, $N = 600$ r.p.m. $p_1 = 1.013$ bar, $T_1 = 27°C = 27 + 273 = 300$ K, $p_2 = 11$ bar, $n = 1.25$, $C = 0.05$, $\eta_{mech} = 0.8$.

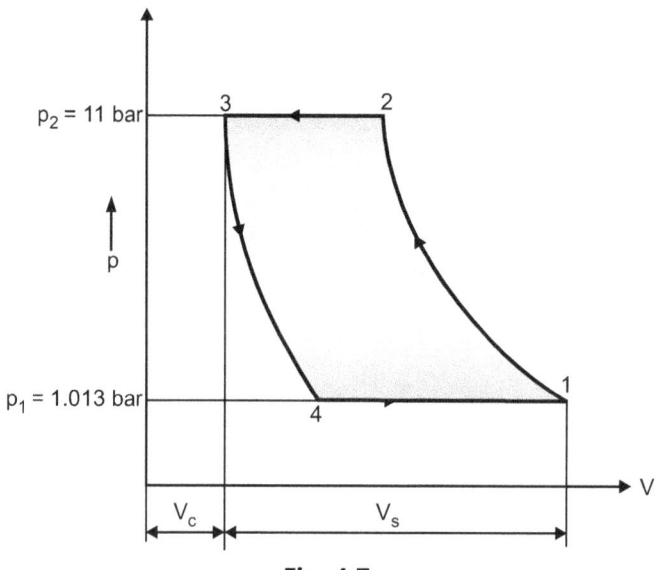

Fig. 4.7

$$\text{Stroke volume} = \frac{\pi}{4} D^2 L = \frac{\pi}{4} \times 0.15^2 \times 0.25$$

$$V_s = 4.417 \times 10^{-3} \, m^3$$

$$\text{Clearance volume, } V_c = C \times V_s = 0.05 \times 4.417 \times 10^{-3}$$

$$= \mathbf{2.21 \times 10^{-4} \, m^3}$$

$$\text{Volume, } V_1 = V_c + V_s$$

$$= 2.21 \times 10^{-4} + 4.42 \times 10^{-3}$$

$$= \mathbf{4.64 \times 10^{-3} \, m^3}$$

For expansion process (3-4),

$$p_3 V_3^{1.25} = p_4 V_4^{1.25}$$

$$V_4 = V_3 \left(\frac{p_3}{p_1}\right)^{\frac{1}{n}} = 2.21 \times 10^{-4} \times \left(\frac{11}{1.013}\right)^{\frac{1}{1.25}}$$

$$= \mathbf{1.489 \times 10^{-3} \, m^3}$$

$$V_a = (V_1 - V_4) = (4.64 - 1.489) \times 10^{-3}$$

$$= \mathbf{3.151 \times 10^{-3} \, m^3}$$

(i) Power required to drive the compressor:

Indicated work done per cycle,

$$W = \frac{n}{n-1} p_1 V_a \left[\left(\frac{p_2}{p_1}\right)^{\frac{n-1}{n}} - 1\right]$$

$$= \frac{1.25}{0.25} \times 1.013 \times 10^5 \times 3.151 \times 10^{-3} \times \left[\left(\frac{11}{1.013}\right)^{\frac{0.25}{1.25}} - 1\right]$$

$$= \mathbf{975.5 \, J/cycle}$$

Indicated power,

$$p = \frac{W \, N_w}{60}$$

$$= \frac{975.5 \times 600}{60}$$

$$= 9755.06 \, W$$

$$= \mathbf{9.755 \, kW}$$

Power required to drive the compressor

$$= \frac{\text{Indicated power}}{\text{Mechanical efficiency}}$$

$$= \frac{9.76}{0.8} = \mathbf{12.20 \, kW}$$

(ii) Volumetric efficiency:

$$\eta_{vol} = 1 - C\left[\left(\frac{p_2}{p_1}\right)^{\frac{1}{n}} - 1\right]$$

$$= 1 - 0.05\left[\left(\frac{11}{1.013}\right)^{\frac{1}{1.25}} - 1\right]$$

$$= 0.713$$

$$= \textbf{71.30\%}$$

(iii) Delivery temperature:

$$T_2 = T_1\left(\frac{p_2}{p_1}\right)^{\frac{n-1}{n}}$$

$$= 300 \times \left(\frac{11}{1.013}\right)^{\frac{0.25}{1.25}}$$

$$= \textbf{483.38 K}$$

(iv) Time required to deliver 1 m³ air:

$$p_2V_2 = m_2RT_2$$

Mass delivered,

$$m_2 = \frac{p_2V_2}{RT_2} = \frac{11 \times 10^5 \times 1}{287 \times 483.37}$$

$$= \textbf{7.929 kg}$$

$$\text{Mass per cycle} = \frac{p_1(V_1 - V_4)}{RT_1} \times N$$

$$= \frac{1.013 \times 10^5 \times 3.151 \times 10^{-3}}{287 \times 300} \times 600$$

$$= \textbf{2.232 kg/min}$$

Time required to deliver 1 m³ volume

$$= \frac{\text{Mass delivered}}{\text{Mass per minute}}$$

$$= \frac{7.929}{2.232}$$

$$= \textbf{3.55 minutes}$$

Problem 4.5: Following data relate to a performance test of a single-acting 14 cm × 10 cm reciprocating compressor.

Suction and delivery pressure = 1 bar and 6 bar.

Suction and delivery temperature = 20°C and 180°C

Mass of delivered = 1.7 kg/min

Compressor speed = 1200 r.p.m.

Shaft power = 6.25 kW

Find volumetric efficiency, indicated power, isothermal efficiency and mechanical efficiency.

Solution: Given: $p_1 = 1$ bar, $p_2 = 6$ bar, $T_1 = 20 + 273 = 293$ K, $T_2 = 180 + 273 = 453$ K, $N = 1200$ r.p.m., $m_a = 1.7$ kg/min, $p_{shaft} = 6.25$ kW, $D = 0.14$ m, $L = 0.1$ m.

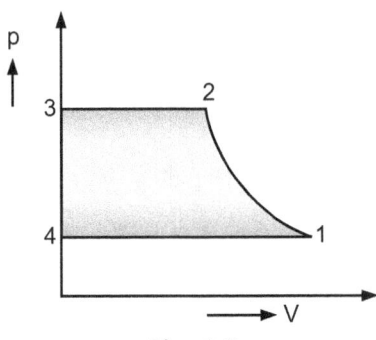

Fig. 4.8

(i) **Volumetric efficiency:**

$$\text{Stroke volume, } V_s = \frac{\pi}{4} D^2 L N$$

$$= \frac{\pi}{4} \times (0.14)^2 \times 0.1 \times 1200$$

$$= 1.8473 \text{ m}^3/\text{min}^*$$

We know,
$$p_1 V_1 = mRT_1$$

$$V_1 = \frac{mRT_1}{p_1} = \frac{1.7 \times 287 \times 293}{1 \times 10^5}$$

$$= 1.4295 \text{ m}^3/\text{min}$$

$$\eta_{vol} = \frac{V_1}{V_s} = \frac{1.4295}{1.8473} = 0.7738$$

$$= \mathbf{77.38\%}$$

(ii) **Indicated power:**

We know,
$$\frac{T_2}{T_1} = \left(\frac{p_2}{p_1}\right)^{\frac{n-1}{n}}$$

$$\ln\left(\frac{T_2}{T_1}\right) = \frac{n-1}{n} \ln\left(\frac{p_2}{p_1}\right)$$

$$\frac{n-1}{n} = \frac{\ln(T_2/T_1)}{\ln(p_2/p_1)} = \frac{\ln(453/293)}{\ln(6/1)} = 0.2432$$

$$n - 1 = 0.2432\, n$$

$$0.7568\, n = 1$$

$$\therefore \qquad n = 1.32$$

---

* **Note :** Unit of V_1 is m^3/min because mass is taken in kg/min.

Work done per cycle is given by,

$$W = \frac{n}{n-1} p_1 V_1 \left[\left(\frac{p_2}{p_1} \right)^{\frac{n-1}{n}} - 1 \right]$$ **(V_1 in m^3)**

Work done per unit time gives power. If V_1 is taken in m^3/sec, the power is given as,

$$\text{Indicated power} = \frac{n}{n-1} p_1 V_1 \left[\left(\frac{p_2}{p_1} \right)^{\frac{n-1}{n}} - 1 \right]$$ **(V_1 in m^3/sec)**

$$= \frac{1.32}{0.32} \times 1 \times 10^5 \times \frac{1.4295}{60} \times \left[\left(\frac{6}{1} \right)^{\frac{0.32}{1.32}} - 1 \right]$$

$$= 5339.59 \text{ W}$$

$$= \textbf{5.34 kW}$$

(iii) Isothermal efficiency:

$$\text{Isothermal power} = p_1 V_1 \, ln \left(\frac{p_2}{p_1} \right)$$

$$= 1 \times 10^5 \times \frac{1.4295}{60} \, ln \left(\frac{6}{1} \right)$$

$$= \textbf{4269 W}$$

$$\eta_{iso} = \frac{\text{Isothermal power}}{\text{Indicated power}}$$

$$= \frac{4269}{5339} = \textbf{0.7995}$$

$$= \textbf{79.95\%}$$

(iv) Mechanical efficiency:

$$\eta_{mech} = \frac{\text{Indicated power}}{\text{Shaft power}}$$

$$= \frac{5.34}{6.25} = \textbf{0.8544}$$

$$= \textbf{85.44\%}$$

4.10 NEED OF MULTISTAGE COMPRESSION

- We have seen that the volumetric efficiency of a reciprocating compressor is a function of clearance ratio C, pressure ratio (p_2/p_1) and index of compression/expansion.
- If clearance volume is fixed, the volumetric efficiency of a compressor decreases with an increase in pressure ratio.
- A stage may be reached when the volumetric efficiency becomes zero as can be seen from Fig. 4.9.

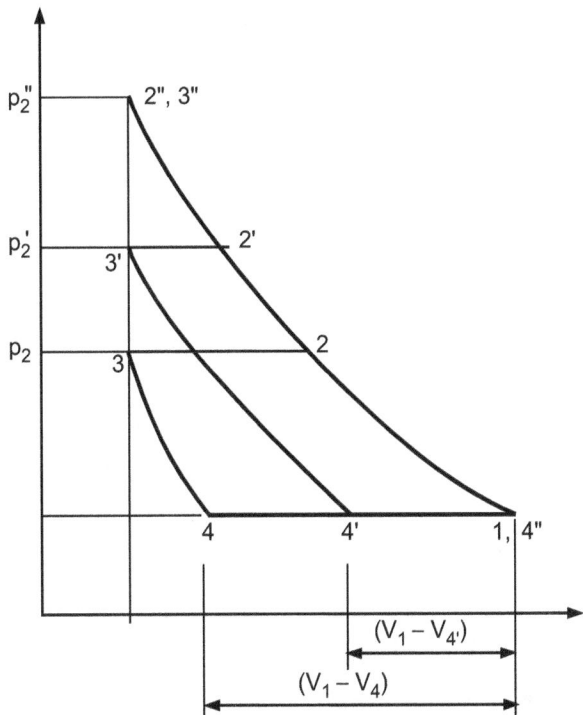

**Fig. 4.9: Effect of increased pressure on
actual air delivered by a compressor at fixed clearance**

- From Fig. 4.9, it is observed that the volume of air admitted in the compressor decreases with increase in delivery pressure for the same clearance volume and fixed intake pressure. At a stage of delivery pressure (p_2''), volume of intake air becomes zero $(V_1 - V_4'' = 0)$ and also the volume of air delivered becomes zero $(V_2'' - V_3'' = 0)$. The attempt made to deliver the air at a high pressure p_2'' would result in compression and re-expansion of same air again and again without any delivery of high pressure air.

- Therefore, the maximum pressure ratio attainable with a single-stage reciprocating compressor is limited by the clearance volume.

In addition to above, it has been observed that, use of single-stage compression for producing high pressure air (8 bar and above) delivers following drawbacks:

- The size of the cylinder and piston will be too large. This will increase the balancing problem and high torque fluctuation will require a heavier flywheel.

- There is rise in temperature of delivery air.

To overcome above mentioned difficulties, multistage compression with two or more cylinders in series with intercooler is used effectively.

The p-V diagram for two-stage air compression without intercooler is shown in Fig. 4.10.

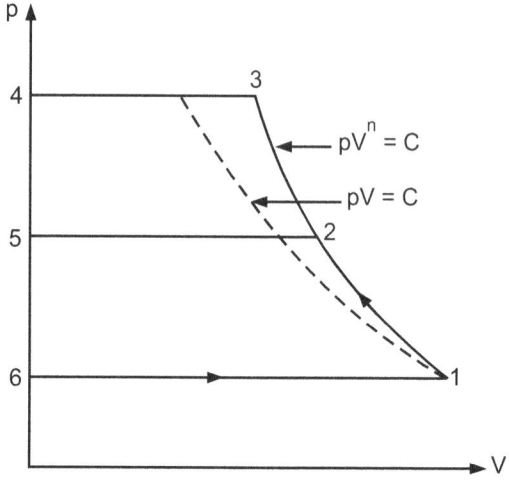

Fig. 4.10: Two-stage compression

4.11 TWO-STAGE RECIPROCATING AIR COMPRESSOR WITH INTERCOOLER

In multistage compression, air cooling after leaving each stage is possible. A two-stage reciprocating air compressor with intercooler is shown in Fig. 4.11. Both the cylinders are mounted on the same shaft and driven by a prime mover.

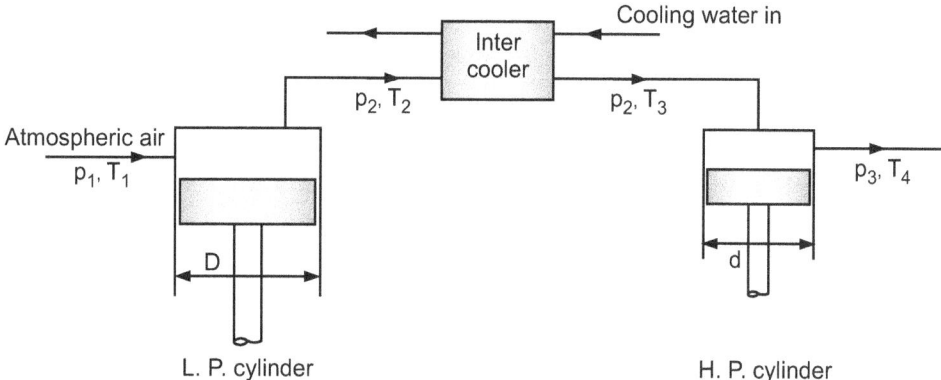

Fig. 4.11: Two-stage air compressor with intercooler

- In two-stage air compressor, first of all, the fresh air from atmosphere is taken into low pressure (L.P.) cylinder at pressure p_1 and temperature T_1. In low pressure cylinder air is compressed (first stage). Then it is delivered to intercooler at pressure p_2 and temperature T_2. Now the air is cooled in intercooler at constant pressure p_2, from temperature T_2 to T_3 ($T_3 < T_2$). Further, air is compressed in high pressure (H.P.) cylinder (second stage) to give pressure p_3 and temperature T_4 and discharged to the receiver.

- The work saved by introducing the intercooler is shown in Fig. 4.12 (a) by the area 2-3-4-6-2. Sometimes a cooler is used to cool the air before passing to the receiver known as after cooler. This reduces size of the receiver and not the work done.

- If the temperature of air leaving the intercooler (i.e. T_3) is more than the atmospheric air temperature (i.e. T_1) as shown in Fig. 4.12 (b), then the intercooling is known as incomplete or imperfect intercooling. Here, point 3 lies on right side of the isothermal curve.

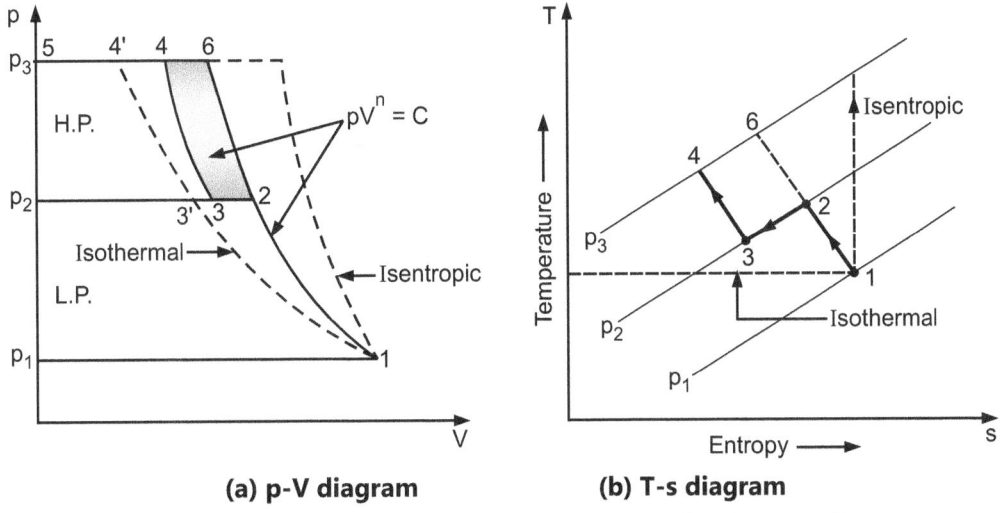

(a) p-V diagram   **(b) T-s diagram**

Fig. 4.12: Two-stage compression with imperfect intercooling

Work done for a two-stage reciprocating air compressor with intercooler: For a two-stage reciprocating air compressor with intercooler, air is compressed in L.P. and H.P. cylinders. So total work done is the addition of the work done per cycle in L.P. and work done per cycle in H.P. cylinder.

$\therefore$
$$W = W_{L.P.} + W_{H.P.}$$

$$= \frac{n}{n-1} p_1 V_1 \left[\left(\frac{p_2}{p_1} \right)^{\frac{n-1}{n}} - 1 \right] + \frac{n}{n-1} p_2 V_3 \left[\left(\frac{p_2}{p_1} \right)^{\frac{n-1}{n}} - 1 \right] \qquad \dots (4.18)$$

4.12 CONDITION FOR MINIMUM WORK OF COMPRESSION OR MAXIMUM EFFICIENCY (PERFECT INTERCOOLING)

Fig. 4.12 shows p-V and T-s diagram for two-stage compressor with imperfect cooling and equation (4.18) gives the work done for the same. In this, temperature $T_3 > T_1$.

When the temperature of air leaving the intercooler (T_3) is equal to the atmospheric air temperature (T_1), then the intercooling is known as complete or perfect intercooling and $p_1 V_1 = p_2 V_3 = mRT_1$.

p-V and T-s diagrams for perfect intercooling are shown in Fig. 4.13.

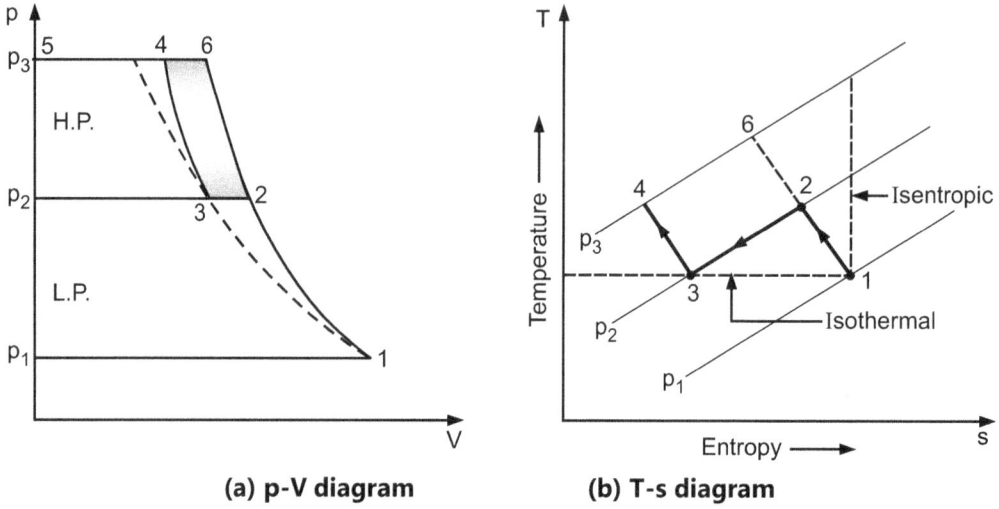

(a) p-V diagram   (b) T-s diagram
Fig. 4.13: Two-stage air compressor with perfect intercooler

The work done for two-stage air compressor with perfect cooling (i.e. $p_1V_1 = p_2V_3 = mRT_1$) is given by,

$$W = \frac{n}{n-1}mRT_1\left[\left(\frac{p_2}{p_1}\right)^{\frac{n-1}{n}} - 1\right] + \frac{n}{n-1}mRT_1\left[\left(\frac{p_3}{p_2}\right)^{\frac{n-1}{n}} - 1\right] \qquad \ldots (4.19)$$

$$= \frac{n}{n-1}mRT_1\left[\left(\frac{p_2}{p_1}\right)^{\frac{n-1}{n}} + \left(\frac{p_3}{p_2}\right)^{\frac{n-1}{n}} - 2\right]$$

$$= a \cdot mRT_1\left[\left(\frac{p_2}{p_1}\right)^{a} + \left(\frac{p_3}{p_2}\right)^{a} - 2\right] \qquad\qquad \left(\because \frac{n-1}{n} = a\right)$$

If the intake pressure p_1 and the delivery pressure p_3 are fixed, then the intermediate pressure p_2 for the minimum work done to drive the compressor is determined by,

$$\frac{dW}{dp_2} = 0$$

$$\therefore \quad \frac{d}{dp_2}\left(a \cdot mRT_1\left[\frac{p_2^{a}}{p_1^{a}} + \frac{p_3^{a}}{p_2^{a}} - 2\right]\right) = 0$$

$$\frac{d}{dp_2}\left(a \cdot mRT_1\left[\frac{p_2^{a}}{p_1^{a}} + p_3^{a} \cdot p_2^{-a} - 2\right]\right) = 0$$

$$\therefore \quad a \cdot mRT_1\left[\frac{a \cdot p_2^{a-1}}{p_1^{a}} + p_3^{a}(-a) \cdot p_2^{-a-1}\right] = 0 \qquad (\because p_1 \text{ and } p_3 \text{ are fixed})$$

$$\therefore \quad \frac{a \cdot p_2^{a-1}}{p_1^{a}} - \frac{ap_3^{a}}{p_2^{a+1}} = 0$$

$$\therefore \qquad \frac{p_2^{\frac{a-1}{a}}}{p_1} = \frac{p_3^{\frac{a}{a+1}}}{p_2}$$

$$p_2^{(a-1+a+1)} = p_1^a \, p_3^a$$

$$p_2^{2a} = p_1 \cdot p_3^a$$

$$p_2^2 = p_1 \cdot p_3$$

$$\therefore \qquad p_2 = \sqrt{p_1 \cdot p_3}$$

or $\qquad\qquad \dfrac{p_2}{p_1} = \dfrac{p_3}{p_2}$ $\qquad\qquad\qquad\qquad$ ... (4.20)

Above relation shows that for minimum work required or for maximum efficiency, the intermediate pressure is the geometric mean of initial and final pressure ($p_2^2 = p_1 p_3$) or pressure ratio in each stage is same $\left(\dfrac{p_2}{p_1} = \dfrac{p_3}{p_2}\right)$.

4.12.1 Work Done

Now, substituting $\dfrac{p_3}{p_2} = \dfrac{p_2}{p_1}$ in equation (4.18), we have minimum work required for two-stage reciprocating air compressor.

$$W = \frac{n}{n-1} p_1 V_1 \left[\left(\frac{p_2}{p_1}\right)^{\frac{n-1}{n}} + \left(\frac{p_2}{p_1}\right)^{\frac{n-1}{n}} - 2 \right]$$

$$= \frac{n}{n-1} p_1 V_1 \left[2 \cdot \left(\frac{p_2}{p_1}\right)^{\frac{n-1}{n}} - 2 \right]$$

$$= 2 \times \frac{n}{n-1} p_1 V_1 \left[\left(\frac{p_2}{p_1}\right)^{\frac{n-1}{n}} - 1 \right]$$

$$= 2 \times \text{Work required for each stage}$$

and minimum work required for X-stage compressor,

$$W = X \cdot \frac{n}{n-1} \cdot p_1 V_1 \left[\left(\frac{p_2}{p_1}\right)^{\frac{n-1}{n}} - 1 \right] \qquad\qquad ... (4.21)$$

or $\qquad\qquad W = X \dfrac{n}{n-1} p_1 V_1 \left[\left(\dfrac{pX+1}{p_1}\right)^{\frac{n-1}{X_n}} - 1 \right]$ $\qquad\qquad$ ... (4.21 (a))

Similarly, we can write for pressure ratio,

$$\frac{p_2}{p_1} = \frac{p_3}{p_2} = \frac{p_4}{p_3} = \dots \frac{p(X+1)}{p(X)} \qquad\qquad \text{... (For X-stage compression)}$$

4.13 HEAT REJECTED PER KG OF AIR

If the air is cooled to its initial temperature ($T_3 = T_1$), all the work done is rejected to the cooling medium (partly during the compression process and the remaining after compression), and there is no change in internal energy. (i.e. $\Delta u = 0$). Then, we have,

Heat rejected per kg of air = Work done per kg of air

$$Q = W$$

$$\therefore \qquad Q = \frac{n}{n-1} RT_1 \left[\left(\frac{p_2}{p_1} \right)^{\frac{n-1}{n}} - 1 \right] \qquad (\because m = 1 \text{ kg})$$

$$= \frac{n}{n-1} RT_1 \left[\frac{T_2}{T_1} - 1 \right] \qquad \left(\because \left(\frac{p_2}{p_1} \right)^{\frac{n-1}{n}} = \frac{T_2}{T_1} \right)$$

$$= \frac{n}{n-1} R (T_2 - T_1)$$

$$= \frac{n}{n-1} (c_p - c_v)(T_2 - T_1) \qquad (\because R = c_p - c_v)$$

$$= \left[c_p + c_v \left(\frac{\gamma - n}{n-1} \right) \right] (T_2 - T_1) \text{ per kg of air} \qquad \dots (4.22)$$

$$\left[\textbf{Note :} \frac{n}{n-1}(c_p - c_v) = c_p + c_v \left(\frac{\gamma - n}{n-1} \right) \right]$$

$$Q = c_p (T_2 - T_1) + \frac{c_v (\gamma - n)}{n-1} (T_2 - T_1)$$

Heat rejected per kg of air = Heat rejected to the coolant in the intercooler + Heat rejected to the coolant during compression process

In a single-stage compression, no cooling is done after compression, so first term will disappear.

4.14 CAPACITY CONTROL OF COMPRESSORS

Compressors are not running at their maximum rated capacity at all the time. To run them depending on demand, the controlling arrangement is required to balance demand and supply. Following are the common methods to control the compressors:

(i) Throttle Control:

Fig. 4.14 shows typical arrangement for throttle control. When the demand for high pressure air is less, pressure in the receiver increases and pushes spring loaded piston in downward direction. Thus, closes partly the suction valve and air intake is partly throttled. The reverse valve movement takes place to meet increase in demand of high pressure air.

In throttle control, fresh air flow from atmosphere to low pressure cylinder is controlled as per demand. Air taken through separate connection from receiver is used for valve movement.

(ii) Blowing Air to Atmosphere:

When the excessive pressure built-up in the receiver due to decrease in demand, the air from last stage cylinder is directly blown off to the atmosphere. Fig. 4.15 shows the arrangement for blowing air directly to atmosphere. High pressure air from receiver operates the relay piston against dead weight, and opens the port at B. High pressure air flows from B to C, and pushes piston at C in downward side. This causes opening of blows off valve at D, and air from high pressure cylinder is directly released to the atmosphere instead of supplying air to receiver.

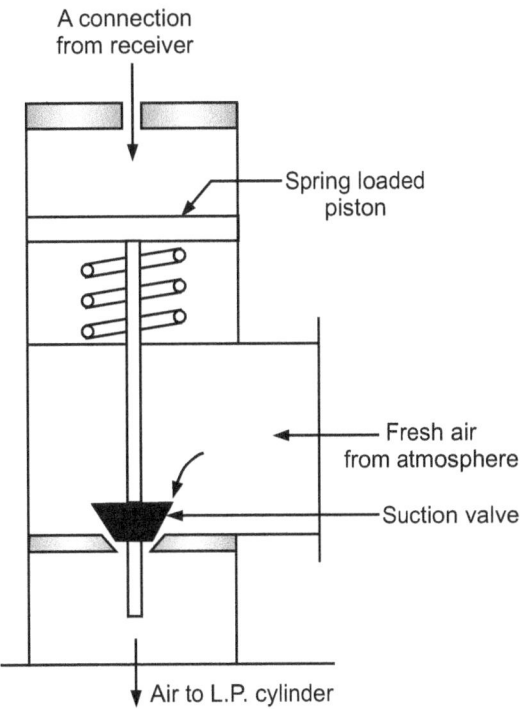

Fig. 4.14: Throttle control arrangement

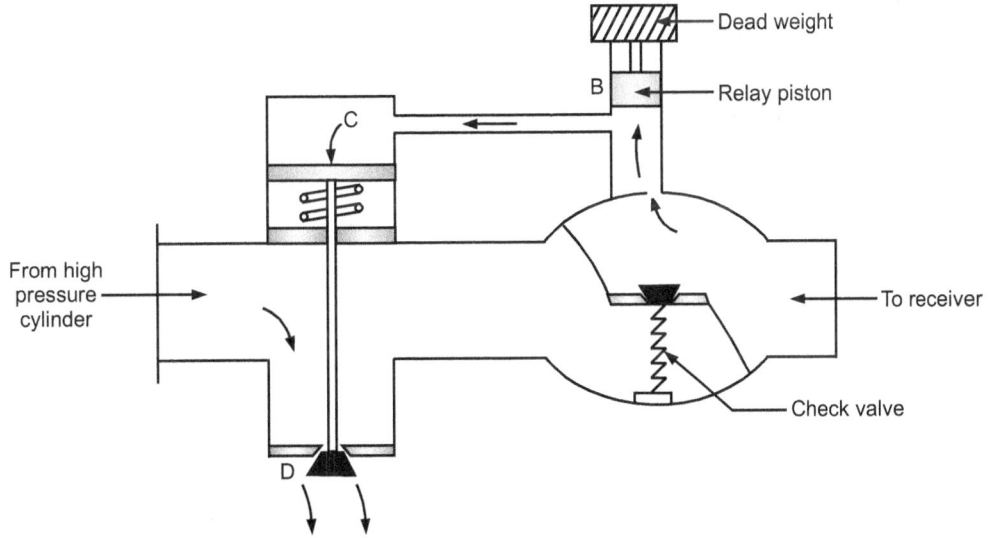

Fig. 4.15: Blowing off air to atmosphere

(iii) Clearance Control:

In this method, the volumetric efficiency is changed in proper proportion to control the output. This is achieved by having air pockets (clearance pocket) adjacent to the cylinder which is brought into communication with the cylinder by automatically operated valves.

4.15 DIFFERENCE BETWEEN INTERCOOLER AND AFTERCOOLER

Intercooler	Aftercooler
1. The cooler which is placed in between stages is called as intercooler.	1. The cooler fitted between last stage and receiver is called as aftercooler.
L.P Cylinder — Inter-cooler — H.P. Cylinder	H.P. Cylinder — After-cooler — Receiver
2. It reduces work done required for compression in next stage.	2. Aftercooler reduces size of the receiver and not the work done.

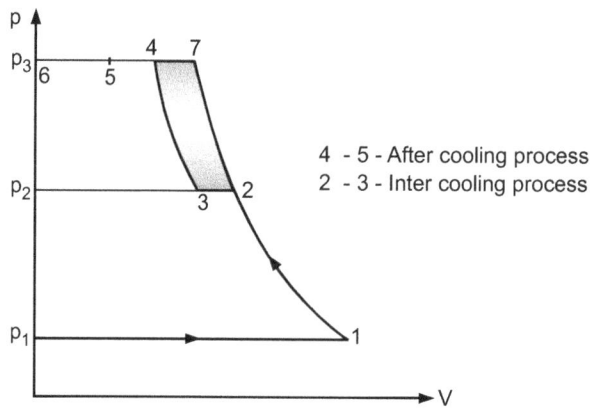

Fig. 4.16: Intercooling and aftercooling on p-V diagram

4.16 THEORETICAL AND ACTUAL p-V (INDICATOR) DIAGRAM FOR TWO-STAGE COMPRESSORS

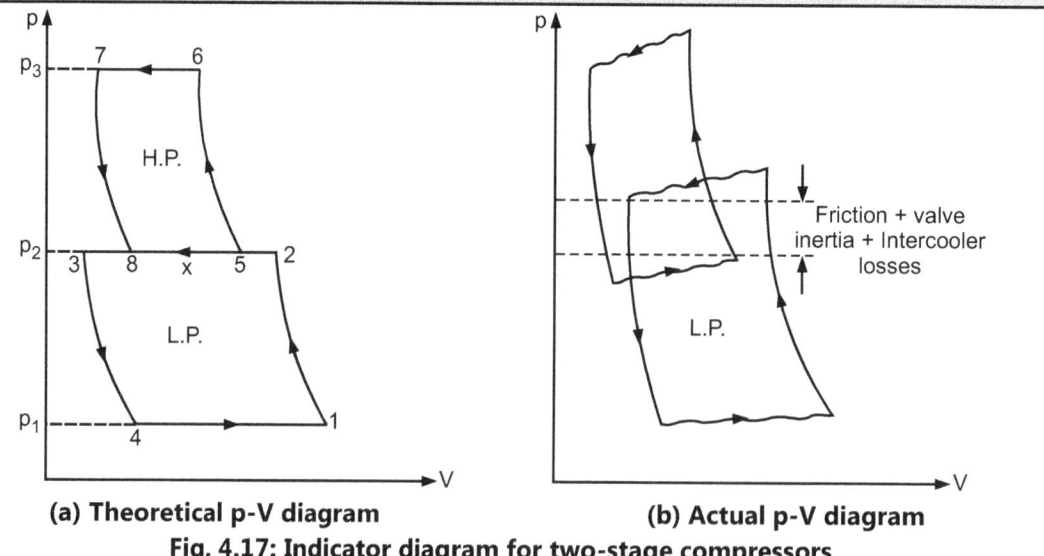

(a) Theoretical p-V diagram **(b) Actual p-V diagram**

Fig. 4.17: Indicator diagram for two-stage compressors

4.17 CYLINDER DIMENSIONS OF MULTISTAGE COMPRESSORS FOR PERFECT INTERCOOLING

$$V_{s1} \cdot \eta_{V_1} \cdot p_1 = V_{s2} \cdot \eta_{V_s} \cdot p_2 = V_{s3} \cdot p_3 = \ldots\ldots$$

η_v, V_s = Volumetric efficiency and stroke volume respectively.

4.18 ADVANTAGES OF MULTISTAGE COMPRESSORS

The advantages of multistage compressor with intercooling between stages are listed below:

1. The work done per kg of air is reduced by using an intercooler between two stages compared with single-stage compressor for the same delivery pressure.
2. Low pressure and temperature range in each stage results in
   (a) Reduced losses due to air leakage.
   (b) Effective lubrication due to lower temperature range.
   (c) The low pressure cylinder is designed to withstand low pressure and high pressure cylinder is designed for high pressure. This reduces cost of the compressor.
   (d) Improved volumetric efficiency.
3. Multistage machines have better mechanical balance, gives smooth torque diagram.

Disadvantages:

A multistage compressor with intercooler is more costly in initial cost than a single-stage compressor of the same capacity.

SOLVED PROBLEMS ON MULTISTAGE COMPRESSORS

Problem 4.6: A single-acting, two-stage air compressor with perfect intercooling delivers 15 kg/min of air at 25 bar pressure. The air from atmosphere is sucked in compressor at 1 bar and 15°C. The compression follows the law $pV^{1.25}$ = C.

Calculate:
(i) Indicated power
(ii) F.A.D.
(iii) The isothermal efficiency.

Solution:

Given: X = 2 (two stages), n = 1.25, m = 15 kg/min, p_3 = 25 bar, p_1 = 1 bar,

T_1 = 15°C = 15 + 273 = 288 K, n = 1.25.

For perfect intercooling,

Intermediate pressure, $p_2 = \sqrt{p_1 \times p_3} = \sqrt{1 \times 25}$ = 5 bar

(i) Indicated power:

$$\text{I.P.} = X \cdot \frac{n}{n-1} \cdot mRT_1 \left[\left(\frac{p_2}{p_1} \right)^{\frac{n-1}{n}} - 1 \right]$$

$$= 2 \times \frac{1.125}{0.25} \times \frac{15}{60} \times 287 \times 288 \times \left[\left(\frac{5}{1}\right)^{\frac{0.25}{1.25}} - 1 \right]$$

$$= 78467.34 \text{ kW}$$

$$= \mathbf{78.467 \text{ kW}}$$

(ii) Isothermal efficiency:

$$\text{Isothermal power} = mRT_1 \ln\left(\frac{p_3}{p_1}\right)$$

$$= \frac{15}{60} \times 287 \times 288 \times \ln\left(\frac{25}{1}\right)$$

$$= 66514.85 \text{ W}$$

$$= \mathbf{66.515 \text{ kW}}$$

$$\eta_{\text{iso}} = \frac{\text{Isothermal power}}{\text{Indicated power}}$$

$$= \frac{66.515}{78.467} = 0.8476$$

$$= \mathbf{84.76\%}$$

(iii) Free Air Delivered (F.A.D.):

$$p_1V_1 = mRT_1$$

$$1 \times 10^5 \times V_1 = 15 \times 287 \times 288$$

Free air delivered,

$$V_1 = \frac{15 \times 287 \times 288}{1 \times 10^5}$$

$$= \mathbf{12.398 \text{ m}^3/\text{min}}$$

Problem 4.7: A two-stage, single-acting reciprocating air compressor draws in air at 1 bar and 300 K. The delivery pressure is 12 bar. The intermediate pressure is ideal for minimum work and the intercooling is perfect. The index of compression is 1.3. Flow rate of air through the compressor is 0.15 kg/sec. Determine:

(i)   Power required to drive the compressor,

(ii) Saving in power compared to single stage,

(iii) Isothermal efficiency for multistage and single stage,

(iv) Heat rejected in intercooler if c_p = 1 kJ/kg·K and R = 0.287 kJ/kg·K.

Solution:

Given: X = 2 (two stages), p_1 = 1 bar, T_1 = 300 K, p_3 = 12 bar, n = 1.3, m = 0.15 kg/sec, c_p = 1 kJ/kg·K, R = 0.287 kJ/kg·K.

For minimum work and perfect intercooling,

Intermediate pressure, $p_2 = \sqrt{p_1 \times p_3} = \sqrt{1 \times 12} = 3.4641$ bar

(i) Power required to drive the compressor (multistage):

$$\text{Indicated power} = X \frac{n}{n-1} mRT_1 \left[\left(\frac{p_2}{p_1} \right)^{\frac{n-1}{n}} - 1 \right]$$

$$= 2 \times \frac{1.3}{0.3} \times 0.15 \times 0.287 \times 300 \times \left[\left(\frac{3.4641}{1} \right)^{\frac{0.3}{1.3}} - 1 \right]$$

$$= \textbf{37.166 kW}$$

(ii) Saving in power compared to single stage:

$$\text{I.P. (single stage)} = \frac{n}{n-1} mRT_1 \left[\left(\frac{p_3}{p_1} \right)^{\frac{0.3}{1.3}} - 1 \right]$$

$$= \frac{1.3}{0.3} \times 0.15 \times 0.287 \times 300 \times \left[\left(\frac{12}{1} \right)^{\frac{0.3}{1.3}} - 1 \right]$$

$$= \textbf{43.34 kW}$$

$$\text{Power saving} = \text{I.P. (single stage)} - \text{I.P. (multistage)}$$
$$= 43.34 - 37.166$$
$$= \textbf{6.17 kW}$$

(iii) Isothermal efficiency:

$$\text{Isothermal power} = mRT_1 \, ln \left(\frac{p_3}{p_1} \right)$$

$$= 0.15 \times 0.287 \times 300 \times ln \left(\frac{12}{1} \right)$$

$$= \textbf{32.09 kW}$$

For multistage,

$$\eta_{iso} = \frac{\text{Isothermal power}}{\text{Indicated power}}$$

$$= \frac{32.09}{37.166} = \textbf{0.8635}$$

$$= \textbf{86.35\% (multistage)}$$

$$\eta_{iso} = \frac{32.09}{43.34} = 0.7404$$

$$= \textbf{74.04\% (single stage)}$$

(iv) Heat rejected in intercooler:

Temperature after first stage,

$$T_2 = T_1 \left(\frac{p_2}{p_1} \right)^{\frac{n-1}{n}} = 300 \times \left(\frac{3.4641}{1} \right)^{\frac{0.3}{1.3}} = 399.62 \text{ K}$$

Heat rejected in intercooler,

$$Q = mc_p (T_2 - T_1) = 0.15 \times 1 \times (399.62 - 300)$$
$$= \textbf{14.94 kJ/sec}$$

Problem 4.8: A four stage compressor works between limits of 1 bar and 115 bar. The index of compression in each stage is 1.28. The temperature at the start of compression in each stage is 35°C and intermediate pressure are so chosen that the work is divided equally amongst stages. Neglecting clearance, calculate:

    (i)   Pressures p_2, p_3 and p_4.

    (ii)   Isothermal efficiency.

    (iii) Delivery temperature in each stage.

    Solution:

    Given: X = 4, p_1 = 1 bar, p_5 = 115 bar, n = 1.28, T_1 = 35°C = 35 + 273 = 308 K.

    Here, inlet temperature for each stage is 35°C, so cooling is perfect cooling.

(i)   **Pressures p_2, p_3 and p_4:**

    For perfect intercooling,

$$\frac{p_2}{p_1} = \frac{p_3}{p_2} = \frac{p_4}{p_3} = \frac{p_5}{p_4} = k$$

$$p_2 = kp_1$$

$$p_3 = kp_2 = k^2 p_1$$

    Similarly,

$$p_5 = k^4 p_1$$

$$\therefore \quad\quad 115 = k^4 \times 1$$

$$\therefore \quad\quad\quad k = 3.27$$

    p_2 = 3.27 bar, p_3 = 10.69 bar, p_4 = 34.96 bar.

(ii) **Isothermal efficiency:**

    Indicated power,

$$\text{I.P.} = X \cdot \frac{n}{n-1} mRT_1 \left[\left(\frac{p_2}{p_1} \right)^{\frac{n-1}{n}} - 1 \right]$$

$$= 4 \times \frac{1.28}{0.28} \times 1 \times 0.287 \times 308 \times \left[\left(\frac{3.27}{1} \right)^{\frac{0.28}{1.28}} - 1 \right]$$

$$= \textbf{478.22 kJ/kg}$$

$$\text{Isothermal power} = mRT_1 \ln \left(\frac{p_5}{p_1} \right) = 1 \times 0.287 \times 308 \times \ln \left(\frac{115}{1} \right)$$

$$= \textbf{419.43 kJ/kg}$$

    Isothermal efficiency,

$$\eta_{iso} = \frac{\text{Isothermal power}}{\text{Indicated power}} = \frac{419.43}{478.22} = 0.877$$

$$= \textbf{87.7\%}$$

(**Note:** Here mass flow rate is considered as 1 kg/sec and indicated power and isothermal power are calculated. If mass is taken as 1 kg then, we get, work done per cycle. Ratio of work done will give same isothermal efficiency.)

(iii) Delivery temperature in each stage:

Temperature at suction and work done for each stage is equal, so delivery temperature in each stage is same. It is given by,

$$\frac{T_2}{T_1} = \left(\frac{p_2}{p_1}\right)^{\frac{n-1}{n}}$$

$$\therefore \qquad T_2 = \left(\frac{3.27}{1}\right)^{\frac{0.28}{1.28}} \times 308$$

$$= \mathbf{399.2\ K}$$

Problem 4.9: A two-stage compressor running at 210 r.p.m. delivers free air at 2.2 m³/min. The pressure and temperature of air at the suction are 1 bar and 298 K respectively. The delivery pressure is 55 bar. Clearance for both the cylinders is 5% of the stroke. Strokes of both cylinders are equal to the diameter of the L.P. cylinder. The index of compression and re-expansion is 1.3.

Determine:

    (i)   Minimum power required to run the compressor when intercooling is perfect,

    (ii)   Stroke and diameters of cylinders,

    (iii) Ratio of cylinder volumes.

Solution:

Given: $X = 2$, F.A.D. $(V_1) = 2.2$ m³/min, N = 210 r.p.m., $p_1 = 1$ bar, $T_1 = 298$ K, $p_3 = 55$ bar, $C = 0.5\% = 0.05$, n = 1.3, $L_{L.P.} = L_{H.P.} = D_{L.P.}$

$$p_1V_1 = mRT_1$$
$$1 \times 10^5 \times 2.2 = m \times 287 \times 298$$
$$\therefore \qquad m = 2.57\ \text{kg/min}$$

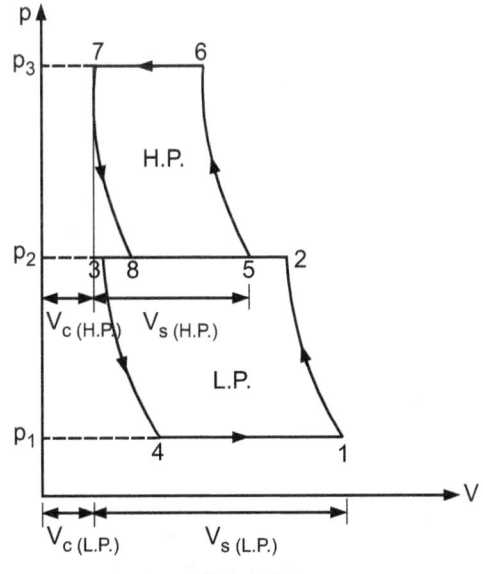

Fig. 4.18

For perfect intercooling,

Intermediate pressure,

$$p_2 = \sqrt{p_1 \times p_3} = \sqrt{1 \times 55} = 7.42 \text{ bar}$$

(i) Minimum power required to run the compressor:

$$\text{I.P.} = X \cdot \frac{n}{n-1} mRT_1 \left[\left(\frac{p_2}{p_1}\right)^{\frac{n-1}{n}} - 1 \right]$$

$$= 2 \times \frac{1.3}{0.3} \times \frac{2.57}{60} \times 0.287 \times 298 \times \left[\left(\frac{7.42}{1}\right)^{\frac{0.3}{1.3}} - 1 \right]$$

$$= \textbf{18.67 kW}$$

(ii) Stroke and diameters of cylinders:

The volumetric efficiency of L.P. cylinder is given by,

$$\eta_{vol\,(L.P.)} = 1 + C - C \left(\frac{p_2}{p_1}\right)^{\frac{1}{n}}$$

$$= 1 + 0.05 - 0.05 \left(\frac{7.42}{1}\right)^{\frac{1}{1.3}}$$

$$= 0.8164$$

$$= \textbf{81.64\%}$$

Also, volumetric efficiency is given by,

$$\eta_{vol\,(L.P.)} = \frac{V_{a\,(L.P.)}}{V_{s\,(L.P.)}}$$

$$V_{s\,(L.P.)} = \frac{2.2}{0.8164} = \textbf{2.6947 m}^3\textbf{/min}$$

$$V_{s\,(L.P.)} = \frac{2.6947}{N} = \frac{2.6947}{210} = \textbf{0.0128 m}^3$$

$$V_{s\,(L.P.)} = \frac{\pi}{4} D_{L.P.}^2 \, L_{L.P.} \qquad\qquad (\because L_{L.P.} = D_{L.P.})$$

$$= \frac{\pi}{4} D_{L.P.}^3$$

$$\therefore \qquad D_{L.P.}^3 = V_{s\,(L.P.)} \times \frac{4}{\pi}$$

$$= 0.0128 \times \frac{4}{\pi}$$

$$\therefore \qquad D_{L.P.} = 0.2538 \text{ m} = \textbf{25.38 cm}$$

$$L_{L.P.} = 0.2538 \text{ m} = \textbf{25.38 cm}$$

The volumetric efficiency of both cylinders is same because $\dfrac{p_2}{p_1} = \dfrac{p_3}{p_2}$

and clearance is same.

$$\eta_{vol\,(L.P.)} = \eta_{vol\,(H.P.)}$$

$\therefore$
$$D_{L.P.}^2 \, p_1 = D_{H.P.}^2 \cdot p_2$$

$\therefore$
$$D_{H.P.}^2 = \dfrac{D_{L.P.}^2 \cdot p_1}{p_2}$$

$$= \dfrac{(0.2538)^2 \times 1}{7.42}$$

$$D_{H.P.} = 0.0932 \text{ m} = \textbf{9.32 cm}$$

(iii) Ratio of cylinder volumes:

Points 1 and 5 are on isothermal line, we have,

$$p_1 V_1 = p_5 V_5 \qquad (\because V_1 \text{ and } V_5 \text{ cylinder volumes of L.P. and H.P.})$$

$\therefore$
$$\dfrac{V_1}{V_5} = \dfrac{p_5}{p_1} = \dfrac{7.42}{1} = \textbf{7.42}$$

Problem 4.10: A single-acting, two-stage compressor with complete intercooling delivers 6 kg/min of air at 16 bar. Intake air conditions are 1 bar and 15°C. Compression and expansion follows law $pV^{1.3} = C$.

Calculate:

(i)   Power required to run the compressor at 420 r.p.m.,

(ii) Isothermal efficiency,

(iii) Free air delivered per second,

(iv) Swept volume for each cylinder if volumetric efficiency of both cylinders is 90%,

(v)   Net heat transferred in L.P. and H.P. cylinders during compression and also in intercooler.

Assume $R = 0.287$ kJ/kg·K, $C_v = 0.71$ kg/kg·K.

Solution:

Given: $X = 2$, $m = 6$ kg/min, $p_3 = 16$ bar, $p_1 = 1$ bar, $T_1 = 15°C = 15 + 273 = 288$ K, $n = 1.3$, $N = 420$ r.p.m., $\eta_{vol} = 90\%$, $R = 0.287$ kJ/kg·K, $c_v = 0.71$ kJ/kg·K

$$\text{Intermediate pressure, } p_2 = \sqrt{p_1 \cdot p_3}$$

$$= \sqrt{1 \times 16} = 4 \text{ bar.}$$

(i) Power required to run the compressor:

$$\text{Indicated power} = X \cdot \dfrac{n}{n-1} mRT_1 \left[\left(\dfrac{p_2}{p_1}\right)^{\frac{n-1}{n}} - 1 \right]$$

$$= 2 \times \frac{1.3}{0.3} \times \frac{6}{60} \times 0.287 \times 288 \times \left[\left(\frac{4}{1} \right)^{\frac{0.3}{1.3}} - 1 \right]$$

$$= \textbf{27 kW}$$

(ii) Isothermal efficiency:

$$\text{Isothermal power} = mRT_1 \, ln \left(\frac{p_3}{p_1} \right)$$

$$= \frac{6}{60} \times 0.287 \times 288 \times ln \left(\frac{16}{1} \right)$$

$$= 22.92 \text{ kW}$$

$$\text{Isothermal efficiency, } \eta_{iso} = \frac{\text{Isothermal power}}{\text{Indicated power}} = \frac{22.92}{27} = 0.8489$$

$$= \textbf{84.89\%}$$

(iii) Free air delivered:

$$p_1 V_1 = mRT_1$$

$$V_1 = \frac{6}{60} \times \frac{287 \times 288}{1 \times 10^5}$$

$$= \textbf{0.08265 m}^3\textbf{/sec}$$

(iv) Swept volume:

$$\text{Swept volume}_{(L.P.)} = \frac{F.A.D}{N \times \eta_{vol}}$$

$$= \frac{0.08265}{\dfrac{420}{60} \times 0.90}$$

$$= 0.01312 \text{ m}^3$$

$$V_{s\,(L.P.)} \cdot \eta_{vol\,(L.P.)} \cdot p_1 = V_{s\,(H.P.)} \cdot \eta_{vol\,(H.P.)} \cdot p_2$$

But,

$$\eta_{vol\,(H.P.)} = \eta_{vol.\,(H.P.)}$$

$$\therefore \qquad \text{Swept volume}_{(H.P.)} = \frac{V_{s\,(L.P.)} \times p_1}{p_2}$$

$$= \frac{0.01312 \times 1}{4}$$

$$= \textbf{0.00328 m}^3$$

(v) Heat transferred:

Temperature T_2 is given by,

$$\frac{T_2}{T_1} = \left(\frac{p_2}{p_1} \right)^{\frac{n-1}{n}}$$

$\therefore$ $\qquad$ $T_2 = \left(\dfrac{4}{1}\right)^{\frac{0.3}{1.3}} \times 288 = 396.58 \text{ K}$

and $\qquad$ $c_p = c_v + R = 0.71 + 0.287 = 0.997 \text{ kg/kg·K}$

also $\qquad$ $\gamma = \dfrac{c_p}{c_v} = \dfrac{0.997}{0.71} = 1.404$

Heat transferred in L.P. cylinder

$$= m \cdot c_v \frac{\gamma - n}{n - 1} (T_2 - T_1)$$

$$= \frac{6}{60} \times 0.71 \times \frac{1.404 - 1.3}{1.3 - 1} \times (396.58 - 288)$$

$$= \textbf{2.6725 kJ/sec}$$

Heat transferred in H.P. cylinder

$$= \text{Heat transferred in L.P. cylinder}$$

$$= \textbf{2.6725 kJ/sec}$$

Heat transferred in intercooler $= m \cdot C_p (T_2 - T_1) = \dfrac{6}{60} \times 0.997 \times (396.58 - 288)$

$$= \textbf{10.825 kJ/sec.}$$

Problem 4.11: A two-stage, double-acting air compressor, operating at 220 r.p.m. takes in air at 1.0 bar and 27°C. The size of the L.P. cylinder is 360 × 400 mm. The stroke of H.P. cylinder is the same as that of L.P. cylinder and the clearance of both the cylinders is 4%. The L.P. cylinder discharges the air at a pressure of 4.0 bar. The air passes through the intercooler so that it enters the H.P. cylinder at 27°C and 3.8 bar, finally it is discharged from the compressor at 15.2 bar. The value of n in both the cylinders is 1.3, $c_p = 1.0035$ kJ/kg·K and R = 0.287 kJ/kg·K.

Calculate:

(i) Heat rejected in the intercooler,

(ii) Diameter of H.P. cylinder,

(iii) Power required to drive the H.P. cylinder.

Solution: Given: X = 2, Double acting, N = 220 r.p.m., p_1 = 1 bar, T_1 = 27°C, $D_{L.P.}$ = 360 mm = 0.36 m, $L_{L.P.}$ = 0.4 m, $L_{H.P.}$ = 0.4 m, p_2 = 4.0 bar, C = 0.04, p_5 = 3.8 bar, T_5 = 27°C = 27 + 273 = 300 K, p_7 = 15.2 bar, n = 1.3, c_p = 1.0035 kJ/kg·K, R = 0.287 kJ/kg·K.

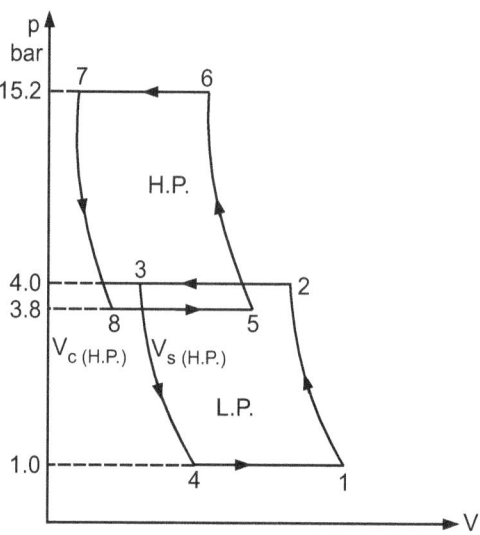

Fig. 4.19

Swept volume of L.P. cylinder $= \dfrac{\pi}{4} D_{L.P.}^2 \times L_{L.P.} = \dfrac{\pi}{4} \times (0.36)^2 \times 0.4$

$$= 0.04071 \text{ m}^3$$

Volumetric efficiency of L.P. cylinder,

$$\eta_{vol\,(L.P.)} = 1 + C - C\left(\frac{p_2}{p_1}\right)^{\frac{1}{n}} = 1 + 0.04 - 0.04 \times \left(\frac{4}{1}\right)^{\frac{1}{1.3}}$$

$$= \mathbf{0.9238 = 92.38\%}$$

Also, $\eta_{vol\,(L.P.)} = \dfrac{V_1}{V_s}$

$\therefore$ $V_1 = V_s \cdot \eta_{vol\,(L.P.)} = 0.04071 \times 0.9238$

$$= 0.03761 \text{ m}^3$$

$V_1/\text{min} = V_1 \times 2 \times 220$ (2 for double acting)

$$= \mathbf{16.54 \text{ m}^3/\text{min}}$$

Also, $p_1 V_1 = mRT_1$

$$m = \frac{p_1 V_1}{RT}$$

$$= \frac{1 \times 10^5 \times 16.54}{287 \times 300}$$

$$= \mathbf{19.22 \text{ kg/min}}$$

(i) Heat rejected in the intercooler:

$$\frac{T_1}{T_2} = \left(\frac{p_2}{p_1}\right)^{\frac{n-1}{n}}$$

$\therefore$

$$T_2 = T_1 \times \left(\frac{p_2}{p_1}\right)^{\frac{n-1}{n}} = 300 \times \left(\frac{4}{1}\right)^{\frac{0.3}{1.3}} = 413 \text{ K}$$

$$Q_{intercooler} = m\, c_p\, (T_2 - T_5) = \frac{19.22}{60} \times 1.0035 \times (413 - 300)$$

$$= \mathbf{36.37 \text{ kJ/sec}}$$

(ii) Diameter of H.P. cylinder:

Volume of air drawn in H.P. cylinder per minute,

$$V_{5\,(H.P.)}/min = \frac{mRT_5}{p_5} = \frac{19.22 \times 287 \times 300}{3.8 \times 10^5}$$

$$= 4.355 \text{ m}^3/min$$

$$\frac{p_2}{p_1} = 4, \quad \frac{p_6}{p_5} = \frac{15.2}{3.8} = 4$$

i.e.

$$\frac{p_2}{p_1} = \frac{p_6}{p_5}$$

and

$$C_{L.P.} = C_{H.P.} = 0.4$$

$\therefore$

$$\eta_{vol\,(H.P.)} = \eta_{vol\,(H.P.)} = 0.9238 = 92.38\%$$

$\therefore$

$$V_{5\,(H.P.)} = \frac{V_5}{\eta_{vol\,(H.P.)}} = \mathbf{0.0107 \text{ m}^3}$$

$$V_{5\,(H.P.)} = \frac{\pi}{4}\, D_{H.P.}^2 \times L_{H.P.}$$

$$0.0107 = \frac{\pi}{4} \times D_{H.P.}^2 \times 0.4$$

$$D_{H.P.} = 0.1847 \text{ m}$$

$$= \mathbf{18.47 \text{ cm}}$$

(iii) Power required to drive the H.P. cylinder:

$$T_6 = T_2 \text{ and } T_5 = T_1$$

$\therefore$ Power required to drive the H.P. cylinder,

$$= \frac{n}{n-1}\, mR\, (T_6 - T_5)$$

$$= \frac{1.3}{0.3} \times \frac{19.12}{60} \times 0.287 \times (413 - 300)$$

$$= \mathbf{45 \text{ kW}}$$

EXERCISE

1. Describe the working of a single-stage reciprocating air compressor.

2. Derive the expression for work in case of single acting single-stage air compressor.

3. Derive an expression for volumetric efficiency of a reciprocating air compressor in terms of clearance ratio, pressure ratio and compression index.

4. Define 'clearance ratio' in air compressor. What is its effect on work and volumetric efficiency? Also comment on effect of pressure ratio and compression index on volumetric efficiency.

5. Explain the methods to improve isothermal efficiency of an air compressor.

6. Derive expression for compression ratio to give maximum compressor efficiency

7. Explain in brief:
   (a) Isothermal efficiency
   (b) Volumetric efficiency
   (c) Mechanical efficiency
   (d) Free air delivery
   (e) Mean effective pressure

8. What are disadvantages of compressing air in single stage compressor through large ratio? Explain with the help of p-V diagram. How are they overcome in multi-staging?

9. Prove that, for multistage reciprocating air compression, the intermediate pressure, with perfect intercooling and for minimum work output, is geometric mean of its neighboring pressures.

10. Explain throttle control of compressor.

11. How actual indicator diagram for a single stage compressor differs from theoretical indicator diagram?

PROBLEMS FOR PRACTICE

1. A single-stage reciprocating air compressor is required to compress 60 m^3 of air from 1 bar to 8 bar at 22°C. Find work done by the compressor, if the compression of air is:

   (a) Isothermal   **(Ans.** 12.5 MJ**)**

   (b) Isentropic with isentropic index as 1.4   **(Ans.** 17 MJ**)**

   (c) Polytropic with polytropic index as 1.25   **(Ans.** 15.5 MJ**)**

2. A single-stage, double acting reciprocating air compressor compress air from 1 bar to 7 bar according to law $pV^{1.2}$ = C. Indicated power is 11 kW. The average piston speed is 150 m/s. L/ D = 1.5. Neglecting clearance volume, determine cylinder dimensions.

    (Ans. 156 mm, 234 mm)

3. A single acting, single-stage reciprocating air compressor compress air from 1 bar at 20°C to 5.5 bar according to law $pV^{1.2}$ = C and clearance volume is 5% of the stroke volume. The bore and stroke of compressor are 200 mm and 300 mm respectively. Determine

    (a) Mean effective pressure   **(Ans. 1.807 bar)**

    (b) Power required to drive the compressor at 500 r. p.m.   **(Ans. 14.19 kW)**

4. A single acting, two stage reciprocating air compressor compress air from 0.1 MPa at 16°C to 0.7 MPa. The air is taken in at the rate of 0.2 m³/s. The intermediate pressure is ideal and intercooling is perfect. The compression index in both stages is 1.25 and the compressor runs at 600 r. p. m. Neglect effect of clearance.

    Determine:

    *   The intermediate pressure,   **(Ans. 0.2646 MPa)**

    *   The total volume of each cylinder,   **(Ans. 0.02 m³, 0.0076 m³)**

    *   The power required to drive the compressor, and   **(Ans. 42.97 kW)**

    *   Rate of heat rejection in the intercooler   **(Ans. 15 kJ/s)**

                                                                              ✴✴✴

UNIT V

ROTARY AIR COMPRESSORS

INTRODUCTION

Air compressors are used for various purposes as described in previous chapter. Different types of compressors are designed and used according to pressure and quantity requirements. Three important types (roots blower, vane type, screw type) of rotary compressors with their features are described in this chapter.

5.1 CLASSIFICATION OF COMPRESSORS

Compressors are classified as follows:

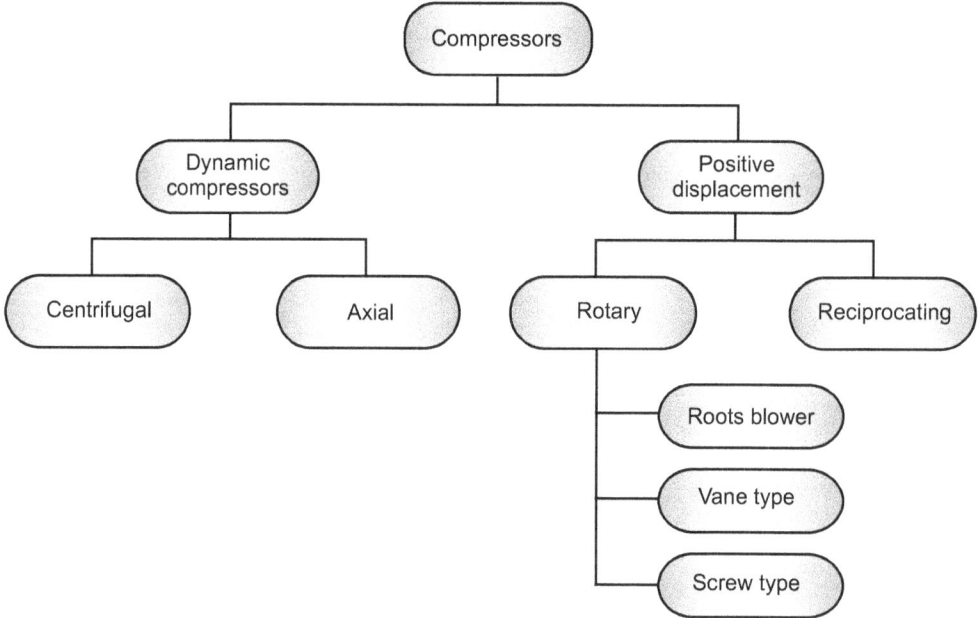

1. Positive Displacement Air Compressors:

In positive displacement air compressors, the air is trapped in specified boundaries and delivered at regular interval to the receiver after compression.

  (a) Reciprocating Air Compressors: In reciprocating air compressors, the air pressure is increased by means of variation in the cylinder volume with the help of moving piston.

  (b) Rotary Air Compressors: In these compressors, the air is entrapped between two sets of engaging surfaces, and pressure rise is either by back flow of air (roots blower) or by both squeezing action and back flow of air (vane type).

2. Dynamic Compressors:

These are also known as steady-flow or non-positive displacement compressors. In these compressors, air flows continuously and steadily. The energy from the impeller is transferred to the air as the air flows through the system and increases pressure mainly due to dynamic effects.

5.2 DIFFERENCE BETWEEN RECIPROCATING AND ROTARY COMPRESSORS

Reciprocating Compressor	Rotary Compressor
1. These compressors are suitable for high pressure with low volume.	1. These compressors are suitable for low pressure with large volume.
2. Receiver is required because of intermittent delivery.	2. No need of receiver delivering air at uniform rate.
3. For the same flow rate, size of compressor is large and weight is more.	3. For the same flow rate, size of compressor is small and it is light weight.
4. They are subjected to heavy vibrations.	4. Comparatively, these face low vibrations.
5. Maintenance cost is more.	5. Maintenance cost is less.
6. Leakage problem is more.	6. Comparatively low leakage.

5.3 DIFFERENCE BETWEEN COMPRESSOR AND BLOWER

Compressor	Blower
1. Compressor is a device for compressing air or gas at high pressure.	1. Blower is a device for blowing air or gas. They relatively operate at low pressure.
2. Compressor compresses gases and increases their pressure or internal energy.	2. Blower is capable of providing kinetic energy to the gases.
3. It may be reciprocating or rotary type.	3. It is rotary type with axial flow or radial flow.
4. Some types of compressors need cooling arrangement.	4. Cooling arrangement is not required for blowers.
5. Compressors are used to supply compressed air for various applications such as rock drills, machine tools, etc.	5. Blowers are used for low-pressure applications such as agitation, pneumatic conveying or combustion air.
6. They consume more power.	6. They consume less power.

5.4 ROOTS BLOWER COMPRESSORS

- A roots blower compressor consists of two lobe rotors in an air-tight casing as shown in Fig. 5.1. For higher pressure ratio, three or four versions are used.
- The lobes of rotor are of involute, epicycloid or hypocycloid profile to ensure correct meeting.

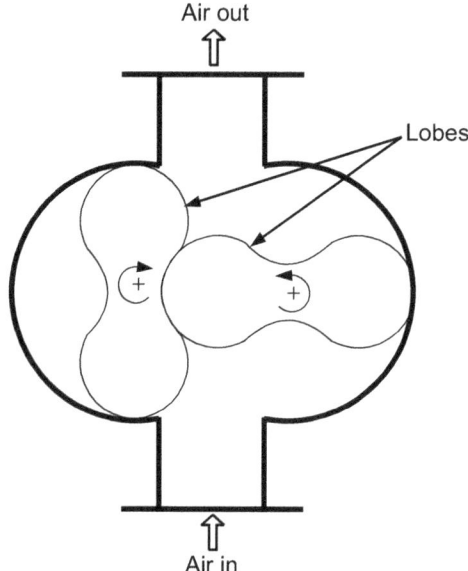

Fig. 5.1: Roots blower compressor

- One of the rotors is connected to the drive and the second rotor is gear driven from the first.
- As the rotors rotate, the air at atmospheric pressure, is trapped in pockets formed between the lobes and casing.
- The rotary motion of the lobe delivers the entrapped air to the receiver.
- Thus, more and more flow of air into the receiver increases its pressure.
- Finally the air at higher pressure is delivered from the receiver.
- When the rotating lobe uncovers the outlet port, some air from the receiver flows back into the compressor pocket. This is termed as backflow process. The back flow air is mixed with entrapped air in the pocket. The back flow stops when pressure in the pocket and receiver becomes equal. Thus the pressure of the air entrapped in the pocket is increased at constant volume entirely by the back flow of the air.
- There is clearance between casings and lobes to reduce wear. But this clearance causes leakage. This leakage affects efficiency of compressors with increase in pressure ratio.

  The p-V diagram for roots blower is shown in Fig. 5.2.

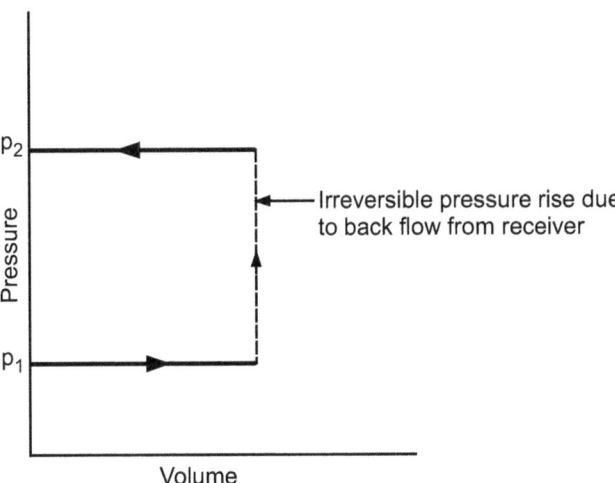

Fig. 5.2: p-V diagram for roots blower compressor

Let,

$$p_1, p_2 = \text{Intake and discharge pressure of air}$$
$$\gamma = \text{Isentropic index for air, and}$$
$$V_1 = \text{Volume of compressed air}$$

Theoretical work done in compressing air is,

$$W_t = \frac{\gamma}{\gamma - 1} \times p_1 V_1 \left[\left(\frac{p_2}{p_1} \right)^{\frac{\gamma - 1}{\gamma}} - 1 \right]$$

and actual work done, $W_a = V_1 (p_2 - p_1)$

Efficiency of roots blower is given by,

$$\eta = \frac{W_t}{W_a}$$

$$\eta = \frac{\dfrac{\gamma}{\gamma - 1} \times p_1 V_1 \left[\left(\dfrac{p_2}{p_1} \right)^{\frac{\gamma - 1}{\gamma}} - 1 \right]}{V_1 (p_2 - p_1)}$$

$$= \frac{\gamma}{\gamma - 1} \times \frac{\left[(r)^{\frac{\gamma - 1}{\gamma}} - 1 \right]}{(r - 1)} \qquad \text{where, } r = p_2/p_1 \text{ pressure ratio}$$

Also,
$$\frac{\gamma}{\gamma - 1} = \frac{C_p}{R}$$

∴
$$\eta = \frac{C_p}{R} \times \frac{\left[(r)^{\frac{\gamma - 1}{\gamma}} - 1 \right]}{(r - 1)}$$

From above equation it can be seen that efficiency of roots blower decreases with increase in pressure ratio. For high pressure, two or more roots blowers are arranged in series and intercoolers are used at each stage.

This compressor has number of demerits but it is suitable for scavenging and supercharging of internal combustion engines.

5.5 VANE BLOWER COMPRESSORS

• A vane blower compressor consists of a rotor mounted eccentrically in an air-tight casing as shown in Fig. 5.3.

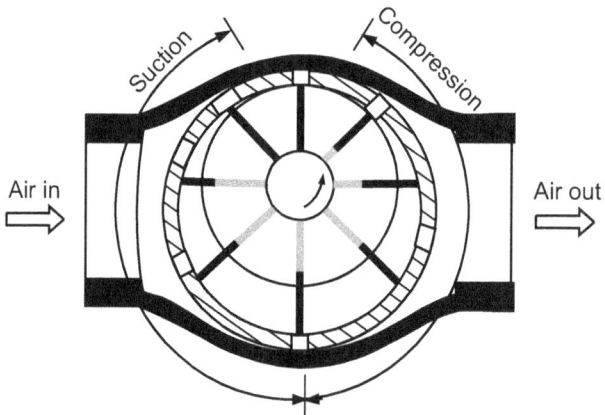

Fig. 5.3: Vane blower compressor

• The rotor has number of slots containing vanes.

• When the rotor rotates vanes are pressed against the casing and forms air-tight passage. The air is trapped in the passage formed between the vanes and the casing.

• When the rotating vanes uncover the exist port, some air under high pressure flows back into the passage. The backflow air mixed with entrapped air in this passage.

• The back flow stops when pressure in the passage and receiver becomes equal.

• Thus, the pressure of the air entrapped in the pocket is increased first by decreasing the volume and then by the back flow of the air. The p-V diagram for roots blower is shown in Fig. 5.4.

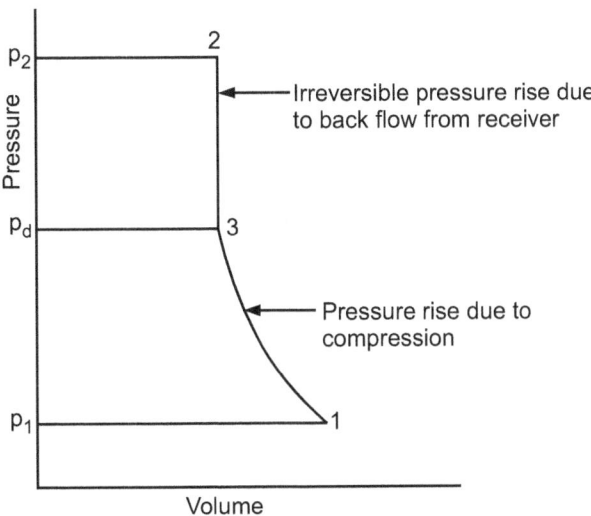

Fig. 5.4: p-V diagram of vane blower compressor

Theoretical work done due to compression (1-3)

$$W_1 = \frac{\gamma}{\gamma - 1} \times p_1 V_1 \left[\left(\frac{p_2}{p_1} \right)^{\frac{\gamma - 1}{\gamma}} - 1 \right]$$

and actual work done due to backflow (3-2)

$$W_2 = V_2 (p_2 - p_d)$$

Total work done, $W = W_1 + W_2$

Efficiency of roots blower is given by,

$$\eta = \frac{W_2}{W_1 + W_2}$$

5.6 ROTARY SCREW COMPRESSORS

- Rotary screw compressors consist of two rotors within a casing where the rotors compress the air internally. There are no valves. These units are basically oil cooled (with air cooled or water cooled oil coolers) where the oil seals the internal clearances.
- Since the cooling takes place right inside the compressor, the working parts never experience extreme operating temperatures. The rotary compressor, therefore, is a continuous duty, air cooled or water cooled compressor package.
- Rotary screw air compressors are easy to maintain and operate. Capacity control for these compressors is accomplished by variable speed and variable compressor displacement.

- For the latter control technique, a slide valve is positioned in the casing. As the compressor capacity is reduced, the slide valve opens, bypassing a portion of the compressed air back to the suction. Advantages of the rotary screw compressor include smooth, pulse-free air output in a compact size with high output volume over a long life.
- The oil-free rotary screw air compressor utilizes specially designed air ends to compress air without oil in the compression chamber yielding true oil-free air. Oil-free rotary screw air compressors may be air cooled and water cooled   and provides the same flexibility as oil flooded rotaries when oil-free air is required.

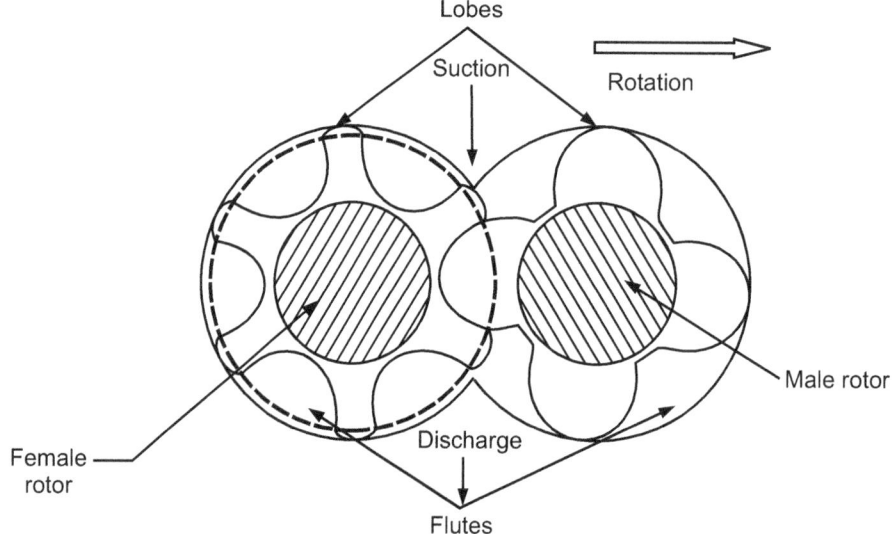

Fig. 5.5 Rotary screw compressor

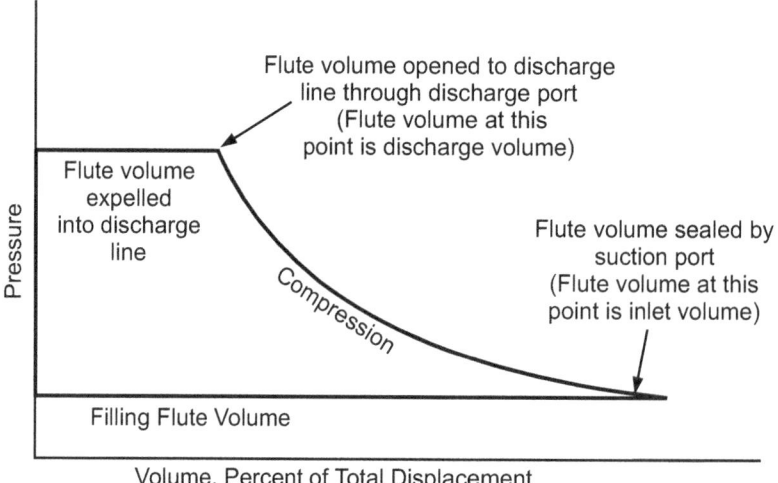

Fig. 5.6: p-V diagram of rotary screw compressor

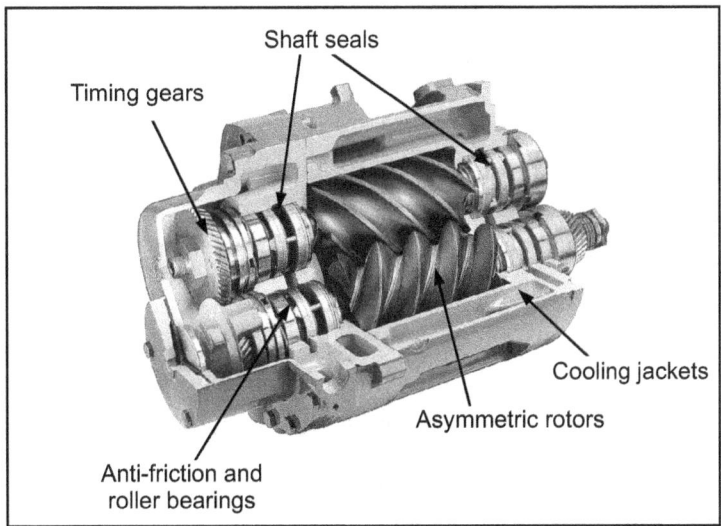

Fig. 5.7: Rotary screw compressor

A rotary screw compressor has no clearance, so there is no clearance expansion at the end of the discharge event. Theoretically, a rotary screw compressor would have 100% volumetric efficiency, but there is not a gas-tight seal between the rotors and between the rotors and the housing. This causes leakage between flutes and lowers the volumetric efficiency. Leakage is a function of compressor tip speed and pressure difference, and will decrease the inlet volume to about 90% of displacement.

5.7 FANS

A pressure difference required to produce a continuous flow of air and combustion gases, from the furnace to the stack, is called a draft. Early and small capacity steam generators used natural draft produced by the chimney, or the stack alone. This draft is created because of the density difference in the hot air column of the stack and equivalent cold air column of atmospheric air.

In modern boilers, large quantities of air and combustion gases are to be handled in short time. The gas passages are very long with bends and baffles. Also there are various heat exchangers like superheaters, reheaters, economizers and air preheaters which offer resistance to the gas flow and cause pressure losses. The stack alone is not able to provide the necessary draft. An artificial on mechanical draft system in the form of fans is to be used. The stack is used to assist the fans in overcoming the pressure losses and to help disperse the flue gases high into the atmosphere to protect the neighbouring area from pollution and ash fall out.

The fans used by the modern boilers are of two types forced-draft (FD) and induced draft (ID) fans. When either one is used alone it should overcome the total air and gas pressure losses in the boilers.

Forced draft fans are used alone in many large boilers especially marine boilers. They are installed at the air entrance to the air preheater and put entire system upto the stack entrance under positive gas pressure. They handle cold air and therefore have following advantages over ID fans:

1.   Lower maintenance problems.

2.   Low power requirement. A fan is a steady flow system. Hence W.D. = $\int$ Vdp. Since cold air, has lowest specific volume, the WD and hence power required is low.

3.   Reduced load. Since there is no fuel, the load of the gas equivalent of fuel is absent.

4.   Low capital and operating costs.

Disadvantages:

The disadvantage is a positive gas pressure is present throughout the furnace. Therefore hot and obnoxious gases leak from the boiler to the outside. A gas tight furnace construction is necessary, especially so, for the inspection and furnace doors, soot blowing boxes etc. This adds to the cost.

Normally, two FD fans running in parallel are used.

Induced draft fans are located in the flue gas passage between the air preheater and the stack. They suck the gases from the system and discharge them at atmospheric pressure to the stack. They create a negative pressure in the system. They handle hot flue gases which contains air supplied, gas equivalent of fuel and leakages into the system. Their power requirement is therefore greater than that of FD fans. They have to handle corrosive combustion products and ash and need air/water cooled bearings. ID fans are rarely used alone.

Modern boilers use both FD and ID fans together. FD fans pushes air through air preheater, dampers, air ducts and burners into the furnace while ID fan suck the combustion gases fxom the furnace and through the superheaters, reheaters, economizers and air preheaters. The furnace in this case is said to operate with a balanced draft. The pressure kept in the system is atmospheric or slightly less than atmospheric to ensure an inward leakage if any.

The fans used have very large capacities. For example, 1000 m^3/s of volume flow at static pressure of 1500 mm water column (0.15 bar).

The types of fans used are:

1. Centrifugal fans
2. Axial flow fans.

Fans produce very high noise and are often enclosed in thick masonry acoustical enclosures.

SOLVED PROBLEMS

Problem 5.1: A roots blower compressor compresses 0.08 m^3 of air from 1.0 bar to 1.5 bar per revolution. Determine the compressor efficiency.

Solution:

Given: V_1 = 0.08 m^3, p_1 = 1.0 bar, p_2 =1.5 bar

We know theoretical work done in compressing air is,

$$W_t = \frac{\gamma}{\gamma - 1} \times p_1 V_1 \left[\left(\frac{p_2}{p_1}\right)^{\frac{\gamma - 1}{\gamma}} - 1 \right]$$

$$= \frac{1.4}{1.4 - 1} \times 1 \times 10^5 \times 0.08 \times \left[\left(\frac{1.5}{1.0}\right)^{\frac{1.4 - 1}{1.4}} - 1 \right]$$

$$= \textbf{3438.89 N-m}$$

and actual work done $W_a = V_1 (p_2 - p_1)$

$$= 0.08 \times (1.5 \times 10^{-5}) = \textbf{4000 N-m}$$

Efficiency of roots blower is given by,

$$\eta = \frac{W_t}{W_a} = \frac{3438.89}{4000.00} \times 100$$

$$= \textbf{85.97\%}$$

Problem 5.2: A roots blower and a vane compressor having same induced volume of 0.03 m^3 per revolution. The inlet and outlet pressures are 1.013 bar and 1.52 bar respectively. For vane type compressor internal compression takes place through half the pressure range. Compare the work input required for these compressors.

Solution:

Given: V_1 = 0.03 m^3, p_1 = 1.013 bar, p_2 = 1.52 bar

1. Roots Blower:

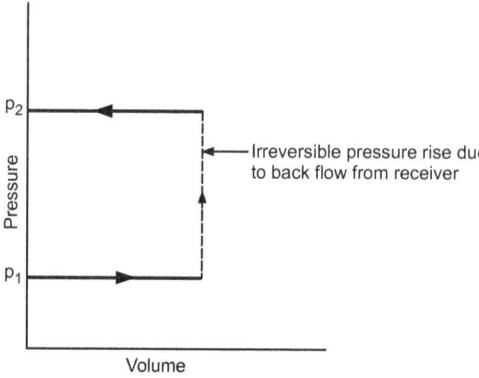

Fig. 5.8

For roots blower, actual work done

$$W_a = V_1 (p_2 - p_1)$$
$$= 0.03 \times (1.52 \times 10^5 - 1.013 \times 10^5) = \textbf{1.52 kJ}$$

2. Vane Blower:

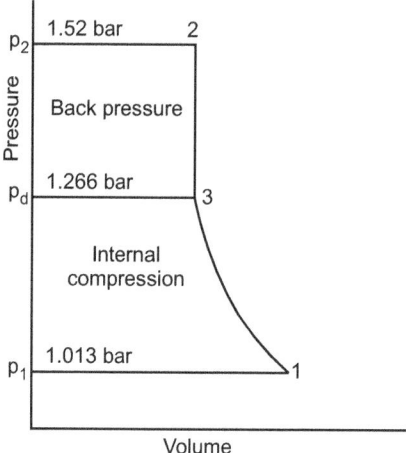

Fig. 5.9

The pressure, $p_d = \dfrac{1.52 + 1.013}{2} = \textbf{1.266 bar}$

Theoretical work done due to compression (1-3)

$$W_t = \frac{\gamma}{\gamma - 1} \times p_1 V_1 \left[\left(\frac{p_d}{p_1} \right)^{\frac{\gamma - 1}{\gamma}} - 1 \right]$$

$$= \frac{1.4}{1.4 - 1} \times 1 \times 10^5 \times 0.03 \times \left[\left(\frac{1.266}{1.013} \right)^{\frac{1.4 - 1}{1.4}} - 1 \right] \text{kJ/rev}$$

$$= 0.702 \text{ kJ/rev}$$

The volume, $V_2 = V_1 \times \left(\frac{p_1}{p_d} \right)^{1/\gamma} = 0.03 \times \left(\frac{1.013}{1.266} \right)^{1/\gamma} = 0.0256 \text{ m}^3$

and actual work done due to back flow (3.2),

$$W_2 = V_2 (p_2 - p_d)$$
$$= 0.0256 \times (1.52 \times 10^5 - 1.266 \times 10^5) = 0.65 \text{ kJ/rev}$$

The total work done $= 0.702 + 0.65$

$$= \textbf{1.352 kJ/rev}$$

Comparison:

Sr. No.	Compressor type	Work input required
1.	Roots blower	1.52 kJ/rev
2.	Vane blower	1.352 kJ/rev

EXERCISE

1. What is the difference between rotary and reciprocating compressors?
2. Derive an expression for efficiency of a roots blower in terms of pressure ratio and ratio of specific heat.
3. Derive an expression for efficiency of a vane type compressor.
4. How compressors are classified?
5. How you will differentiate compressors with blowers?
6. Explain working of following rotary compressors with neat sketches. Also draw p-V diagrams for them.
    (i) Roots blower   (ii) Vane type compressor   (iii) Rotary screw compressor
7. Compare fan and blower.

PROBLEMS FOR PRACTICE

1. A vane compressor compresses 4.5 m^3 of air per minute from 1.0 bar to 2.0 bar when running at 450 r.p.m. Find the power required to drive the compressor when:
    (i) If there is no internal compression, and
    (ii) There is 50% increase in pressure because of internal compression.
    (**Ans.** (i) 7.5 kW, (ii) 6.03 kW)
2. A roots blower compressor compresses 0.06 m^3 of air from 1.0 bar to 1.45 bar per revolution. Determine the compressor efficiency.   (**Ans.** 87.11%)

✱✱✱

www.ingramcontent.com/pod-product-compliance
Lightning Source LLC
Chambersburg PA
CBHW080955020726
47505CB00009B/2204